The New Cadet:
A Young Woman's Journey in a Man's World

The New Cadet:
A Young Woman's Journey in a Man's World

Destiny Jennifer Ringgold

iUniverse, Inc.
Bloomington

THE NEW CADET:
A YOUNG WOMAN'S JOURNEY IN A MAN'S WORLD

iUniverse books may be ordered through booksellers or by contacting:

iUniverse
1663 Liberty Drive
Bloomington, IN 47403
www.iuniverse.com
1-800-Authors (1-800-288-4677)

Because of the dynamic nature of the Internet, any web addresses or links contained in this book may have changed since publication and may no longer be valid. The views expressed in this work are solely those of the author and do not necessarily reflect the views of the publisher, and the publisher hereby disclaims any responsibility for them.

Any people depicted in stock imagery provided by Thinkstock are models, and such images are being used for illustrative purposes only.

Certain stock imagery © Thinkstock.

ISBN: 978-1-4759-7793-6 (sc)
ISBN: 978-1-4759-8071-4 (hc)
ISBN: 978-1-4759-7794-3 (e)

Printed in the United States of America

iUniverse rev. date: 2/19/2013

"I'm very proud you did this. I know perhaps better than others what courage it took not only to write, but to face it all as well. What an accomplishment." – Julia Halo Wildschutte, part of the 2nd class of women at VMI.

"Any military brat or Veteran can relate to DJR's life changing experiences as she takes you through the terrifying, humorous, and enlightening journey through the military's often kept secret initiation world."
– T. Harman, USAF Veteran, VMI '01

"Having attended a southern military school, I can relate to the image expertly painted by Destiny Ringgold. She was there, she lived it. If you ever wondered what goes on behind the walls, I recommend this work." – MAJ D.W. Gray, VMI '01

"There are so many wonderful books telling stories of military experiences. It is even more wonderful to get the perspective from a woman in the military. Our voices are still emerging at a slow pace. This is beautifully written, descriptive, and truthful."
– Kelly Ann Harkness, PO2 USN

"Destiny- Thank you for your courage in publishing this book. The book reminded me of the sacrifices young cadets made in pursuit of something greater than themselves. The chronological encounters of your ratline jogged my faint recollections and my own experiences as a young cadet. I personally believe that The Institute brought out the worse and the best in aspiring cadets. I want to note that your perseverance to rise to the challenge speaks volumes. Perhaps the harsh conditions subjected were the catalyst that enabled you to embark upon a spiritual journey to greater personal discovery and personal growth. Your book epitomizes the struggles that we all endure during our soul-search endeavors for meaning and value. You should keep writing because your gift is inspiring and will change someone's life one entry at a time." Sincerely, – Kenny Harman, VMI '01, Capt, USAF

In loving memory of Benjamin Jones,
June 25th 1978 to September 1st 2000

Table of Contents

Acknowledgments

I would like to first and foremost thank my parents:

Timothy Devall Ringgold & Gina Ann Ringgold, for all they have done and continue to do to support their children and grandchildren.

Secondly, I'd like to thank: my sweetheart, Keith J.E. Moore; my best friend, Kelly Ann Harkness; my sisters; my spiritual teacher, Carol Dunning; my VMI friends, especially Kenny Harman, Tom Harman, David Gray, and Salmaan Khawaja; and all those who have read, commented, and supported this book. Thank you from the depth of my heart.

Note to Readers:

This book is portrayed as fiction, but the story is real, based on real events. Most are my own experiences, and the rest are based on former classmates' personal experiences. When I wrote this book, I had no idea how it would be received. I attended Virginia Military Institute, as part of the 2nd class of women, and I was prepared to have some people react to the honesty of the book. Wonderfully, though, I have received lots of powerful compliments from readers who have connected emotionally with the story. This includes a number of VMI alumni and military friends. As a result, I am putting this 2nd edition out specifically to have more authenticity. Some of the characters' names have been changed, mainly because some of the people—who the characters were based off of—requested to have their names in the book. The college also now takes place in Virginia, and the book comments have been added.

For any reader who picks up this book, it is my greatest hope and desire that you are moved deeply by the story.

-Destiny J. Ringgold

Destiny would enjoy hearing from her readers.
Please contact her at destinyringgold@ymail.com

Chapter 1: Matriculation Day

The release from high school brought relief, an end to the monotony of petty drama and cheap gossip. I was not motivated by school, so I spent most of the year waiting for graduation. The achievement of scholarly grades felt empty, and I deeply longed to be challenged beyond the rote memorization and regurgitation of facts for multiple choice exams. I excelled in music, yet the idea of choosing one profession for the rest of my life felt like a death sentence. I wanted meaning.

During my senior year, Dad took me to his college, the United States Military Academy (USMA), at West Point for the first time. Suddenly my eyes opened to a new world, and I was instantly intoxicated. The gray stone buildings that lined the Hudson River vibrated with history and tradition. The cadets walked with an air of superiority as if they had a secret. I was forever changed.

I had never considered joining the military, but military school would test me. Instead of applying to USMA, which required a military commitment following graduation, I researched and found a state-funded military school without the required military obligation.

The College of Armed Forces (CAF), traditionally an all-male school, was forced by a 1996 Supreme Court decision to integrate women. The first class of women entered CAF in 1997, during my senior year of high school. CAF is located in the mountains of Virginia, far from home, but I applied and was accepted into the second class of women. My mind was made up.

1

⌒

The day of enrollment at CAF finally arrived, the day that would change everything.

Entering Mackenzie Hall, my parents and I came to a few tables guarded by CAF cadets dressed in all-white uniforms and thick black belts. Standing straight in their miraculously clean and heavily starched uniforms, the cadets looked like perfect human beings. The boxes on the table were labeled in alphabetical order: A-H, I-P and Q-Z. I stood in line behind the Q-Z box.

"What's your last name?"

I cleared my throat. "Randall, sir," I answered, standing straight and acting confident. I didn't know if it was appropriate to say "sir" or not.

The cadet handed me a number and a few registration forms. I walked over to my parents. Dad patted me on the back in encouragement.

"Shall we?" his hand gestured toward the stadium. The door was open and sounds of voices traveled out. I took the lead while Mom and Dad followed closely behind.

In the stadium, three hundred of my new classmates sat waiting with their relatives and friends. We arrived at a good time. Today was the beginning of the Tick Line, the first year at CAF and the year of initiation.

"Alicia, there's a few seats," Mom pointed.

"Okay." I nodded and looked around. I was very aware that many of my future classmates had brothers or fathers that were alumni of the college. It was very much an 'old boy's school' with many children having been geared toward cadetship from a young age. Entering as a woman was going to be tricky.

Everyone was talking, and I could feel the excitement and anticipation in the room.

I turned to Mom. "Do you notice how all the mothers look sad, but the fathers are all beaming?"

She looked around. "Well, it's our job to be concerned," she said defensively.

"Gina, there is nothing to worry about. Our girl here," Dad said, grabbing my shoulders to reassure me, "has a good head on her shoulders. We've raised her well."

"Yes, Dad." I patted his hand that rested on my left shoulder.

"I know, but if *I'd* chosen the school, I would've chosen one that was closer to home," she explained.

Here we go again, I thought, and rolled my eyes.

"She should be going to college for music, not entering this Tick Line. What happened to all those years we paid for piano, violin, and saxophone lessons?" She shook her head in despair.

"Oh, Mom, those lessons didn't go to waste. Hey, I'm going to be in Band Company." I smiled brightly, trying to cheer her up.

"Don't worry about your mom, Alicia. She'll be proud of you no matter what you do," he encouraged with a wink.

I looked at him and smiled back.

Over the summer, I'd received videos from CAF that showed what to expect during the Tick Line. The videos portrayed Ticks running around Barracks, doing push-ups, being yelled at by Cadre, and flying through obstacle courses in muddy uniforms. It was intense, but equally invigorating, to watch.

I can handle it, I reminded myself in an attempt to calm my nerves that were building to a crescendo. I observed the Upperclassmen in gray blouse uniforms—distinguished by the rank on their arms and shoulders—walk around the center of the stadium, chatting with each other and hungrily eyeing the "fresh meat" of 2002.

"Numbers fifty-six through sixty," a voice announced over the intercom.

I looked down at my number: 205. There was plenty of time before I would be called. Feeling unsettled, I quickly explained to my parents that I needed a moment and stepped outside for some fresh air.

～

I wished my brother was here. I always pictured entering CAF with his encouragement.

I inhaled, looked at Barracks across the street, and observed the coming and going of students. For the past year, I'd thought about CAF every day and desperately desired to be a cadet. I'd worn T-shirts that read, "Future CAF Cadet." A T-shirt at the CAF Cadet Store said, "If you want a true CAF experience, *date one.*" Not everyone was in favor of women being here. Despite all objections, I felt I had chosen the right path.

~

The moment came when my number was called. I signed the large Matriculation Book, adding my signature to those cadets that had come before me. I was one of thirty-six females matriculating in the second class of women. It was simply a matter of time before I would make my mark in this world.

"Good job," Dad said, smiling at me. "Now we need to unpack the car and take your things to your room."

~

With my arms full, I entered Barracks through the famous Stonewall Jackson Arch. I hesitated when I first entered because I expected to be yelled at. I could hear the echoes of footsteps and voices all around. I envisioned the Ticks squished together along the railing of the fourth stoop, the fourth floor, as I had seen in the Tick videos. I straightened my back and walked ahead while my eyes continuously scanned my surroundings.

"I can't believe I'm finally here, and this is really happening," I said, turning toward Dad.

"Yes, this *is* really happening, Alicia. You'll do fine." He nodded at me. As a USMA grad, he knew firsthand what it was like to be a freshman at a prestigious military college. His assurance calmed me.

After climbing three flights of stairs, we quickly found my room. One of my roommates was already there dropping off her stuff.

"Hi, I'm Caroline."

"I'm Alicia."

She appeared to be sweet. I could tell her father was dreading their separation. I treasured the last moments talking with my own parents, knowing our separation would soon come. I hugged Dad and both of us squeezed, and the five of us headed to the Chapel to say our good-byes.

~

"This is it. There's no turning back. You show them what you're made of!" Dad cheered.

"I promise to learn how to do e-mail, so I can write you," Mom said. "We love you."

"I love you too," I said.

One by one, the speaker called the individual Companies that each Tick was assigned to, starting with Alpha Company and then Bravo Company, with Band Company being called last. In my white T-shirt, blue shorts, and sneakers, I walked outside with Caroline to join our new Fellow Ticks.

Heavenly

Gripping the covers tightly in fists

Wide-eyed with ears perched

Laying erect like the wooden boards our bodies laid upon

Stomachs dancing to the tune of fright

Anticipation escalating as the echoes intensified

BOOMMM!

The dramatic opening of our sacred room was safe no more.

Bolts of lighting zapped us into consciousness

We rushed to accomplish simple tasks

Like tying a shoelace while tripping over inanimate objects

Our vital organs vaulted with liquid adrenaline

And we mumbled illogical motivation as forever bonds conceived

Promising each other to leave as *one*

Sprinting out to join our fellow bald classmates

Standing elbow to elbow

Arms pinned at our sides and shaking involuntarily

As pictures of the holocaust flashed through our minds

The morning darkness portrayed our inner fears

It was only natural to wonder the origin of this desirable choice.

We prayed to God who seemed lifetimes away

Wishing to be anywhere but *here* right *now*.

Chapter 2: Meeting Cadre

Before I could catch my breath, I stood in the courtyard of New Barracks with my Fellow Ticks awaiting the arrival of Cadre, our instructors of the Tick Line, who would teach us drill and ceremony. Cadre were essentially the tormentors of the Tick Line, whose goal was to indoctrinate the new Ticks with the military traditions of CAF. In awaiting the arrival of Cadre, I felt lucky to be in the center of the four neatly lined rows of Ticks in Band Company.

We already had our haircuts and stood there as equals, stripped of the accoutrements of our former lives, looking young and vulnerable. At least the females were not bald. Our hair stood at a ½" on top and a ¼" on the sides, longer than the first class of women. Because of outside influence on the school, the requirements for the second class of women changed slightly. The public did not like female cadets resembling little boys. There was one female Tick who'd cried as her three feet of hair was cut off, as though every lock of hair was a piece of her identity. Personally, I felt like Demi Moore in the movie *G.I. Jane* and was thrilled to discard the obligation of having to maintain hair.

Around our necks hung a thin rope holding a paper nametag that read in black printed letters, "If I am lost, please return me to Cadre," with our last name, first and middle initials marked as our identification. I was no longer Ms. Alicia P. Randall, but Tick Randall, AP.

"Just wait until Cadre gets here!"

"You're going to get it!"

I looked around. Upperclassmen were swinging from the first and second stoops, the first and second floor, like hysterical monkeys, hollering their excitement and making fun. Their screaming was intimidating and my heart began to beat faster.

The scene resembled a barbaric medieval execution, where the accused were chained and dragged out while the audience taunted them.

My Fellow Ticks and I were strangers, but we were flimsily bound together by our mutual choice to matriculate into CAF. We were here, not because we were forced to be, but because we chose to be. I knew we'd come to rely heavily upon each other as the year went on; how could we not? People become united against a common enemy and now we had one: the Upperclassmen.

"You're dead, Ticks. You're dead!" an Upperclassman yelled.

"You're going to wish you were never born!" another chimed in.

I briefly glanced at some of my classmates. I was surrounded by males, with only a few females in Band Company. Everyone looked uneasy. I noticed Caroline in the line behind me, and our eyes met. She gave me a half-smile, her face reflected my own feeling of nervousness. I returned the smile and faced forward, questioning my sanity for choosing this college. Did I really know what I'd signed up for?

As the screaming and ranting continued, I stood there shifting from my right leg to my left leg and back again. My anticipation about meeting Cadre grew. An undertone of fear permeated the Tick mass; one could almost taste it. All summer I'd kept my fears about the Tick Line at bay, using pep talks to convince myself that whatever happened, I could handle it. The pep talks were more convincing at home. Now I was starting to feel scared.

I awoke from my absorbed attention of the crazy Upperclassmen and my fear-filled pondering when the drums started.

Boom ... boom ... boom ... left ... right ... left ... Boom ... boom ... boom ... left ... right ... left ...

The steady drums pounded in unison to the clicking of the shiny black shoes, announcing the entrance of the infamous Cadre. The collective hammering of the cement shook the ground beneath us. I stood there mesmerized, watching the scene unfold in slow motion. Cadre marched in step to the beat, backs straight, and arms moving

8

mechanically. They looked powerful and in control—and they scared the shit out of me.

An electrical charge ran through Barracks. I felt panic well up inside me, and I suddenly wanted to run, yet my feet were bolted to the ground. Besides, where would I go? I had no choice but to wait out the experience, to surrender and allow it to happen.

With the final beat of the drum, the procession of Cadre stopped at once in the center of the courtyard, while the individual Tick companies stood along the perimeter.

"*Ticks—*" a voice spoke, commanding the full attention of Barracks.

Our awareness was drawn to the second stoop where the President of the First Class stood to give the traditional welcoming speech. Mr. Thomas Carr spoke loudly and clearly. He was in charge. We had entered *his* kingdom.

"*Ticks, these are your Cadre. They are your new instructors. They will mold you into the ideal CAF cadet that we require you to be. You will obey them, surrender to them, and give them your absolute obedience.*" He paused and took a deep breath. "*Ticks, they will teach—and—you—will—learn!*"

The drum beat twice, and Cadre turned with military precision to face us, their company of Ticks.

Oh no! Shit, shit! My Fellow Ticks and I have become *prey*.

I looked straight ahead, trying to hide behind the taller Tick in front of me. I wished to blend in. I couldn't hide the fact I was female, but I could do my best to be "one of the guys."

My insides tightened in anticipation of the oncoming slaughter. I took a shallow breath in the silence and held it briefly. Then Cadre were set loose—on the Ticks—on me.

The antics of the Upperclassmen climaxed. As the voices bounced off the wall, the situation turned to madness. No one initially came up to me, then—

"*You think you're good enough to go to my school?*"

He was in my face within seconds. I kept my mouth closed, but my eyes widened in surprise. I didn't answer and hoped silence was the best response.

"*You don't belong here, Tick. I'm going to make your life a living hell.*

Do you understand that, Tick? Do you understand? You're a nobody. I'm going to haunt your dreams until the day you die!"

Chills ran down my spin. The screaming was so loud it made my head spin.

"Would you like me to give you a quarter, Tick?"

I was confused.

"So you can call home to ask them to pick you up! You don't belong here!" He laughed and growled in my ear.

"On your face, Tick!"

I paused, not knowing what "on your face" meant. He knocked me down, and I quickly figured it out and started pushing.

"I'm your Second Corporal, Tick, Mr. Gray." His body was crouched down, and he yelled directly into my ear. His feet were a few inches away from my face. His shoes were so shiny and perfect that I wanted to spit on them.

"You don't belong here. I'm going to work you out every day until I run you out of here. You're pathetic!"

I pushed slowly, pacing myself.

"What the hell are you doing? Push, Tick, push! You can't even do push-ups right. You're worthless!"

The smell of his overpowering cologne made my stomach turn. I could feel my face turning red. My heart was pounding out of my chest. The chaos and noise was overwhelming.

"Push, you wretched worm. Push! Push! Push, damn it, push!" His hand slammed the ground in emphasis of every word.

My arms weaken and started to shake. I couldn't push anymore. I knew—at that moment—the Tick Line was going to be hell.

~

Cadre were now in control of every aspect of our lives. I felt my freewill taken, sucked out of my body, and handed to them.

We were moved outside, forced to form up in four rows with approximately ten people in each row, and set off for a welcoming run. Caroline and I, along with the other two females in Band Company, were put at the front of formation.

"Pack it in Ticks!" one Cadre member yelled.

I didn't realize until now how much I hated to get yelled at. The run started off slowly, but the pace picked up immediately. When the run reached full speed, I was left coughing in the dust. I shamefully watched my company of Ticks pass me by. I kept running, though, putting my head down, lowering my body, and widening my stride.

I looked up and noticed a few of my classmates had fallen out of formation, too. I saw Caroline and sighed relief. An overweight Tick stopped jogging and was breathing heavily. I caught up with Caroline.

"Hey," I said.

"*No talking, Tick! That was an easy run and you fell out! You might as well quit now. This is just the beginning!*" a voice spoke a few feet ahead of us, heading in our direction.

I cringed at the sound of his voice, a voice I'd now recognize anywhere.

"*Now I have to babysit you, you weak creatures. Keep moving!*" Mr. Gray demanded.

I was pleased that Caroline and I jogged at the same pace. We kept our mouths shut and finished the run. Unfortunately our Fellow Tick, the overweight one, wasn't in good enough condition to catch up. I felt so bad for him. I wanted to run back and walk with him, encourage him to keep moving, but Mr. Gray was on our tail.

~

After the run, Cadre took us up to the fourth stoop, outside of our rooms, and instructed us on our new lives at CAF.

"You're forbidden to look around, to glance at us, or around Barracks. You must keep your eyes forward at all times."

"*That means eyes front, Ticks!*" Mr. Gray barked. "*Now on your face!*"

We jumped down, squished together, trying to get enough room to do push-ups. While pushing, I focused my eyes on the ground and noticed the cracks in the concrete. I pushed slowly; no point burning myself out at the beginning.

"Tick, why are you here?" a Cadre member spoke to me.

I kept pushing; he kept talking.

"Do you want to be a soldier? Are you a God-damned feminist trying to prove women belong at the College of Armed Forces?"

The questions rolled out. I didn't know which one to answer first. *It's just a game. They don't give a damn what you think. Just do as you're told.* I heard Dad's words echo in my head.

"I just felt called, sir," I answered.

"Very well," he said and moved on.

"Get up Ticks!" Mr. Gray commanded.

"In a moment, you are to go to your rooms," one Cadre explained. "In each room, there is a Blue Book which includes all the rules and regulations of CAF. You're required to unpack your clothes and set up your wall lockers to the specific standards described in the book. Dismissed!"

I ran to my room. When the door closed behind me, I felt instantly relieved that Cadre were on the other side.

"Those motherfuckers," one of my new roommates mumbled under her breath. She was short with stubbly red hair and a bitchy attitude that was refreshing.

I smiled and nodded in agreement.

Chapter 3: Hell Week

"God! What have we signed up for?" I asked.

"What do you mean—this isn't fun for you?" my spunky, red-headed roommate asked sarcastically.

I stopped in my tracks and looked at her with one eyebrow turned up.

"I know this is just the beginning, and I was expecting some sort of culture shock entering the Tick Line, but I have to say—holy shit!"

"Ha!" she answered back and held out her hand. "I'm Brenda Jones from Alabama."

I shook her hand and addressed her and the other girl I didn't know. "I'm Alicia Randall from Texas."

"I'm Dawn Buxbaum from … around here, actually. I grew up in Waynesboro."

Our attention turned to Caroline. "Caroline Allen," she spoke softly, pointing to herself. "I'm from L.A."

"California? Wow, you're a long way from home," Brenda said.

"Yes, I am," she answered and looked down.

"I guess we're the only females in Band Company?" I asked.

"Seems that way," Dawn said.

"So, we're supposed to be organizing our room right now?"

"Yeah, did you get that list of everything we were supposed to bring?" Brenda asked.

I nodded.

Weeks before matriculation, I'd received the list of required items: twenty-four white sports bras, thirty pairs of white underwear, twenty white T-shirts, twelve pairs of white socks, fifteen pairs of black socks, two white pillow cases, one solid-colored blanket, and a fan. Illegal items like CD players, walkmans, CDs, DVDs, non-academic reading material, nail polish, make-up, and all civilian clothes were stored in the basement, to cleanse us of our individualities. We were allowed personal laptops, but we were required to remove all Instant Messengers, like AOL and Yahoo IM.

I walked over to the windows. "It is beautiful up here!"

The back of Barracks overlooked the plentiful mountains of Virginia. I opened the windows wider to examine the view.

"Yeah, it's a stark contrast to the reality we face within these walls," Dawn said.

Our four desks were pushed together in the center of the room, making a square, with our wooden chairs the only place to sit. Caroline was already sitting down and surfing through the regulation book, the Blue Book.

I inhaled deeply, enjoying the scenic view, and then went to one of the chairs and sat down. There was work to be done.

Two wall lockers adorned the width of the right and left walls. We designated wall lockers and desks to the four of us. On the right side was Brenda's wall locker and then mine, and directly across were Caroline's and Dawn's.

The wall lockers held the majority of our possessions. On the left side of the locker was a bar for hanging uniforms: our class uniform which included our white shirts and blue-gray pants, our Battle Dress Uniforms (BDUS), the camouflaged pants and top for Field Training Exercises (FTX), and our gray blouses and starched white pants for formal occasions like Saturday parades and going into town. The Blue Book described how the hangers were required to be placed two fingers apart in measurement.

Under our hung uniforms, we neatly lined up our shoes: our black dress shoes, sneakers, and combat boots. On the right side of our wall locker were two medium-size rectangular shelves and two bottom drawers. We folded all our clothes to the extreme CAF regulations described in the book. On the shelves, we displayed a set of matching sport bra and underwear, one yellow physical training (PT) T-shirt and red shorts, and a gray sweatshirt with matching gray sweatpants. In the drawers, we stacked the rest of our perfectly folded sport bras and underwear, two pairs of PT uniforms, and another pair of sweats.

To the left of the door to our room, a rifle rack stood with four M-14 rifles. Next to the rifle rack, on the adjacent wall, was a sink and mirror, located a foot from Brenda's wall locker. To the right of the door, our laundry bags hung on sturdy hooks. Above our laundry bags, we posted the white document of CAF rules with tape.

We had entered a totalitarian environment that enforced a perfect world of order and obedience.

❧

Outside our room, we were only known by our last names: Allen, Buxbaum, Jones, and Randall. I knew what my roommates looked like because—within the sanctity of our rooms—we could look around and talk. At all other times, we were required to remain silent and to keep our eyes locked straight ahead. As a result, I knew many of my classmates' names, but few faces.

Roll call was taken frequently: in the morning on the stoop, on the parade field before physical training (PT), and before and after meals. During roll call, Cadre yelled the last names and the first and middle initials to those who shared the same last name, hence to distinguish Smith, JD from Smith, TA. I was only Randall.

❧

Hell Week is one of those experiences that has the potential to make you shit your pants, literally. After noticing how stressed I was the first evening, the Band Director Colonel Bryant took me aside and showed me a letter from a CAF graduate. In the letter, the former cadet explained how he had puked in the sink of his room during Hell Week because of his nerves. I could relate.

On the second day, during morning PT, a male Tick went right up to Mr. Gray and asked to be excused to the bathroom. Mr. Gray laughed and then barked, *"Williams, get back in line! We are going for a run! You'll have to wait!"*

During the run, Tick Williams raised his hand and again asked for permission. I had no idea what his face looked like, but by the tone of his voice everyone could tell it was an urgent request. We saw him fallout as a Cadre member escorted him to the latrines, near the baseball field.

That evening while we were supposed to be cleaning our rooms, Dawn and I snuck out of our room and went next door to see if we could find Tick Williams.

When Dawn and I first bolted in, our Fellow Ticks jumped to attention. When Cadre enters a room, Ticks are required to assume the position of attention.

"It's just us," Dawn said, breaking the ice.

They relaxed. None of us were used to each other yet, and some of the guys especially acted strange to us females.

"Do you know where Williams lives?" Dawn asked.

Two of the guys chuckled.

"I'm Williams," one spoke up.

"Oh, ah well, we were wondering how you survived this morning?" she asked.

Williams' face turned red. "I didn't make it to the bathroom in time, if that's what you're asking—*and* I had to shower shit off of me in front of Mr. Gray too!" He sounded somehow proud. This obviously wasn't the first time he told the story.

We were horrified.

"Damn," Dawn said. "So sorry, man. That must've sucked. We all felt bad when you left formation." Her gaze traveled from his face to the window where his shorts hung to dry. "Your shorts must be …"

"Eeeww." I chuckled.

"Yep, I tried to rinse them off the best I could with just hand soap."

"Well, your shorts aren't much worse than the rest of our uniforms." Dawn and I both glanced down at our own yellow shirt and red shorts colored with grass stains and dirt. "We all stink."

"It's comes with being scum of the earth, don't you think?" I laughed.

~

Hell Week involves a lot of yelling, pushing, and a smell that permeates everything, known as "Tick-nastiness." The smell was a combination of sweet grass mixed with body odor. It comes from wearing the same uniform day in and day out without having the chance to take a shower or do laundry.

Sixty second showers mocked our desire to become clean. Because there were so few females, the females were heard throughout Barracks chanting "We just took a shower—we just took a shower," while we waited for the male Ticks to finish "showering."

We were required to be properly dressed at all times which was annoying, especially in the middle of the night, when we wanted to use the bathroom. We couldn't just go barefoot, but had to put on our socks and sneakers.

Over the years, many male Ticks had been caught pissing from their bedroom window, a choice made to avoid exiting the safety of their rooms. By leaving our rooms, we instantly drew unwanted attention from Upperclassmen and Cadre, who wanted nothing more than to work us out.

As a result, my roommates and I designated one of our CAF drinking cups as a pee cup. Squatting down with our shorts around our ankles, urinating in front of each other, and pouring our remains down the sink was a natural everyday occurrence. It only became a problem when we forgot which cup was the designated cup. Sanitation was definitely not the priority.

~

Cadre were our new instructors, the men we so easily hated. They constantly drilled us, and we only had the occasional thirty-second water and bathroom break. There was no room for failure; each mistake was answered by the wrath of Cadre. Cadre swarmed around the weaker ones like bees on honey with vengeance in their eyes.

No one wanted to be singled out. This happened constantly to those poor souls who missed a step in formation or accidentally got caught whispering something to their neighbor.

Fear and obedience were driven into us day and night. I hated the mornings the most.

"Here they go again," Dawn mumbled sleepily on the third day.

I stared at the ceiling above me. I'd barely slept. I was so on edge and tense. I had no notion of what time it was. It was obviously still dark. Watches and alarm clocks were contraband to Ticks; one more link to our old reality removed from us.

"Ticks, get on the stoop—" We heard voices of other Cadre members echoing throughout Barracks. The echoes were too far away, so we knew it was not Band Company Cadre.

"I've really started to question my sanity in choosing this school," I said. I was flat on my back. It was too hot to use a blanket, which was crumbled at the bottom of the wooden rack known as my bed.

"*Get on the stoop now!*" I jolted at the recognition of Mr. Gray's voice a few doors down.

"Sounds like Band Cadre finally woke up," Brenda yawned.

We were required to stay in our beds until Cadre specifically banged on our door. The waiting was sickening.

I slept with my contacts because I wanted to be ready for anything, at any time. We typically had thirty seconds to be fully dressed and prepared.

"*Get on the stoop now!*" Our thick wooden door flew open and closed with an abrupt slam. We obediently jumped out of bed, knowing we only had a few moments before a Cadre member would be back to check on us.

With no makeup, buzzed hair, and dressed in the uniformed T-shirt and shorts, we looked very androgynous. The main thing that distinguished us physically from the guys was our breasts. My roommate Dawn taught me the benefit of wearing two sports bras in order to hold everything securely in place. My roommates and I left the room together while I gathered the courage to get out onto the stoop.

It was still dark out, and we lined up with our backs against the metal bars. With my eyes locked ahead facing our room, I felt the burden of leaving the safe haven behind.

I was nervous and vulnerable during these morning hours, as if the lack of sunlight naturally brought out my inner demons. This must be like prison or a work camp.

Once every Tick was accounted for, we ran down the three flights of stairs until we reached the parade field to join the other company of Ticks for morning PT.

At o-dark-thirty, the dreary black sky covered Earth like a blanket. The distant Barracks shinned like a fortress with random lights flickering from the bedrooms of those cadets getting a head start on their day.

The PT instructors wore black T-shirts with the bold red C-A-F letters, green Battle Dress Uniform (BDU) pants, and combat boots. The PT instructors gave direct orders, and everything was executed in a military manner.

"Line it up!" one Cadre yelled.

We stretched and paired up for sit-ups, taking turns holding each other's feet. Our shorts got stained with dirt and the pungent scent of grass. After completing multiple sets of push-ups and jumping jacks, we lined up in formation for our morning run. By this time, the sun peeked over the horizon, marking a new day.

~

"Hey, look over here, Mr. Rouge. I think we have a smartass. This young Tick seems to have a problem with being worked out after lunch. Wouldn't you say that's true, Randall?" Mr. Gray's voice oozed sarcasm; he enjoyed the privilege of power.

My arms shook and sweat dripped down my nose onto the concrete floor inches from my face. *What an asshole*, I thought.

I attempted to answer and cleared my throat instead.

Instantly Mr. Rouge and Mr. Harman were there to participate in the event.

"Look, her arms are shaking!" Mr. Gray said.

"She can't even do a real push-up," Mr. Harman chimed in.

I continued holding my arms steady. I knew if I attempted to do another push-up, I was going to fall on my face. Instead, I tried to muster up as much sternness as I could under the circumstances. Part of me wanted to laugh; I knew I looked pitiful. My lower back and butt were beginning to lower to the floor. With my face looking down, I kept my head up. I didn't have to look up to know who was standing next to me; I recognized their voices.

"Go ahead and do some girly push-ups on your knees. You probably think the standards here should be different for a girl, don't you?" Mr. Rouge tormented.

"No, sir!" I yelled.

"Well, I have a question, Randall. If you only had one bullet, which of us would you shoot?" Mr. Rouge asked slyly. The other Corporals chuckled.

Mr. Gray crouched down and whispered right into my ear, "Which would it be, Tick? Which one of us would you like to see dead?" the warmth of his breath sickening me.

"Mr. Gray, sir!" I screamed.

Mr. Gray jumped to this news. He casually walked around me, using his carefully executed steps to grate my nerves.

"Which one did you say, Randall?" Gray asked again.

"Mr. Gray, sir!" I screamed louder.

"Well," he said and paused for a long time. "At least you have guts!"

"*Get up, Tick!*" Mr. Harman barked.

My knees dropped, and I ungracefully got to my feet and stood at attention. I was sweating like a pig and faced the door to my room, keeping my eyes forward. I avoided making eye contact with my roommates—who I knew were watching me—because it would ruin my focus.

"Look, do you understand why you got worked out today?" Mr. Rouge asked.

"Yes, sir!"

"I expect we won't be having any more trouble from you, otherwise we'll have to continue with these workouts on the stoop. You need to get rid of that damn smirk on your face! If you continue to need an attitude adjustment, I'm your man. I'm sure you wouldn't want that to happen now, would you?"

"No, sir!"

"Good, now go tell your roommates. Tell them how easy we went on you today. It's only going to get worse if you keep up with that attitude."

I ran into my room, out of breath.

"What the hell happened out there, Alicia? Why did they stop and work you out?" Brenda asked.

"I don't know. They're probably just testing me. They made up some crap about how I was looking around Barracks, but I think they just wanted to find out what I was made of. If they think a stupid workout is going to frighten me, they have another thing coming…. Those crazy assholes." I smiled to myself.

"Well, we almost joined you out there, but it looked like everything was coming to an end, once Mr. Harman told you to get up. Did you really tell them you'd shoot Mr. Gray?" Caroline asked, her eyes wide.

"Yes."

"Damn, girl. You're in for some trouble later!" Dawn laughed.

"Well, I expect we all are. That was a short workout. To be honest, though, I'm tired. It's like … what now? Day four or five here?" I said, yawning.

"Nope, Randall, it's day three. Welcome to *fuckin'* Tick Year!" Dawn said.

"Just day three! Damn! … So what are we supposed to do now? Clean our rifles?" I asked.

"Yeah, that's what they said, but I think Cadre's just getting ready for something bigger," Dawn muttered.

I took a deep breath and fell into my chair. "I bet you're right. This week is full of surprises." I feigned enthusiasm.

Suddenly we heard a bang in the room. All of us turned toward the sound and saw the cabinet door under our sink flung wide open. Brenda got up and looked under the sink.

"Hey, look a here, I think we have some company," Brenda giggled, crouched down, and waved.

Caroline and Dawn went over to the sink. I stayed in my seat, with no desire to move.

"There's a hole between our walls and one of our Fellow Ticks used a broom to knock the door open!" Dawn laughed.

Right then, the door to our room was kicked open and Caroline yelled, "Attent—tion!"

I immediately jerked up, hitting my left knee on the top of the desk, trying to get to standing position. I heard a groan behind me and concluded that Brenda had hit her head on the top of the sink.

With my eyes forward, I couldn't tell which Cadre member it was. The Upperclassman walked in, footsteps barely making any noise, and took in the scene of the room. I stood staring at the wall lockers in front of me. The footsteps approached.

"You-lousy-yellow-belly-wimpy-lazy-stinking-lice-invested-lolli-pop-lickin'-nerdy-all-for-nothing-Dave-Mattehews-lover-band-geek-pink-wearing-girly-girl-cheerleader-bastard-of-a-child-coward-Tick…"

Noticing the hoarse female voice, I broke attention and instantly right-fisted her in the jaw.

My roommates stood in shock, as their eyes darted to see us laughing.

"How the hell did you find me?" I asked.

She chuckled. "Well, it wasn't that hard, knowing you're in Band Company."

"Hardee-har-har. I'd better introduce you before my roommates think I've gone mad," I said, turning to them. "Guys, this is Lalita. My dad introduced us over the summer. He had a friend, who had a friend, who had a daughter that was part of the first class of women here."

"Well, that's Ms. Doyle to you, Randall," she said, punching me in the arm. "Did you know that it's rumored that this room, 482, had a Tick who hung himself to death?"

"No, I didn't know that. Ouch, you bitch!" I slapped her back, making us laugh. "That's Caroline there, Brenda, and Dawn," I said, pointing to each of them.

"How ya gals doin'?" Ms. Doyle asked, exaggerating her southern accent.

They relaxed, but before they could answer I interrupted, "What are you doing here already? Classes haven't started yet."

"Well, you know how it is with being short-staffed on female Upperclassmen. They needed someone to be around to take the females in Bravo Company to the bathroom."

"Oh, right …" I said.

"Look, I know everything is crazy right now. That's how the school is. Welcome!" She chuckled deviously. "At least you have one good guy…I mean gal," she winked at me, "behind enemy lines. I'll be watching out for you." She turned to my roommates. "I promise. Alicia knows me well enough to know I'll do my best to help you guys out.… It's just a game. Once you learn how to play by the rules, you'll be okay." She sighed. "And, if it makes you feel any better, Third Class Year is supposed to be worse than Tick Year. No more mistakes—we're apparently supposed to know our shit—whatever that means," she said, rolling her eyes.

"That's cool," Brenda said.

"Yeah, definitely," Caroline added.

"Do you have an okay Guide?" Ms. Doyle asked.

"We haven't met our Guides yet," I answered. Each Tick had a Guide, a first classmen mentor. Having a Guide had advantages and disadvantages. The Guide could make a Tick's life good or bad.

"Oh, well, you will soon. Anyhow, I've got to go. I'm not even supposed to be in here, but I wanted to check on you," she explained. "And don't forget, you're making history as the first women here! Ciao," she said and left the room.

"Ciao, bella!" I replied.

"She seems cool," Brenda said.

"Yeah, she is," I said.

Over the summer, Ms. Doyle told me horror stories of her Guide making her do push-ups with a wooden rack on her back. She had to fight from two angles, from two prejudices, as a black woman in a southern all-male school. Because of her endurance, stubbornness, and personal strength, she got through Tick Year, paving the way for future female cadets, paving the way for us.

It was rumored that the first class of women had an easier Tick Line than the second class of women would. The reasons made sense. Law suits were not desirable and neither was getting kicked out for sexual harassment, listed under Title IX, the Sexual Harassment code. In 1997, when the first class of women entered, it was a huge transition for the school. Many of the male cadets, including the Cadre, chose to avoid females because leaving them alone was safer than getting in trouble. With the school being integrated for a year now, we assumed our class of women would be challenged more, but this of course was just speculation.

Chapter 4: Hell Night

I lay in bed each night staring at the ceiling. My roommates slept or pretended to. It was Friday night, our fifth night here, and I still couldn't sleep; my body was on autopilot. I felt on guard, never knowing when I'd be called to action. This constant state of readiness drained me; it sapped away my strength and will. Part of it was surrendering to a greater power, the power of the school and Cadre over our fate.

Lying in bed, my mind went back to thoughts of the past.

I felt his hand caress my face. His Celtic ring created a small cold spot on my cheek. I felt like a traitor.

"I can't leave him. He's my brother and he needs me. He needs both of us. When he wakes up, I have to be there for him, to show him that he has people who love him," my voice cracked.

"Listen, Alicia," Seth said firmly. "It's not up to you to save him. You have a dream. You've talked about nothing but CAF for the past year."

"But things have changed! That dream hardly feels credible. Ethan is lying in the hospital. I want to be here when he wakes up!"

"Oh, I see. You're going to wait around and do nothing—just wait until he wakes up? You'll miss the opportunity to enter with your class, give up your dreams, and when Ethan does wake up—he's going to be the reason for you not going to CAF?"

"Seems like a good enough reason to me," I cried.

"Do you want Ethan to feel guilty for you not completing your dream?

You have to move on with your life. Neither you nor I know what's going to happen. Ethan may not wake up!"

"No—no, don't say that. He's my big brother...."

"And he's my best friend, but shit happens, and Ethan has been through one hell of an ordeal. Don't make him pay for your choices too. The last thing he'd want is for you to stop living your life. Make him proud! Do what you are meant to."

"Okay—I know. You're probably right. It's just so hard for me to accept that I'll be so far away from him. I hate leaving him ... and ... I ... hate ... leaving you too!"

"Look," he said in a tone stopping me dead in my tracks. "I care about you. You know that, but it won't do you any good thinking about us when you enter Tick Year. You need to be strong, focused, and determined like you have been this whole year. I know you. You'd regret not going." He shook his head, looking down at the ground.

I rubbed my left eye that continued to tear up as I spoke. I caressed his chin and made him look at me. "Is it worth it? Is me leaving, worth it?"

"There are no choices here, Alicia. You have your path and ... I have to go—" he said, letting go of my hand.

My heart sank as I sat on the porch and watched him climb into his black sports car and drive away.

~

While lined up on the fourth stoop with our noses pressed to the outside wall of our rooms, a voice ordered me to do an about-face. I obeyed, turned around, and kept my eyes focused forward. Ticks were taught never to look an Upperclassman in the eyes.

"Cut your eyes here," he said, meaning *look at me.*

"Do you know who I am?" he asked.

"No, sir," I said.

"I'm your Uncle Guide," he spoke nicely. An Uncle Guide was my Guide's roommate, but I had yet to meet my Guide.

I took a chance and looked at his nametag.

"Lor-tese," I sounded out.

"That's right. Jamie Fraser's your Guide. You'll meet him tonight."

His voice was so different from the harsh and demanding sounds I usually heard from Cadre.

I relaxed and glanced at him. He was thin, average height, and looked carefree, a guy with a big heart. Maybe he was someone I could trust. Then again—if I did something wrong—I wouldn't be surprised if I saw an instant shift in his character. Everything at CAF seemed unpredictable.

That night I met Jamie Fraser, the handsome and popular redhead who was also the Company Commander (CO) of Band Company. Dawn was one of my co-Ticks, along with Trevor, Quentin, and David. We ate pizza and hung out; it was a luxury.

I sat on Jamie's bed with a soda in my hand. Jamie had three roommates: Brandon Lortese, Kenny Harman, and Toby Palsen. Kenny was Band Company's Executive Office (XO), Jamie's right hand man. Brandon held an even higher position as the 2nd Battalion Commander.

With three out of four of our Guides having rank, I was intimidated by how hardcore they were. They seemed to identify with the school in every way, yet appeared to be so easy-going.

I was thrilled that Dawn was in the same Tick Room since she was Kenny's Tick. Trevor, Quentin, and David were all from different companies. In this tiny bedroom, there were four First Classmen and five Ticks. It was crowded, but so fun.

Having a nice Guide makes all the difference, Lalita had told me. By having a good Guide, Tick Year could run smoothly. However, the opposite could also be true. As a result, it was the Tick's goal to keep their Guides happy.

~

Saturday arrived, and we were finally able to take a real shower. Then we were fitted for our class uniforms. During this time, I got to meet some other female Ticks. We stood there in our white underwear and sport bras, not feeling self-conscious, as the seamstress took our measurements.

"Nice to just be around some females for a change, isn't it?" I said.

"Are you kiddin'? Hell yeah. We don't even get a break when we're in our room." She rolled her eyes in annoyance. "There are only three females in Bravo Company … and all the other Ticks want to be in our room. We're popular, the cool room to be in."

"Yeah, I know what you mean. During those few moments when we're supposed to be cleaning our room or our M-14s … or at the end of the night when we're supposed to be in our racks *sleeping*, it never fails.… One or two of our Fellow Ticks sneak into our room, just to hangout."

"Yeah, I'm past the point of being polite. We've started using our broom as a weapon. Get back! Get back!" she said, pretending to hold a broomstick like a baseball bat.

"Ha! And then there are those Fellow Ticks that act as if we don't exist. I guess I should be thankful that they pretend we're not there. Being invisible is always better than getting messed with!" I smiled.

"Yeah, that's true any time of the day! But those that scorn us, I get it, even if I don't agree with it. To them, it's family tradition to attend CAF, and they grew up knowing they would one day follow the CAF path, and the school has changed."

"I hear ya. Integrating women altered everything. I'm not here, though, because I personally thought the school should change. I'm here because I was accepted, and I wanted to be a cadet," I explained.

"Oh, I know girl, but that doesn't matter to them."

I sighed. "I know, but I still find it odd when any of our Fellow Ticks act weird around me, especially since it's so important to stick together. Our survival depends on our collectivity, our brotherhood!"

"You mean our *sisterhood*?"

"Yeah, that too!" I laughed.

~

Sunday, the rumored last day of Hell Week, consisted of a large picnic down at the Soccer field. I intuitively felt like Hell Week was not over, though. This serene and jovial atmosphere was a complete contrast to what we had experienced previously.

Being given a moment of fun was never truly fun because we always knew we'd soon be returned to Cadre. Cadre were the enemy, and it was easy to fantasize about revenge.

That night, Cadre put us to bed, and Barracks became eerily quiet. I was suspicious and lay in my rack wide-awake and tense. Hours passed and then my eyelids became heavy. As I drifted off to sleep, I was suddenly jerked awake by *machine guns firing and bombs exploding! What the fuck?*

I instinctively wanted to jump out the window. It was a rule, though, that we had to still be in our racks until a Cadre member woke us up. Our door was then brutally kicked in.

"*Ticks get on the stoop now!*"

We were ordered—in the middle of the night—to get up and dress.

"*Fuck!* What is this bullshit?" Brenda asked.

"I guess this is what we'd call *Hell Night*, girls." Dawn shrugged her shoulders and climbed out of bed, like it was an average day.

"*Get on the stoop now!*" Gray banged on our door again.

"Shit. I guess we'd better go." I sighed.

Once all the Ticks were out of their rooms, we were ordered to fly down the stairs and into a line which filed into the Chapel. I glanced up at the night sky filled with stars, and a Cadre member from another company yelled, "*What the hell you looking at? Eyes ahead! No talking!*"

Entering the dark Chapel in the middle of the night ironically created a sense of doom. *Was there no God in this church?* I wondered.

Each company of Ticks filed in, Band Company thankfully all the way in the back. We were ordered to sit on the edge of the wooden benches, with our backs straight, our hands on our knees, and our eyes faced forward.

For a few minutes it was quiet, and the sense of unknown was creepy. Then footsteps pounded their way down the aisle in an orderly manner, and chills ran up my spin. Their shoes clicked so loudly that I felt dizzy. I wished I was back in my hay.

Men marched onto the small stage in front of us, and I could see they were dressed in the gray blouse uniform.

"*Ticks, we are the Tick Disciplinary Committee. We have brought you here tonight to teach you your privilege of being a Tick. From now on, whenever you enter Barracks, you will follow the red lines designated Tick territory. You will square all your corners and double-time all staircases. Within the walls of Barracks, you will at all time—strain!*"

Right then a helpless Tick was pulled from the crowd and dragged up to the stage. I gasped. *God, I felt bad for him!*

The TDC surrounded him and yelled at him right in front of our fear-filled eyes. It was a blur of strong tall men with short haircuts in immaculate uniforms of grayish-blue, woolen tops marked with rank, white pants, and shiny black shoes. Their fierce yells echoed within the walls of the chapel like a horrible dream.

"Shoulders back! Arms in! Forehead back, now! Chin in. Chin in, further!"

Oh, God. What were they doing to him? They twisted the Tick until he was molded to represent the perfect stiff attention position, called a *strain*. All of us sat horrified. The Tick stood there painfully contorted with a double chin, shoulders back, and upper body leaning back. The traumatized Tick was instantly returned to the crowd, and within minutes we were filed out of the Chapel.

Entering Barracks, we walked into the loud vocal demands of Cadre.

"Chin in! Forehead back!"

"Randall, pin your arms in!"

I was startled by the mention of my name. That must've been Mr. Gray. *I hate him.* I obeyed immediately, and hoped I would not hear my name again.

We tried our best to strain properly while Cadre ran their fingers down our spines to check that our shoulder blades almost touched. We kept our foreheads shoved back with our chins in tight. The painful position almost cut off our circulation and respiration, all the while creating a double-chin, with our arms pinned to our sides. Straining was awful! Awkward … excruciating … and just another way for Cadre to humiliate us.

"Walk the Tick Line! Square all your corners!"

"Square your corners!"

In my peripheral vision, I could see the red tape on the concrete floors, lines directing how we were now required to walk in Barracks.

Upperclassmen had returned today, Sunday, in order to start academic classes tomorrow. They waited for us hungrily in New Barracks. Like wolves longing for fresh meat, they eyed us from around the courtyard as we filed in and formed rows. We knew where we stood in this food chain. Barracks was no longer occupied by just the Ticks and Cadre. Barracks was now overflowing with Upperclassmen, and this was our introduction to each class.

"*Ticks, on your face!*" Energy resonated high within Barracks.

Oh shit, this must be our first *sweat party*! I'd learned about sweat parties from watching the Tick Line videos and from what Lalita had told me. This was the beginning of our training to become a unified class. Three hundred of us spread out on the courtyard, in order to get some room on the floor to push.

The First Classmen, the seniors, went first randomly picking their victims. The screaming started, and Barracks echoed loudly with their hate-filled epithets for us.

During our one minute breaks, we squeezed back together, chanting and clapping. "Fellow Ticks!" (Clap, clap.) "Fellow Ticks!" (Clap, clap.)

I prayed not to be seen, but to blend in, to be a "Ghost Tick," doing what everyone else was doing. They were the lucky ones, the Ghost Ticks, who were rarely singled out or put on the spot. It was harder to blend in as a female.

After the short breather, we were introduced to the Second Class. My neck and arms already ached from the workouts all week.

"*High knees, Ticks!*" a voice called.

I responded by kicking my knees up in the air. I held my arms up, trying to balance myself.

"*Higher Tick, higher!*" an unfamiliar voice commanded.

He was in front of me, holding his hand out, palm down, directing my knees higher and higher. My hips, legs, and arms all burned.

"*On your face, Tick! Push!*"

I could feel the heat rise in my face. The smell of unwashed bodies and grass-stained clothes permeated the air.

Lalita had told me that the Third Classmen were the most vicious because they'd been Ticks the previous year, and this was their first opportunity to experience the other side of these sadomasochistic rituals.

During our third sweat party, my arms wobbled, and I could do little more than hold myself in the push-up position. This was really a test of the mind, especially when the body gives out. I could feel myself zoning out, my vision blurring, and my movements shifting to slow motion. With my muscles worn out, it was a matter of waiting out the last workout.

When the sweat parties ended, we were ordered to our rooms. We ran, stumbling on each other, scurrying like frightened animals up the stairs to our rooms, away from the threat as quickly as possible. Many of us wanted to fight back, to yell, "Fuck you!" to all the Upperclassmen for our humiliation and their power.

By the time we got to our room, we were high on adrenaline and drained at the same time. I plopped onto my bed and sat there, letting my legs and arms dangle, not wanting to move.

After such an intense and exhaustive week, many of us wished this was the completion of Tick Year, so we could be initiated as Cadets, but we knew this was just the beginning. Our endurance would have to last throughout the school year, for the end of Tick Line was so far away.

Chapter 5: Life as a Cadet

With the end of Hell Week and the return of Upperclassmen to the school, academics began. The hardest part of the daily regimen for me was the lack of sleep and the absence of alone time.

"Come over here and shine your shoes with us, Alicia," Brenda encouraged.

"Okay," I said, grabbing my polish rag and shoes.

Lights were out at eleven, but my roommates and I often shined our shoes and brass by the light of the moon. Our covers, our hats, had a brass plate with the words "The College of Armed Forces" inscribed on it, which needed to be polished daily, as well as the brass buttons on our shoulder boards. Our black shoes were continually scraped up from doing push-ups in uniform, but we aspired to keep them shiny.

"I can't believe some of our Fellow Ticks have to live on the third stoop. That must suck," Dawn said.

Ticks generally lived on the fourth stoop. Each class occupied a floor with the First Classmen on the first stoop and the Second Classmen on the second stoop. Because of the generous number of freshmen, some Ticks regrettably lived on the third stoop next to Third Classmen.

"Well, I'm sure Administration doesn't think it's a problem, at least not for long," Brenda said.

A large percentage of Ticks were expected to dropout during the first year, especially during Hell Week and the first few months.

"Did you know that around twenty-five percent of those who enter CAF actually stay the whole four years and graduate?" I asked.

"No way!" Caroline said.

"Yeah, I read it on the CAF website."

"I wonder if that percentage will increase with the integration of women," Dawn said. "We women have to prove that we're tougher than the guys!"

"I don't feel like proving anything right now, honestly. It's past my bedtime," I moaned.

~

The mornings were the most difficult for me. We were required to tightly roll our thin, stiff mattresses, our hays, and stack them in alphabetical order. Rolling our hays took two people to do correctly while breaking them in. We stenciled our individual hay with our last name and first and middle initial. To the right of Caroline's and Dawn's wall lockers, we stacked our rolled hays like standing spirals. My roommates' three rolled hays stood vertically, labeled "Allen, CH; Buxbaum, DE; and Jones, BL." On top of the three rolled hays, we folded our blankets neatly and lined them up evenly, largest to smallest. Being last in alphabetical order, my hay was neatly placed horizontally on top of the four folded blankets with my name "Randall, AP" stenciled across.

"Alicia, get up! It's after six," Dawn said.

"*You're* still in bed!" I argued.

"Yep, but I'm getting up," she answered, not moving.

"You're both a bunch of lazy bums. With all we have to do in the morning—get up and help me roll this hay!" Brenda demanded.

"Yes, mom ..." I mumbled.

It was necessary to rise no later than six o'clock, which gave my roommates and I just enough time to roll our hays, stack the wooden boards our hays rested on, straighten our rooms, dress, splash water on our faces, brush our teeth, and leave to wake our Guides. We also had to straighten our Guides' rooms, so the privileged First Classmen wouldn't be written up for "disorderly rooms," before arriving to formation by seven o'clock.

"I personally think we should stop sleeping on our hays," I said. "It would give us a few extra minutes in the morning."

The wooden planks weren't comfortable, but it didn't matter since exhaustion was constant.

"That's a good idea. It's not like I wouldn't be able to fall asleep," Dawn said, walking around the room disoriented like she was sleep-walking.

Because our hair was short and make-up and jewelry were not part of our existence, personal maintenance was minimal.

"Hey, check this out," I said, holding up a pair of black garters.

Over the summer, my dad bought me black garters, commonly called "shirt stays," that attached from my black socks to my shirt. I never thought I'd use them, but it would help to keep my shirt straight.

"You look so nerdy," Brenda laughed.

"I don't care! As long as it keeps my shirt tucked in."

"I'm sure it's better than tucking your shirt into your underwear, like I do." Dawn shrugged her shoulders.

"Can your dad get me a pair of those?" Caroline asked.

"Of course. I'll ask him to send some for Brenda and Dawn too. I wouldn't want them missing out...."

My roommates and I looked like little toy soldiers with breasts.

Having hips and being a woman, I never felt I portrayed the ideal cadet: the male figure with broad shoulders, a thin waist, and a flat stomach.

"Later, gals," Brenda said, exiting the room.

"Bye!" We yelled together.

"Ready, Alicia?" Dawn asked.

"Yes," I yawned. "You okay, Caroline?"

"Yeah, I'm just about ready. See you later."

As soon as Dawn and I exited our room, we immediately strained and walked the Tick Line. We had to walk straight out of our rooms in single file, to the edge of the stoop, and square all our corners. We became robotic, like lemmings, in following the Tick Line. Whenever we went up or down the stairs, we had to "double-time," running and stomping up or down.

Walking through the stoops below was like entering a war zone where Upperclassmen had full privileges to stop us, work us out, and scream at will. In the mornings, though, most Upperclassmen were too preoccupied with getting to formation on time. However, it only took one early riser to make your day hell.

Dawn and I always left together because we had the same Guide room. Our Guides' room was located in Old Barracks, far from us in New Barracks. Dawn and I would stay on the fourth stoop until we reached the closest staircase to their room, in order to minimize our exposure on the other stoops. Often times Quentin, David, and Trevor, our Co-Ticks, beat us to our Guides' room.

Once we got our First Classmen up, Dawn and I would have to stand outside of their room while they changed uniforms. It was the small consequence of being female in a male room. There were no First Classmen female Guides yet.

Outside our Guides' room, Dawn and I stood at parade rest, with our arms behind our backs, our legs spaced shoulder width apart, and our heads straight. We'd carefully dart our eyes while we stood perfectly still, observing the various men walking to and from the bathroom in bathrobes.

It was a strange dichotomy to find any of the Upperclassmen attractive. They held such power over us, and I felt so genderless. I recognized myself as female, but being a Tick I didn't feel cute or pretty. I was a Tick, the scum of the earth, with no power at all, constantly proving my worth.

On laundry days, standing outside of our Guides' room, I stared at the laundry truck in the middle of the courtyard. I dreamt about jumping off the fourth stoop and flying into the laundry below. We were told by our Guides that if a Tick were to do that, we'd be released from the Tick Line immediately and permanently. It was the alluring easy way out, a way to free us.

"Alright Randall, Buxbaum, let's go," Jamie ordered, as he exited his room.

With only minutes to spare, we'd casually walk to morning formation. In Barracks, Ticks strained and walked the Tick Line, except in the presence of their Guide or Uncle Guide.

During formation, accountability was taken to make sure that everyone was on time. Cadre walked around inspecting uniforms, making sure our shirts were tucked in, our shoes were shined, and our brass was polished. They also checked to make sure we adhered to weekly haircuts.

All Companies were called to attention, and each Platoon Leader announced how many cadets were present and missing.

"Band Company Ticks, forty-three present, one missing," Mr. Rouge yelled.

Ticks stood in their own formation, and we were told that later, once we were recognized as Fourth Classmen, we'd be mixed in with the rest of our company.

While Reveille was played on the trumpet, we saluted the flag as it was raised. Then Cadet Battery fired one of the cannons, and we headed off to Crozet Hall where we ate breakfast.

In the mess hall, Ticks strained unless with their Guide. It was painful to strain and carry a tray, especially while waiting in line behind other cadets. It was the same food layout every day. There was a section of cereals, muffins, bread, milk and juice, as well as a buffet of eggs, bacon, pancakes, and French toast.

Sweets were a luxury of the Upperclassmen, I found out one morning. After breakfast, Mr. Gray had worked me out right outside Crozet Hall as punishment for having chosen a dark muffin that had been chocolate, not bran.

During meal times, Ticks were required to push their chairs all the way in, until their stomachs touched the table. We were not allowed to glance around, but were required to keep our eyes down with our foreheads back. Since our plates were pushed up against our chests, we could hardly see the food that we were required to cut into microscopic Tick Bites.

Using the silverware properly, knife in the right hand and fork in the left, we had to put our silverware down on the plate and our arms at our sides, before we could chew. Performing this ceremoniously throughout the whole meal allowed little time to fill with nourishment. As a result, I was hungry most of the day.

After breakfast, we left for classes to attend to our full academic responsibilities.

~

I majored in Psychology, a newly established major, and shared classes with both Ticks and Upperclassmen. In the classes with only my Fellow Ticks, we made light of our situation and came up with different plots on how to destroy Cadre.

"I am going to ball up my Corporal in his hay and throw him over the stoop into the courtyard," one Fellow Tick said enthusiastically.

"I'm going to use my M-14 and shove it up Mr. Franklin's ass." one Tick laughed as another classmate slapped him five.

"Whoa, vicious," I mocked. "If I were to do anything," I lowered my voice conspiratorially, "I'd wait until after Tick Year. I'd come back, looking all feminine and beautiful, and seduce Mr. Gray."

"No way!" a Tick interrupted me.

"And then once I had him where I wanted, I'd cut off his balls with my bayonet!"

"Whoa—stay away from Randall! She's *evil*," one Tick said, stepping back from me.

"Eve should've never eaten that apple," another Tick mumbled, shaking his head.

I laughed and returned to the chemistry experiment in front of me.

~

Many of us fell asleep while the teacher lectured. We only got away with this when all the students in the room were Ticks. If any Upperclassmen were present, like a Third Classman making up a failed academic class, it wasn't a good idea to dose off. They were usually assholes and wrote down the names of the sleeping Ticks, so when they saw them later, they'd have a specific reason to work them out. We Ticks feared the wrath of Upperclassmen more than that of our professors.

I was the only Tick in one psychology class. When I entered the classroom and sat down, the Upperclassman I sat next to would move to another seat. If I hadn't felt discrimination prior to entering CAF, I felt it now. I briefly imagined what it felt like to be black before the Civil

Rights movement. Discrimination makes you feel like a leper, like you're contagious. I knew it was just another aspect of the Tick Line, but it's one thing to be treated as a Tick with your Fellow Ticks, and another thing to fight back the vulnerability I felt when I was alone.

In between classes, I sometimes hid in the bathroom. The quiet and aloneness allowed me some precious solitude and peace. I could take a break from the disparaging looks and stares from the Upperclassmen.

I tried to spend as much time as possible in the library on the computer, escaping to my connection with the outside world. I e-mailed friends and family regularly, craving an update on my brother's condition. Instead of responding to every e-mail, I sent mass e-mail updates. I received copious correspondence via e-mail and snail mail, not to mention the much cherished care packages. If I ever doubted my friends' and families' love for me outside of CAF, my mailbox proved otherwise.

~

One afternoon, I used the pay phone in the library, which was off-limits to Ticks, and called Seth.

"Hey it's me. How's Ethan?" I asked, lowering my voice to the phone, trying to attract as little attention as possible.

"He's the same. I promised you, and I promise you again: I'll call the minute anything changes," Seth said.

"Yeah, but you know how it is here. After calling the guard room, it might be hours before I receive the note. So, how are my parents? I haven't called them. I just don't have the strength to talk to them right now, and my phone privileges are nonexistent. I'm not even supposed to be calling you right now."

"Your mom sits by his side and reads to him from some of the books we got from his room. She misses you and is worried sick…for you both."

"Poor Mom…what about my dad?"

"Well, he stops by twice every day, during lunch and after dinner. He talks to Ethan about his work day and literally begs him to wake up. Your mom's a little different. She cries most of the time. She tells him if he's in a lot of pain, it's okay if he wants to go."

"And what do you tell him, Seth?"

"Oh, you know me. I tell him what a stupid-mother-fucking-asshole he is for having wrecked his truck in the first place. I tell him to get his lazy ass awake, so he can finally beat me at a game of *Risk*."

I smiled. My heart ached for them both. I wanted to be there next to Ethan's bed and talk to him. Talking to Seth was a catch-22. It reminded me of my feelings. It was easier to not talk to him, to not think about him, so I could focus on the duties at hand. At the same time, my heart yearned for him, and I couldn't ignore the reality of my life outside of CAF.

"Hey, Tick, get off the phone," demanded an Upperclassman.

I looked up at him and rolled my eyes in annoyance, instantly regretting my reaction.

"Hey, times up. I'll call again soon, okay?" I said reluctantly.

"Alright, Alicia. Keep your head up."

"Yeah, okay. Tell Ethan I love him. Bye."

I hung up the phone and fought the tug of tears building up inside of me. I went to the nearest bathroom, seeking a sanctuary for my inner turmoil.

I looked at myself in the mirror, my dark brown eyes brightened by the emotional response of having talked to Seth, yet they stared back at me with such loneliness and longing. I blinked a few times, took a couple deep breaths, and tried to calm down.

My long eyelashes and full lips hinted at femininity. The image of a female cadet reflected back at me. I missed my nose ring I'd had in high school. I liked wearing the uniform. I felt good having my dream become a reality. I straightened my white blouse and dusted off my pants.

My life had turned into a trial of frustrations. Randall, get your ass back out there. This is your destiny. There's nothing you can do, but surrender to this path you have chosen, I heard my inner voice saying. Alright, alright! I splashed some water on my face and felt the coolness calm me. I can do this. I can do this. I took a deep breath, returned to my desk, and collected my things. I exited the library and went straight to my Guide's room.

~

I entered Jamie's room, relieved I'd made it there without being stopped, but I was surprised to find it empty. For lunch, Ticks were not required to line up for formation, so the five of us: Dawn, Quentin, David, Trevor, and I; met here daily to go to lunch with our Guides. I suddenly panicked. Where was everyone? Did I forget about somewhere I was supposed to be? I quickly looked at Jamie's clock. I sighed. It was a little after eleven; I'm just early.

We Ticks worshipped our Guides, like puppies adoring their masters. If we behaved and the Guides were happy, life was good. In the mess hall with our Guides, we didn't have to strain and could actually eat a full meal. At other times, when the Guides were disappointed in our behavior, we were worked out after lunch.

It was popular for Guides to work out their Ticks. Guides were known to force their Ticks to drink a lot of milk and horrendous condiment concoctions, so after lunch they could test the strength and endurance of their Ticks, testing them until they threw up; it was awful. Generally, our Guides didn't require this, and they let us relax after lunch. Jamie and his roommates were academic achievers and required their Ticks to get good grades. As a result, they wanted us to use any free time to study.

I went over to my stash of illegal Tick material and grabbed my walkman and small photo album. I plopped onto Lortese's bed, near the window, and listened to Sarah McLachlan. I stared at the trees outside, at the vibrant fall reds, oranges, and yellows that painted the landscape. I was grateful that time was passing. Home felt far away, as if in another galaxy. During these moments of peace, I could easily become content with the fact CAF was now my new home.

I stared at the summer pictures of Seth and me. One particular photo of us in the swimming pool showed how happy we were. Seth was so handsome. I held the picture to my heart. Life was good then, even if it was just a moment. I daydreamed about our imaginary life together until everyone arrived.

~

After dinner, Ticks lined up in formation outside of Crozet Hall and marched back to Barracks. During and after dinner was Cadre time. Because we were Band Company, we were taught to march with our instruments, as well as our rifles. When I marched, I felt a sense of pride, the "espirit de corps," that holds the school together.

Pride stemmed from all the hard work, from upholding tradition, from being part of something special and unique. There was pride in getting up early every day to follow rigid rules, and in giving up the freedom a normal college experience would have allowed. There was pride in not quitting, no matter how stressful or demanding CAF was. Cadets often insult the school when they're there, but brag about it when away on leave. Ticks are linked together by pride. This camaraderie, forged in the fire of mutual discrimination and harassment, can last a lifetime.

All CAF alumni have a common bond no matter when they graduated, making alumni return again and again for parades and football games.

~

Study time began at seven PM, and Barracks generally quieted down then. Brenda often headed to the Engineering building, and I usually went to the library. Sometimes I hung out in our room, but I had trouble studying there because of our popularity. Many male Ticks came over whenever they had free time.

Homework was a daily occurrence, but I didn't always have the motivation or attention span to do schoolwork at the end of the day. I wanted to relax, take a break, and breathe. I wasn't alone in this. Many Ticks were model cadets and survived Tick Year while failing academically. Any one of us could fall into that trap. The goal was to create a balance, to stay on top of all the Tick responsibilities, including any designated Guide tasks, while completing all our required academic assignments. To me, I felt like we were required to be Super Ticks.

The days were long. We experienced as much in one day as a typical college student did in a week. My favorite part of the day was the evening, when I was back in the room with my roommates. We always had stories to tell each other from the day's events.

I especially loved when Brenda was there. We sat by the large windows and smoked cigarettes, staring out into the night. The windows opened to a magnificent view of the Virginia Mountains. I envisioned myself in flight over the rolling hills, over the fall colors that shined brightly in the waning sun. It was our special time, a brief moment of connecting.

Brenda and I shared stories about the men in our lives that we loved. Brenda's boyfriend, Troy, was in the Marine Corp, having gone through the Crucible phase during the exact time we were going through Hell Week. I'd told her what happened to my brother over the summer, and how I'd accidentally fallen in love. We both dreamed about being rejoined with our men; the dreaming and talking kept us going.

Chapter 6: The One Week

The summer before I entered military school, my brother, Ethan, and I decided to spend as much time as possible at our parents' beach house in Crystal, Texas. We were extremely close. Being exactly twenty-two months apart, I often lived vicariously through him, depending on him to get the scoop of what was to come in life.

Ethan left for the University of Texas with his best friend, Seth, two years earlier. They rented an off-campus apartment instead of living in the dorms. Ethan and Seth lived the lives of older college students, working part-time to support their independent lifestyle, while attending classes full-time.

Ethan majored in history and had ambitions to write his dissertation on the Civil War. He was obsessed with the genealogical connection between family members on opposing sides. As a result, he wanted to become a professor because he felt it would give him the freedom to tell stories. I'd always thought he'd end up as a therapist because he understood people so easily, but he told me that he was happier studying the people of the past.

Seth was just as driven and wanted to be a lawyer. Seth tended to come across as confrontational, but he just liked to debate issues. Ethan and Seth were inseparable, and because Ethan and I were so close, I was used to Seth always being around. Now that they were in college, I was lucky to spend any moment I could with Ethan. I wanted to catch up on time missed while we led separate lives. I felt lonely being the only child at home.

Because I was about to leave home for CAF, my focus for the summer was to run every day and to spend as much time with Ethan and my girlfriends. I was determined to enjoy my freedom while it lasted. Every morning I got up and ran three miles on the beach, did one hundred sit-ups and fifty push-ups. I kept the workouts simple. I tried not to stress myself out, but every day I anticipated entering CAF. It was hard not to think about the Tick Line when it was less than a month away.

Following the crowds after Independence Day, I invited my friends Christine, Julie, and Courtney down to my parents' beach house. Our friend Theresa, who completed the tight knit group of the five of us, couldn't make it. Ethan naturally invited Seth. The house was small, with only two bedrooms and one bathroom, but it was located right on the beach in a remote area away from the busy commercial district. We usually ended up camping out on the beach anyway.

~

During the first day, the girls and I drove to South Beach, to the boardwalk, to do what tourists did: we ate a ton of ice cream, shared funnel cake, treasured the frivolous nature of buying things we didn't need, and Christine got a bunny tattoo. In the evening, Ethan created a bonfire in the back of the house facing the shore, and Julie made chocolate martinis for the girls. Ethan was twenty-one, so he provided the alcohol to us seventeen and eighteen year olds.

"Oh yes, this is the life. The breeze off the water feels so good," Julie moaned, as she stretched out luxuriously.

Christine, Julie, Courtney, and I were casually sprawled on our lawn chairs reading *People*, *Oprah*, and *Yoga Journal* magazines while delightfully sipping martinis. I rarely read magazines, but this was the perfect setting for light reading and relaxation.

"I hope you made enough, Julie. I plan to have at least three," I said.

"I can make some strawberry daiquiris," Courtney chimed in, bouncing her eyebrows in delight.

"Oh, that sounds good!" Christine said.

"This is what I call a vacation! Why didn't we do this sooner?" I asked.

"Because Courtney couldn't take off from work until now, *that workaholic*, and Christine had Band Camp. And I, well, could've come down anytime." Julie grinned. "Forget responsibilities! I'm always ready for a good time."

"Well, I have to work." Courtney defended herself. "I didn't get an ROTC scholarship like Alicia, and I don't have rich parents. I need money for college, unless I find a sugar daddy to take care of all my financial needs."

"How's your job at Hess?" I asked.

"Oh, it's fine. People are dumb, though. They don't work as hard as they should, and I'm always having trouble getting them to do their freakin' jobs. Other than that, my job is fine, and my manager told me that in a few months when he moves up to regional director, that he'll put in a good word to get me promoted to manager. I feel like I'm already doing his job, since he's gone most of the time, and it would be nice to get paid for it too!" Courtney turned the pages of her *Yoga Journal*, scanning the pictures.

"That's cool. Who was that tall and handsome guy you were working with Courtney?" Julie asked.

"That was probably Josh," Courtney answered matter-of-factly.

"And have you thought of dating him, hmm?" Julie asked.

"Are you kiddin'? Josh is like a brother to me, my bud, my friend. There is absolutely no chemistry whatsoever."

"Yeah, yeah," I said.

"No, really. To tell you the truth, I'm pretty into this customer that comes in all the time. His name is Anthony," she said, fluttering her eyelashes.

"Really? And what's he like?" I looked at her shocked because I hadn't heard about him before. "Is he smelly enough for you?" I said in a deep husky voice.

"Yeah, he just might be," Courtney laughed. "He's kind of grungy, and he plays drums," she said, as if that explained everything.

"Well, go for it girl, and don't wait around for him to make the first move. No sense in waiting that long."

"I know! But that's not my style, Alicia. I'm not like you, acting all confident, just able to go straight up to a guy and make a move."

"And that's why you've dated … how many guys? There was Kevin, Bobby … two?" I laughed.

"Three," she said. "You forgot Don."

"Well, we're not all hoes like you, Alicia," Julie said.

"Ah!" I threw an ice cube at her. "I've just dated a lot, but I'm still a virgin! I know what I'm looking for, but I just haven't found him yet. In the meantime, I do enjoy experimenting," I said coquettishly.

"Not me," Christine said. "Dating is a pain. All I need to know is that he's rich."

"Okay, Miss Princess," I said, rolling my eyes. "Personally, I don't need him to have a lot of money. I'm looking to connect with the heart … you know … feel something underneath it all?"

"Yeah, I know what feeling you're missing out on," Julie said, poking me in my side.

~

Like a rainbow shinning right after a thunderstorm, an unexpected shift took place: I noticed him. I sat across from my brother's best friend, whom I had known for years, and he suddenly appeared magical, like a two dollar bill. *What had changed?* Ethan and Seth had been doing shots of Jagermeister around the bonfire, and then Seth brought out his guitar. He started playing and singing.

"Would you feel the same … if I saw you in heaven? I must be strong … and carry on … 'cause I know … I don't belong … here in heaven."

I sat mesmerized, suddenly feeling something I hadn't felt before. Seth was so handsome. How did I not notice that before? He sung with sincerity, from an essence deep within. It was lovely.

I couldn't shake the feeling that I'd had an epiphany. I finally saw everything so clearly. I'd always thought Seth was a nice guy, but that was it. He was Ethan's best friend, but now, unexpectedly, he was much more.

～

After everyone fell asleep, I went outside under the stars. I had trouble sleeping with the impending Tick Year around the corner. I sat in one of the lawn chairs, peacefully watching the waves. New emotions were alive within me, crashing my sense of peace with each wave. I wondered if Seth felt anything for me.

If I showed my true feelings, I could embarrass myself. Had I liked him this whole time? I didn't think so, yet these feelings felt familiar. What was the point? I was leaving in just a few weeks anyway.

"Hey, what are you doing up so late?" a voice spoke out of the darkness.

I was startled out of my thoughts of Seth, to see him standing before me like an apparition.

"I couldn't sleep. Lately, I've had trouble quieting my mind. What's your excuse?" I asked.

"Nothing. Just awake," he said. "I wasn't tired, so I wanted to find a movie to watch, but then I saw you sitting out here. You and I haven't had much time to chat recently. How've you been?"

"I'm okay." I nodded.

"Feel like going for a walk?" he asked.

"Sure, why not." I shrugged my shoulders, my heart skipping a beat.

"Okay, sit tight. I have to grab my shoes," he said, walking toward the house.

A few minutes later, Seth returned holding two bottles of water, handing me one. "I thought you could use this."

"I could. Thanks."

We walked along the beach in silence.

"You know, your brother is going to miss you. He'd never admit it, but he's really proud of you. The military environment is not his thing, even though he likes reading about it. He doesn't fully understand why you'd want to put yourself through all that, but he's happy that you found your thing."

"Yeah? Hmm," I said. "I appreciate you telling me that." My heart began racing, hearing his voice so close to mine. I stayed quiet, not sure what to say and then I asked, "Do you like college?"

"It's alright. It suits me."

Then out of nowhere, I felt his left hand glide against my right hand. It took me by surprise. I stopped and looked at him. His lips were parted, and his eyes looked right at me. I reached up and kissed him. I don't know what made me do it.

I felt the warmth of his lips and then my tongue found his. He didn't pull back.

Seth gradually stopped and began undressing. I stood there, hesitant, a little surprised at his initiative. I looked at him. "What are you doing?"

"I'm going to seduce you.…"

"Oh, really? Right here, right now?" I said, my eyebrows rising.

"Yes," he said simply. His black beady eyes pierced through me, as if he could see me underneath it all.

He bent down and kissed me again, this time more passionately. He reached down and unbuttoned my shirt. We sank to our knees.

"Whoa, Seth," I said, pushing him back a little. "I can't give in that easily. You'll think I've gone soft. I'm supposed to be playing hard to get."

"You can try, Alicia, but I know you. You're anything but subtle. You always go for what you want. You're always honest; you can't be otherwise. I can see it all over your face. Try to play hard to get, but it won't last long."

"Humph," I replied. "I don't believe it. My brother's best friend thinks he knows me." I threw my arms up. "Next you'll tell me when we'll be married and how many kids we're going to have."

"Now who is being presumptuous?" he laughed. "Just sit back, shut up, and let me love on you."

I didn't object.

~

I felt I'd finally arrived home. There was something so sensual and sweet about being in his arms. I laid my head against his chest. Is this what people feel the morning after? I wondered how long it'd last. Was it just a night together? In the presence of Ethan, would Seth pretend nothing had happened between us? What use were any of these questions when I would be leaving in just a few weeks?

I gently rubbed my finger around the edge of his belly button. Then I tickled his hair below, the trail leading down. I hadn't intended to wake him, but he stirred under my touch. I actually felt nervous to see his initial reaction to what had happened. Would he regret it?

"Good morning, beautiful," he said.

I sighed with relief. "Good morning. How did you sleep?"

"Like a rock. Your body close to mine relaxed me completely. Or maybe it was the workout you gave me last night?" he smiled. "What are your plans today?"

"Well, first things first. I need my morning coffee, and I need to go for a run. Once I have both and a shower, I'm up for anything. What do you and Ethan have planned today?"

"Oh, I don't know, probably looking for young beautiful women who are susceptible to our charm," he said slyly.

"Ah!" I punched him in his side.

"I'm just teasing. I don't know what we're going to do. We'll see …"

"Well, would you like to jog with me along the beach this morning?" I asked, not expecting him to say "yes."

"I'll think about it." He leaned down and kissed me gently on the lips. "Thanks for last night," he said playfully, grabbing my ass.

"Just leave the money on the kitchen table, and we'll call it even."

"Is that so?" he said, wrestling me to the ground. "Have you forgotten how madly in love you are with me?"

"Oh yes, I forgot…. Well … how about some midnight skinny dipping and margaritas tonight?"

"Alright, now we're talking," he said. "Would you mind if I was the one who told Ethan about us?"

"Sure, I don't care. Why? Worried about his reaction?"

"Not fully. I just need to ask him if it's okay. It's a guy thing."

"Alright," I said, getting up. "Let's go find out if everyone is awake yet. And Seth, I'm so happy about this."

"Me too, love. Me too."

~

"Where have you been? Thank god you're here!" Julie grabbed my arm and dragged me into the house to sit down.

"What's wrong? What are you freaking out about?" I asked, my heart beginning to pound. Seth followed right behind me.

"Well, that answers our questions," Christine said, eyeing us both.

"Alicia, Seth—" Julie took a deep breath. "There's been an accident." She paused, checking to see our reaction. "We don't know all the details yet. Ethan and Courtney went out to get breakfast this morning, for everyone. Something apparently went wrong with the truck, and they swarmed off the highway and slammed into a tree."

"Oh my god! Are they okay?" I choked out the words. I was astonished and frightened.

"We don't know. Courtney called us from her cell phone. She's pretty shaken up."

Time stopped.

"The accident was pretty bad, Alicia." Julie looked at me with concerned eyes. "It was so bad a helicopter flew to the scene."

A helicopter flew to the scene, I thought, trying to process the words. I felt my world crumble.

"A helicopter?" I asked. "A helicopter? Why did they need a helicopter?"

"Because, honey, Ethan's truck caught on fire," she said, probably for the second time.

"What about Courtney?" I asked slowly, my eyes darting back and forth, not truly seeing the things in front of me.

"Courtney's okay. She was able to get herself loose and crawl out of the back window of the truck."

Ethan could not get out of the truck, obviously. Courtney must have watched from the side of the road, horrified and helpless, as the truck caught on fire.

"And Ethan was caught inside," I stated, in an effort to process the truth. "Do my parents know?" I asked, lifting my head to face Julie. I dreaded them finding out, the reality hitting them like an arrow to the heart.

"Yes, they're on their way to the hospital. We should go."

⌐

Julie, Christine, Seth, and I climbed into Seth's car and headed to the hospital.

Mom and Dad greeted us in the waiting room. A doctor came out to talk to everyone. He explained that Ethan was severely burned and in a coma. Over seventy percent of his body had second and third degree burns.

The day's events strongly contradicted the happiness from the night before. Fear and grief ran threw us all. Ethan was in a coma; Courtney was traumatized; and the rest of us felt hopeless and empty. None of us knew what to do. Our one week vacation was abruptly over.

Chapter 7: Drum Out

The College of Armed Forces was obviously not an easy place to go to school, and everyone questioned, at one time or another, why they were there. I was hundreds of miles away from Texas, and I couldn't do anything to help my brother or Courtney. I called and e-mailed, but it never felt sufficient. Dad wrote regularly to update me on Ethan's progress. His most recent letter read:

> *What to say about Ethan? It is really sad and frustrating. He is not doing well at all. He is battling recurring infections, including pneumonia. Some of the infections are bacterial and some are fungal. Burn patients are really susceptible to infections because they are so exposed. The doctors have amputated most of his fingers on both hands and also his left foot. They have not been able to do anymore skin grafting due to him being so sick with all these infections. Two of them are in his lungs so the ventilator is doing most of his breathing. They have him completely sedated. He has not been conscious for over two months now. Dr. Rolland said she does not know how long he will stay this way. She also says that there is a good chance that he may not make it through this. All we can do is wait and pray. Love, Dad*

I stared at his e-mail, stunned with fear, sadness, and bewilderment. Then I read the P.S.

Just so you know I created a website for Ethan with daily updates. This way you can check it whenever you can to know what is happening. I know you are busy at CAF, so no need to write back.

The website Dad had created for Ethan included pictures of Ethan prior to the accident. A picture of Ethan and I hugging in front of the camera stood out more than the others. Another picture showed a bunch of us, including Courtney, with Ethan in the background making a silly face, his tongue hanging out of his mouth like a dead fish.

I stared at the screen, and my throat tightened. I wanted to scream. I wanted to hit the computer with my fists, bludgeon the damn thing, and bash the keyboard against the wall. I hated this. I hated that I couldn't do anything!

I called Courtney one afternoon, and she sounded awful. She was dealing with her own feelings of shock, sadness, and despair like any survivor of a tragedy would. She didn't leave for school like she had planned to, and she quit her job at Hess. Christine and Julie wrote the same e-mails, feeling as hopeless as I felt. They described Courtney as being withdrawn and depressed. It was comforting to know that Courtney had started seeing a therapist. I simultaneously prayed for her healing and for Ethan's recovery.

The best days I had at CAF were when I got so caught up in my life as a Tick that I temporarily forgot about Ethan being in the hospital, about the touch of Seth's hands on my skin, and about the sadness that was deeply apparent in all of us. Pretending to forget was my only option. In order to survive, I had to focus on what I could do, on what I had to do, on my duties at CAF. Every day I waited for word of any change in Ethan's condition.

～

The beginning of October was the hardest for me because I was still adjusting to the demands of CAF. I never felt like I could get ahead. There was always work to be done, formations to attend, and papers to write. I tried my best to keep going, but my body rebelled. I got sick.

When I went to sick call, the doctor diagnosed me with an earache, stuffy nose, sore throat, and a fever of a hundred and two. I was constipated for over a week, which obviously caused a toxic build-up. As a remedy, the doctor gave me a handful of suppositories. When I finished using the bathroom, I had to put an "Out of Order" sign on the door because the toilet stopped up, and I wasn't even embarrassed. My fever went down, and my symptoms disappeared. I even dropped a few pounds.

During moments of weakness, like when I got singled out, I fought the desire to cry and let it all out. I was afraid and felt dangerously close to falling apart.

As a result, I tried my best to keep my fear of losing Ethan at bay. I prayed for him all the time. I suppressed my fear of failure, of not being able to keep up, even though I was spinning in circles with all the responsibilities, never knowing where I was going to land. Survival was the only objective. Some days felt extremely long, and there were moments where I could only take one minute at a time.

I didn't know many of the other Band Ticks yet, but one evening changed that.

"Attention!" Dawn yelled as Mr. Harman entered our room.

"At ease," he said. "I've come to congratulate Tick Randall." He handed me a piece of paper. I glanced at it briefly, slightly confused.

"What's this?" I asked.

"You've been nominated by your Fellow Ticks to be the Band Company Representative, along with Tick Delphine. Report to the Band Room tomorrow evening and your additional responsibilities will be communicated to you."

"Me? I didn't even vote. When was this held?" I inquired, looking at my roommates.

"Too late now, you've been selected. Congratulations," he said and left the room.

I turned to my roommates. "And did you have anything to do with this?"

"Why, aren't you happy?" Dawn asked.

"Um, I'm a little stunned or flattered, actually ... not that I needed any extra responsibilities.... I just didn't know our Fellow Band Ticks knew who I was."

"Everyone knows who the female Ticks are. It's not like we can hide," Caroline said.

"True. Alright, just another thing I have to do. Might as well add it to the list! Band Company Representative. Wow, I feel so popular, and here I thought *I* was the one falling apart," I laughed.

"Nah, you got it going on!" Dawn said.

During breakfast formation, Cadre yelled at some poor Tick for arriving at formation without his roommates. Cadre were trying to teach brotherhood and the importance of working together. Dawn, Caroline, Brenda, and I constantly checked on the welfare of each other, never leaving our room without knowing the other was okay.

Caroline was the most sensitive and idealistic one of us all. She envisioned perfection and everything working out in an ideal order. She dreamed of a white picket fence and an adoring husband while she pursued her career as a veterinarian. Caroline was the symbolic cheerleader who had blonde hair to boot, buzzed as it was now. She was the trophy in her family, the child her parents showed off at Christmas parties and encouraged her to be nothing but the best. This sense of perfection weighed heavily on her. I believed her attendance at CAF was a subconscious plea at rebellion, as well as a continuation along the straight and narrow path.

One afternoon, I caught Caroline throwing up in the bathroom. I waited outside the stall until she finished and confronted her about it, not to criticize, but to show my concern and support. I think it was her way of handling all the stress, all the pressure at CAF. Later I spoke with Brenda and Dawn, and we agreed to support Caroline in any way we could. We all depended on each other.

Brenda was the essence of strength in our room. She was short, wavering barely over five feet with buzzed, reddish brown hair. She was fearless and had a sense of endurance like no other. I fed off her enthusiasm. She was inspiring. She spoke with an inner strength, as if she had known who she was since the day she was born. Her boyfriend, Troy, and she had been a couple throughout high school, and she spoke about him like a lover whose passion never waned. She often sang ditties in the room, distracting herself from the monotony of chores and responsibilities. She faced each challenge with poise and confidence. I knew she would succeed at any path she chose.

Brenda's weakness, if I were to point out one, was her inability to say "no" to herself. She pushed herself constantly, sometimes beyond her physical boundaries. I was concerned that one day she would push herself too far.

Dawn, similar to Brenda, had the type of beauty that shined not just because she was physically fit and naturally beautiful, but because of her self-confidence. Her dark hair and tan skin oozed sexuality, ambition, and independence. Dawn was the spunky one, and the slut, if anyone could be a slut during Tick Year. She flirted and laughed all the time, not with Fellow Ticks, but with the men she met prior to matriculation. Men wrote her constantly, and whenever she had a chance, she was chatting with them online, secretly sending e-mails. It was an escape from the stress and duties at CAF. Her pen pals exchanged naked pictures of themselves, and she loved the attention. Sometimes Dawn shared the pictures with us, and we lived vicariously through her.

Dawn seemed so non-CAF, but somehow fit in fine. She was charming. She followed the rules, played all the Tick games, and excelled at everything. I learned the real reason she was attending CAF was to be a pilot, not just any pilot, but one of the top fighter pilots. She wanted to be one of the chosen ones to fly Stealth Fighters and F-22 Raptors. She yearned to feel the sense of freedom that only flying could create. Her wildness, beyond flirtation, desired to take flight. I pictured her with her own personal plane flying to different ports and meeting various men at each stop.

I adored my roommates and saw myself in each one of them. I saw my sensitivity and hope for everything to fall into place in Caroline. In Brenda, I saw my determination and stubbornness, and I saw my fun side in Dawn's spunkiness. Each of them colored and entertained my world. I knew I could depend on any of them at anytime. We checked on each other constantly and would never have shown up to formation without the other.

⌐

I awoke, in the middle of night, to screaming and the sound of Cadre kicking open doors.

"What the fuck?" I asked sleepily. "You've got to be kiddin' me!"

My roommates and I sat up in our racks, stunned by the abruptness of being pulled from dreams.

"I don't want to get out of bed," Caroline moaned.

"Me neither," Dawn said. "Tell those mother-fucking assholes—we don't care."

Our door was kicked open. *"Ticks, dress and get on the stoops, now!"*

We looked at each other solemnly, not wanting to leave the warmth of our blankets and face the wickedness that lay beyond our doors. I slowly got up and put on my sweats and sneakers. I didn't even look in the mirror or attempt to flatten my bed-head buzz. I did put in my contacts because whatever the reason was that we were rudely woken up, I wanted the safety of being able to see clearly. I sat back down and waited for my roommates to finish getting ready.

"Alright girls, ready for battle?" Brenda asked.

"No," Caroline said weakly. "How about you go and report back to me later with what I missed."

"Yeah, like Cadre is going to allow that. Let's get to it and get this bullshit over and done with, so we can return to our racks," Dawn said confidently, as if our speediness affected our return to our room.

I followed my roommates out of the room. All of Barracks was awake, and Ticks lined the entire fourth stoop. Once roll call was taken, Band Company Ticks were ordered to Old Barracks. All the Ticks squashed together along the fourth stoop and were ordered to face the courtyard.

A loud drum beat startled us from our sleepy states, and chills ran down my spine, despite the warmth of my sweats.

The President of the Honor Court stood in the courtyard, dressed formally in all white.

"Tonight, the Honor Court of the College of Armed Forces met," he yelled, addressing the whole school slowly and distinctly. *"A jury formed by the peers of Mr. Brian Larkshire has held trial and he has been found*

guilty—on one count—of cheating. He has shamed the school and has been kicked out indefinitely. His name will not be mentioned within the four walls of Barracks—ever again," he emphasized. *"You—are—dismissed!"*

At that moment, I felt the push of Ticks as they ran back to their rooms. I stood motionless, staring down at the courtyard. There was something so unnerving about this undue ceremony. Brenda grabbed my arm and pulled me along. We ran back to our room, shaken by the experience.

"So *that* was a Drum Out? How eerie!" Brenda said, mimicking my thoughts.

"Couldn't they've waited until morning to do that?" Caroline asked, annoyed.

"That scared the shit out of me," I mumbled.

"Which was the reason for doing that in the middle of the night," Dawn said. "You'd think twice about breaking the Honor Code."

"Yeah," Caroline said.

"Does anyone else feel like we're living in a cult?" I asked.

The four of us crawled back in our racks and tried to resume sleep.

Chapter 8: Tick Challenge

Ticks were required to participate in Tick Challenge three days a week. Tick Challenge consisted of Field Training Exercises (FTXS), as well as weekly runs. The harassment died down during this time, and Cadre took on a more professional mode as instructor.

Tick Challenge consisted of rock climbing, bridge crossing, and obstacle courses. We repelled from towers, learned first-aid, blew shit up, and low-crawled fields while live rounds were fired ten feet above our heads.

One afternoon on a clear sunny day, Band Company Ticks marched in Battle Dress Uniforms (BDUS) with our Gas Mask Pack strapped to our right sides. We were on our way to the Gas Chamber; another experience to aid to the list of the fun activities offered at CAF! We formed up according to height, so my roommates and I were always together in the front.

I wore my glasses because contacts could be permanently stuck to my eyes in the Gas Chamber. I rarely wore my glasses and wasn't used to the extra weight on my face, as they had a tendency to fall down my nose.

Band Company Ticks got in line, behind another company of Ticks, to enter the depressing black shack in the middle of the woods. All the windows were boarded up, and the entrance door was painted red. The exit door was on the other side and was the only place we were allowed to exit.

"Looks like Mr. Gray's home," Dawn whispered in my ear.

"Yeah, I have a feeling he's not that great of a host," I said.

"I think a few glasses of tequila might loosen him up."

"I'd hope so, but I doubt it," I laughed.

As ten people entered, the next ten prepared by putting on and sealing their gas masks. My roommates and I were part of these ten. I became nervous when half of the first squad came running out of the entrance door, the wrong door, coughing and wheezing.

"What a bunch of wimps!" Brenda chuckled and breathed hard through the gas mask, sounding like a robot.

The four of us looked at each other through our own gas masks and giggled. We could see nothing but each other's eyes and upper part of our checks.

"You look so dorky!" I said to Brenda, my voice muffled by the plastic and metal.

"No, you do!" she laughed.

I rechecked my mask to make sure it was sealed securely before we were ordered to enter the little shack. Mr. Rouge was inside instructing everyone to form a circle around the center and to remove our masks.

Those that had no common sense took a deep breath of tear gas. Those with a little more sense held their breath, until they could put their masks back on and reseal it properly.

All exposed skin felt like sunburn, especially the back of my neck. Then it burned a little more, and my eyes started to water. I looked over at the girls. Their eyes were watering too, and Caroline started to jump up and down, anticipating a quick egress from the shack. I closed my eyes, forced myself to calm down, even though a natural panic stirred inside me.

To my relief, the door finally opened.

I yanked off my gas mask and *could not* see where I was going. My eyes had glued shut, and I felt snot running down my nose.

"Randall, just keep walking straight. Flap your arms. This stuff wears off after a minute or two," a Fellow Tick said.

Sure enough, the burning sensation wore off after a minute, and we spent the next hour watching others exit the gas chamber like blind flocks of birds in agony; it was hilarious.

There was one dumb male Tick who decided to go through the Gas

Chamber twice. He wanted to see how much he could stand since the first time had not affected him much. During round two, though, he came out of the chamber distressed, with swollen eyes, a red face, and snot everywhere.

~

Some of the experiences during Tick Challenge were specifically gender-related. My roommates and I were completely grossed out at the bug-infested, spider-webbed, porter-potties. The males, on the other hand, were generously rewarded with indoor male latrines.

While waiting in line for the porter-potty, I undressed as best as I could before jumping in and out to make the time spent in the disgusting bathroom as short as possible. I never felt clean after that, and it was inevitable that we'd all have to go to the bathroom; we were ordered to drink water out of our canteens constantly because of the heat and our high activity level. So when we had to go, we had to go right away because we'd be drinking more water soon.

Sometimes we'd have to run into the woods to relieve ourselves when there weren't any porter-potties around. The guys could easily run into the woods, but the four of us went together to make a square perimeter, each of us pulling our pants down at the same time, with our backs facing each other.

"Who do you think has the biggest ass?" I asked, zipping up my pants.

"That is a given, Ms. Wide-hips," Brenda said, her eyes moving up and down my body.

"Well these wide hips of mine may come in handy one day."

"Like when you have a baby?" Dawn asked.

"Yeah, like then. Other than that, my hips are here just to allure men to the bedroom," I said.

"It's the way you move your hips that does the trick," Dawn said, all-knowing as usual.

"I'll take your word for it," I said.

I couldn't help but laugh as Dawn rolled her hips as if she were in the middle of a giant hula hoop.

⌣

I was often asked by family and friends if I thought men and women were treated differently at CAF. Some people have the assumption that life at CAF is harder for women. Truthfully, CAF was mentally and emotionally challenging for us all. The constant intensity of adhering to Cadre and Upperclassmen was overwhelming and frustrating. Just entering Barracks was like entering a battlefield with Upperclassmen having full authority over the Ticks.

But of course, it is obvious that men and women are built physically different. During marches and runs, I had to take wider steps to keep up with the men's natural stride. Push-ups were probably harder, but that didn't matter much because we each pushed until we couldn't push anymore. We were all hard-pressed to move beyond our physical limitations. When we took long marches, we were sometimes ordered to hold our M-14s above our heads, which I struggled with, but we all did our best.

Requirements for the CAF physical training test stayed the same with the integration of women. I could only do two pull-ups, but by CAF standards, I was required to do five, just like the men. The PT test included pull-ups, sit-ups, and a two mile run. I passed the run okay and the sit-ups with flying colors, but I still failed the test because of the pull-ups.

Many Alumni felt the standards at CAF had weakened since women entered. To me, it seemed like old men telling their stories about walking to and from school in eight feet of snow, uphill both ways. The longer it had been since they attended CAF, the harder their Tick Year had been, or so the story goes.

The fallacy, that the standards at CAF had weakened since women entered, assumed that standards changed specifically *because* of the integration of women, rather than the natural progression of changes in society. CAF was influenced and pressured by society, since it was a private school. However, CAF was so meticulous about adhering to tradition that I doubted the school had changed much over the years. Sometimes older alumni stopped me outside of academic buildings to tell me how proud they were to have me there. It was touching.

One afternoon, I attempted to get to my room to collect some books. I was determined to get there without being stopped, so I strained and hauled my ass upstairs.

"*Stop, Tick!*" a male voice commanded.

Damn, the third stoop …

"*Chin in, forehead back, Tick!*" he yelled, placing his hand in front of my face to get my forehead back.

I don't have time for this shit.…

He walked around me, grabbed my left wrist, and tugged. So many Upperclassmen did this. He was trying to determine if I was straining hard enough. When he pulled my wrist, he got resistance.

"*Elbows in tight!*"

My arms were pulled in tight against my body with my CAF book bag in my right hand. He slowly slid his finger down my back, along the spine, and stopped between my shoulder blades.

"I don't feel your shoulder blades pinching together. Don't you know how to strain correctly, Tick?" he asked, as I stood there in the most uncomfortable and belittling position.

My neck ached from the opposing pressures of pushing down my chin with my forehead back. I could care less what he wanted. I just needed to get to my room, so I could study. *Doesn't he have anything better to do with his time?* He must be bored.…

"What's your name, Tick?" he asked.

I couldn't help rolling my eyes. It was a military school, and I was in uniform with a nametag.

"What, did you forget your name already?"

What an idiot.…

"I'll remind you, Tick. Your name is Ran-dall," he said rolling his r's. "I've heard of you. You play saxophone in Band. So you're a blower, not a beater," he laughed at himself.

All the Upperclassmen asked the Band Ticks, at one time or another, whether they were a "beater" or a "blower," the remnants of an all-male school strictly in place.

"*Get on your face now, Tick!*" he ordered.

I dropped my bag and assumed the push-up position. I began the tedious task of pushing at once.

"*Get up, Tick! High-knees.*" He held out his hand, palm down, in order for my knees to touch his palm. As I did high knees, his palm rose higher and higher. I quickly began to wear out.

"*Down, Tick!*" he yelled again.

Back down I resumed the position. My cover had fallen off by this point, and my naked head revealed my short, spiked brown hair. I did one push-up and then he yelled, "*Up, Tick!*"

"*Down, Tick!*"

"*Up, Tick!*"

"*Down, Tick!*"

Finally back down, my arms felt the burden. I pushed again, and he whispered in my right ear, "*You're such a turd, Randall,*" and walked away.

I kept pushing, not completely sure if I was let go. Then I quickly glanced right and saw no one. I got up, grabbed my cover and bag, and ran up the last stoop, not stopping until I reached my room.

I barged in, startling Dawn and Tick Anders. I was red-faced and sweating.

"That asshole called me *a turd*," I said, looking at them and began to laugh. "I hadn't heard that word since grade school."

"At least he didn't call you a 'Superstar with a big mouth,'" Dawn said, still looking at her computer. "That's apparently my new nickname."

"Why? In the newspapers, again?" I asked. "That's a charming name. I think it fits you." I grinned.

"Well then, you're a *big fat turd* …"

"That may very well be true." I slumped into my seat. "Now why did I come back to this room? That's the question…. And what are you doing in our room, Anders?"

"Buxbaum is smarter than I am at Calculus, so I'm studying with her."

"Gotcha," I said, nodding. "How's Tick Year been for you? You and your roommates surviving okay?"

"Yeah, we're fine. My Guide sucks, though. He gave me an atomic wedgie in front of my Co-Ticks. It wasn't fun."

"A … what?"

"An atomic wedgie. I don't think they do that to girls here. It's when they pull our underwear from the back—hard enough until it tears off," he explained.

I was astonished. "What the hell for?"

"It amuses them." He shrugged his shoulders.

"Damn," I said. "I'd rather be worked out and called a turd any day."

~

That night Upperclassmen had the privilege of giving us another sweat party.

"When are these sweat parties going to end?" I asked while tying my shoe.

"When Tick Year is over, my dear," Dawn said.

We could hear the chaos below, as the Upperclassmen prepared to work us out, *again*.

The four of us filed out of our room, resigned to the reality of another workout. We joined our Fellow Band Ticks on the fourth stoop, briefly, before we were herded down to New Barracks courtyard, where all three hundred Ticks lined up together.

"*Ticks, you have proven how worthless you are. You haven't learned how to unify as a class. Tonight is your punishment. It is time you learn to work together!*" Mr. Thomas Carr, the President of the First Class, addressed us.

The screaming started, and the Upperclassmen were let loose.

"*You, you, and you,*" one Upperclassman said to me, Dawn, and another Tick.

Like a line of baby ducks trailing the mama duck, we followed the Upperclassman to the corner of Barracks where the shouting diminished a little.

"Randall, tell me what the CAF mission statement says."

Oh fuck, he's asking about the Tick Bible. During Hell Week, we were given a small book full of CAF history, rules, and the 1998-1999 Chain of Command. At all times, we were required to carry our Tick Bible with us in our covers.

"It is the mission of the College of Armed Forces to—"

"Buxbaum, do you know who your First Battalion Commander is?" he inquired, cutting me off.

She stuttered.

"Buxbaum, you disappoint me! I'm your First Battalion Commander," he yelled over the noise of Barracks. "The three of you, cut your eyes here." He pointed to his nametag. "What's my name, Buxbaum?"

"Bromley, sir," she sounded off.

"Very good, Tick. Now remember that name because I now know who you are, and I expect the three of you to hold up the standards and traditions of this school. *Now get on your face!"*

We pushed until the bell sounded, signifying a short breather. We immediately got up, ran toward the center of New Barracks, and started chanting, "Fellow Ticks," and clapping. The bell rang again, and our one minute recovery was over. Then I heard a familiar voice.

"Randall, Buxbaum, follow me," Ms. Doyle ordered, taking us to the side of the courtyard. "Do what you like, but keep moving."

Dawn and I assumed sit-up position, our favorite exercise.

"How are you both doing?" she asked.

"Fine, ma'am," we said.

"Good, glad to hear it. Thanksgiving break is around the corner. Where are you going for Thanksgiving, Randall?" she asked.

"I don't know, ma'am," I yelled.

"What about you, Buxbaum?"

"I'm going home, ma'am. I'm from Waynesboro," Dawn answered, short of breath.

"Very well. Randall, you're coming to my house for Thanksgiving. I'll be in touch."

"Yes, ma'am. Thank you, ma'am."

We did sit-ups until the bell sounded, and then we rejoined our Fellow Ticks.

When the bell rang again, my Guide Jamie got me. He took me aside and had me stand for a minute, while he yelled into my ear.

"Randall, I want you to cut your eyes there," he said, pointing. "You see that Tick doing push-ups with a one arm cast. That's Tick Moore. He's hardcore, and the epitome of a CAF cadet. Now cut your eyes at two o'clock. You see that Tick standing there while the rest of his classmates get worked out?"

I glanced at a Fellow Tick with a white note pinned to his T-shirt, obviously from the nurse's office, excusing him from participating in any workouts.

"That's Tick Bigelow, and he has a GIM tag for shin splints!" All "worms" were detested. "Unfortunately, he's in Band Company. Now it's your job, as Band Company representative, to get his act together."

I sighed in resignation.

"Do I make myself clear, Randall?"

"Yes, sir!"

"Very good, now get on your face until the bell rings. I'll see you in the morning," he said and walked off.

Chapter 9: Stone Soup Bookstore

"Alright, it's Sunday!" Caroline gleamed.

"I don't like Sundays," I mumbled.

"*What?* How can you not like Sundays, crazy woman?" Caroline asked, shocked. "It's the day of freedom—to go to town, to church, and eat some *real* food. I want to go to that cute purple café, near the Civil War Museum," she said excitedly.

"Sounds cheerful …"

"What's your problem?" Brenda asked. "Attempting to diffuse Caroline's happiness in an effort to make her as miserable as you are?"

"No," I answered. "Sundays are always so bittersweet. I've gotten excited about getting away from Barracks before, eating good food, and calling home. The truth of the matter, though, it's all so damn depressing. Tomorrow always lingers in the way. Tomorrow we return to Cadre and continue all this bullshit."

"Yes, I agree, it is bittersweet, but why ruin today, Alicia? You might as well enjoy the freedom, even if it is temporary," Brenda said.

"*Need me to give you a knuckle sandwich?*" Dawn said, pounding her fists together, mocking Cadre.

I threw my pillow at her. "No, Buxbaum, but thanks … so kind of you to ask." I sighed and climbed out of my rack.

"So who's going to the cute purple café with me?" Caroline asked.

I wished I had another pillow to throw at her.

"I'm in," Brenda said.

"Okay, me too. It's a café, right? Well it's got to have chocolate, and I'm always up for that," I said.

"I can't guys. I'm sorry. I'm going to my host family, Mr. Penchard's house today," Dawn said. "Pick me up some yummy dessert, though, would you?"

"Well, we'll have to draw straws on who's going to bring dessert back into Barracks and get worked out for it," Caroline said.

"Nah, I'll do it. Barracks is usually quiet on Sunday. I'll even bring back another dessert, something pinky and girly for myself, to make it all worth it!"

"Ha! Awesome. Thanks, Randall."

~

On Sunday mornings, we had the opportunity to attend church; that was the freedom designated to Ticks. Going to the purple café wasn't necessarily allowed, but since Ticks were allowed to go into town for church, we could easily get away with leaving campus.

Before my roommates and I left, we collected our shower gear and headed to the bathroom to get our weekly scrub down. During the week, the four of us often took bird baths from our room, washing our face, hair, and underarms, as well as shaving our legs by the sink. With buzzed hair, all I needed was a bar of soap and a razor. It was normal for us to see each other naked, and we never felt embarrassed by it. It was a necessary part of survival at the school.

A week before, I had a horrendous rash on the inside and tops of my legs and lower part of my stomach. Because of one of the Tick Challenge events, I'd remained in a wet, muddy uniform too long, which irritated my skin. I looked reptilian.

I'd gone to Sick Bay, but they only prescribed me Benadryl, and I knew if I took the medicine, I'd pass out, so I didn't take it. With the open female showers, the rash was seen by many eyes, but it was the least of my concerns. This was one bullet in the ass, like straining, that I had to put up with.

"Looks like the rash is healing," Brenda said.

"Yep. How come none of you broke out into a rash?" I asked, suddenly curious.

"Because we're not as much of an animal as you are, Randall," Dawn teased.

~

Caroline, Brenda, and I walked into town, sparkling like three shiny new pennies. The town was accustomed to CAF cadets adorning their streets and shops. However, female cadets were still an oddity. We easily found the purple café Caroline was talking about. It was attached to the Stone Soup Bookstore.

I squealed with pleasure the moment we walked in. I loved books. I cherished the way they looked on the shelves, how they felt in my hands, and even how they smelled when first opened. I was in heaven. We'd only been at CAF for a few months, but it felt like I'd been away from the outside world for years. I happily skimmed my fingers along the edge of the bookshelf.

"You like books, huh, Alicia?" Brenda asked.

"You could say that. Books have always been my friend, my first love," I said dreamily.

"Well, do you want us to leave you two alone?" Caroline asked.

"No …"

"I'm going to get a cup of coffee. Come join us when you're ready," Brenda said.

"Okay," I said, watching Caroline and Brenda leave the room.

I looked around to find the Psychology section. I began reading the titles, but my attention quickly diverted elsewhere. I didn't feel like reading instructional books, since I was now studying it in school. I looked around and the romance novels caught my eye; easy reading that allowed me to briefly escape reality.

"Can I help you?" a kind voice asked from behind me.

I glanced up to see a stunningly gorgeous woman with long, flowing black hair. She wore vivid makeup, dressed like a hippy, and looked in her element in this cute, purple bookstore. I felt so strange being in uniform. We came from two different worlds. Her jet blue eyes sparkled when she glanced at me, and I quickly looked away.

"No, I'm okay. I'm just looking." I then realized, "This must be your store."

"Yes, it is. I see you enjoy books as much as I do."

"I do."

"Well, if that's the case, may I recommend some books to you?"

"Sure, but right now being at CAF, I haven't even found time to keep up with my school work."

"That's okay. Sometimes just having the books themselves can have the power to uplift you."

"I fully agree."

"Since you are in the fictional section, have you read Diane Gabaldon's *Outlander* series?" she asked.

"Yes. Actually, I only read the first book, *Outlander*, and loved it," I said, taking my hand to my heart.

"Did you know she came out with a fourth book in that series?"

"No way! What's it called?"

"*Drums of Autumn* and it's rumored it's not her last."

"Oh, that's fantastic! I'll have to read the second book this summer."

"*Dragonfly in Amber*," we said at the same time.

"I'm going to save Gabaldon's books for when school's out because they're so detailed."

"I understand. Her last book was over six hundred pages," she said. "Well, have you ever read any New Age books?"

"No, not really. That was never my thing, but what do you recommend?"

She thumbed through the bookshelf, looking for something. "*The Fifth Sacred Thing*, by Starhawk. It's one of my favorites," she said, handing it to me. "Just return it when you're done."

"Are you sure?" I asked.

"Positive. It's used, anyway. Just promise me that you'll tell me what you thought, when you've finished it."

"Okay, sure. Thanks! Well, I guess I'll go join my roommates in the café now. Thanks again …" I said, holding the book up.

"Hey soldier, what's your name?"

That stopped me in my tracks. No one had ever called me a *solider* before. I turned around.

"I'm Alicia."

"Well, it's nice to meet you. I'm Cathleen. I guess I'll be seeing you around then?"

"Yes, definitely!"

Chapter 10: Ethan

I entered Barracks burdened by all that I carried. It had been a while since Jamie took me to get my laundry and mail. It was mandatory for Ticks to have their Guides present whenever they checked their mailbox. There had been a note in my box that a package needed to be picked up. I had gone to the front desk and was handed a massive care-package, from my parents.

Since Ticks were required to carry book bags in their hands, like a briefcase, I entered Barracks with my book bag in my right, my laundry bag in my left, and the huge cardboard box in between my arms. I could barely strain and walk the Tick Line, nevertheless see over the box.

When I reached the first set of stairs, I attempted to double-time. I reached the third stoop without any interference, and then I heard my name.

"Hey, Randall, need any help with your things?" a Third Classman asked. "Nah, you're just a nasty Tick, and we don't help Ticks, do we?"

"Hey, Randall," another voiced chimed in. "Have any Twizzlers in that box?"

I stood there in an awkward strain, eager to get to my room.

"Wow, looks like someone sure loves you," the voice said, coming closer. "I don't remember the last time I was sent a care-package. Come to think of it, I don't think my parents ever sent me one. *Do you feel sorry for me Tick?*" he said, pouting.

I stood there annoyed, my arms tiring.

"If you have any red Twizzlers ..."

"Or any snicker bars ..." the other voice spoke again.

"Yeah, if you have any Twizzlers or Snickers bars, bring them to room 352. We'll make it worth it for you."

I sighed. *Is he going to let me go or what?*

"Get on your face, Tick!" someone yelled, far off.

"Nah, don't listen to him. You're free to go."

I ran up the stairs, relieved when I finally reached my room. I barged in and happily released everything to the ground. No one was there. I sat down, began to look for my scissors, and noticed the yellow note on my desk.

Randall, Rm. 482 Please call home as soon as possible, it read.

Ethan is awake.

Oh my god. Oh my god! Ethan's awake! I turned around the room, looking for someone to tell. Phone. I need a phone. Okay, think Randall. Think. I could go to Jamie's room and get him to take me to the Lounge—but he's at class. What about my Uncle Guides? *Hell ...* I could run to Sick Bay—and use the phone down there....

I grabbed my cover and took off running. I didn't even strain. I just kept running, faster and faster, down each flight of stairs. I exited Jackson Arch, quickly saluted the statute, and took off past the cadets walking to and from class.

Ethan was awake! *I couldn't believe it.*

As soon as I entered Sick Bay, I had to stand in line to sign in. A thin, dark-haired woman was handing paperwork to a cadet in front of me. My right leg started to shake, impatiently.

I looked around to see if there was another nurse on duty, someone I could ask to allow me to use the phone. I was so anxious; I could hardly contain my excitement. Finally, I was directed down the hall to a line of payphones. I was so relieved to find no one around.

I pulled out the calling card that was almost torn to threads by my tight grip on it, and began dialing. 1-800-942 ... and then I dialed the eight digit personal code.

"Please press '1' for the United States, otherwise dial the extension for the country you would like to call," the recorded operator said.

I quickly pressed "1" and then dialed Ethan's hospital room number.

It began to ring. And ring.

I stood there nervously, hoping I had dialed all the numbers correctly. Then I heard his voice.

"Hello?" Ethan answered gruffly.

"Hey, it's me," I said, choking back tears.

"Well hey, how's my favorite Tick?"

"Oh Ethan! It's so good to hear your voice," I said, gasping for breath. I willed myself to calm down. I took a deep breath, letting it out as slowly as I could.

"You too, Alicia. How's the Tick Line?"

"It sucks, you know—I don't care. I want to know how you are," I said, sounding pathetic and needy.

"Don't even think you're going to cry on me. I've had enough pity and Mom, oh god. Mom wouldn't stop crying. It's like I woke up and God came down from the heavens and looked upon us...."

"Oh, shut up!"

"Really, I'm okay. Whatever. I'm alive."

"And thank *God* for that. I'm going to come see you as soon as I can."

"Don't worry, you silly girl. I'm not going anywhere, anytime soon."

"Are Mom and Dad there with you now?"

"Dad's here, but he stepped out to get some coffee, so you caught me alone." He sighed. "I hear you're having a pretty rough time being a Tick."

"*Who told you that?*" I snapped.

"Dad read me your mass e-mails. I know it's tough. It has to be. I wouldn't willingly put myself through that bullshit, but you're different. Some sort of gluten for punishment, you are."

"Well, you know me. I can't enjoy life unless I'm challenged."

"I'm proud of you, kid. You have some nerve. Promise me one thing, Alicia. Please finish Tick Year. No matter how much bullshit you have to go through, how many hoops you have to jump through, finish what you started, okay?"

"Of course!"

"Alright, my nurse Shelly just came in. She's the one who gives me the drugs, so I'd better go. I'm glad you called," he said.

"Well, I'm glad you're awake," I said stupidly. "I love you, Ethan."

"Love you too."

We hung up, and I instantly regretted that I didn't ask him about his health. I'll have to get the scoop from Mom and Dad the next time I talk to them. I was just so relieved Ethan was awake.

I looked down at my watch and noticed it was minutes before Super Roll Call (SRC), so I quickly signed out and ran back to Barracks.

After dinner, Cadre let us go, so I went to the library to get online. I had to do it secretively. I pretended I was composing a paper for my latest assignment, keeping a Microsoft Word document available, to disguise doing e-mail. I immediately checked Ethan's website.

> *Today we received the news we've been so desperately waiting to hear. Ethan has woken up. He seems to be of good spirits, and talks non-stop. It is as if nothing has changed, though everything has. His face is so swollen from the burns it is hard to recognize him. His body is all bandaged up. Unfortunately, the doctors had to amputate most of his fingers on both hands and also his left foot—*

My heart stopped. Ethan didn't tell me any of this!

> *but this doesn't seem to concern Ethan. He has pneumonia, but the doctors say he is recovering. For the moment, things seem hopeful. God has given Ethan back to us, and his mother and I are overwhelmed with joy. The entire family is very grateful to everyone for their support through phone calls, e-mail, prayers and cards. Let's pray for a speedy recovery. Thank you.*

I felt relieved. It looked like everything would be all right. Thank God!

I went about my daily life at CAF feeling lighter, happier, and inspired. Life felt okay again. I started to attack my studies with full force, surprising myself. I was just *so thankful* that Ethan was alive and well.

Chapter 11: The Memoriam

"You have to hear this, Randall," my co-Tick Quentin said, as I entered our Guide's room. "One of our Fellow Ticks jumped off the fourth stoop into the laundry bags!"

"No way! Who was it?"

"Tick Thompson, from Golf Company. He sprained his ankle, that stupid mother-fucker, but he's now the hero of all the Ticks," he laughed.

"That's awesome! Man, I can't believe someone actually had the nerve to do that!"

"Too bad our Tick Year isn't over…." He shook his head in disappointment. "Oh well, Tick Thompson has some big balls as far as I'm concerned."

"Sure does! Some *big brass balls* …"

Jamie looked up from his studies. "Looks like you're in a good mood, Randall?"

"I am. My brother Ethan is awake," I said, grinning from ear to ear.

"Well, that's wonderful! We should celebrate. Y'all feel like going to the Lounge for some pizza?"

"Sure!" I said, like any of us would turn him down.

~

I talked to Jamie about going home. He told me that I could get an Emergency Furlough in order to visit Ethan in the hospital. During lunchtime the next day, Jamie walked with me over to the main office and helped me with the paperwork. Jamie even called a friend he knew in town that would drive me to the airport. Then I contacted Dad. He searched hours on the Internet to find a reasonable price and within days, I was on my way home.

~

Wednesday, I got up at 0'dark thirty. With my bag in hand, I left my roommates behind, still sleeping in their racks. I walked out of our room into the cool morning air. I ran down the three flights of stairs, rounding, instead of squaring, my corners while barely straining; no Upperclassman was around to watch my every move. I walked out of Barracks, surprised to find groups of cadets doing PT on the parade ground.

I sat on a bench in front of the science building and watched the cadets do stretches. A silver Buick drove up in front of me, and the driver rolled down his window.

"Alicia?" he asked.

I immediately jumped up and climbed inside.

"Hey, I really appreciate you taking the time to help me out," I said.

"It's cool. Jamie and I have been friends a long time. I know you're tired, so sit back and relax. I'm taking you to Regan International, so we have a little over a three hour car ride. Your flight departs at 11:25 AM, right?"

"Yep. Thanks so much. I can't believe this. I'm going home!"

"Yes, you are. I'm sorry about what happened to your brother. I hope he's okay."

"He is now," I said, rolled over, and went to sleep. I could fall asleep anywhere, at any time.

A couple of hours later, I woke up to the sound of a voice over an intercom in a drive through.

"Hey, you're awake. Want breakfast?"

"Sure," I said, rubbing my face. I could feel where I had drooled and felt self-conscious. "Anything is fine, but definitely coffee. Coffee, with lots of cream," I said happily. I hadn't had real coffee since before matriculation.

At the airport, I gave him a big hug good-bye, even though I didn't know him; I just felt really grateful for his assistance. I quickly got out of the car and grabbed all my gear.

"Need any help?" he asked.

"No, thank you. I got it."

"I'm sure you do," he said confidently, like any woman that goes to CAF must be hardcore. "Alright, I'll see you tomorrow night."

"Yes! Thanks again."

~

On the flight, I drifted in and out of consciousness. Normally, I'm really friendly and outgoing. This time, though, I kept to myself. I was in uniform and received some curious glances. When I took off my cover, I became aware that my appearance, with extremely short hair for a female, seemed out of place. I didn't care. I was happy that I was on my way home.

~

Mom and Dad greeted me off the plane. They looked really tired, aged with the stress and burden of the past four months. We hugged and kissed.

"How was your trip, sweetheart?" Dad asked.

"I slept most of the time. It seems like now I can fall sleep wherever and whenever I want."

"You sound like your father," Mom said.

"I can't wait to see Ethan!"

Mom and Dad looked at each other, debating who would speak first.

"*What's wrong?* Why are you acting strange?" I said, suddenly worried.

"Honey, uh, we need to talk, but let's go to the car first."

"*About what? What's wrong?*"

Dad took a deep breath and let it out. I immediately sat down where I was, which was in the middle of the airport, with people swarming all around us.

"I'm sorry to tell you this, but—"

"No! No! No! Don't. Don't tell me anything is wrong with Ethan. I just spoke to him. *He's fine!*"

"No, honey, he's not," Mom spoke up.

"Today Ethan took an unfortunate turn for the worse," Dad explained. "The pneumonia was more than his body could handle."

I stared at him, shocked.

"He began respiratory failure this afternoon," he continued, "and Ethan passed away shortly after five this morning."

"*What?*" I couldn't believe what I heard.

"The doctors at Brooke Army Medical Center did all they could, but they weren't able to save him. It is God's will," Mom tried to explain.

"Fuck God!" I yelled, embarrassing my parents.

"It's time to go, Alicia. Get your bag. It's time for you to say good-bye to your brother," Dad ordered, taking control.

~

My parents, unbeknownst to me, had made the quickest funeral arrangements known to man, so I could be there during my brief emergency furlough; the funeral was scheduled for the following morning.

That night I barely slept. In the morning, I had to actually decide what to wear to my brother's funeral. How do I plan for that? I looked through my closet and saw all my old clothes, feminine apparel, but nothing seemed to represent who I was now. I decided to go with the formal uniform I'd brought. It would really make Ethan proud to see me in that.

I carefully ironed my white pants, polished my shoes, and shined my brass. Looking in the mirror, I noticed the dark circles under my eyes and baggy eye lids.

I didn't say much that morning to my parents; I was simply overwhelmed. Besides, there was little to say during this solemn time.

My parents asked me if I wanted to speak at the funeral, after the priest spoke. I hesitated. I wanted to honor Ethan, to express what a warm and caring brother he had been, but how would I stand up in front of all those people and express my feelings? I didn't want to feel so vulnerable, so I told them I'd think about it.

At the funeral home, I walked cautiously over to Ethan's casket. It was open, but the man inside didn't resemble Ethan at all. The head was larger and covered with a baseball cap. His face was lightly plastered with make-up, and his eyes were closed. *That's Ethan*, I told myself, even though I questioned my logic. Is he here … floating in this room, watching us?

I placed a CAF uniformed teddy bear in the casket, with my good-bye letter, and a picture of the two of us. Seeing Ethan, I decided I would say a few words, in case he was listening.

The man I looked at wasn't smiling. Ethan always smiled. Where was his gold chain? I felt slightly panicked until I noticed it sticking out from under the buttoned shirt.

My attention was brought to the past, during my sophomore year at school. Ethan had told everyone it was my birthday and forced everyone to say "Happy Birthday" all day, to his younger sister. I smiled in reminiscence. He wasn't embarrassed by me, like older siblings normally were of their adoring younger brothers and sisters. He took care of me. We were very close.

I stared at the figure lying in front of me. Ethan was dressed in a suit and tie, so unlike the casual guy he was. I wanted to touch him and wished I had the courage to lean over and hug him—but I was scared. He's dead. I hadn't really encountered death before. Oh, how I yearned for one more conversation, a way to say a good-bye that felt complete. I was numb with grief, numb from innocence so quickly defiled, and I couldn't comprehend how this came to be.

I treasured my last moments with Ethan. With a certain amount of privacy, I tried to say good-bye.

"I'm sorry you had to leave so soon, my brother," I whispered. "But

I'm glad you're not suffering anymore." Tears streamed down my face. "*None of this makes sense to me....*" I suddenly wanted to scream ... and instantly controlled myself. "I wished ..." and sighed. "Just know ... I love you ... and I will miss you, *forever.*" I briefly put my hand on his stomach, took a deep breath and let it out, and then went and sat down next to Mom.

I turned around and eyed Julie, Christine, and Theresa. The three of them looked at me with such concern and pity in their glistening eyes. They knew Ethan well. It was clear that life would never be the same again.

I looked around the room and wondered where Seth and Courtney were. Ever since the accident, Courtney had changed. I received an e-mail from her a few weeks ago, expressing her stress, and how she had turned into someone she didn't like and others didn't want to be around. She was obviously scared, hurt, and psychologically wounded. I wished I was closer to help. I wondered if she was getting the love and support she needed from her family. I knew our friends didn't exactly know how to help her. It was so important that the five of us, Christine, Julie, Theresa, Courtney and I, remain close. We had to get through this tough time together.

I noticed Seth sitting alone in the back of the room. I didn't have the strength to get up to greet him. I just stayed where I was as the funeral started. Mariah Carey and Boys to Men sang *One Sweet Day* over the speakers, causing me to cry.

The funeral felt like a dream. I didn't hear the words spoken by family and friends. I zoned out, wondering why this had happened. How was Seth coping with the situation?

Mom's voice called me back.

"Alicia flew from Virginia, interrupting her Tick Year at the College of Armed Forces, to join us today." I thought her remarks were silly, but I knew she was just showing how proud she was of me.

I got up and walked slowly to the podium. I felt completely bewildered.

"Um, hi everyone," I said self-consciously. "I came home yesterday, excited that I was going to see my older brother." I paused and looked at the audience. "I didn't expect him to die. It didn't even cross my mind. The only question I held in my mind was *when*. When was Ethan going to wake up? When was I going to be able to see him?" I expressed. "Most of you knew who Ethan was. He was sweet … caring … and a lot of fun to be around. He had a big heart and loved telling stories." Tears rolled down my face. "It just feels so wrong that this was his time to go," I said, my voice cracking.

I glanced at my friends. Their love for Ethan was reflected in their eyes. I looked at Mom. She sat red-faced with tear stains on her checks. I gently smiled at her. Dad handed me a tissue. I looked at him for a minute, my vision blurring from the tears, before I took it.

I was in a daze. "I don't know what to say…." I mumbled. "I don't have words to express …"

"It's okay, Alicia," Dad whispered, standing next to me for support.

"I guess all I want to say is that Ethan was a great brother." I swallowed hard. "And I will love him always."

~

At the end of the service, I walked down the aisle past Seth. I couldn't look at him, but I knew he saw me. My fingers gripped my CAF hat, and my heart leaped. I found the water fountain in the hallway and drank long gulps, trying to refresh my sense of self and steady my nerves.

Christine, Julie, and Theresa came out to the foyer looking for me. They were my friends, people I had known for years, and who loved me. As close as I felt toward them, I felt disconnected from everyone. I felt alone, beyond a sense of loneliness; I no longer felt like me, but a stranger to myself.

They found me and each hugged me, expressing warm words of sorrow.

"Courtney's not here, is she?" I asked.

"No, she told us it'd be too hard for her to come," Christine said.

Julie rubbed her hand up and down my back. I could feel her hand, but it didn't bring comfort. Feeling *anything* was undesirable.

I had a moment where I too wanted to die—to just fade away—but it passed quickly.

I tried to convince myself that I was strong enough to see Seth, that it would somehow be okay.

"I need to face Seth," I said softly. I'd had dreamt about seeing him, ever since I left, but I had not dreamed of seeing him like this. Not at my brother's funeral. Ethan wasn't supposed to have died!   "Okay." Julie nodded.

"Is there anything we can do to help?" Christine asked.   "You're here. That's all that matters," I said, holding back the tears.

"Seth's still inside." Theresa nodded toward the door.

"I know. I just don't know how I'm going to do this. Part of me has been dying to see him the past couple of months, but I don't know if I have the strength...."

"It's okay. You'll be fine," Julie said.

"You have my back, right girls?" I said, smiling a little.

"Of course we do," Christine said.

I walked with them, hand and hand, outside to our cars to drive to the cemetery.

❧

Two bagpipers played Celtic dirges as everyone collected around the burial site. Their music helped create a truly sentimental atmosphere.

Seth came over to where I was standing with my friends and hugged me. My heart stopped. He hugged me for a very long time. I felt so serene in his arms, as if we created our own vortex. I began to melt as I listened to his words of love.

I tried to stay calm, but my tears disobeyed my orders to be strong. I wished he could comfort me forever, to massage my heart, and convince every part of my being that things were going to be okay. I no longer wanted to fight so hard to survive—I just wanted to be with him.

He loosened his embrace, and—somehow I instantly knew that—this wonderful moment ... was *over*. That's all Seth had to give.

❧

Amazing Grace played solemnly and beautifully on the bagpipes while Ethan's brilliant white casket, shinning like pearl, was lowered into the ground.

When the burial ceremony ended, I said brief good-byes to my family and friends. I sat in the backseat of my parents' car, feeling empty.

I stared out of the window as we left and briefly saw my reflection. I hardly recognized myself. My eyes were swollen and my cheeks and lips were so puffy. With my buzz cut, I felt unattractive and stripped of my feminine beauty. I realized I must've looked quite different to Seth, not the cute and spunky girl from the summer. I knew that was going to be the last time I saw him for a while.

~

My parents drove me to the airport with little time to spare. I was thankful I didn't have the opportunity to hang around the house, as people gathered to mourn my brother. I didn't think I could have handled it.

I left Texas feeling utterly depressed. When I arrived in Baltimore, Jamie's friend was patiently waiting to drive me back to CAF. During the car ride, he let me sleep again.

When I woke up, I didn't feel better. I mourned the loss of Ethan, no longer having my older brother, my greatest companion, and Seth. I felt so alone.

I no longer cared about anything. The most important aspects of my life had been taken from me, stripped from my heart and soul, and left me naked and extremely vulnerable.

I entered Barracks exhausted. I forced myself to strain when what I really wanted to do was hit somebody or run away.

No one stopped me on the stoops. Maybe the look on my face told them to back off. I got to my room and collapsed in my chair.

Brenda looked up from her computer and asked, "How are you?" even though she could tell what the answer was.

"Well, I'm still breathing," I replied, as if that was a positive thing.

"Want a cigarette?"

I nodded. "Ethan's dead."

"*Oh … no …*" Brenda instantly pulled a chair up next to me.

Chapter 12: Tick Rescue

I laid on my rack thinking and couldn't fall asleep. My mind was playing tricks, doing cartwheels, running around in circles. Feeling was painful enough, and now I had to think, too. Maybe I could just float, ride the wind, and fly over the mountains. I'd feel so free. Then there wouldn't be any pain; there wouldn't be any hurting.

⌐

I awoke up with puffy eyes and a sore throat. I felt so raw; my body ached as if recovering from a fever. My roommates were getting ready for morning formation, zipping by all around me. I was stuck in slow motion; it felt like being under water. Maybe I should just climb back in my rack and forget morning formation. Could I get away with it?

"Randall ... *Randall!* Come on now, you need to get ready. It's about time to go down to our Guide's room," Dawn insisted.

I stared at her, as if not knowing her face or comprehending what she said, and then looked down at my apparel. Well, I'd at least gotten my shorts off, but I was standing there in a T-shirt and underwear, not ready as I should be in class uniform. I snapped back into awareness. I can do this.

"Um, tell Jamie to excuse me, this one time. I'm not all here, but I'll be at formation on time. Just go without me."

Dawn hesitated, looked at my disheveled appearance and said, "Okay, but I hope you're there. Come back from wherever you've been! You have responsibilities here, and you'll only make it worst for yourself if you get in trouble."

"I know. Alright, alright. I'm moving...."

"Okay, see you later," she said, and the door slammed shut behind her.

I put in my contacts, seeing clearly at once, but feeling a sense of doom in facing the day.

"Do you need some help?" sweet Caroline asked.

"No, I'll be okay ... *really.*" I nodded, trying to convince her and myself of this notion.

"Alright, well, hang in there. Things will get better," Caroline said, the cheerful and optimistic one. She smiled, gathered up her books, and headed out the door.

Brenda had already left that morning for Marine ROTC PT, so I was left to fend for myself.

Alright Randall, it's time to get your act together. I quickly changed, put on my shoes—*shit*. My shoes weren't even shinned. My brass looked like crap. Oh, fuck me. Well, I can't do anything about it now because I'm going to be late if I don't leave pronto.

I grabbed my cover, my CAF backpack, and left.

At formation, we were given a surprise inspection. Shit, shit, shit! I thought, as I stood at attention.

"Well, look at what we got here. Hey, Mr. Fraser, you might want to see this. Looks like we have a slacker, a nobody, a looosssserrr," Mr. Harman said, rolling his r's in exaggeration.

Jamie walked over cautiously. "Leave her alone," he ordered and turned closer to Mr. Harman and whispered, "Her brother just died."

Mr. Harman paused, clearly surprised.

"I'm sorry to hear that, Randall," and moved on with the inspections.

"I'll see you later, okay?" Jamie spoke gently to me.

I nodded.

~

I went about my day trying desperately to hide my soiled appearance, but it seemed to have the opposite effect. In between classes, I tried to run to my room without being stopped, but I didn't make it.

The First Classman who stopped me didn't seem too invested, just bored, as if he just felt like making an ass out of someone, and it happened to be me. He made me do a dozen push-ups, a couple high-knees, and then let me go.

I took off up the staircase, but was stopped again on the third stoop, this time surrounded by three or four Third Classmen.

They're hungry, I realized. They saw me alone and surrounded me like a pack of lions about to have a zebra snack. I listened to their commands and pushed.

"*Faster, Tick!* Where do you think you are, West Point? This is C-A-F! You have to work here. *Push! Fuckin' Tick, push!*"

I was sweating profusely at that point.

"Go home, Randall. We don't want you here," one of the cadets said matter-of-factly, like it was truth, not just because I was a Tick, but because he really didn't like *me*.

I knew I was taking things too personally, but I couldn't help it.

There was one Upperclassman female that was especially nasty to me and nicknamed me "Fatty Randall." I wanted to shoot them all with a 9-millimeter, or better yet, stab them with my bayonet one by one to watch them all die a slow, painful death.

I tried to block out their remarks by daydreaming, by pretending I didn't hear what they said. I continued to strain while sweat rolled down the back of my neck. I felt dirty and knew my shirt was covered with grim from the concrete floor. I could feel my face turning red as my fists tightened with rage.

The group of Third Classmen continued to grow, as if no one was in class, and all were hanging out in Barracks. I knew they could smell my weakness, as if I reeked of defeat and hopelessness.

"*You should go home, Randall. Find a nice state college to attend and just be an average student because there is nothing, I mean nothing, special about you!*"

"You're not fit for this school! You don't even deserve to be a worthless Tick, maggot!"

"You don't even care enough to shine your shoes!"

"You should just quit now!"

The screaming got to me, and it felt like they'd never let me go.

"You don't belong here!"

"Go home, Randall!" the voices repeated.

"Fuck You!" I screamed, not realizing it was my own voice that I heard.

Then I felt a hand grab my right arm, and I reacted immediately, thinking I was going to be hit. I swung, but only hit the air around me. It was actually one of my Fellow Ticks who grabbed my arm, pulling me out of the madness, trying to save me.

"Run, Randall, run!" he yelled.

I felt him pull me toward the stairs. I pushed past the cadets and ran up the steps to our home base, the fourth stoop, away from the screaming, away from the yelling and torments of the vicious cadets below. I ran to my room, like a mad man that had just been ravished by Indians on the warpath. I ran past Brenda who was alone typing on her computer, and fell to the floor in the corner.

"Those fucking bastards," are the only words I got out, as I rocked back and forth, shaking from the shock of it all.

The Fellow Tick who had saved me, who had performed the Tick Rescue, walked over to Brenda.

"It was the Third Classmen. They all ganged up on her. It was quite a show!"

I looked up from my stupor and, a bit throaty, said, "Thanks, Khawaja," and put my head back down. He left the room, and Brenda came to my side.

"Damn, girl. I had no idea it was you! I heard the noise and knew something crazy was going on the stoop below, but I had no idea it was *you*! I'm *so* sorry. Are you okay?"

"I'll be okay in a minute. That fuckin' sucked, but it would've been worse if Khawaja didn't get me. I was about to start swinging. I got so angry. I wanted to kill them, for real! I wanted to *kill*."

"Yep, that sounds about right. Well, get cleaned up. Let's hide you under there," she said, pointing to the desk closest to the window. "Let yourself calm down before dinner formation."

I pulled down the shade on our door and started stripping. I stood in front of the mirror in my sports bra, my skin flushed and damp. I washed my face and head with cold water, splashed water down my back, and took deep breathes to calm myself. In the background, I heard Barracks settling down, as cadets left for their classes.

"How can you study in here? The echoes in Barracks would distract me. Don't you get interrupted constantly?" I asked her, amazed at her fortitude and concentration.

"Nah, I zone out, and people don't generally come in because they don't think anyone's here. Most people are at lunch or in class. My Guide doesn't always eat lunch, so I sneak up here, eat from my food box, and study until SRC."

Once I was dressed, I grabbed my blanket and crawled under Dawn's desk which faced the windows and kept me out of sight. I stared dreamily out the window, comforted by the enclosure. My mind drifted.…

I saw Ethan in his casket, lying there, not looking like him. I couldn't feel his presence and that scared me. I remembered the feeling of Seth's arms, how safe I'd felt, and my heart ached to feel them again.

I swallowed. I'm going to have to put *all of that* in the back of my mind, *for now*. I need to concentrate on surviving here; otherwise I'm not going to make it through the Tick Line.

"Do you think about Troy a lot?" I asked Brenda, not seeing her, but heard her sigh.

"Yeah, I sure do. We were together for two years in high school. When you're used to being with someone every day, it's hard to picture time apart."

"When do you think you'll see him next?"

"I have no idea. His life is the Marines now, and I'm here."

"I saw Seth at Ethan's funeral," I explained. "It was painfully sweet. I felt so desperate. I wanted so badly to run away with him, to forget our lives and just run away from the pain and sorrow. I can't seem to shake it. I carry it all with me … Ethan's death, my yearning for Seth, and my sadness for Courtney. I don't know what to do. If I'm not careful, I'm afraid I'm going to fall apart.…"

"You're a lot stronger than you think you are, Alicia."

"No matter what, Brenda, don't let me leave here. I have to make all this worth it." I looked out the window, hoping the beauty of the sky and the mountains below would give me strength. "Don't ever let me leave...."

"I promise. You're going to be fine. One day at a time, right?"

"Yeah."

⌐

I heard that CAF does not necessarily get better as the time goes on. I asked my Guide Jamie what his favorite year at CAF was. As a senior who was about to graduate, I was shocked when his answer was "Tick Year." *What?* In my mind, being a Tick sucked. To him, though, it was his favorite year. It was the year people cared, family sent care-packages, and friends wrote letters. It was the year Cadre "babysat" you, and no matter what you did, it was okay because you were just a Tick and still learning the system.

By the time you're a Third Classman, everyone expects you to know your shit. Everyone expects you to know the rules, to follow them, and to be completely independent, like being instantly thrown into the world of adulthood after only a brief time in infancy.

Third class year was described to me as the hardest of the four years at CAF. It is the year girlfriends are known to break up with CAF cadets because long distance relationships are no longer desired, a CAF schedules are too demanding to allow time for romance. It is the year family stops paying so much attention because they think their cadets no longer need it, after having surviving Tick year.

With the combined stress of cadetship and academic responsibilities, along with the lack of emotional support, Third Classmen often become desperately depressed. This also explained why the Third Classmen were the most brutal to Ticks.

⌐

When Khawaja rescued me from the madness that afternoon, I'd felt like I had some support, like someone was looking out for me. When life is rough and there seems to be no end in sight, sometimes the world throws a bone, something to keep you going.

I went to Economics class the next morning and daydreamed during a discussion about gas prices going up in relation to the Iraqi conflict. I looked down at my bag and noticed the book the woman, Cathleen, had given me at Stone Soup Bookstore. I smiled. I cherished books, especially ones that were recommended to me.

After class, I went to the library and descended the three flights of stairs to the basement, where few students studied. The seclusion allowed me time to collect my thoughts and read in peace. Reading had always been an escape for me, allowing my mind to move beyond the confines of the present moment.

I had homework to do and papers to write, but I took a moment and allowed myself to enjoy something outside of CAF. I opened the book and began to read.

The book immediately drew me into another world. This may be exactly what I need to help me survive the Tick Line.

Chapter 13: One Ends One Begins

I stared at the letter in my hands, not fully comprehending the meaning of it. It was from Seth. When I received it, I clutched it to my heart and concealed it away. Now in the privacy of my Guide's room, I took it out. I held the letter like a precious stone, protecting it and cherishing it. Seth was my lifeline. I thought of him incessantly, especially during the tough moments where thoughts of him brought me comfort.

I focused my attention on the letter before me. The letter only contained a few lines of his scribble.

> *Alicia, you are a remarkable person and I care for you deeply. Since Ethan has died, I am no longer the same person. I do not want you to count on me any longer, for I am afraid that I will only disappoint you. I am so very sorry. —Seth*

Tears welled up, but I choked them back. I didn't want my Guide to see me cry. Besides, tears didn't help. The purpose of crying only let my guard down. Tears merely brought me shame and exhaustion. I had to keep my emotions in check. There was no purpose in losing control anymore. Apparently, I can no longer yearn for Seth; that was obviously the point of his letter. I felt this at the funeral, but I was reluctant to let go.

As much as I loved Seth and dreamed of him, the distance was painful. I wouldn't be able to see him until Christmas break and then not again until next summer. That was obviously not enough to him, not enough to keep our relationship going.

I was surprised by how easily Seth could let go. Maybe it was better this way, I wondered. I didn't want to give up the dream, though, the existence of what we had together and of what could be. Dreaming of him was an escape for me, happiness in the dreary sleep-deprived and stressful existence, with the lack of alone time and the continuousness of duty and performance.

The thing with tragedies, though, is everyone handles them differently. Sometimes people are brought closer together, like my roommates and I in our struggle for survival at CAF. But in this instance with Ethan's death, it was too much for Seth. I could understand his need to break free, not just from me, but from my whole family, to not be reminded daily of our loss. He had to move on with his life.

Even with my logic, my heart ached. I looked around the room, my eyes wide and my lips pressed hard together, and suppressed the urge to fall apart. In many ways, I needed to cut off my emotions in order to make it here.

I looked at Jamie reading at his desk. He was always studying. He had mastered the art of controlling his emotions, always appearing astute and strong. CAF had taught me I must become humble, no longer valuing my desires, but succumbing to the desires of those with power, to those with authority.

I wanted to lie back on the hay and allow the comfort of a pillow to caress me, to allow the blanket to swallow me, but I couldn't. I shook the feelings of weakness that were about to overcome me. I got up and walked around the room. I looked over Kenny's shoulder. He was juggling playing a video game and chatting on Instant Messenger while smoking a cigarette.

"Would you mind, Kenny, if I had one?" I asked.

"Nope," he said, as a cigarette dangled from his mouth.

I stood by the window and observed the cadets outside of Barracks walking to and from class. It was so easy to pick out the Ticks. It wasn't just the obvious missing bars of rank on their shoulder boards, but the way they walked and interacted. Ticks were not allowed to talk to their classmates outside of academic buildings; that was an Upperclassman privilege. Ticks walked with more purpose, trying hard to follow the rules. The fear of attracting trouble loomed like a dark cloud over each Tick's head.

I lit my cigarette, fully enjoying the smell and immediate flavor. Upperclassmen, especially Seconds and Firsts, walked with an air of casualness and superiority, knowing they owned the school. Most were busy getting to class, so they rarely took the time to correct disobedient Ticks, like those whispering to each other in passing. The Third classmen also walked with a similar arrogance, but were more eager to catch Ticks red-handed, like bullies ready to extort lunch money from nerds.

I enjoyed the cigarette and savored the fumes. I looked down at my watch and saw that I had to be in history class in ten minutes. I chuckled at the irony of that, since Seth and I were now *history*.

⁓

On Sunday, I was surprised to find myself alone. Dawn went to her host family, Mr. Penchard's house, again. Brenda was overwhelmed with homework, so she decided to use this time to catch-up. Caroline went with her Guide to church and a barbeque. I decided to head into town to Stone Soup Bookstore.

When I entered the bookstore, the small bell on the door chimed, announcing my entrance. I looked around and didn't see anyone, so I browsed the bookshelves. Since I was currently enjoying *The Fifth Sacred Thing*, I went over to the New Age section.

"Well, it looks like my recommendation put you on a new trend."

I turned around to see Cathleen beaming from ear to ear.

"*The Fifth Sacred Thing* is awesome so far, a good escape, though my current reality parallels the militaristic society described in the book."

"What are you trying to escape from?"

"Well …" I hesitated and looked up. "I've been through some crazy changes in the past couple of months." I shrugged it off like it was no big deal.

"I hear the Tick Line can be pretty grueling."

"True, but that's not just it.…"

"Really? What else has been going on?" she asked, giving me her full attention.

I felt comfortable enough, and she seemed nice enough, so I continued. "My brother died."

"Oh," Cathleen said, as a sudden look of worry crossed her face.

"Yeah, it hasn't been easy. Ethan and I were very close."

"How are you feeling?"

"I feel like I've lost a huge part of myself. And you know what was weird? As all this was happening … the funeral, seeing my family and friends talk about Ethan, I began to like … become the observer rather than the participant of my life. Has that ever happened to you? Maybe it's a coping mechanism." I looked up, concerned I'd been sharing too much to a person I didn't know.

"No, it's okay. Go on, Alicia, I'm listening."

"Well, I see my brother lying there in the casket, and I don't see him. It's obviously his body, but I don't connect with it being Ethan."

"You didn't feel his presence, the presence of his energies."

"Exactly, but then when I get home, and I go to my room, I feel him right in the room with me, as if he was standing there next to me." I felt self-conscious telling her this.

"I know what you mean."

"You do?"

"Yeah, sure. My mom died when I was six. I don't remember much because I was so young, but there are moments when I strongly feel her presence. It's random too, like when I chose to open this store. I was completely at a loss for a location. My mom came to my dreams and told me to move here, so I listened. This town is full of so many people connected to The College of Armed Forces which made me think my store wouldn't survive here, but it's doing okay."

"That's cool. Does your mom come to your dreams often?" I asked.

"Most of the time I just feel her presence. I know she's watching out for me."

"I see. Do you believe in angels?"

"Yeah, I certainly do."

"Well, I haven't told anyone this yet, but—" I was unsure how to begin. "I went to the scene where my brother's accident took place. I stood next to the tree that his truck hit. I went there alone, but then a man pulled up. He told me he'd been there when the accident

96

occurred," I explained. "He told me that the rear wheel of my brother's truck had come off, which is why Ethan lost control of it! After listening to the man, I tried to envision the scene myself. When I turned around to inquire more about it, he was no longer there. I didn't hear him get into his car or drive off or anything. He was just nowhere in sight. At the time, I was still in the fog of shock and mourning, and it didn't dawn on me until later how odd the whole encounter was," I said, getting chills at the memory.

"Whoa, sounds to me like you'd been visited by an angel."

"That's the only sense I can make of it, though I feel like I imagined the whole thing. And, as silly as this sounds, I thought Ethan would've come to my dreams by now, to tell me he was okay … to have communicated somehow with me. That probably sounds dumb."

"It doesn't sound dumb at all," Cathleen said. "But you did say you felt his presence. Maybe that was his way of saying good-bye."

"Yeah, maybe … Anyhow, this reading has done me some good. It gives me a break from the constant military duties and allows me to think about other things."

The room became quiet, so I refocused my attention on the books around me. After some time, Cathleen spoke up.

"May I ask you a personal question?"

I nodded.

"Why did you choose to attend CAF?"

"Well … I wanted to do something special and unique. I guess you could say I was drawn here."

"Well, what exactly were you drawn to?"

"I liked the seriousness of military school. I like to be challenged, to experience something greater than myself." I shrugged.

"Is it what you expected?" Cathleen looked at me straight on.

"Um, yes and no. In some ways, it's harder than I thought it was going to be. I obviously didn't expect—" I stomped my foot in annoyance at the fact I all of a sudden became teary-eyed, with thinking of Ethan. I cleared my throat. "I didn't expect Ethan to leave this world so soon, to leave me all alone."

The air in the bookstore suddenly felt thick, burdened with my emotion.

"I'm so sorry," she said.

"No, I'm sorry. I don't mean to be so emotional around you. I just, for some reason, feel real comfortable talking to you."

"Oh, I'm glad! I feel the same way. We must've been friends in a past life," she said, winking at me.

"So you believe in reincarnation?"

"Sure do, doesn't everyone?"

"I don't know. I've never discarded it. Personally, I wasn't raised with much of a religious background. My dad's religion could probably be called *the military*. He's a retired army officer," I explained. "And my mom, she always told me to think for myself, to ask many questions, and to seek answers."

"Yes, you definitely have to ask your own questions. Your mom sounds like a Buddhist." She smiled.

"Since Ethan died, I've been thinking more about God. I keep asking: why did this happen? I know I'm still in shock. I'm trying to get some control of my life, but everything is so out-of-whack."

"That's the funny thing about hard times. It usually brings us back to God," Cathleen said. "Whatever *God* is to you...."

"Yep..."

"I sympathize that you feel overwhelmed at school."

"Thanks. CAF *is* a lot to handle. The death of Ethan is even more than I can handle, but what can I do? I have to survive and try to move forward, regardless."

"Now I understand why escaping is so important to you."

"Yeah, reading books ... they don't feel like a burden or a responsibility; I've always loved to read. Reading is something I can do for myself, separate from the school. I read quickly, so it's always been a joy."

"That's why I love books too! Well, if you don't mind, I have other books I'd love to share with you. I have a special stash," Cathleen said, lowering her voice, as if sharing a secret.

"Really?"

"Yeah, but it will have to be off hours. Next week is Thanksgiving, and I will be closed Friday. Will you be around?"

"Yeah, I'm not going home since I just came back from Texas, after going to Ethan's funeral," I explained. "So I'll be around."

"Well, come over to my place. It's not far from here." Cathleen pointed up. "I live upstairs, kind of convenient and all."

"Oh, awesome. Sure. What time would you like me here?"

"Noon? We can have lunch, and I'll show you my treasure. Sound good?"

"Sounds fantastic."

"Great!"

"Okay. I'll see you Friday," I said and left.

Chapter 14: Tick Riot

When I arrived back at Barracks, I went to Jamie's room to what was going on.

"Just the Tick I was looking for...."

"What now?" I asked unenthusiastically.

"Well, we've been talking," he stated, clearly referring to his roommates, but only Kenny was present. "You see, we have two problems."

I sat down at the nearest seat, Jamie's hay.

"First, as Band Company Commander, I need the Ticks to step up."

I looked at him, waiting for him to continue. He looked deep in thought, so I asked, "And what do you intend for us to do?" I really wasn't up for surprises.

"You see, this Tick Line, the goal of it is to create a unified class. The trouble is some Ticks are living for themselves, showing up to formation without their roommates or are getting ready for room inspection without helping each other. And there are those Ticks that have been worked out regularly, without their Fellow Ticks showing support," he explained.

When a Tick is singled out by Cadre, it is expected that his Fellow Ticks voluntarily join him in the process, which sometimes helps end the workout prematurely, showing Cadre that the Ticks are working together.

"Some Ticks are even attending Tick Challenge without any notion of teamwork! That simply has to change."

"I don't disagree. What would you like me to do about it?" My roommates and I depended on each other so fiercely; I couldn't imagine fending for myself alone.

"Well, I'm thinking a Tick Riot would do the trick."

"I see …" I said with a concerned look on my face.

"And I want *you* to run it, but I want you to put Tick Bigelow in charge to execute it."

I sat looking at him with my mouth open. "Are you serious, Jamie? You want Tick Bigelow—" My protest was quickly interrupted.

"Yes, I want that little worm to step up to the plate."

"Hasn't he been stepping up to the plate?" I was fully annoyed by this obligation, but as Band Company Representative, it was expected.

My mind travelled back to when Jamie first ordered me to oversee Tick Bigelow. Tick Bigelow was the GIM who "wormed" out of sweat parties and Tick Challenge with the pathetic excuse of shin splints. The first thing I did was barge into Tick Bigelow's room and ordered him to remove the GIM tag.

"But I'm injured," Tick Bigelow protested.

"That's nice, Bigelow, but that's not going to work for me." I got in his face. "You're one of my Fellow Ticks, and I expect you to work as hard as every other Tick in this school! You're not going to worm out of sweat parties, Tick Challenge, or Cadre workouts anymore. It's not going to be tolerated!"

"Who do you think you are, Randall?" he asked quietly, not looking at me.

"I'm Band Company's representative and my Guide is Mr. Fraser, our CO, so …" I took a deep breath. I should try to relate to him, show him I care, rather than belittle him. Time to use a carrot rather than the stick, I thought. I grabbed one of his roommate's chairs and pulled it up beside him. "Alright … you're obviously strong enough, fit enough," I said, observing his approximate trim five foot ten build. "You don't have a weight problem. You're of good health, so what gives?"

He immediately took offense, looking at me angrily, but I spoke to him with a gentle voice, hoping I could somehow connect.

"What's going on, Bigelow? Anything I should know?"   "No..."
he said, not giving an inch.

"Do you think you have it hard here?" I asked seriously. "We all do.
It's the Tick Line. It's a ton of bullshit, but we all have to pull our own
weight. Okay, look. This is what I'm going to do. Every morning I'm
going to check on you at six thirty, before I head down to my Guide's
room, to make sure everything's okay. In the evenings, Tick Delphine
is going to check on you."

"I don't want—"

"You don't really have a choice now, do you? But then again, you
could get your act together. For starters, get rid of that GIM tag. It
makes you an easy target because it makes you look weak."

"Excuse me, did I ask for your help?" he asked rudely.

"Not really, but you obviously need it. Look, I've been put through
the mill these past few months. It's truly been hell." I instantly thought
about Ethan and Seth. "But, I've talked to my roommates. They are
my support system. Do you have anyone you can talk to? How's your
relationship with your roommates?"

"It's okay," he spoke softly.

"Well, if you ever need to talk, I'm available and so are my roommates.
We're a bunch of girls, so we're good at talking. Seriously, we're all in
this together. You can't do this alone; none of us can."

He looked at me. There was a hint of a smile beneath his stubborn
face.

I patted him on the back. "Well, I'll see you tomorrow morning," I
said as I got up, putting his roommate's chair back in place, and left.

~

"Alright Jamie, you want the Tick Riot to be tonight?" I asked.

"Yeah, that'd be good." He clicked his tongue.

"What time?"

"Let's make it ten. Most of the Upperclassmen will be back by
then."

I sat waiting for him to continue. He was clearly still thinking this
through. "Well, that solves the first problem. The second problem is the
Christmas Hop."

I looked at him, not sure where he was going with that.

He cleared his throat. "I was wondering … if you had any friends who'd like to come?"

I stared at him, not sure what to say.

"Brandon is the only one with a date. He's been seeing this girl from Mary Baldwin College for the past year. However, Kenny, Toby, and I don't have dates."

Now, fully comprehending his dilemma, I began to chuckle, but quickly stifled it. Jamie, the Commander of Band Company, was tall and stunningly handsome with red hair. He stood proudly in his uniform, looking astute and powerful at all times, especially when formally dressed for parades. He commanded Band Company with clear leadership, ruling those beneath him fairly modestly. He had brains, wit, and charm. He was the epitome of a CAF cadet. To any woman, he was quite a catch, and he wanted *me*, his Tick, to find him a date!

I cleared my throat and attempted to speak nonchalantly, but my voice ignored my requests. "And what type of woman are you looking for?" I asked, pressing my lips together in an attempt to suppress a smile.

I looked over at Kenny who had raised his head, instantly drawn into our conversation. "Don't go playing Cupid on us now. We just need dates for the dance, more for show than anything else."

"How do you expect me to come up with these dates?"

"Don't you have any friends, Randall?" Jamie asked.

"Ah, why yes, I do have friends, but they're all in Texas."

Jamie looked over at Kenny. Their faces said it all, and with a nod of the head, the exchange of information was complete.

"Okay, yes, that's fine. Three women. Each of us will foot the bill for their flights."

I mulled over this situation. Julie, Christine … both single. And yes, my friend Theresa was single as well, and they'd all totally be up for the trip; I know they would.

"Okay, Jamie. I'll see what I can do."

"Very good, Tick. Your services will be very much appreciated," Kenny smirked.

"No rest for the weary, eh?" I looked at Jamie.

"I don't expect you to disappoint," he said and resumed his attention to his desk.

"Alrighty …" I said and left the room, straining and smiling to myself. At the very least, I'd get to see my girlfriends!

~

While arranging the Tick Riot, word spread through the fourth stoop exactly what we were planning. At the strike of ten, the Ticks were to execute a massive riot throughout Barracks, to show the growing strength and unity of our class.

"Put this on," Brenda said, handing me shoe polish.

"*Are ya kiddin'?*" I asked.

"No … Just put some streaks on, to conceal your identity."

Brenda and I were a sight to see. Brenda stood there in her red shorts over her gray uniform trousers. She wore her white undershirt, black suspenders, and her camouflaged hat backwards. I stood looking similarly out of place with my red shorts, combat boots, untucked white blouse, and helmet to complete my ensemble.

Brenda had used the shoe polish to put streaks of black across her cheeks like a football player.

"Does this stuff come off?" I asked.

"Probably not, but it'll be worth it," she laughed.

"Alright, Brenda, give me the shoe polish!" I dabbed some on my nose.

Caroline and Dawn were next door checking to make sure that everyone was decked out for tonight's event. I was late in my personal preparations because I'd been disseminating orders throughout Band Company Ticks.

I'd first met with Tick Bigelow, who originally hesitated to take power. The past month had assured some trust between us, so after a little thought, he willingly stepped in place as the leader. His getup was hilarious too. He wore his gray sweatpants with his tighty-whitey underwear on the outside. He didn't wear a shirt, just his black suspenders. He took real camouflage from his own personal military stash and colored his skin with streaks of black and dark green.

"Everything's in place," I said.

"Who's preparing the water balloons?" Brenda asked. After debate on this issue, I resolved and put Tick Bigelow in charge of two operations: the filling of the water balloons and the collecting of all food items for throwing.

"Bigelow's group. Now, what food can we spare from our food boxes?"

Tick Delphine, the other Band Company Representative, had divided the company into three groups. Tick Bigelow's group was to cause destruction. My group's mission was to raid the third stoop and throw as many hays into the courtyard as possible. With careful consideration, Tick Delphine and I decided Mr. Rouge, our First Corporal, should be his group's objective. Their mission was to grab Mr. Rouge, roll him up in his own hay, and drag him out to the stoop for everyone to see.

Ten o'clock came quicker than anticipated. I signaled to Delphine three doors down that we were ready. Bigelow signaled they were ready also.

Bigelow, followed by his roommates, ran out first with water balloons aimed toward the third stoop. I almost died laughing when I saw one of the balloons hit an Upperclassman standing in the courtyard. Within seconds I signaled my group, and we ran out screaming, down the stairs, like a bunch of banshees. Instantly, Barracks erupted in chaos. Ticks ran wildly, disguised in motley uniforms. One group of Ticks wore their sweatshirts with the hoods up, shading their faces, like a bunch of hoodlums.

My group was instantly met with resistance as we barged into an unknown third classman room. I kept my head down and charged forward; I was glad I had my helmet on. I grabbed the closest hay and immediately felt hands on the other end, pulling it back.

I screamed louder, startling the cadet who wouldn't let go. I yanked with all my might and the hay was set free. I awkwardly ran out of the room, with the hay waddling on my side, and heaved it over the railing to the courtyard below. I could feel how the rush of adrenaline made me stronger. Other Ticks had been quicker with their implementation, as a handful of hays already lay below.

Upperclassmen everywhere were screaming at the Ticks. The Ticks pushed forward, determined to complete their mission. The stoops looked wild and alive. Ticks were running throughout Barracks while the firing of water balloons continued from the fourth stoop. One balloon barely missed me as it smashed onto the door to my left. Commotion was all over as the Tick Riot was in full execution.

I heard Brenda yell behind me, "Over here!"

I followed her into a female third classman room. The women were wicked and pushed us violently, but we met them with equal resistance as five or six other furious Ticks entered the room.

"You can't do that!" one female cadet yelled.

I helped grab the nearest hay, and my Fellow Ticks and I easily got it out of the room and over the railing. I ran back in, and the mob of Ticks slammed me hip first into the center of desks. I winced in pain, but kept moving. The hay to the left, by the window, had already been taken, so I went right. The female cadet sat on it possessively, refusing to give it up. I immediately pulled her arm, but she was strong. Brenda grabbed her other arm, and we held her together, struggling to hold her back while another Tick hauled her hay out of the room. I followed and scanned the barracks, trying to decide where I should head next.

"*We got him!*" a Tick screamed on the other side of Barracks. I squinted and looked across, trying to distinguish where the announcement had come from. I then realized that Tick Delphine's group had balled up Corporal Rouge! It was awesome.

"*Ticks, get back to your rooms! Now!*" a voice ordered over the loud speakers. I looked around and saw many Ticks stop in their tracks. I continued to run around third stoop, the long way to my room, to see if there was anything else I could do before retreating to my room.

The courtyard looked clouded over with white hays scattered in piles, mixed in with colorful pieces of broken balloons, and puddles of water. There was food: Twinkies, muffins, bananas, and milk cartons, all smashed along the walls and cement of the third stoop. Barracks was a mess.

I gazed up at my room and saw Band Company Cadre commanding Ticks back to their rooms. I ran up, winked at Mr. Gray with a smirk on my face, and scurried into my room.

We did well. Jamie should be pleased.

Chapter 15: The Release

I rolled over in my hay, waking to the smell of cigarette smoke. I didn't immediately open my eyes; the smell of smoke was typical in our room. I assumed Brenda was smoking by the window.

I moaned and stretched leisurely, knowing my alarm clock had not gone off yet. I opened one eye toward the window and saw not Brenda, but a dark figure at my desk. It took me a minute to process what I was looking at. Then suddenly it dawned on me, and I sat up instantly.

"What the hell?" I said, ready for a fight.

The figure stared at me and blew a second cloud of smoke in my face.

I brushed it off with my hand. "What's your problem?"

As my eyes adjusted to wakefulness, I could see the outlines of a body slumped on my desk, but the figure remained silent. His eyes glared at me, and I stared back with equal determination.

My roommates stirred around me, moaning with the grumpiness of being woken up to face another day at CAF.

"Randall, will you please shut up!" Dawn mumbled.

"I have my eyes on you," the dark figure said in a deep voice, clearly wanting my roommates to hear as well.

I noticed why I couldn't see who exactly he was. He wore a black ski mask and seemed very determined to frighten me. As I was partly still in a dream state, I wasn't scared. I was more annoyed, annoyed at being woken up before my alarm clock buzzed.

"The next time I see you, the next time you're on my stoop," he said, "you're mine, Tick!" He then rudely flicked his cigarette, ashing on the floor.

He stood up, took one more puff of his cigarette, and flicked it in my direction. I flinched, immediately shielded my face, as he walked out the door.

"What the hell was that about, Alicia?" Brenda asked, sitting up in her rack. "What did you do?"

"What did *I* do?"

"Well, he didn't come in here for no reason, so what did you do?"

"Hell if I know," I said, shaking off the chills that ran through me.

"Well you need to learn how to be a *Ghost Tick*."

"I'm trying, but it's not working!" I rubbed my hand through my buzzed hair and scratched the bottom of my head. "I don't even know who that was! Anyone recognize his voice?" I looked around the room.

I glimpsed at Caroline still laying down, shaking her head, hesitant to get out of the bed.

"That was creepy," she said.

I nodded. Thoughts raced through my head about events of the past week. "Maybe something happened at the Tick Riot?"

"Nah, that can't be it," Brenda said.

"Well, I'm clueless. I'm sure I'll find out eventually.…" I tried to shake off the last remaining tension in the room. "Let's get up. There's work to be done. Who cares about that coward of an Upperclassman who didn't even have the courage to show us his face!" I dismissed him with the wave of my hand. "It was probably a Third.…"

"Alicia, I'm worried about you. Aren't you going to do anything about what just happened?" Dawn asked.

"What can I do about it? Report him? To whom, Jamie?"

"Jamie might be a good start," Dawn suggested.

"I'll think about it.… Get up, you lazy butts." I climbed out of bed and folded my blanket.

"Did you screw one of the Upperclassmen?" Dawn asked, suddenly enthusiastic, like she had finally hit the nail on the head.

"Noooo!" I threw my pillow at her. "Are you fuckin' kidding me? No pun intended...." I laughed.

"Just makin' sure!"

⌁

Sex in Barracks was forbidden; it was well known that cadets of all grades could be dismissed if caught doing the act in Barracks.

I barely thought about sex. *Who had the time?* In the evenings, if I did dream about sex, it was usually about Seth. It was so easy to dream about him, like a comfort, my mind always going to him at the first thought of arousal. But Seth was no longer my man, and the thought of me longing for him made me angry. I tried to hate him, to envision throwing daggers at him, but I was always left with a feeling of sadness, of deep remorse.

There were no locks on any of the doors. All rooms had shades draped on the doors, a new addition with the integration of women. It was expected that when a cadet was changing clothes, the shade would be drawn down, and at all other times the shade would be up.

In the mornings, Caroline or I pulled the shade down because we were closest to the door. After we changed and were properly dressed, I always hesitated to pull the shade back up. The few minutes of privacy created a sense of protection, of peace, separating us from the loud and chaotic life on the other side.

With women being so recent to CAF, we didn't hear many stories of female and male cadets caught fornicating in Barracks. There was one story, though, about a woman from the first class of women who left in October, just weeks ago. She was nicknamed "Pussy Cat." It was speculated that she was loose and had slept with many other cadets. We didn't know if she was kicked out or had chosen to leave.

I didn't think Pussy Cat, whatever her name was, left voluntarily. I couldn't comprehend why anyone who had gotten through Tick Year, would choose to leave. Because I didn't know the truth behind it, I fought the urge to assume the worst, to blame her. If Pussy Cat had truly slept around with other cadets, she was the type of woman that made the rest of us look bad. All of us female Ticks wanted to do well at CAF; we did not want to be accused of attending CAF "to meet guys."

We were there because we wanted to be, to be cadets, to succeed in a system that wasn't naturally created for us.

~

The quiet times haunted me the most. I heard Ethan's voice occasionally, as clear as the sound of a voice being spoken a few feet away. I often caught myself wondering where he was and what he was doing. Then I would remember the truth: Ethan was dead.

I frequently found myself staring off into space when I was supposed to be studying. The material I was learning seemed so pointless, so insignificant to what was necessary for real life survival. Where was I going to learn how to heal a broken heart?

I felt burdened by my life and pretending, or essentially denying, that I didn't have a life outside of CAF gave me temporary moments of ease. I was a Tick, and thus all I had to think about was reporting for duty, completing homework, and obeying the Upperclassmen. At brief moments, it was easy. I could fall into the routine of CAF, not thinking, not remembering, and not reflecting on what had happened.

When I did remember, Ethan's funeral ran over and over in my mind like a nightmare. His death ate away at my heart and thoughts of Seth increased my feelings of abandonment. I felt stained by rejection and betrayal, like the stench of a skunk that lingers too long. That's why I preferred denial.

One afternoon, I was ordered to check with Tick Bigelow to make sure he'd completed all his assignments. I sat next to him, like a good Tick, and asked him about his work. When he answered me, my mind drifted to another place. I saw Seth standing there, looking at me, and I kept hearing my voice ask, *Why? Why Seth, did you choose to give up on us?* Unwelcome tears welled up, and I chocked them back, suddenly aware of where I was sitting.

"Do you need my help anymore, Bigelow?" I asked, turning away from him, so he couldn't see my face.

"No, Randall, I think I'm good."

"Good. Good," I said, talking more to myself. "Then you don't need my services any longer...." I got up and walked toward the door.

"Hey, Randall ... whoever broke your heart was an idiot."

I looked at him, straightened my posture, and blinked back the tears. "Thanks, Bigelow, I appreciate it," I said and ran to my room, to finally cry.

~

I didn't think I'd ever stop crying. I pulled my chair up to the window and placed my feet on the window pane. I wrapped my arms around myself and rocked back and forth, as tears poured down my face. I grabbed at tissues, quickly wiped my nose, and discarded the crumpled tissues in heaps around me.

"Oh, I'm so mad at you, Seth!" I said, between clenched teeth. "How could you! You bastard! You told me you loved me.… I let you touch me. I let you in, and then you walked away!"

I felt completely empty inside, like God had cleaned out every good thing in my life and left me hollow. I envisioned myself flying over the mountains of Virginia. Somehow flight seemed so liberating, to finally let go of grief's powerful grip, and release all that had happened.

One by one my roommates returned to the room. Each pulled a chair up beside me. We sat in silence, looking at each other, and communicated with a nod or look. I continued to cry while Brenda passed around cigarettes. We smoked in silence, like a ritual, a coming together of women for the purpose of healing, similar to a sacred circle. Any time a Fellow Tick came to our room, they were shooed away. We smoked slowly, each blowing big puffs of smoke into the night sky, temporarily creating a cloudy entity, a ghost of welcomed condolence.

When the cigarettes were finally discarded, I got up, wiped my face, and put my rack down. I unfolded my hay and climbed into the comfort of blanket and pillow. The three girls walked around the room, got ready for bed in silence, and each of us succumbed to the darkness.

Chapter 16: Thanksgiving Break

I awoke with a headache like I was hung-over. I splashed water on my face, observed my puffy eyes, and wished I had access to cucumbers, a chocolate martini, and some time off. Thankfully, I only had one more day until Thanksgiving leave.

The morning went smoothly. The atmosphere around Barracks was less lively than normal due to the upcoming break. Upperclassmen left as soon as their classes were completed or skipped out a day early, having requested early leave. Jamie was still around, finishing assignments due that day, and finalizing the itinerary for the CAF Jazz Band. A performance for the Jazz Band was schedule the week after break.

For some, Thanksgiving break was a time to leave the life of CAF behind. For others, it was a time to catch up on academics. For those with rank, dodging responsibilities was not an option.

I entered Jamie's room to find him slumped at his desk, forehead in the palm of his right hand, deep in thought.

"Trying to make a decision about something?" I asked.

"No, just frustrated …"

"Anything I can do to help?"

He looked up at me, paused for a minute, thinking. "You play piano, right?"

"Yep."

"Well, you may be just the person who can help then," he said, suddenly uplifted. "Would you be willing to accompany the Jazz Band for one song?"

"You know that I'm already in the Jazz Band, don't you?"

"Oh, I knew that…. Well, then, that won't work. You're playing second lead on saxophone, right?"

"No, I'm first sax, but I could ask Mr. Harman to play my part," I suggested.

"Yeah, or get one of the Tenors to play your part."

"That's fine with me. How difficult is the piano part?"

"I can't tell, since I don't play myself, but I'll ask Col. Bryant to leave the music for you. Are you going to be around this weekend?"

I nodded.

"Excellent! Well, that solves one of my problems. Next I need to find a bagpiper who's willing to learn the music last minute and play for the Christmas parade in a few weeks. Know anyone?"

"Ah, no," I said, realizing that might be more difficult to come by.

"I know, I know," he said, clearly aware of the complications. "So, Randall … you kicked some ass during the Tick Riot."

I smiled, feeling a surge of pride.

"You should've seen Mr. Rouge's face when he was unrolled from his hay!" he laughed. "Anyhow, shit … I have so much to do. I need to find my Arabic professor and see if I can get an extension on my paper that's due today." He got up, clearly busy with the rattling to-do list inside his head.

I watched him leave and was glad to be alone. Because Jamie and I had developed a nice relationship over the past few months, I'd been granted permission to use his computer when I desired. Upperclassmen had Internet access for academic purposes, while Internet connections were denied to Ticks, due to regulations. With wireless access, this rule was continually broken, especially by Dawn. The Administration was trying to prevent Ticks from chatting online, skimming porn sites, and occupying themselves with e-mails rather than doing homework.

I opened the browser and brought up the Yahoo homepage. E-mails had diminished slightly the past month in comparison with the beginning of the Tick Line. Since Ethan's death, I'd received a bunch of condolence letters, but that had faded away as well. I chose not to check my e-mail as frequently now, not only because I didn't have time, but because there wasn't any pressing need to. It was also important to stay focused at CAF by speaking with my outside life as little as possible, but I did have a mission that needed to be completed. My Guide and two of his roommates wanted dates to the Christmas Hop. I opened a blank e-mail and wrote to Julie, Christine, and Theresa.

> *Alright girls, this is an odd request, but one that has the potential to be really fun. Being a Tick, I have a Guide, a first classman mentor that I report to daily. His name is Jamie. He has three roommates, all guys that I have come to know, truly like, and respect. His roommates are Brandon, Kenny, and Toby. Jamie, Kenny, and Toby are really great guys: handsome, sweet, and funny. They are all hardcore leaders at CAF and are very smart.*
>
> *The reason I am telling you all this is because Jamie, Kenny, and Toby all need dates to the CAF Christmas Hop. Would you be willing to come to VA and be their dates?*
>
> *Of course you would! You'd be crazy not to. The three of them will pay for your flights. I recommend you stay at the local Comfort Inn and share a room to cut expenses. You should fly in the day before the Hop, so you can get settled, spend some time with me, and have plenty of time to get ready for the dance. The Hop is the second Friday in December.*
>
> *Tell me what you think! This would be a big help to me and my Guide/Uncle Guides. Besides, it's a free ride to come see me and my school!*
>
> *Love you all,*
> *Alicia*

I reported to an easy Economics test. Then I attended my Science class and finished my lab from Monday. Everything was running smoothly, or so I thought, until I attended my Psychology class and realized that I hadn't finished my paper. I stayed after class to ask Professor Cain for an extension.

Professor Cain looked me up and down, debating whether he should be flexible to a Tick's silly mistake.

"Professor Cain. I'm so sorry. I look irresponsible, but I assure you that I made a mistake, not because of slacking." I decided not to specifically explain what the reasons were that made my life so difficult. I was obviously a Tick, but that truth didn't hold any power here.

"Well, given the fact that all your other assignments were turned in on time, and you have been receiving adequate grades, I'm willing to extend this one assignment. Since Psychology is your major, Tick Randall, I expect you not to repeat this behavior. Is that clear?" he asked, with one eyebrow turned up.

"Yes, sir. This will not happen again." I hoped it was true. I hated groveling, especially when it was an accident. I had a schedule book that I heavily relied on. It contained all my class assignments and exam days. I filled it out in August when all the professors handed us our class syllabus for the semester.

When I left the classroom and ran back to my room, I took my schedule book out. Wednesday, the day before Thanksgiving, "Psychology paper due" was clearly marked in red ink.

How did I miss that? Oh, forget it. I know how I missed that…. Crying all last night had left me in a fog. I'd better use this time over Thanksgiving to catch up. It shouldn't be too bad, though. I just have to write a Psychology paper and practice the piano. I took my pen out and wrote in "meet Cathleen" on Friday at noon. Tonight, I planned to hang out with Lalita.

As if summoned by my thoughts, Lalita walked in. I looked up from my desk and observed her appearance in civilian clothes.

"Wait a minute. You're a woman?" I teased.

"Don't I clean up nicely?" she turned to and fro, allowing her skirt to swing gently back and forth. Because she was a Third Classman, regulations allowed her to grow out her hair, which hung down to her chin, after having grown out since her Breakout last May, six months ago.

"Do you have make-up on?" I asked, peering closer to her face.

"Yes, I do. Now, we need to get your clothes from the basement and get out of here. I have plans for us tonight," she said, beaming.

"What are you up to?" I asked suspiciously.

"Tonight, we're going in to town."

"What town? There's no night life in Farmington, is there?"

"No, not really, but we're not staying in Farmington. We're going to Mechanicsville where I grew up. It's not far from here, but I know this hole-in-the-wall that serves minors. It'll be fun. Let's get going!"

I followed Lalita down to the basement where we found my small brown suitcase that I hadn't seen since matriculating. It felt like a lifetime since I had packed that suitcase.

We arrived at her family's house thirty minutes later. I got out of her small truck and was instantly greeted by a curious pack of dogs, their tongues lolling, and their tails wagging in excitement.

"Morgan, back off!" Lalita ordered. "Morgan's the alpha male." The yellow lab sat obediently for a millisecond before he resumed his happiness by energetically wagging his tail. The other two dogs sniffed me gingerly, one pawing me.

"Down, Bear!" Lalita ordered. "That's my brother's dog. He's in Afghanistan right now, and Bear really misses him."

"And who's this darling?" I asked, scratching behind the ear of a tiny dog resembling Toto from *The Wizard of Oz*.

"That's Samantha, my mom's dog." She sighed. "My parents separated while I was in high school. Even though Dad bought Samantha for Mom, she didn't have the heart to take her away from the other dogs," she explained, picking Samantha up.

Morgan barked jealously over the gesture. Samantha nuzzled Lalita's face as she hugged and petted the dog affectionately.

In comparison to the greeting we received from the dogs, we found the house rather unwelcoming. The door was unlocked, but the lights inside were off.

"Dad?" Lalita yelled. I followed closely behind. "Dad? Are you here?"

I looked around. The house was warm with a feminine touch. Her mother was clearly still living here, even if she wasn't physically present.

"I'm going upstairs to see if he's in his study. My dad has a tendency to zone out when he's on his computer. If the house caught fire, he probably wouldn't even notice!" She rolled her eyes and ran upstairs.

I walked into the living room and scanned the family pictures hanging on the walls. There was a picture of a man, who I assumed was her brother, posed in a Marine uniform on the hearth of the fireplace.

I thought of my own parents. Since Ethan's death, life had drastically changed for both of them. I hadn't called home since the funeral, except to briefly tell them I'd arrived safely. I didn't want to call home. I didn't want to revisit the memories. Tomorrow will be hard for them both, celebrating Thanksgiving without either of us home. I made a mental note to call them.

"Dad, I'd like to introduce you to my friend, Alicia," I heard Lalita say, as she came down the stairs.

"Hi, Mr. Doyle. It's a pleasure to meet you." I offered my hand. Mr. Doyle stood slightly shorter than the average man, with a gentle face and deep brown eyes. His hair was disheveled, having clearly come from a bout of deep thought. He wore a white undershirt and no shoes or socks in the comfort of his home.

"Dad's a computer geek, an "IT" guy," she said, tousling his hair. "He likes to go for the mad scientist look."

Mr. Doyle smiled at his daughter, his affection evidently showed on his face. "I'm so glad you're here, Alicia. Lalita doesn't have any friends," he teased, getting smacked in the arm by her.

"I do so!"

"Ah, yes, well ... maybe a few. Nevertheless, I'm glad you're here. I need someone to eat the food I prepared for tomorrow. I rarely cook anymore because it's no fun cooking for one," he said solemnly, the obvious result of divorce.

"Dad makes the best Thanksgiving meal you've ever tasted. He makes this great cranberry chutney and spinach casserole. Yum! My mouth is watering just thinking about it."

"That sounds wonderful. It sure beats mess hall food and having to eat little Tick bites." I smiled.

"Well yes, but no more talk about CAF. We're on vacation, and tonight we're going out!"

"Oh, you're not staying for dinner?" Mr. Doyle asked, disappointed.

"No, Dad. I'm sorry. Save all your culinary skills for tomorrow. Tonight I'm taking Alicia out to Ming Garden!"

"Ming Garden? You're taking me to a Chinese Restaurant?"

"Yes. It's not what you think, though. Besides having the best pork egg rolls, they have fantastic cheap beers." Her eyebrows bobbed up and down as she smirked.

"Well, that does it. I'm in!"

"Great. Now, let's get you something to wear."

~

I looked suspiciously at her. "Are you freakin' kiddin' me?" I asked, looking at the long v-cut down the front of the red shirt she held up for me. "How much cleavage do you expect me to show off?"

"Lots! … I know it isn't Breakout, far from it, but after *my Breakout*, I went crazy. I had a list. I was determined to cut loose and feel like a woman again."

"And what did the list say?"

"Number one, get laid. Number two, get a tattoo. Three, get a belly ring. Four, get a manicure. Five, buy a sexy black dress. And six, go dancing!"

"And did you accomplish everything on the list?"

"Oh, hell yeah, and more."

I laughed. "Well, you'll have to tell me all about it tonight."

"I will. So … I think you should wear something that makes you feel powerful, like a woman in charge. You need to remember you're not a Tick. You're a woman. It's time to par-taaay!"

"Okay, fine." I surrendered to the peer pressure and searched her closet. I knew I didn't have anything in my suitcase I could wear, so I didn't even bother to open it. "It's very hard for me to feel like a woman with *no hair*."

"Ah, forget that. Many women cut their hair short these days."

"Well, I do look kind of cute.…"

"That's my girl! Keep it up. You look hot and now shake that thing." She slapped my ass which made me jump.

"*Ah!*"

I tried on a bright blue spaghetti strap dress. The dress was cut low, but not too low, revealing a lot of pale skin. Lalita is slightly taller than I am and a little rounder at the bosom and buttock areas, but other than that, her clothes fit perfectly.

I couldn't come to grips with wearing heels, so I chose a pair of simple silver flats that complimented the dress nicely. Lalita gave me a pair of silver hoops and a few decorative rings. I used a little hair gel in a desperate attempt to gain body out of a near buzz cut. I did apply some makeup, using a little mascara and lip gloss, and then I was all set to go.

Lalita wore her little black dress, the one she had bought last summer after Tick Year. She went all out with black heels, a silver ankle bracelet, and bracelets. She wasn't shy about makeup and colored her lips in a deep rouge.

"I can't believe you talked me into this, but I'm glad you did," I said, as we entered Ming Garden.

I felt a little foolish getting all dolled up to go to a Chinese Restaurant, but my concerns quickly faded when I looked around. The restaurant was clearly a Chinese Restaurant, but it had a Lounge as well, with a wall separating the family restaurant from the darkened atmosphere. We chose to sit at the bar, wanting to be in the center of any activity.

Looking at the menu, I was surprised to see typical American entrees in addition to the Chinese food.

"They sell burgers and fries to attract more people, and it has clearly worked," Lalita whispered in my ear.

"And pizza too?" I said, laughing. "China meets Italy."

"What can I get you ladies?" a bartender asked, directing the question at Lalita.

"Hey, Freddy, I brought a new girl to town."

The bartender looked at me and realized at once where Lalita met me. "Yes, I can see that." He extended out his hand.

While I gave his hand a good shake, Lalita said, "We definitely want your pork egg rolls and two pints of Guinness."

"Coming right up," he said with a nod.

"Wow, Guinness. Nice touch." I happily looked around. "Obviously not your first time here, huh?"

"Um, no, this little place was my safe haven when my parents fought, and it wasn't pleasant to be home."

"I see, but it looks like you have a nice relationship with your dad."

"I do. He's just lonely.… Ever since Mom left, he's retreated to the computer."

Freddy arrived with the beers.

"Ah, yum!" I said, taking a sip of ale.

Tap … tap … tap … I looked up. A man appeared behind Lalita, his huge CAF ring pounding obnoxiously on the counter.

"Doyle, what do you think you're doing?" a deep voice addressed her.

Lalita eyed him casually. "Franklin, so nice to see you. Would you care to join us?" she asked, raising her glass in invitation.

"No, thank you. I just want to know *why* you brought this little *Tick* here."

"Oh, drop it. It's Thanksgiving. We're not on campus, so you can quit being a smartass."

"Well it's better than being a dumbass," he replied and chuckled.

"Funny. So what do you want?" she asked calmly.

I felt his eyes on me, but I focused on Lalita, feeling very uncomfortable.

"You think you can dress her up, like *your own puppy dog?*"

"Don't you have anything better to do? Go back and sit with your friends." She dismissed him with the wave of her hand.

"Leave you alone? But I'm just getting started," he said and started pointing at me. "I have my eyes on you, Tick, and I expect you to behave, otherwise …" he drifted off, losing his focus.

"Sit down, Franklin! I can smell the whiskey on your breath. Leave us alone, *now!*" she ordered, startling him.

I watched as he tried to think of a comeback, but changed his mind and turned, stumbling to a group of guys in the corner.

From where I was sitting, I saw that some of the guys were from CAF, but not all. A few curious glances headed our way, and I turned around, pretending I didn't see them.

"Aren't you concerned about being seen with me in public?" I asked.

"Absolutely not! Don't worry about those guys. They're harmless.

There's nothing wrong with us hanging out off campus during school break," she laughed.

"What's so funny?"

"Franklin is a pure example of the guys that attend CAF. He's a great cadet, but when it comes to functioning outside the school, he *is completely lost.*"

"What do you mean?"

"Some guys have trouble separating the two. CAF is built on a specific system, a certain code of rules, like a separate culture."

"I fully agree."

"And when they leave school, even temporarily, they have trouble readjusting back into mainstream society, not as bad as soldiers coming home from war, but it's similar. They have to be socially reconditioned." She took a sip of her beer.

"Here you go ladies," Freddy said, handing us two plates of miniature egg rolls with dipping sauces.

"Thanks, Freddy," Lalita said.

"Let me know if you need any help with those guys," Freddy said, like an older brother looking out for his baby sister.

"Does it look like I need help?" Lalita said with a little attitude.

"No... but in case you do, just ask." Freddy winked.

"K, thanks." Lalita smiled and flicked her hair back, enjoying the attention.

"You see, Alicia, many guys completely give up who they are, in order to become part of the system. The challenge is not to allow yourself to be completely transformed by CAF. You can still be a cadet without giving up who you are."

"I hear ya. Thanks. These egg rolls are fantastic!" I said with my mouth full. "What's their secret?"

"My guess is because it's fresh. Freddy told me they bake them, instead of frying."

"You know, and please keep this between you and me," I said, munching happily. "My Guide and his roommates are the epitome of CAF cadets, and they asked me to get three of them dates for the Christmas Hop! That's exactly what you're referring to as great cadets, but a little dysfunctional in their social skills, right?"

"I can't believe that! That's hilarious," Lalita chuckled. "I'm not surprised, though."

"Yeah, I'm trying to get my girlfriends from back home to come."

"Well then, it might work out for all of you."

"Yeah, it will be a nice to see them after all that has happened...."

"All that has happened with the Tick Line?" she asked.

"That too." I said.

"What else?"

"It's a long story."

"We have all night, honey."

~

That night I told Lalita everything. We drank, played pool, flirted, got a few numbers, and walked home with our bellies fully content. I felt free. We were women out on the town, not necessarily in search of men, but in search of fun and togetherness.

Lalita told me about the breakup with her boyfriend, how he hadn't been supportive about her choice to attend CAF.

We bonded because we knew what each other was going through, about the challenges of CAF. Being part of the integration of women at CAF was hard to describe to outsiders. Only those who experienced it could fully understand the implications.

We stayed up late watching *Titanic,* which had come out earlier that year, and finally fell asleep while the sun rose over the horizon.

Chapter 17: Solitude

After devouring a delicious homemade Thanksgiving dinner, Lalita dropped me off at Barracks. She was heading to her mom's house for an evening together, and I had excused myself, suspecting it would be better that she went to her mom's alone. Besides, I was looking forward to some alone time.

Entering Barracks, I didn't strain, but my body physically responded to habit and my heart beat increased as I ran to my room. Barracks was eerily quiet.

"It's just me," I said out loud, as if greeting a pet. The room was exactly as we had left it, patiently waiting for our return. I found the immediate emptiness surprisingly gloomy.

I took a deep breath and put my suitcase down. I grabbed my smokes and pulled a chair up to the window, ceremoniously welcoming myself back. For the next three days, I was free to come and go as I liked. It was almost incomprehensible knowing I could spend my time however I pleased. I enjoyed the few minutes by the window, lazily smoking my cigarette before I became productive.

Finishing my Psychology paper should be first on my list. I didn't want the task to weigh on me the rest of the weekend, so I turned my computer on and began the laborious task of writing. The more I learned about Psychology, the more I understood how often people could be labeled dysfunctional. I enjoyed Psychology, though I had no idea what I was going to do with the degree, upon graduation.

~

After completing a rough draft, I decided to take a break. I walked outside to the chilly air, glad I was in sweats, and went to the Band building. I entered the Band Room and sat down at the piano. I found the piece of music Jamie had told me about. The music had a yellow post-it on the first page that read, "Randall, I really appreciate your help, Col. Bryant."

I skimmed the music, noticing how simple the melody was. I played it a couple times through and then pulled out my own personal stash of music. Playing the piano is an excellent escape from stress. Because I'd been so busy, this was the first time I played since matriculation. I felt rusty, so I warmed up with scales. I learned that practicing slowly and correctly was the secret to becoming a great musician because of instant muscle memory within the fingers. I concentrated as my curved and strong fingers moved up and down the keyboard in a slow and controlled manner.

My favorite piece from high school was Rachmaninoff's *C sharp minor Prelude.* The first section of the piece allowed me to bang on the keys, letting me get out any pent up frustrations. The section contrasted with soft piano parts, forcing me to be gentle. My fingers remembered the music, as if no time had passed, since I'd last played four months ago.

The middle section of the *Prelude* was my favorite. In listening to a professional recording of the song, I was always disappointed with the speed pianists performed this section. Playing too fast sounded chaotic, as the magnificent melody disappeared to a sound of jumbled notes. In slowing down, I could accentuate the rise and fall of emotion. It was beautiful.

The last section of the *Prelude* held an array of melody and harmony, bouncing back and forth in competition, a more powerful version of the first section. The piece ended with the sound dying off into the distance, as if retreating over a hilltop. I played the last cord gently and held my hands there until the sound diminished completely.

When the song ended, I felt as if I had awoken from a dream. I took a deep breath and released my hold. Playing Rachmaninoff always refreshed me, allowing me to enter another world, a world of sound, emotion, and beauty.

I closed the piano case, stood up, and pushed in the piano bench. I looked around the band room at the empty stands, chairs, and the drums and tubas in the back, awaiting their owners' return. The band room felt like a ghost town, with the sounds of marches and Colonel Bryant's voice echoing just beyond hearing.

I felt uncomfortably out of place, as if I was supposed to be somewhere I had forgotten. I put my piano music back in my cubbyhole and left.

I slowly walked back to my room, listening to my stomach grumble. When I got to my room, I took down my depleted food box. I had just enough food to get me through the next week. I made a peanut butter and jelly sandwich, the staple of my diet.

Living in an environment like CAF made me more appreciative of the little things, like climbing the stairs to my room without straining or being worked out. It made me more appreciative of my friends because their constant encouragement helped so much. It also made me value the simplicity of uniforms, allowing me to forget fashion and the feminine demands of presenting myself in a pretty manor.

I didn't have to do laundry, cook meals, clean dishes, or work a part-time job. I didn't need much money here. The little money that my parents deposited into my account more than covered any additional expenses. Compared to a typical university, I was separated from pop culture, college parties, and daily news. I was literally in a world of its' own. I only had to focus on meeting the standards of a cadet, pleasing my Guide, and completing academics.

Nevertheless, life at CAF was full, full of responsibilities that never seemed to end, full of rules and regulations, and full of stress. I learned to expect the worst, not so much from a pessimistic attitude, but to always be prepared. Life was no longer completely in my hands, and even my best efforts barely kept me afloat.

～

After my food digested, I went for a run. The sun was setting, my favorite time of the day, where the sky beamed with color. Even though I missed my roommates, I really enjoyed the alone time. I jogged slowly down the path, into the woods behind Barracks, as the sounds of chants echoed in my head.

When my grandma turned ninety-two, she did PT better than you.
When my grandma turned ninety-three, she did PT better than me.
Left—right—left.
Left—right—left.

I tried to hear the silence. I just wanted to let go and surrender to the sound of nothingness, to be with the woods and animals, and feel peaceful. I jogged a little faster, feeling as though the further I ran away from school, the more I returned to myself.

I climbed the hill, lowering my head as if to fight a non-existent wind, and pushed myself to climb farther and farther.

Little hill … little hill. The old chants continued in my head.

Once at the top, I felt my legs warm up. I wanted to feel free, to experience what it was to let go of worry and responsibilities, so I ran. Nothing existed around me except trees, dirt, rustling leaves, and animals hidden in the bushes.

My mind wandered. What would I be doing today if I wasn't here at CAF? Would I still be in Texas with Seth? Would I be hanging with my girls?

Sweating now, I breathed deeply and slowed my pace to a comfortable jog. I enjoyed the quiet of the night and the solitude established by the darkness and separation from society.

I jogged to a bench and slowed down to stretch. My legs were very tight. I bent forward and touched my toes, and felt the warmth running up and down my legs. I held my ankles and then moved to the yoga downward dog position, stretching my back, arms, and calves as I lengthened. One at a time, I put each foot on the bench and stretched my hamstrings.

I gently pulled myself up. I sat on the ground and very slowly did sit-ups, counting each one with my out breath. Feeling satisfied with half my normal count, I completed my workout with a few sets of twenty push-ups. I felt good.

I walked back to Barracks at a near crawl, not anxious to return, nor looking forward to leaving the solidarity and peace I'd found in the woods.

Barracks loomed in the darkness. The stone structure resembled a castle or an old fashion mansion. It was beautiful, yet deceiving. I knew the truth of what went on inside Barracks, unlike the locals or visitors that were merely awed at the sight of the magnificent structure.

How odd it was that the school upheld tradition, and yet society was always changing. Whenever news cameras were around, Ticks weren't required to strain and after-lunch workouts were banned. Of course people were curious about what happened inside Barracks, but they weren't given the true story. Why? Was the school afraid of being forced to change?

I entered Barracks and walked quickly to my room. Even though it was break, my room still felt the safest place to be. Some Upperclassmen and a few Ticks remained at the school. Many of them were international students, like the Tick from Sweden, and home was too far away to travel for such a short time.

How people were raised definitely affected their capacity to withstand CAF cadet life. Obviously, personalities and sheer willpower affected their ability as well. If one had an easy-going childhood, especially in a comfortable middle-class household like I'd experienced, one probably did not develop the survival skills needed to withstand CAF. However, if life was hard growing up, one probably developed the independent will to endure hardship which made cadet life more manageable.

I took out my journal. I could finally write about how much my life had changed.

～

I woke a few minutes before six. It was natural for me to wake up before my alarm clock now. I closed my eyes again, aware that I did not have to be anywhere until noon. I could fall back to sleep, so that's what I did.

I woke some time later to shouts in Barracks. Voices echoed so easily through the hollowness of the courtyard and hallways. The protection of the night left with the morning sun. I suddenly felt a stir of panic. It was not from logic, but from instinctual fear that I'd be yelled at for sleeping in. This, of course, was foolish, but I quickly got out of bed anyway. I would feel embarrassed if anyone entered my room while I was still in my hay. The last thing I wanted to portray was laziness. I looked at the clock and saw it was shortly after eight.

I put on my shoes. I was already wearing my sweats, to keep warm through the chilly hours of the night. I shivered slightly after exiting my room, bar of soap, razor, towel, and flip-flops in hand. I glanced around and followed the voices below. I peaked gently over the railing and spotted two Third Classmen shouting to each other across the center of New Barracks. I quickly turned away, not wanting them to notice me.

I entered the female bathroom and felt the slight humidity. There must be another female Tick in Barracks. I dropped my things off in front of the showers and went to the toilet stalls. Everything felt eerie. I suddenly wished my roommates were here, their voices and presence were a comfort. I quickly showered and climbed back into my complete sweat uniform.

When I returned to my room, I opened my suitcase. I was looking for a suitable outfit to wear to visit Cathleen. There were a couple of T-shirts and shorts, one pair of jeans, a few books, and a small framed photograph. It was the picture of the five of us; Julie, Christine, Seth, Ethan, and I; at the beach house that Courtney had taken prior to the accident. I immediately sat down, not trusting my legs to hold me. I felt so empty, the healing wound torn open again. We all looked so happy, and I was instantly reminded of the one week that changed everything.

I took a deep breath, sighed, and buried the picture under my clothes. I pulled out the pair of jeans and put them on over my white underwear. Each pair of underwear, bra, and clothing had my laundry number, B-1465, marked on it in black permanent marker. I took out one of the T-shirts, the one that said CAF class of 2002, and put it on. I put on my CAF sweatshirt over the T-shirt and then quickly took it off. If an Upperclassman were to catch me wearing the CAF sweatshirt, I could be accused of improperly wearing my uniform.

I stared at the open suitcase. It was an old brown leather suitcase without wheels. I liked the well-used worn look, the same way I liked old furniture and old pianos. Why didn't I think to add a sweater or jacket to my suitcase? I was annoyed at my poor planning. Well, at least the cold will keep my feet moving.

I took a good look in the mirror and assessed my appearance. I didn't have any makeup and had short hair. Cathleen knows I'm a cadet, so I'm sure she's not expecting any miraculous transformations because I'm out of uniform. There was a rule, though, that whenever cadets were in town, they had to be in dress uniform. Because it was officially break, I hoped wearing civilian clothes were allowed—unless some jackass Upperclassman saw me. Anything was possible. Ignoring my own thoughts, I left determined to have a nice breakfast before meeting Cathleen at noon.

~

When I reached town, I noticed a few curious glances. People were always curious about the women who attended CAF. My short hair immediately gave away my status. I was also blatantly wearing CAF clothes which confirmed their questions. I smiled and kept to myself; I didn't feel like engaging in small talk.

Looking in the windows of the shops, I noticed this was really an older generation kind of town. The tiny town was surrounded with Civil War paraphernalia, and pictures of General Robert E. Lee displayed throughout, along with other well-known American heroes. There were no trendy boutiques, or even pubs to watch TV, just one antique shop after another. The country shops closed at three PM with little or no night life. It was as if time stood still in Farmington, never entering the twentieth century; the memories of the distant past were still prominent everywhere.

Many of the shops weren't opened yet, but I knew one cute coffee shop, so small that it only had four tables, that would be open at this hour. "Fresh muffins, made daily," the sign in front said. I ordered a western omelet and a large cup of coffee with chocolate syrup and lots of cream, like I used to make at home. I grabbed a newspaper and sat down. I was clueless about all that was happening in politics, domestic and international.

Once within the walls of Barracks, no world outside of it exists, I heard Cadre say in my head.

I needed to call home, to touch base with someone who knew me, I thought in alarm. I was feeling too disconnected from the real world.

After eating, I walked a few blocks to the nearest 7/11 and used the payphone.

"Hey!" I said when Christine answered the phone.

"Alicia?"

"Yeah, it's me."

"Hey! We miss you so much here. How are you? How's the Tick Line?"

"Ah, well, it's what it is. It sucks—but I'm okay. I'm surviving. How are you? How are the girls?"

"Well, things have definitely changed.... Going out with just the three of us isn't the same."

"Have you seen Courtney? How is she?" I asked, pressing my head again the payphone.

"She's not so good, I'm sorry to say. She's backed off from the rest of us, and we've haven't seen much of her."

"That's a shame...."

"Yeah, she just hasn't been right since the accident. And after Ethan's funeral ... she's just closed off from us," she explained. "She stopped wanting to hangout, no matter how much we asked. There was always some excuse.... Things have really changed, Alicia."

"Tell me about it." I sighed.

"Have you spoken to your parents lately?"

"Yeah, I called them yesterday for Thanksgiving."

"That's good. You'll be home for Christmas break, won't you?"

"A few more weeks, and then I'll be home. It'll be good to get away. Um, Seth wrote me a letter ending our relationship," I said, finally able to admit it out loud to myself.

"Oh... no. That bastard! I'm *so sorry*."

"Yeah, so it goes."

"Well, I'm not dating anyone and neither is Theresa or Julie. This must be the first time we're all in the same boat!"

"Does that mean y'all are coming to the Christmas Hop next month?"

"We're definitely thinking about it. I've already replied to your e-mail."

"Oh, good. I haven't read it yet. I'm not online every day," I explained.

"Well, I'm in. Julie's in. We're just waiting for Theresa to get off work. It shouldn't be that big of a deal, except Western Bar gets extremely busy this time of year. She's doing her best to pull it off, though, so let's just say the three of us are in, shall we?"

"Awesome! That means a lot to me, thank you. Besides, who'd have thought I'd be playing matchmaker for my Guides?" I smiled to myself.

"The Hop is on the fourteenth, right?"

"Yep. Since the Hop is Saturday, I'll be able to see you Friday night. Jamie will call me out of dinner formation, and then Saturday morning you can see our parade. You'll have plenty of time to walk around town and get ready for the Hop. Come to think of it, Jamie will probably take you guys out to lunch, so y'all can have a casual time getting to know each other."

"Now Jamie is your Guide, right?"

"Yep. He's handsome and tall, perfect for Theresa. You and Julie can fight over Kenny or Toby. They're both really cool and good-looking."

"Sounds great to me … should be fun."

"Yeah, and make sure to tell me every last detail when it's all over!"

"A lady doesn't tell, though I'm sure Theresa will tell you everything!"

"Ha! Alright, so I'll see you guys in two weeks. Keep in touch by e-mail. I rarely have the luxury to call, so tell Julie and Theresa I said *hello*."

"Alright girl, you go kick some butt."

"I'll do my best," I said and hung up the phone.

Chapter 18: My Extended Education

I spent the next couple of hours strolling around the local park, observing families and happy children climbing all over the playground. It was turning out to be a lovely day in November, and leaves were already scattered on the ground. The air felt crisp; I wished I had a jacket.

When it was time, I arrived at Stone Soup Bookstore, ready for warmth and to see Cathleen. I noticed how much the store stood out, the old Victorian house that Cathleen had converted into a cozy bookstore, with off-white paint and a purple trim. It was no wonder she questioned her choice for location, but the store did add a lot of charm to the old town of Farmington.

As I approached the front door, it opened; Cathleen had been looking for me.

"Hey," I said, smiling.

"You're not in uniform."

"No, but this isn't much better." I looked down at my apparel. "I've been freezing. I was wondering, could I borrow a sweatshirt or coat?" I rubbed my arms.

"Yes, of course, but let's head upstairs. It's warmer there anyway, so you might not need one."

Cathleen looked beautiful. She was dressed in a turquoise, long-sleeved shirt that framed her body and a long vibrant skirt, one which resembled a modern-day painting. When we entered her apartment, she took off her shoes. The skirt skimmed the top of her maroon-painted toenails which shimmered from the silver toe-rings that adored them. So feminine, unlike how I felt in my CAF T-shirt, jeans, and sneakers. A pang of envy shot through me. I was jealous of her femininity and how she walked with such self-assurance. I suddenly felt self-conscious.

I took off my sneakers and walked into the living room. Her apartment was an explosion of color and feelings of comfort. There were bright mosaic tapestries on her walls and huge pillows that ornamented her plush, tan couch. A deep blue rug lay in the center of her wooden floor.

"I'll be right back," Cathleen said and then returned with a woolen brown sweater. "Sorry, I don't own sweatshirts, but I thought this would be comfortable."

"Thanks. I appreciate it," I said, putting it on.

"Well, we're going to have lunch in a minute, and since it is a holiday, can I get you something to drink, like a glass of wine?"

"Sure!"

"Great."

I walked over to the window. I had butterflies in my stomach. This was weird. Why would I be nervous talking to another female? I can usually talk to anyone.

"How was your Thanksgiving?" Cathleen asked, coming back into the room. She handed me a pretty pink glass of white zinfandel.

"Um, it was fine. Nice, actually. Wednesday night a friend of mine from CAF took me out. It was the first time I felt feminine since I entered military school," I said, sipping the wine. "Nice ..."

"Yes, I like it too. Light wines are my favorite. So," she chuckled. "You haven't felt feminine since you started the Tick Line? It's no wonder ... but you're definitely a woman," Cathleen said, smiling at me.

I felt slightly embarrassed. "You know what I mean. I really think it's the hair more than anything else. I like not worrying about hair while I'm at CAF, but once I'm in society, I do feel different." I rubbed the top of my head.

"I bet you do. I wouldn't cut my hair, ever." With her right hand, she grabbed her long, dark hair from behind and pulled it to the front.

"Your place is wonderful. It has such a nice view up here," I said, looking down on Main Street.

"Yeah, I got lucky. My home is my sanctuary. I don't let too many people up here, honestly. I definitely have to keep work and home separate."

"That makes sense."

"I'd like to show you my secret stash." She walked over to a large trunk, covered with silver moons and stars. "This is my precious book collection. I do sell many of them downstairs, but I'm still getting a feel for what the people here like to purchase. There's no point in buying books that never sell. This is my personal assortment, each with my own writing in it."

She opened a book titled *Women Who Run with the Wolves* and showed me the red ink that decorated the pages. "I always use red, like a school teacher."

I walked closer and sat on the edge of the couch, sipping the wine and watching her.

"Did you go to college?" I asked.

She looked up. "No, I never felt called to. I've read so many books since I was little and never felt like I had to pay to get an education. With a library card, I could pick up books in any subject for free. When I was small, I read any book I could get my hands on. Besides, I've kind of been a loner, never really felt like I fit in," she explained, without a hint of remorse.

Cathleen seemed so neat, even magical. "You seem like you really know yourself. You're only a few years older than I am, right?"

"I'm twenty-two," she said.

I nodded. "You said your mom died when you were six, so you were raised by your dad?"

She nodded.

"So you learned to stand on your own feet from a young age."

"In some ways, but I've always been a little adult. My dad's a good dad. We had to rely on each other a lot, since it was just the two of us. Everything changed when he remarried." She swallowed. "It wasn't bad because I always had books. It's just he was less available to me, so I read." She smiled.

"Well, thanks for sharing your favorite ones with me."

"My pleasure. You see here, this book, *The Four Agreements* by Don Miguel Ruiz, is so simple, so easy to understand and incorporate into your daily life. You can read it in an afternoon and it can change your life forever."

"Really, what's so special about it?"

"Well, the first agreement is 'Be impeccable with your word,'" she explained. "So many people tell you what they think you want them to tell you. Personally, I would rather be told the truth. We live in a world where honesty is not a guarantee. Whether it is politicians, your neighbor, or even your best friend, honesty is not used by everyone. For example, you have a planned time to meet your friend, and she calls to say she's running late. You're like, no problem; she's only ten minutes behind schedule. Then the ten minutes pass and your friend is thirty minutes late. By that time, you're annoyed because you expected her to be there like she said. You could've planned differently, if you knew you had thirty minutes to spare, instead of just ten, but your friend wanted to look good in your eyes and didn't want to make you mad with the truth, so she lied. It's not a big lie, but the truth would have been better," Cathleen explained.

"I know what you mean."

"I'll give you another example. Often times when we are angry, we suppress our anger, thinking we are holy or the better person. Anger is an ugly emotion, so we'd rather not express it and just pretend we didn't feel it. Instead, that anger rots inside of us, ferments, and makes a permanent wound. It creates a sense of distrust, so the next time that friend or parent does something that hurts us, we either explode or decide to cut off the relationship completely. This is why many relationships end, leaving the other person confused. If we'd been honest and confronted our friend, we would've had the potential to heal the anger and make the relationship stronger or better, but many people don't think that way. As a result, most conflicts are because of misunderstandings from lack of communication."

"I agree. I try to be very honest and upfront with my friends about how I feel. That way they know they can trust me and don't have to play games to figure out what I'm thinking."

"And your school promotes honesty with a code of ethics, right?"

"Yes, 'A Cadet will not lie, cheat, steal, nor tolerate those who do.' It's good. I can leave money sitting on my desk and no one will touch it. Cadets are kicked out for breaking the Honor Code," I explained.

"Wow. Well, most people haven't figured out the importance of honesty yet. White lies are an acceptable part of our society. People prefer to avoid confrontation when confrontation, as painful as it seems, can actually be a loving and positive thing."

"My parents don't like confrontation. When my mom gets angry with my dad, she brings up things that happened before I was born. That's anger held in for twenty years!"

"Yeah, if your mom addressed the issues when they first happened, it could've been healed, and would be less likely to occur again."

"That's true. So what are the other agreements in the book?"

"Well, I want to tell you about the third agreement first because it is kind of part of this discussion. The third agreement is 'Don't make assumptions.' I believe most conflicts are from misunderstandings. I'm angry because I think you did so-in-so to hurt me, when in reality your reasoning could've been completely different. This is another reason why confronting issues honestly is so important—to clear misunderstandings. Communication is the key to healthy relationships."

I nodded.

"The second agreement is 'Don't take anything personally.'"

"Well, I'm really going to have a problem with that agreement!"

"Why is that?"

"Because I'm singled out constantly at CAF, and it's hard not to take it personally. I know it is part of the school's culture, but I wish sometimes I'd get a break. I attract harassment like I have a kick-me sign on my back."

"Well, maybe you do. Maybe you have a victim sign on your forehead too!"

"What do you mean by that?"

"Well, have you read the book, *The Secret*?"

"No, but first finish the last agreement."

"Okay, I'll get back to *The Secret* in a minute. The second agreement, 'Don't take anything personally,' seems perfect for you to learn about now." She opened the cover of the book and read out loud.

"Nothing others do is because of you. What others say and do is a projection of their own reality, their own dream. When you are immune to the opinions and actions of others, you won't be the victim of needless suffering," she said, closing the book. "You see, we all live in our own little world. Our views are filtered through our thoughts, emotions, experiences, and our interpretations of reality. It's a wonder we can have relationships at all! So, if you can, try to learn not to take all that stuff at CAF personally. It's not about you, I assure you."

"Yeah, right!" I rolled my eyes.

"It's okay. You don't have to believe me. The fourth and last agreement says 'Always do your best.' If I'm doing my best, that's all I can do. As I continue to grow, my self confidence will grow too. If we are honest with ourselves and others, don't take other people personally, ask questions, and do our best ... then we can change our lives for the better."

"I understand exactly what you're saying. That sounds like a great book."

"Good, because I want you to read it, so I'm lending it to you," she said, laying it in a pile on the floor. "I'm not trying to overwhelm you. You can take or leave any of the books. I'm just sharing them with you, okay?" Cathleen looked up at me.

"Okay. I really appreciate it. I've been enjoying *The Fifth Sacred Thing* and hope to finish it over Christmas break. This is awesome. No one has ever taken such an interest in sharing books with me, like this. Thanks."

"No problem."

"So tell me about the secret book," I encouraged.

"Oh, yes! *The Secret* is about the Law of Attraction."

"Okay ..."

"Well, the Law of Attraction is about what we draw into our lives. It comes from the understanding that we are *one* with God or the Goddess, however you view the ultimate universe. Since we're all connected, we draw to us exactly what we desire. At the same time, we draw to us what we don't want. We just need to become aware of the energy we are sending out, and then change our thoughts and emotions, in order to attract the life we desire."

"Our minds are that powerful?"

"Absolutely. Our minds, not just our brain, but our consciousness, the essence of who we are, has the power to draw to us *anything* we desire."

"So, if I focused on attracting a mansion with my mind, would I *poof* have a mansion show up in my life?" I asked.

"Sort of, but not exactly. You see, your heart wouldn't be in it because you don't really want a mansion, at least I don't think you do."

"Yeah, you're right, but what does that matter?"

"It matters most of all. The *emotion* behind the thought is the fuel that runs the car," she explained. "You attract what's in your heart."

"Okay …"

"It's one thing to want a million dollars or the perfect marriage, but if there are conflicting thoughts or emotions, like unworthiness or doubt, then you won't draw it into your life," she explained. "Instead, you'll draw experiences which reflect your doubt. Does that make sense?"

"I think so.…"

"This is a big topic to jump into. We'll talk more about it later. For now, I'm going to pass on this book to you. Read it. Take your time to process it, and then we'll talk about it later."

"Sounds good!"

"Shall we have lunch?"

"Sure."

"I'm going to warn you. These books have the power to change your life," she said.

"I'll take my chances."

I followed Cathleen into the kitchen. It was small and cozy, like the rest of her apartment. There was no room for a kitchen table. Instead, there was a small counter with two bar stools. There were already two plates set on the counter, along with two sets of silverware and a basket of napkins.

Cathleen pulled out two containers of food from the refrigerator.

"I'm not a vegetarian, but I don't eat a lot of meat. I hope you don't mind this meal is meatless," she said.

"Oh, I don't care. Anything other than mess hall food or peanut butter and jelly sandwiches is fine with me."

"It was so nice to prepare food for more than one person." She handed me a plate of interesting food. "That's a brie, pear, and honey sandwich and a black bean salad. All of it goes perfectly with the wine, I promise."

"Looks yummy."

"Care for a refill?" she asked, holding up the bottle of wine.

"Why not?"

"Why not!" she said, filling my glass to the rim. "Let's go outside. It's a little too small to eat in here, so I often sit on the fire escape. It's not elegant by any means, but it is nice to be outside in the fresh air."

~

With our legs dangling over the edge a few stories up, we held our plates on our laps and ate with our arms through the metal bars. It felt freeing to be out there.

"Why aren't you put off by me being in a military school?" I asked.

"Well, my dad was a Vietnam Vet. He'd encouraged me to go into the military," she chuckled, "but it didn't appeal to me. I'm somewhat familiar with the military mentality, with how hardcore and dedicated most soldiers are. Just because it isn't my path doesn't mean I can't relate to it."

"You're right.... This is a great sandwich. What made you put these ingredients together?"

"It's my favorite sandwich. My dad used to make it for me when I was growing up," she said, handing me some napkins. "The honey makes your hands really sticky."

"So, what else do you do, other than run your own bookstore?"
"Well, I'm very spiritual, as you probably can tell. See, I have this tattoo," she said, lifting up her shirt. An Ohm symbol with a lotus flower adorned her lower back. "The Ohm symbol is the sound of God."

It was pretty.

"I attend yoga classes, and volunteer at the local monastery with the Buddhist monks."

"Wow, I've never done anything like that before. What are the monks like?"

"They're nice." She laughed.

Cathleen was interesting. I felt like maybe she was flirting with me, but what did I know? Cathleen never mentioned a boyfriend or anyone significant like that.

I told her briefly about Seth, not wanting to dive too much into it. Cathleen and I could have talked for days; it felt so comfortable.

"So what are you doing tomorrow?" she asked, as if reading my thoughts.

"I don't have any plans."

"Great. Would you like to come over again, after I close the store?"

"Sure."

After the meal, I collected the books and said my good-byes. Cathleen gave me a big hug and gently kissed me on the lips. I left in a daze and walked back to Barracks a little foggy-brained from the wine.

It took me a couple of minutes to comprehend that Cathleen had kissed me. Does she normally kiss her friends good-bye? It seemed so natural, not a big deal at all. I wasn't even put off by it. That thought suddenly startled me. Was I a lesbian and I didn't even know it?

Cathleen was cool, magnificent really, and simple at the same time. I was very intrigued by her beauty and intelligence. Maybe kissing her back wouldn't be such a bad thing. I had felt really comfortable there, maybe *too* comfortable.

Chapter 19: A Strange Encounter

It was dark out by the time I reached Barracks. I went up to my room, changed into my sweats, and went for a short run, for the exercise and to clear my head. My body was sluggish. My legs felt like they were made of metal, from the wine and from surrendering to relaxation. I have to be careful with alcohol, I noted to myself.

I ran around the baseball field, leaving footprints in the sandy dirt. I heard voices in the distance, but I couldn't see them in the dark. I reduced my pace to a walk, letting my heartbeat slow a bit, and walked over to a bench. It always felt good to do long and deep stretches when my muscles were warm.

I stood with my feet underneath the bench and grabbed the top with both hands and pulled back, stretching my back and legs. I did the same stretch again, with my legs further away and enjoyed the fullness of the stretch. Then I stretched my calves and hamstrings. I hadn't worked my arms too much the past couple of days, so I got down in the dirt and pushed, keeping my eyes on the ground in front of me, as my chest skimmed the dirt. I concentrated on my breathing, breathing in as I lowered my body and breathing out when I pushed up.

Nothing like exercise to get me feeling focused and centered again. Sweating, with the release of toxins and stress from the day, felt so calming. Jogging also had the side-affect of making me feel powerful, like I could do anything.

I stood up and dusted the dirt from my hands. I heard voices again, but this time they were closer, so I headed in the opposite direction. I didn't feel like running into any Upperclassmen.

"Hey, Tick!"

I stopped in my tracks. Great, just great … I didn't feel I had to obey, with it being a holiday, but I didn't want to risk it. The Tick Line was run by the Upperclassmen—not the Administration—like it is at the academies, Lalita has told me.

I slowly turned around. I didn't recognize the male voices. The moon was over half full which allowed enough light to catch the outline of two cadets. I wondered how they could tell, in the dimness of the night, that I was a Tick.

They walked toward me, and I wanted to run, but I hesitated. Before I knew it, they stood a few feet away, close enough that I got a whiff of the alcohol on their breath.

I remained silent and focused on their every move; I didn't trust them.

"Who the fuck do you think you are, Tick?"

"You're the one who called me," I replied, without thinking.

"Oh, we have a live one here," the Upperclassman said, chuckling, and took a step in my direction.

I looked at the other Upperclassman and realized, by the lack of focus in his eyes, that he was just as lit, or more so, than his companion. I stepped back, not wanting either to come any closer, but he grabbed my left arm, and I reacted instinctively. I jabbed my right hand, straight and rigid, at an angle and down into the side of his neck. He winced in pain, releasing his grip and stepping back, startled.

I took off running, hearing the muffled words, "Bitch, I will get you!"

I kept running until I reached my room. I ran so fast back to Barracks and up the stairs that I had to catch myself before I ran into Caroline's desk. I instantly felt a wave of nausea from having sprinted the whole way.

I forced myself to keep moving, to breathe, as I walked circles around my room, allowing my heartbeat to slow. Because I was so tense, it took a couple of attempts before I could breathe deeply.

After I felt myself calm down a bit, I went to the sink and ran my hands under some cold water. I was still shaking and had trouble keeping my hands steady. I filled my CAF cup and sipped, swishing water around my mouth and wetting my dry lips. Shit … shit … why did I do that? Because it was two against one, that's why. Besides, I didn't know what he … *or they* were going to do. I was just protecting myself.

It wasn't a normal occurrence for an Upperclassman to touch a Tick; there were rules. All throughout the Tick Line, whenever Cadre came up to me, to adjust my salute or the way I was carrying my saxophone, they always asked, "Permission to touch, Tick?" I had to say "Yes, sir," before Cadre could briefly shift my position, though I doubted any Tick ever said "No."

Over the summer, I started taking the contraception pill, which was required to enter the Tick Line. I wondered why females had that regulation.… The reasons for the requirement had not been made clear. I initially speculated that it was to regulate the women's menstrual cycles, just to make sure the women continued to have monthly cycles with all the stress of the Tick Line. Now I questioned if it was to prevent pregnancy if rape did occur.

I pulled down the shade to my door, stripped, and left my wet clothes in a pile on the floor. I put on fresh sweats, grabbed my M-14, and got in my hay with it. Our rifles were not loaded, but the solidness of the weapon comforted me, especially since I was alone. The weapon could provide a good defense, just by the weight of it.

I instantly fell asleep, the combined effort of the run and the waning adrenaline made me fatigued.

~

My bladder woke me up in the middle of the night. I stumbled out of my rack, put my sneakers on, and quickly made my way to the bathroom. Barracks was quiet, except for the occasional sounds, creaks, and windblown hums that echoed in the hollow structure, making vague whispers sound like tormented wailings. It was as if Barracks cried out in pain from all the suffering that had occurred within. There were plenty of ghosts, people who had come and gone, even aspects of my own Fellow Ticks who had left.

The past played in the present, like a time warp, repeating the same situations over and over, the essence of upholding tradition. I knew others had faced the same challenges I dealt with today, and that many would in the future.

When I returned to my room, I grabbed my blanket and wrapped it around my shoulders. I pulled a chair up to the window and sat peacefully, listening to the noises streaming in from my window. The crickets chirped, and I heard the hoot of an owl. The window was always open to allow a slight breeze, and I opened it wider to expose the night air. A light flickered from a house far off in the distance. I heard a car pass underneath.

My mind drifted to thoughts of Seth.

"Seth," I whispered. "Seth, Seth …" I sighed and envisioned him hovering before me, like an apparition. I felt different. "I just want you to know, everything's okay. I'm okay," I said, addressing him. "Thank you for loving me. Thank you for the time that we had together."

At that moment, in the middle of the night, I could honestly say that I was fine. An epiphany opened my eyes to how difficult it must have been for Seth to stay connected to me, a girlfriend so far away, and one that reminded him of our loss. It was important for him to move on, just as much as it was for me to.

"I want you to know—I get it. You're free to go. I love you, probably always will.… Good-bye, Seth. Good-bye."

I inhaled deeply and exhaled more than my breath, but my emotional attachment to him. True love *is* loving enough to let go.

I left the windows slightly ajar and returned to bed. I'd made it this far in the Tick Line, and I was going to complete what I'd started; I knew that for sure now. I felt content, not high or low, but okay, like a straight line across the horizon.

⌒

I stayed in my room the next morning, not feeling the desire to leave or run, but to hibernate and be by myself. I opened *The Four Agreements* and soaked in the words of wisdom.

Halfway through, I set the book down and took out my journal. Everything in the book made sense. I wrote a declaration to myself. I wanted to acknowledge this moment.

I am choosing growth, to be aware of who I am, and these books are going to help. From now on, I choose to be empowered. I don't fully know what that means or how I'm going to accomplish it, but that's what I'm going to do, even while I'm a Tick. I will play the game, but I will not process the degrading comments. I can choose what to focus on. Am I going to play the victim and feel sorry for myself because the Tick Line is hard? No. I want to be here, even though I may not like all the bullshit that goes along with it. I will be an Upperclassman one day. I have survived the Tick Line so far, and I've done an okay job despite everything, despite losing Ethan.

I have three weeks left until Christmas break. Everything is going to be okay—this is my mantra. If the Tick Line has taught me one thing, it is that I'm a survivor.

I closed my journal and picked up the book again. *The Four Agreements* talked about how our world is a dream, a dream based on false thoughts. My life doesn't feel like a dream. It feels very real to me, but I wonder … if I change my thoughts, can I change my dream? I must first be aware of my thoughts.

Awareness comes from being honest with yourself which is why I keep a journal. To anyone who opened it, the scribbling would appear incoherent. I don't record my day's events; I record how I am feeling. It gives me the opportunity to hear my own voice, to bring my subconscious thoughts and emotions to the forefront, so I can understand myself better.

I opened my journal to the back cover and wrote down a quote from *The Four Agreements*. "Death is not the biggest fear we have; our biggest fear is taking the risk to be alive – the risk to be alive and express what we really are. Just being ourself is the biggest fear of humans." (17)

It is hard to be myself in a school that breeds collectiveness and uniformity. Was there a way I could continue to be my unique self while at the same time fulfilling the role as a CAF cadet?

I don't know. I continued to read.

"Humans punish themselves endlessly for not being what they believe they should be," (19) which is similar to how Cadre punish Ticks for not living up to a specific standard.

Who do I think I should be? I think I should be physically fit and emotionally strong, I wrote again. "Our image of perfection is the reason we reject ourselves; it is why we don't accept ourselves the way we are, and why we don't accept others the way they are." (21)

Do I have an image of perfection? I probably expect too much from myself, I wrote and closed my journal.

~

I got up and stretched. It was eleven o'clock, and I hadn't eaten anything yet. I pulled down my food box and opened it to find there wasn't much left: a box of Ritz crackers, yogurt covered raisins, a protein bar, packets of hot chocolate mix, instant coffee and a little peanut butter. I was out of bread and jelly, so no PBJ for me.

I went over to the sink and turned the knob to hot. The water pouring out of the faucet steamed, so I made myself a cup of coffee with cocoa mix, and opened the protein bar, a complete set of amino acids. Well, it wasn't the best breakfast, but it would do.

Chapter 20: Integrated Energy Therapy

I showed up at Cathleen's apartment that evening, to find a note on the door which told me to let myself in.

"Cathleen?" I called from the doorway, but I didn't get an answer.

I found Cathleen in a daze, as if she hadn't heard me enter her bedroom. However, her mannerisms were not surprised by my appearance. She was sitting by the window and peering outside, as if she was looking somewhere else, rather than the scenic view of mountains and shops below.

"Hey, what are you doing?" I asked.

"Just meditating …"

"Oh … are you okay?"

"Yeah, yeah. I was in a deep mediation, and I'm allowing myself to gently come out of it. How are you?" she asked softly, still not looking at me. With night approaching, I could see part of her reflection in the window. This was my favorite time of day, as the sun began to wean, when night and day were in equal balance.

"I'm good. I read *The Four Agreements*, and even did some self-reflection on it," I shared proudly. "All the books you have recommended have been wonderful."

"Oh, I'm so glad. I was thinking about you earlier, about everything you are going through, and wanted to offer you something that might help."

"What's that? Psychedelic drugs? A séance?" I teased.

"No, no …" She smiled and turned to me. "I'm certified in Integrated Energy Therapy (IET), and I thought you'd enjoy a session. It might help alleviate some stress."

"Really? What's that?"

"IET helps shift energy, so in the end you feel more empowered. It's a wonderful, life-changing technique."

"Well, my life has already changed a lot," I replied, a little defensively. "It's just," I sighed, "I don't know. Tell me more about it. What would I have to do?"

"Let's go into the kitchen," she encouraged. "And get something to drink."

I followed her, noticing her long, flowing turquoise dress that tapered at the waist, complimenting her slender hourglass figure. Her wide sleeves were long enough to cover part of her hands and they danced as she walked. She looked beautiful, like always. I was wearing the one and only civilian outfit that I had with me, my jeans and CAF T-shirt, along with Cathleen's wool sweater that I hadn't given back yet.

"Wine, soft drink, or juice?" Cathleen asked from behind the refrigerator door.

"Whatever you're having is fine."

"I was going to make a juice bubbly … juice and carbonated water. Sound good to you?"

"Sure, that's fine." I propped myself on one of the stools.

I watched Cathleen as she brought out apple juice and cherry flavored seltzer. She opened the cabinet door, pulled out two large clear glasses, and filled them to the brim with ice.

"We Americans do love our ice," I said.

"Yes, we do," she said, handing me a glass.

"Thanks."

"So …" she said, sitting down on the other stool. "I've been having energy work done on me for the past five years. I have a wonderful mentor, Willa. She's guided me through some very challenging moments in my life. She does the energy work on me, and then last summer I got certified."

"That's cool."

"I continue to have IET sessions with her a couple times a year, along with phone consultations every other month. I truly believe everyone needs a mentor, someone they can talk to. Life can get complicated, so it's always helpful to get some guidance."

"Ah … yes. When I talk to my girlfriends back home, they understand my pain about Ethan and Seth, but they don't truly understand what I'm going through here. No one does, except my roommates, but they didn't know my brother, so I don't feel like anyone *truly* understands everything I'm going through."

"Yeah, I can only fathom.…" Cathleen shrugged her shoulders.

"I journal when I can, which helps me vent."

"That's cool. Journaling is wonderful. I've been writing since I was a kid."

"Me too."

"With Willa, I felt I'd finally met someone who understood me. The talks I've had with her have been insightful and very much needed. I also owe a lot of my changes to the energy work itself. Willa is a powerful healer and has done a lot of work on me. I've changed so much, but I've become more of myself, if that makes sense. It's the whole point of being on the spiritual path, I think."

I nodded.

"Have you heard of the Golden Buddha analogy?"

"No …"

"Well, we are all Golden Buddhas, you see, our essence, our souls. The reason we don't naturally see that, is because we are covered in mud—the sadness, doubt, disappointments, and grief in our lives. Most of us feel so disconnected from the Divine. We have to wash away the mud, to reconnect with ourselves and the Higher Power, so we can be our true selves and shine like the polished Golden Buddhas we are. It's not that we are *to become* the Golden Buddha; we *already are* the Golden Buddha. Does that make sense?"

"Sure, I get it."

"Clifford Mate created the practice of IET, through the guidance of Angel Ariel. He was ordained at The New Seminary, in New York City, which is why I chose to go there myself. I was ordained last spring as an Interfaith Minister. So, with the guidance of Angel Ariel, Clifford Mate discovered the IET cellular memory map and the IET integration points. These points are not recognized by traditional acupressure systems. Using these points, he created a type of therapy where the specific IET points on the body are triggered and suppressed energy, hence lower energy vibration, is released."

"He received all this information from an angel?"

"Yes."

"That's neat. I've never heard of IET before. Wait a minute ..." I turned around. "Is that picture over there, Angel Ariel?" I asked, pointing to a picture in the hallway.

"You're very observant. It is!"

"Well, how does he know what Angel Ariel looks like?"

"Because a friend of his can see angels and painted the picture for him."

"Oh, this all sounds ... *different*. You believe in all this?"

"Yes, definitely. I've experienced it firsthand and know the power of IET."

"That's cool. Well ... I'm open."

"That's good enough for me." She smiled and continued. "So, IET is a form of angelic healing. When I do a session on a client, I, as an energy worker, act as a channel between my clients and Angel Ariel," she described, using her hands to accentuate her speech. "When the IET points on the body are triggered, suppressed energy is released. Then Angel Ariel fills the void with a higher energy vibration."

"Wow. That sounds intense."

"It is, but the session itself is very gentle. Yet, the outcome of the work can be life-changing, just like the books I passed on to you."

"I see, but what do you mean by energy vibration?"

"Everything in our world is energy, and individually we each vibrate at a certain frequency. For example, the spirit realm is all around us, but on a different dimension, a higher plane of existence, vibrating at a faster speed than this realm. Angels vibrate faster, so fast that most of us do not see them. Think of a fan. When a fan is spinning on high, the blades seem to disappear to our eyes."

"Oh yeah ..."

"Here, in this third dimensional world, we vibrate at a slower speed. When we grow spiritually, we raise up in vibration. We may one day be able to see angels. Besides, the veil between these two dimensions has thinned tremendously."

"I too believe the spiritual world is all around us. That's why there are moments I feel Ethan's presence. I don't see him, but I know he's there. I don't believe he hangs around like a ghost, more like he comes to visit, and then returns to his new home. Do you know what I mean?"

"Of course, that makes complete sense. You see, our soul is energy. Our emotions are energy. Thoughts are energy, and our physical body is energy. Actually, our physical body is the densest energy we work with."

"I never thought of it that way."

"So, if you were to create an illness—"

"What do you mean, create an illness?"

"Yes, Alicia. Nothing in this world is random. We don't just magically receive an illness. An illness comes about because of an energetic pattern, whether the illness is caused by lifestyle choices or has been passed down energetically through generations, it is still an energetic pattern that has been present for a long time. The cool thing is, though, an illness can very much be a blessing. Since our physical body is the densest form we operate from, an illness is generally a way for us to heal at a very deep level."

"Wow, I never looked at disease that way before."

"Generally, I think most health problems stem from suppressed emotional wounds. If we hadn't been able to heal a broken heart, we might manifest a heart palpitation; or if we had trouble forgiving and releasing pain, we might manifest colon cancer. Who knows? We are complex Beings."

"Really?"

"Sure. Think about it. Think about what we say. How many times have you heard someone say "I can't stomach it" or "he made my head hurt" or "I'm so in love it made my heart skip a beat." Where in your body do you *feel* the most?"

"Well, I know when I get yelled at a lot, my stomach tightens up, and when I'm stressed, my shoulders hurt."

"The stomach is your solar plexus. It's where we hold our personal power; that's why punching someone in the stomach is so violating. It's the center of us, the middle chakra, where we stay balanced. So, when Cadre yells at you, you may feel like your personal power is being taken away from you."

"Uh, huh," I agreed.

"And the shoulders represent what you feel you *should* be doing. It's probably because you feel the weight of the world on your shoulders."

"You know what? I just thought of something. When my aunt and uncle broke up, after thirty-something years of marriage, my aunt broke out in a rash—medium size, red bumps everywhere—and she used to call them her *anger spots*."

"You see, your aunt knew. Her suppressed emotional pain finally came out to be released."

"Yeah, I just never thought about that before. Interesting …"

"So, with IET, we release suppressed energy from our physical, mental, emotional, and spiritual planes. It's important to understand that our personal experiences are a reflection of the energy we send out into the world. We draw to us experiences that mirror our beliefs, feelings, and expectations about ourselves and about life. As a result, when we change the energy we send out, we change what is reflected to us and what we receive."

"Okay, I hear what you're saying. *The Four Agreements* talked about how all of us live in our own dream world, how we see the world through our personal filters of experiences and beliefs."

"Exactly. Our thoughts and emotions are very powerful. So, for example, if you were raised with the belief that you're not very smart, you'll habitually recreate scenarios in your life that will reflect this belief. You may not fully apply yourself to your studies, thinking it's a lost cause anyway, and as a result you receive poor grades, once again reflecting the belief that you're not very smart. It's cyclical. Our beliefs create our reality, and our beliefs are re-enforced by our experiences."

"How do you know what specific thoughts are creating situations in your life that you don't want?" I asked.

"Through self-reflection. Most of our thoughts and emotions live in our subconscious mind, where we're not aware of their influence. By taking personal responsibility for our lives, we bring those subconscious thoughts and feelings to the conscious mind. It is a lifelong practice. Once we become aware, we can choose how to think and feel. For example, the thought 'I'm always the victim,' will change to 'I have control of my destiny; I have choice; and I have the power to create any life I desire.'"

"Well, that makes sense, moving from a negative thought to a positive thought."

"With IET, we can transform a lot of thoughts and emotions without having to dissect each individual thought and emotion. It's a quick, efficient, and powerful form of healing. The session itself is gentle, but for up to two weeks afterward, you integrate the new energy. That two week period can be chaotic, but everyone is different. I've had some clients sail through the two weeks without any problems. For me, though, it was hard. During my first few years of working with Willa, I felt like I was constantly in the midst of a tornado—my energies shifted so much. Now, it's much easier," Cathleen said, getting up to stretch.

"So, why did you continue to have sessions if it disrupted your life so much?"

"Because I always ended up in a better place. The thing with energy, when you're in the midst change, you can't see clearly…. You can't see the forest for the trees. But once the new energy is integrated, it's usually pretty apparent what energetic pattern had been present before, what had been released."

"That's cool. Sign me up! I'm more curious than anything."

"I thought you'd like it. Let's have dinner first, and then we can have a session. Sound good to you?"

"Sure, how can I help with dinner?" I stood up and refilled my glass.

"Well, the chicken should be ready. We're having honey-curry chicken, wild rice, and green beans. How does that sound?" Cathleen asked, handing me a plate.

"Great!"

Chapter 21: The Session

"Follow me to my sacred space, my healing room. Feel free to discard the wool sweater for now. I put a blanket down for you." Cathleen pointed as I entered the room.

The lights were turned off, but the small room was illuminated by candlelight. Some candles were in holders that were nailed to the wall while others adorned a white bookshelf. A colorful flag was draped across one long wall. It consisted of numerous small flags, all connected by a thin, black rope.

"That's my Interfaith Flag," Cathleen said, reading my thoughts. "The Goddess flag," she said, pointing to a robust female figure. "Native American Spirituality," she said, pointing to the dream catcher on the second small flag. "The yin-yang sign for Taoism; the star for Judaism; the balanced cross for Christianity; and the Om symbol of many religions, but represents New Age Spirituality to me."

"It's beautiful."

I glanced around and saw three angels high on the bookshelf lit up electronically, glowing and shimmering as their wings moved gracefully back and forth. In the center of the small room was a massage table with a pink blanket, embroidered with a large white angel.

"This room seems magical," I said, taking off the sweater and placing it underneath the table.

Soft music played in the background and a light, sweet scent garnished the room.

"Do you mind if I burn a little sage?" Cathleen asked.

"Not at all." I stretched out on the massage table and put the blanket over me.

"That's right. Lie on your back and put your arms at your side. Feel free to fully relax. I'll do the work. You can sleep or meditate if you want to."

"Alright," I whispered, placing my head on the small feathered pillow.

"I'm going to start by working on your head. If I lift your head, don't feel like you need to help me. Just relax."

"Okay. I'm probably going to fall asleep."

"That is perfectly fine. Most people do." Cathleen closed the door and took her place at the head of the massage table.

Cathleen raised her arms and faced heavenward. "I call the presence of my guides and my angels. I call the presence of Alicia's guides and her angels." Cathleen took a deep breath. "I also call the presence of Angel Ariel for this healing today. May this healing be in Alicia's highest and best interest, and may this healing contribute to the healing of the world. Amen. Blessed Be." Cathleen bowed once, as if honoring the spirits before her, and began the healing session.

~

"Now come back into your body," Cathleen spoke lightly. "And when you're ready, open your eyes."

Did I leave my body? Whoa, I must have. It felt like coming back from somewhere far away. I tried opening my eyes, but my eyelids felt very heavy.

"Don't push yourself, Alicia. Allow yourself to gradually wake up."

The music stopped. I could hear Cathleen blowing out the candles. I eventually peeled my eyes open and stared at the ceiling.

"That was an intense session," I heard Cathleen say from the side of the room. I tried sitting up, but failed. Cathleen walked over and placed a hand under my lower back to assist me.

"What did you do to me?"

Cathleen laughed. "Welcome to Integrated Energy Therapy 101," she teased. "Be kind to yourself. No reason to push through the energy."

I sat up with my legs dangling over the side of the table.

"Sit there for a moment," Cathleen said, rubbing my back, helping me feel my body again. She touched the air around me.

"I'm smoothing out your aura," she stated matter-of-factly.

"Oh …"

"Go ahead, stand up, and wait there a moment. I need to ground your energies." Cathleen crouched down on the floor by my feet. She pressed two points on each ankle. "I'd like to thank Angel Ariel for the healing work today. I'd like to thank Alicia for choosing this healing, which is for the better of her soul's growth and the healing of the world. Amen. Blessed Be." Cathleen stood up, and with her hands folded in prayer, she bowed towards me. Then she gave me a big hug, and I squeezed back with appreciation.

"You're okay, and you're going to be okay," she said, taking a deep breath and letting it out. "Shall we go out to the fire escape and chat a minute before you go?"

"Sure."

~

"How do you feel?" Cathleen asked after we'd settled ourselves comfortably outside.

"I feel a little disoriented."

"That was an *intense* healing session. Sometimes I'm shown pictures, scenes of what is being released. Would you like me to share anything I saw?"

"Sure, why not." I listened intently. Why put any restrictions on my night now?

"Well, my angels communicate with me regularly. During your session, I saw chains around your wrists and ankles. I removed some energy there. Hopefully that will allow you to walk more in your power and be less controlled by those around you."

I laughed. What power did I have being a Tick in the Tick Line?

"At the top of your head, I felt your guilt, guilt over leaving for school while Ethan was in the hospital. I was shown a picture of Ethan lying in bed alone, and you being far away. You're not to feel bad about this. It was part of his journey, and this is part of yours." She took deep breath and closed her eyes, trying to remember. "Your throat chakra was blocked, not allowing you to fully express yourself, whether with your family or at school. Many people have trouble with their throat chakras. It's okay. As you become more of yourself, you'll naturally clear that."

I sat and listened. Ever since I was little, I had reoccurring sore throats. I'd even had a sore throat at the beginning of the Tick Line.

"You carry much weight on your shoulders, hence the tension you've been feeling in your shoulders. You'll clear those blockages when you start fully living your life for you," she said casually and took another deep breath. "Your heart is wounded, but okay.... You'll love again." She opened her eyes. "How do you feel now?"

"I feel okay. I should get back to Barracks. Tomorrow everyone will return, and this is my last chance for some alone time." I smiled. "I really appreciate the work you did on my tonight. It was very sweet of you. Thank you for dinner and everything."

"It was my pleasure, Alicia. I really enjoy talking with you. It's so nice to share things like IET with a friend," she said, following me to the door.

I turned and gave Cathleen another hug. "I feel so connected with you, so relaxed. I'm glad that I can be myself here."

Cathleen looked at me, "Yes, it's quite magical, the connection we both have."

"Yes, it is! Thanks again and good night," I said and walked out the door.

"Auf Wiedersehen," I heard Cathleen utter as I descended the staircase.

Chapter 22: Tradition

I walked along the streets, dazed by what I'd experienced. Cathleen was incredible. I was amazed by her experience working with the angels and by her wisdom. She lived in such a different world than I did.

I could see Barracks in the distance. Back to *my* world.

As I walked closer, my vision blurred and the crystal-clear imagine of Barracks turned to a gray haze. Then my vision focused again. The Barracks is energy. Everything around me is energy. I am energy. The energy in Barracks is of obedience, control, and order. My vision blurred again. I held the blurred vision longer, making the sky and ground one big blur with Barracks.

I suddenly felt myself as part of the whole, no longer an individual fighting through the system. I was One with the mass of Fellow Ticks, all of us collectively surrendering to tradition and surviving a system put in place long before us, a system that will sustain long after we were gone. I was here in this segment of time, a brief moment, as a flicker of light that is extinguished within an instant. Suddenly my life didn't seem so significant, but at the same time my life felt very special. I felt drawn to this place, to this specific experience, to this school that challenged me so.

The energy of the school was like a tornado: strong, cleansing, and damaging. I felt the great power the school held, the honor and dedication of the cadets, professors, and alumni. CAF was a world of its own, a world I'd chosen to enter, and a world I was determined not to let consume me.

I looked up at the sky and felt peaceful. I closed my eyes and felt One with the Great Force, the entity too large and grand to describe.

Since entering the Tick Line, I'd felt like a pawn on a chest board, being moved around carelessly. I wondered if I could somehow surrender to the system without losing myself.

I walked through Jackson Arch and up to my room. There were voices all around me, echoing words I didn't catch. I jogged up each flight of stairs, feeling so light, as if my feet didn't fully touch the ground. No one confronted me. I entered the sanctity of my room without being noticed. I felt very connected to myself, a feeling difficult to retain while immersed in the stressful, chaotic, and unpredictable life of CAF. I cherished this private time. If only I could hold on to this connection with myself, this connection to the Divine *forever*, then I'd know peace.

I sat down at my desk and turned on my lamp. I took out my journal and wrote whatever came to mind, whatever I felt, not worrying about grammatical errors or disjointed thoughts; this way I heard my inner voice without interruption.

~

The next morning, I woke up when Brenda entered the room.

"Hey, lazy bones. How was your break?" Brenda asked cheerfully, putting her bags down. She stretched her arms high and jogged in place, as if trying to re-acclimate herself to Barracks life.

"It was interesting...." I answered groggily, stretching my legs one at a time. "I missed you and the girls. I've had a few quiet nights here, if you can believe it."

"That must've been trippy. Want to have a smoke?" Brenda asked, surfing through her bag.

"What time is it?" I was surprised by the bright sunlight. "After nine, I guess," she said, opening the windows wider.

"Damn, I haven't slept in this late since summer. I must've passed out from yesterday's experience," I said, trying to motivate myself to get out of bed. "It sure feels good to have you back." I walked toward the window and grabbed a cigarette from her desk.

"What did you do with yourself while we were gone?" Brenda asked, staring out the window.

"Oh, a little of this, a little of that." I smiled. "I'll tell you more when I'm awake."

"I bet they're going to beat the shit out of us tonight." Brenda inhaled some smoke.

"Sweat party?" I asked, one eyebrow raised in questioning. "I should've assumed. Did your Guide tell you that?"

"Nah, I just know the school enough by now to know better." She grinned.

"So, what did you do over break? Any good stories?"

"I saw Troy," she said, briefly sounding happy. "But not that long … Long enough, though …" She smirked.

"Oh … I see … Did you see your girlfriends too?"

"Yeah, but not a lot. I mostly spent time with the horses. I miss them when I'm here, so I went for long rides. I didn't have much to say to my friends, honestly. You'll feel it when you go home for Christmas. It's not that I don't care about them, but how can they understand the bullshit we go through here?"

"Heck if I know."

"Troy understands, though. He's been through a hell of his own in the Marines. He was lucky enough to be home for Thanksgiving because in two weeks he's off to Afghanistan."

"No kiddin'? Man, that's rough," I said, shaking my head.

"You're tellin' me! It's his thing, though. He wants to go." She sighed.

"Know when you'll see him next?"

"Nope. Have no idea. We're just going to have to wait it out, though it looks like our lives are heading in two different directions," she said, flicking her bud out the window.

"I understand how that feels." I looked out the window to the bare trees. "I'm so glad winter is almost here." I breathed in the scents coming through the air.

"Why is that?"

"Because it means time has passed, and we are one season closer to the end of the Tick Line. Hoo-ah!" I said, smacking my thigh.

~

"*Ticks, welcome back!*" the familiar voice sounded over the loud speaker.

I looked straight ahead. Ticks stood on all sides of me, and I was comforted by the sheer presence of them all. We were in this together! Brenda was to my left and Caroline and Dawn were close by, probably right behind me.

"*It is the tradition of the College of Armed Forces to hold a party for the Ticks, to remind them of their rightful status in our school. All Ticks, resume the position!*"

We got on our faces, tripping over each other, and spreading out to get room on the floor. Upperclassmen remained on the perimeter, waiting to work us out. I liked the feeling of unity when all of the Ticks pushed together.

A few Ticks called out numbers, mainly the hardcore guys who wanted attention. I pushed slower, pacing myself. I felt the solid concrete and dirt underneath my hands. I focused on a small mark in the floor and reminded myself to breathe. All around me, Ticks were grunting and sweating, and even some were chuckling.

"*Push Ticks, push!*"

I held my arms straight, in the up position, and slightly turned my head to the left to see how Brenda was doing. She grinned, her face red from the excursion.

"Having fun yet?" I asked her.

"Never better!" she yelled back.

I looked around. We were right on top of each other. The sneakers of a Tick in front of me were just a few inches from my face. Ticks' shirts came untucked, and I saw a lot of hairy legs, and some other things I didn't wish to see from this position. I continued to push, but we were all slowing down.

"*Ticks, it is now time to go for an evening run. Get in file formation, now!*"

Brenda and I looked at each other, alarmed. We stood up, got in line, and huddled together.

"*Left-face!*"

It was after ten and we were going for a run? What the heck?

Brenda moved in front of me, and I instinctively followed. We exited Barracks in single file through Marshall Arch. We moved quickly, trying to stay in line, and then found ourselves smack against the person in front of us as the line slowed unexpectedly, the mass of our bodies moving like a human accordion.

There was no formation, just a gaggle, with the Ticks being split up into groups randomly. Luckily Brenda and I remained together. Even though we didn't have a chance to talk, we knew where each other was and that was a great comfort. I followed my new group—directed by two Upperclassmen I did not know—down the hill toward the street below. It was late, so there was barely any traffic. We ran across the street to the Track and Field.

My body pumped out adrenaline in the midst of the unknown, as my guard was up.

"They're messing with us," Brenda said as we ran.

"Tell me something I don't know."

We kept moving, ending up in front of the bleachers. We were all breathing heavily and were glad for the opportunity to catch our breath.

"This sucks," I whispered to Brenda.

She nodded.

"*Ticks, this is your mission. Starting at the beginning, all the way to your left, you are to run up and down each bleacher until the end,*" he pointed right, "*and then you will be rewarded with the opportunity to return to your racks for a good night sleep. Until then, your mission must be completed. We are watching you—go!*" commanded one of the Upperclassman. He then pushed the Tick closest to him, demanding him to begin.

"*Go! Go!*" the other Upperclassman yelled. They were dressed in class uniform, obviously not planning to exert themselves tonight.

The Ticks ahead of us started up the steep steps to the top of the outdoor stadium. I took a few quick deep breaths, trying to prepare my body for this ungodly task, my peace left behind in our bedroom.

I jogged right behind Brenda, thankful for her presence, and felt my legs grow warmer. The first few steps were easy and gave me a sense of hope. Once reaching the top, though, my legs began to burn. I was keenly aware that this was not a task given to the weak. Going down was slightly better, but the third climb up the stairs left my legs shaking. I couldn't wait for it to end. By the fifth repetition, Brenda and I were both hurting and walking. I wanted to crawl, but I forced my wobbly legs to keep moving.

"Come on, girl. Only three more flights to go, and then we can head back to our room!" Brenda said.

"You better have chocolate in your food box...."

"I have something better than that," she said breathless.

"What's that?"

"A little weed ..."

"Yeah, right!" I smacked her arm.

By the time Brenda and I finished, we were ordered by the Upperclassmen to motivate the last Tick to finish.

Fellow Tick Custer was overweight and having severe trouble finishing the last two flights of stairs.

"Let's help him," Brenda said, grabbing my arm.

I was sitting in the dirt, stretching my hamstrings. "Are you freakin' kiddin' me? I can barely walk now!"

"Come on," she said, pulling on my sleeve and forcing me up.

"You are too fuckin' hardcore for me, woman!"

We barely made it up the stairs to join him. Tick Custer was breathing hard and looked embarrassed.

"We're here to help. Just lean on us," Brenda said, wrapping her right arm around him and anchoring his left arm on her shoulders. I followed her lead on his right side. He leaned on us—and I thought I was going to die.

"Come on Custer, you can do it!" Brenda said.

"That's right, Custer. You can—just a few more steps," I said.

We dragged him and ourselves up the last two flights of stairs. By the time we reached the end, I felt my lower back about to break. Custer let go, and I slid to the ground. I put my face in the dirt, feeling the hard surface and relaxed into it. I didn't want to get up ever again. I didn't care how dirty I got; I was already sweaty and smelly.

Next thing I felt was massive pressure on the side of my face, pushing me down farther into the dirt. A pain shot through my ears and head. I grabbed with my right arm, but I was weak and the pressure was strong.

"Hey! Leave her alone!" Brenda yelled.

"Randall, the next time you want to be a hero, I'd suggest you run!" I heard the voice say, muffled as it was with one ear in the dirt.

My head pounded, and I could barely breathe. I was scared, starting kicking, and tried to wiggle free from the pressure of his foot on my face.

"Do you know who I am, Tick?" he asked. "I'm the Upperclassman you hit near the baseball field. I told you I'd find you." He finally released his grip on my face.

I coughed, barely getting breath back into my lungs. I didn't look up; I was afraid of any repercussions.

"Are you okay?" Brenda asked, crouching down next to me.

"Line up, Ticks!"

I didn't move, but felt Brenda's arm lift me, and we slowly got back in line. I could still feel the painful imprint of his shoe on my right cheek and jaw.

We marched back to Barracks in silence. My head hurt. Once we passed under Stonewall Arch, we immediately strained and walked the Tick Line. I followed Brenda to our room, feeling the burning sensation in my legs and the aching in my head. We slammed the door to our room, and I collapsed on my hay with my sneakers still on.

~

"Get up, Alicia," Brenda whispered. It was morning. "I can't believe he did that to you!"

I looked up at her enraged expression and stared back with a blank face.

"Aren't you angry?" she egged me on.

I rubbed my eyes and tried to wake up. I pressed my fingers along my face to assess the damage.

"I know that we only have so much power as Ticks, but come on— that was uncalled for. He's not playing by the rules," she continued.

"I don't disagree," I murmured, letting out a big yawn as I moved my jaw back and forth, feeling the internal bruising.

"What happened?" Caroline asked in a whisper. "Why was that guy so mean to you?" Obviously Brenda had filled them in.

I told them what had happened in the woods over Thanksgiving break, when I had gone for a jog alone in the woods. Nothing occurred, obviously, except me striking a drunken Upperclassman, a reaction to him grabbing my arm.

"It was purely to prevent anything from happening," I repeated.

"That makes sense to me," Dawn said. "I'd have kicked him where it hurts—if he'd touched me."

"Something happened with us last night too," Caroline said.

Our attention shifted to Caroline.

"My group was taken to the woods for a run, like we do during Tick Challenge, but it was so dark out, we could barely see. Then we heard screaming—"

"*What?*" Brenda asked.

"Yeah, it sounded like a few of our Fellow Ticks were yelling out in pain," Dawn added.

"We didn't know what to do, but it scared the hell out of me. We just kept running ..." Caroline said.

"It's like they created groups of unfamiliar Ticks to put us at a disadvantage," Dawn said.

"That makes sense. Do you have any idea what happened?" Brenda asked.

"No idea. The yelling didn't last long, but it was really freaky. The Upperclassmen kept yelling at us to go faster, and I was barely keeping up...."

"It wasn't our fault, Caroline," Dawn said.

"I know ... but it makes me feel so powerless...."

"I know." Dawn nodded.

"I'm going to talk with Jamie and see what he says. Maybe we can get some answers. I've been meaning to talk to him about that guy with the ski mask that had come to our room." I sighed. "It seems the shit never ends around here!"

~

"Jamie, that's messed up! This is supposed to be a college. I can't believe what you're telling me!"

"It's true, Randall. It was just a test to see if your class is unified or not.... That's it. Drop it. There's no reason to get your nose out of joint over what your roommates said happened." He was clearly irritated by my inquiries.

"But you obviously don't understand. I believe them, *and* I know what happened to me in the baseball field *and* what happened to me last night at the track!" I looked at him, hoping for some sort of validation. "What the *hell* is going on here?"

Jamie flicked his pencil across the room in pure annoyance. "Randall, drop it! You weren't hurt. Your roommates weren't hurt. You have absolutely *nothing* to complain about."

"But this doesn't make any sense. Why are you defending that type of behavior?"

"All of the Upperclassmen that you talk about have been through the system. They know what they're supposed to do, and I don't need to question their judgment or their actions."

I looked at him in shock.

"Randall, look ... When I was a Tick, when it was an all-male school, things happened that you wouldn't agree with.... My Guide made me do push-ups with a rack on my back while he held a bayonet upright underneath me."

"*That's fucked up.*"

"And my Guide used to do push-ups on my head. He'd place his hands on my head and drive me into the concrete while he pushed. I had bruises all over my face from that. One time I even thought he broke my nose." He chuckled. "Sometimes I was required to do push-ups while holding a coat hanger. The coat hanger would dig into my fingers, which was intensely painful and made my fingers bled."

"Ah! *What?* If that's what you went through during your Tick Year, why don't you force me to do that stuff?" I asked curiously, instantly wishing I could take it back; I didn't want to encourage anything.

"Because I don't think abuse is right, or necessary, in order to build leadership. I don't believe in torturing Ticks—unless they step out of line."

"I see," I said, as chills ran up and down my spine.

"Randall, the thing is … many of your Fellow Ticks are going to go through experiences like this. Who am I to judge or do anything about it? Honestly, I don't care. I have too much to think about and too much to do. It's part of the system. This is how the school is run."

"I understand." I felt suddenly empty.

"So if I were you, I'd drop it."

"Okay. Thanks for talking to me about it," I mumbled, feeling defeated, and grabbed my bag on my way out of the room.

Chapter 23: The Hop

"I hate Guard Duty!" Caroline whined, as she polished her brass.

"Yeah, we already don't get enough sleep here," Dawn yawned in exaggeration, as she sat there looking like a beautiful toy solider. She was decked out perfectly in a gray blouse.

"Well, it's about time, eh? I think all the other Band Ticks have served two or three times by now. This is only our second time. I wonder why?" I asked.

"Heck if I care. I have two papers due in the morning and a Physics exam that I don't feel ready for." Brenda rubbed her red eyes.

"I know. I'm barely passing my classes this semester," I said, shrugging my shoulders. "I guess it's typical for being a Tick. How can we prioritize academics when we have all this other shit to do?"

"Guess what I heard?" Brenda said, suddenly grabbing everyone's attention. "My Guide told me that the last week before Christmas break, we don't do anything but study. No Tick Challenge; no random Upperclassmen workouts; no sweat parties; no TDC morning workouts; and no Cadre workouts!"

"No kiddin'! So all we have to do is prepare for finals?" I asked.

"*Exactly*. The school doesn't want us flunking out."

"Sweet." I sighed and rolled over in my hay. "Caroline, wake me up when I need to report for duty...."

"No, girl. You better set that alarm! You need to be dressed and ready to relieve me downstairs!"

"I know, I know. I'm just messin' with you…. I'll be ready."

Shortly after, Dawn and Caroline left for guard duty. Caroline guarded Old Barracks, and Dawn guarded Southside of Barracks in front of Lee Arch. I had to be up and ready in one hour. It almost felt pointless to go to sleep, but I was exhausted and wasn't going to give up any opportunity for rest. I set my alarm for 11:45 PM.

"Good night, Brenda."

"Good night, Alicia."

Brenda had already served guard duty today, as she'd been the Supernumerary, the Guard who delivers messages to all the cadet rooms. It was an exhausting job that required her to go up and down the stairs all day long. Today she had delivered a few notices to Fellow Ticks and Upperclassmen to report to the General Committee, the committee that enforced the Class System. Being written up to the General Committee as a Tick meant you did something big; otherwise, they'd just write you up to the Tick Disciplinary Committee. Brenda also delivered the TDC notices to Ticks, as unpleasant as it was. Luckily none of us had been written up to the TDC yet. We would all eventually be written up to the TDC, regardless of behavior, and we hoped to be sent together.

~

When my alarm went off, I reluctantly got out of bed. I splashed water on my face, and then holding onto the sink and lowering my body, I stretched my back. I was exhausted all the time. I had entered the state of sleep deprivation where I could fall asleep instantly, as well as wake up and respond instantly. I slowly changed into my Guard uniform, trying not to wake Brenda. I grabbed my M-14 and headed out the door. The one benefit to serving Guard duty is that Ticks didn't have to strain.

I walked down the three flights of stairs and signed in at the Guard Room. I relieved Caroline, winked at her, and took post. She could go to sleep now, that lucky girl. I holstered the rifle on my left shoulder and walked gingerly the small perimeter from the center of Old Barracks to the end and back again.

It was a quiet evening. There were a few lights on, including the one in the Guard room. Most of the light that did shine came from the almost full moon in a clear sky.

It wasn't so bad, to be alone in the center of Barracks, to be under the stars and moon, in the middle of the night. The cold helped keep me awake. I enjoyed the silence. It sure beat the chaotic echoes and yelling that usually penetrated these four walls. This was the part of the day I cherished, the quiet and darkness which allowed me to hear my innermost thoughts.

I enjoyed my own mind. Most of the time we were instructed how to think, how to act, and where to report. It was nice to at least have something that was my own.

"Shhh, man, come this way...."

I glanced toward the sound, without thinking. Two Upperclassmen were stumbling in under Lee Arch. By the way they hung off each other, they were clearly intoxicated.

I looked straight ahead, pretending I hadn't noticed anything. My thoughts diverted to Cathleen. I wondered what she was doing right now. Well, probably sleeping, I thought to myself.

She's amazing, so beautiful, and sweet. She was opening me up to a whole new world, a world of spirituality. Maybe that's why I've been so drawn to her, to her sense of connection with the Divine.

I'd snuck in the books she'd given me, books that felt alive with ideas: *The Camino, The Four Agreements*, and *The Secret*. Cathleen had told me that if anything I read seemed too far fetch, to act like it was fiction, so my imagination could guide me.

Cathleen was so cool, so beautiful ... I was happy when I thought about Cathleen, mainly because she was so different from me. I'm a cadet and I'm straight.... Or am I? I don't know, I don't know. I always thought I was and now ... *shit*. So, hypothetically-speaking ... what if I liked a *girl*? I don't know.... I never thought— Nah, Alicia, you're just tired and thinking too much. You're cool, I thought to myself.

Fellow Tick Bigelow's presence brought me back to awareness. He was there to relieve me from duty, and I was free to go. He smiled; I nodded in response and left my post.

~

"*Alicia!*" a high-pitched voice screamed my name.

I felt immediately uncomfortable with attention being drawn to me, but I couldn't contain the excitement that broke-out on my face. I was in uniform and had trouble leaving the Tick Line behind, even when I wasn't on campus.

I smiled and waved.

"Hey, we made it. We thought we were lost, driving down Route 63, but Theresa figured it out," Christine exclaimed in one breath.

"Yeah, we're lucky we made it alive! Christine drives erratically when she doesn't know where she's going. I wanted to grab the wheel from her multitude of times!" She shook her hands in front of her like she wanted to strangle Christine.

I laughed, knowing the personalities of my friends.

We stood outside of Applebee's, one of the few restaurants in Farmington. Jamie was with me, and he stood silently behind me, as if intimated for the first time in his life.

I hugged each of my friends, fully aware that I was breaking the PDA code, the code against showing public displays of affection while in uniform. Luckily, Jamie ignored this oversight.

"Alright, girls," I cleared my throat, "I'd like you to meet Jamie, my Guide," I said calmly, grinning from ear to ear. I was finally able to show my friends my new life.

It was a strange thing, to incorporate my old life with my new reality. I showed Jamie off like a trophy, briefly allowing the hierarchy between us to fall apart. I hoped he didn't mind. Besides, he did ask *me* to find dates for *him* and his roommates. Maybe this time he'll treat me as an equal, appreciating the mission I'd accomplished.

"Hi, I'm Theresa," she said confidently, walking toward Jamie, holding out her hand. Theresa was tall, had strikingly thick, dark hair that hung to the middle of her back. She always found dating tiresome because none of the men were tall enough for her, but Jamie stood over six feet, towering over her.

"And this is Julie." I pointed to my stylish friend. Julie was spunky and flirtatious like Dawn. "I'm loving your hair, honey." Her hair was newly cut, fashionable layered, and dyed in three different colors:

purple, hot pink, and black. I chuckled at the thought of how much attention she was going to get at the dance.

"You too! Let us see your hair, again." Julie said.

"You saw it last month," I said, but took off my cover anyway.

"I know! But I'm still not used to seeing you that way!" Julie said, petting the top of my head.

"You have guts, girlfriend!" Theresa clapped.

"You could get this special haircut too if you chose to attend CAF," I said, winking at them.

"Yeah, no thanks," Julie replied.

I put my hat back on. "And Jamie, this is Christine." Christine was blonde, short, and adorable. She resembled a younger Paula Deen. She was the bubbly one of the group and danced as she walked.

"Shall we go inside and get a table?" I asked. "Kenny and Toby will be joining us soon. They're both finishing up finals."

"Yes, definitely, but I need to go to the bathroom—*now*," Christine said wide-eyed and grinning.

"Christine wouldn't stop once, even though she'd been hopping up and down in her seat the past hour; she was afraid we'd be late," Julie said.

"Well then, go in!" I demanded. Christine excused herself and flew into the restaurant. Theresa stayed by Jamie's side.

"So, how was your flight?" I asked.

"It was fine. It was direct, but we had a little trouble renting a car because you have to officially be twenty-five. So, Christine called her dad and he set up everything over the phone. We almost had to walk here!" Theresa said.

"Oh, I'm sorry. If I'd known, I would've had a friend pick you up from the airport, instead of y'all going to the trouble," Jamie said.

I looked from Theresa to Jamie and then at Julie with a crooked grin, surprised by this immediate sense of attraction.

Julie's eyes replied back.

"Shall we?" Jamie directed us inside.

"How many will there be?" the hostess asked, looking up from her podium.

"Six," Jamie answered, taking control.

Julie elbowed me in my side. "You look great in your uniform. I forgot to tell you that, when I saw you at Ethan's funeral."

"Thanks." I smiled back. "It's the perk of attending a military school."

"Yeah, and what are the other perks?" she asked.

"Um ... hmm ..." I said, looking at Jamie. "Cute guys in uniform," I whispered, "but I'm scared of most of them." As usual, Jamie displayed a controlled manner, preventing me and others from observing what he was thinking or feeling. I was the only one in uniform. Jamie was there in a causal blue collared T-shirt, jeans, and brown loafers.

Christine rejoined us, and I followed them to their table.

Seeing to my friends' safe arrival and introduction to Jamie, I quickly said my good-byes, took Jamie's car, and halfheartedly returned to school. It wasn't yet time for me to socialize. I had my Psychology and Calculus finals that afternoon. Jamie promised me time with my girlfriends Sunday morning, before they flew back to Texas.

Sunday morning arrived along with gray skies. The weather turned as the onset of winter rapidly approached. My roommates and I slept with our windows barely open. There were no heaters, just like there were no air conditioners during the summer.

Bundled up in my year-round blanket, I looked out the window from my cocoon. It was dim outside; making it feel like it was earlier than it actually was. Staying in bed was tempting, like it always was, but I got out of bed eager to see my friends.

"How was it seeing your friends on Friday?" Brenda asked, noticing I was awake.

"It was fun, but brief. I miss them and really wanted to stay and hangout, but responsibilities, responsibilities..." I said rolling my eyes. "And seeing them was also a little strange. They're so carefree!"

"Um, hm ..."

"When you went home for Thanksgiving, did you—all of a sudden—feel like an outsider?"

"With my friends, yes, but my horses always recognize me." She smiled, thinking of them. "And with Troy ... we understand each other, not just because of our history, but because we're both going through similar challenges. Honestly, I didn't tell many of my friends that I was coming home," she said, stretching her neck with her eyes closed. "I knew the time was short, and I just wanted to relax, see Troy, and be alone. It's not like we ever have alone time here."

"True. I was allowed to stop by the hotel to see them last night, before the dance. They were running around the hotel getting ready, looking chic and gorgeous, while I stood there in my uniform feeling dorky, like an alien among the group."

Brenda laughed.

"You know, I think I'm jealous!" I looked down at my hands and wringed them uncomfortably. "They're getting to know my Guides as dates, as men, not as Upperclassmen, not as their superiors. They got to act all frivolous and girly. I miss feeling so young and feminine," I whined.

"Have you aged in the past few months?"

"Yes! Haven't you?"

"Yeah, certainly. You're right."

For a moment, I could understand my mom, who got pregnant at nineteen, before she was ready to give up her youth. She told me she'd lost friends, mainly because they were off living the college life and she was single and trying to cope with the reality of raising a family. Our situations were different, but both colored with sacrifices.

"Yeah, you were put in an interesting situation, that's for sure. I don't know if I would've had the guts to bring my friends here and set them up with my Guides."

"Why not?"

"I don't know. Like what you're talking about.... I've developed such a special bond with my Guide. It's obviously not romantic—it's professional—but I don't know if I'd be willing to share him." She laughed. "Are women always this territorial?"

"Apparently!" I said as we both laughed.

Chapter 24: Trip Home

A week before Christmas break, academics became our top priority. Finals determined thirty percent of our grades, which gave us an opportunity to bring our grades up if we had fallen behind or to hurt them if we blew it. Like Brenda had predicted, Barracks became suddenly quiet, and even though we were still Ticks, no one harassed us during finals week.

I left CAF with some ironic apprehension. I was nervous about going home, nervous about facing an empty house. The airport was full of people traveling over the holidays. The weather was colder now, but Texas would be warmer than Virginia. I remained in uniform on the flight, in my white blouse, gray pants, and black military jacket. It wasn't required, but that's what felt most natural to me, to present myself as I was now. I held my cover with my left hand and carried my rucksack over my right shoulder.

When I got off the plane, I took a deep breath and began searching for my parents. I didn't immediately see them and felt relieved; I was hesitant to face the reality that Ethan was truly gone. I knew I hadn't stopped grieving. It was easier to stay focused at a school that instigated a separation of oneself from one's emotions.

I walked slowly, allowing people to scurry past. I went into the ladies' room and heard the stall doors banging and the toilets flushing. It was a busy time of year. I felt surprisingly vulnerable and desired not to be noticed. How many times this past year had I wished I was invisible? It was time for a break, a break from all the stress. I wanted to disappear for a little while. For a second, I saw myself in another country, in a place where no one knew me.

I walked to the end of the sinks and flung my rucksack down. I'd become a lot stronger and trimmer these past few months. I looked good physically, especially in uniform. My face, though, told a different story. I saw dark circles under tired and sunken eyes. I had aged. I was deeply sleep-deprived and mentally and emotionally wounded from my first semester at CAF.

I knew, once I arrived home, I could fall into the oblivion of rest. I could crawl under my comforter, surrender to the warmth and solitude—and sleep the next three weeks away—if I wanted to.

I turned the faucet and put my hands under the running water. I stood there a minute, allowing the water to fill my open palms, enjoying the gentle sensation as it ran through my fingers. Water is such a commodity and so sacred.... I splashed it on my face and ran my fingers through my hair, spiking the ends and making me look tough.

I didn't think I'd dread going home as much as I did now. I was here at this same airport, just a few months ago, when I'd received the news of Ethan's death. It dawned on me that putting up with the bullshit at CAF *was easier*—than facing this loss. I'd rather be running, doing push-ups, getting yelled at, than feeling the deep emptiness I felt when I thought of Ethan.

I left my rucksack and cover next to the sink and entered one of the bathroom stalls. I wasn't worried about anyone taking my stuff.

I left the bathroom and walked toward the waiting area. I didn't see Mom and Dad anywhere; it was weird. I looked at my watch and it read 5:36 PM East Coast Time, meaning it was 4:36 PM Central Standard Time. My flight was a little late which would've given them extra time to get here.

The airport was decorated with holly and reefs, making me think of Christmas past. On Christmas mornings, Ethan used to wake me up early and tried to convince me to sneak downstairs with him to see all the gifts before Mom and Dad woke up. It was Randall tradition that we weren't allowed downstairs until they were ready. Mom and Dad wanted to experience our excitement, I realized, smiling at the thought. This year would be different: a Christmas without Ethan.

I wasn't in a rush, so I walked leisurely through the crowds.

He was leaning against the large white column, his body slouching with his right hand hanging out of his jean pocket. He stood staring at me. Just seeing him stopped me in my tracks. He wore his construction boots, a flannel jacket open with his school T-shirt underneath. He didn't put much thought into his cloths, but somehow he always looked good.

I stared back, not able to conceal the smile that ran across my face. I stopped there, as people scurried by, feeling like I couldn't move. He stood up, inviting me to join him. I started to walk toward him, not looking where I was going.

"Jesus!"

"I'm so sorry. Excuse me," I muttered.

"Watch it, eh?" an older gentleman complained and hurried on.

"Hey, Tick," he beckoned me.

He'd better not try to be sweet with me, I thought, defensively. I couldn't hide the fact, though, that I was happy to see him.

"What are you doing here?" I asked, not intending for my voice to sound harsh. Being mean was easier than being nice. I needed to immediately establish my boundaries—by not allowing him to get too close again.

"I came to see my most favorite Tick in the whole world...."

I rolled my eyes and sighed.

"I see you haven't changed much." Seth laughed at me.

"Ah, screw you! What do you know?"

"I know you," he answered and grinned.

I took a deep breath and handed him my rucksack. "Well, if you're here, you might as well be useful."

He nodded, grabbed my bag, and I followed him outside. Once outdoors, I immediately put my cover on and stood up straighter. I was representing CAF, *my* school.

Seth opened the passenger seat door, and I climbed in. I sat quietly, trying my best to pretend my insides weren't jumping all around. Things had changed, I reminded myself. We weren't together anymore. Still, it was only natural my feelings hadn't completely vanished.

Seth climbed in, briefly smiled at me, and put the car in reverse. He held his right arm across the back of my seat and looked behind as he shifted gears, and we were off.

God, please help me. Give me some peace! I thought to myself.

"Well, you're looking good," he said

"Thanks," I said, tightening the grip on my hat.

Seth put on some music, and Aerosmith began to play in the background.

"How's school?" I asked causally.

"It's not the same without Ethan," he said, glancing at me.

"Did you get another roommate?"

"No, not yet. Your parents have been very kind to pay his rent. I'm advertising for spring semester."

"I see."

"How's CAF?" he asked in a baritone voice, accentuating the seriousness of my choice in schools.

"Well … stressful," I answered and looked out the window. It was only five months ago when I'd happily rode in his car—in love. The time we'd spent together had been bittersweet since the accident. The prognosis of when Ethan would wake up was always unknown, and we had both felt powerless about the whole situation.

"So, are you dating anyone?" I was curious and didn't care if it was rude to ask.

He cleared his throat and swallowed hard. "Ah, no," he said, taking a deep breath and blowing it out through his nose.

"I see." I wasn't convinced. He must at least be sleeping with someone, someone who doesn't know him well—a simple girl, not too demanding or needy—just someone to have fun with. Then he wouldn't have to face anything that had happened; he wouldn't have to truly *feel* anything.

We rode in silence the rest of the way. There wasn't much to say anyway.

When we arrived in front of my house, I got out and grabbed my bag from the backseat.

"Alicia, the reason I picked you up—" he tried to get the words out, "was because I wanted to see you."

I nodded. He looked so sincere. In that moment, I looked at someone I loved, a handsome guy, and the closest connection I had to the brother

I lost. Seth was right. He did know me, and I was very aware of my feelings for him, but what was I supposed to do? It didn't matter. There were no words of apology from his mouth, no words of us getting back together, or of him supporting me through my current journey at CAF. He'd set his intentions and wasn't willing to give much. I clearly wasn't part of his plan.

The second I felt tears well up in me, I broke the gaze and turned around. I quickly mumbled, "Thanks for the ride," and walked away from the man I loved. When I heard his car pull away, my heart sank, and I felt like a million broken pieces, but a very microscopic part of me was also relieved that he was gone.

Chapter 25: Emotions and Logic

I was actually thankful that no one was home. I climbed the staircase and entered my room glad to close the door behind me, hoping not to be interrupted. I took out my journal, kicked off my shoes, and laid belly-down on my bed. I opened to a blank page.

Dear Diary,   *Friday, December 18, 1998*

It was so strange to see Seth. My heart leaped when I first saw him, but I had to rein in my feelings. As much as I wanted to grab him and kiss him, I love my sanity more. I couldn't allow myself to be hurt by him again, at least not now, when I have so much at stake.

In times of suffering, we look to a higher power and ask 'why.' Why am I going through this? How can I make it better? Suffering is such a huge part of human existence. I feel like I have been suffering a lot.

I chose a school that causes suffering. And taking it well is considered ... honorable. We're expected to conform and follow regulations, even if our spirit is compromised.

I understand suffering forces us to grow. If suffering causes us to look within, maybe the whole point of suffering is to find ourselves.

I chose CAF because I knew it would challenge me and force me to grow. I liked striping away the material aspects of life, because then the only thing that separates cadets are personality differences, like how hard someone is willing to work.

I wonder how emotions play a role at CAF? There, we are taught to be responsible, tough, and mentally strong. We are taught to move beyond the pain, to push ourselves past limits. We look at injuries as inconveniences or as part of our personal failure. We're not taught to listen to our bodies; we do not rest when it says rest, or stop when we feel pain.

If we are not taught to listen to our bodies, we create a sort of disconnection with our physical body ... do we not? If we are not fully in touch with our bodies, how can we truly feel anything? When we disconnect, whether as a temporary survival mechanism or permanently, we block our ability to feel deeply. We become more mind-oriented, more of a thinking-individual, rather than a feeling-individual. BUT, isn't it our feelings that make us human? If we only think, we are similar to machines. With our feelings, we are human.

I wonder ... are we supposed to control our feelings? Or are we supposed to value and listen to our feelings? How come we don't value our feelings and logical mind equally?

I feel other people's emotions very strongly. At CAF, when I hear another Tick getting worked out, I ache, as if I was getting worked out too. It is beyond compassion; I can tap into other people's pain.

I am tough and determined to succeed at CAF, but now I'm learning to shut down my ability to feel so deeply. With Ethan's death, I feel like I've gone numb. I keep busy, constantly moving, with continuous duties and chores ... but sometimes I feel like I'm running away from myself.

CAF and the military teach us to become more logical and less emotional. Is this a good thing?

I read the book The Camino, *by Shirley MacLaine, on the plane ride, and this quote got me thinking:*

"Those scientists of human behavior who refused to observe through their own emotions were missing the point of reality. Individual feelings received no respect in their world. They had dehumanized human feelings and emotions, disregarding them in favor of what they term collective observations, which were agreed upon in the world. They didn't even give themselves permission to be human. If they were not rational and "scientific" in their observations, they were ostracized. Even the expression of emotion was unseemly in their world. Though they claimed to be seeking truth about its inhabitants, in reality they were establishing a new mind-set that refused the capacity to feel.... The new enslaver of truth is science, and we are seeing its effect on human behavior everywhere. Without the recognition of the soul's journey within us, we are lost and only part of what we were intended to be." (MacLaine, 9-10)

Our world values logic over emotions, and as a result, we've become less human.... Personally, I believe our spirit, the essence of who we are, is connected to all people and God. The way our spirit communicates with us is through our feelings, carrying the truth that our logical mind only touches upon, while the logical mind helps get things done. If our emotional side is our connection to God, why have we chosen to devalue that aspect of ourselves? Probably because understanding our emotions is abstract and is often difficult. Sometimes it can be stressful and overwhelming to truly allow ourselves to feel deeply.

Take grieving, for example. I try to avoid thinking about Ethan while I'm at CAF because it's easier not to feel. -Alicia

I sat up and stretched. I was so tired. I got up, closed the blinds to my room, and crawled into bed. I fell asleep easily. I slept deeply and without dreams, my mind and body finally able to relax within the comforts of a safe space—home.

~

"Alicia? Are you home?" my mother called from downstairs.

I awoke groggily. I tried to move, but felt as if a huge weight was pressing me down.

"Alicia?" I heard my mother's footsteps on the stairs. "Alicia?"

"Yes, I'm here, Mom," I mumbled.

Light shined in from the hallway, and she sat down on the bed next to me.

"Hi, honey. You must be exhausted," she said in a concerned tone. I felt her hand on my forehead.

"Yeah, CAF has worn me out." I sighed.

"Well, I'm going to make dinner. Come down in a little bit, and we can eat together," she encouraged and kissed me on the forehead.

"Okay," I whispered.

I felt like I had fallen asleep on the bottom of the ocean and had to swim to the top in order to wake up fully; it took a lot of strength to move. CAF had sucked the life out of me.

⁓

"Hey, Mom," I said, entering the kitchen.

"Hi, honey. Dinner's about ready, so just sit and relax."

I obeyed without question. "How are you doing?"

It had been a while since we spent time together, alone. The last time we spoke was on Thanksgiving. Since Ethan's funeral, I'd kept a safe distance, calling home only when necessary.

"Oh, Alicia, you know I'm fine." She shrugged good-naturedly. "Your dad is not coming home tonight. He's in Washington, D.C. for meetings over the next few days. We should expect him back by the beginning of next week."

"Oh," I said disappointed. "Didn't he know when I was coming home?"

"Of course he did, but you know how his business is. He's always running here and there. I barely see him anymore myself."

"That's a shame.... How's teaching? How are your students?"

"Fine. I've been playing a lot. I'm in the County Orchestra, and I'm doing a lot of gigs. You'd be surprised how many people are having Christmas weddings. I have a wedding to play at tomorrow, as well as on Sunday. Would you like to make money while you're home?"

"No thanks, Mom. I'm rusty. I've only played the piano a few times and haven't touched my violin all semester. All I want to do over break is rest."

"That's what I thought."

"Thanks for asking, though."

⁓

Dear Diary,   *Saturday, December 19, 1998*
   It seems I have a lot of time to write. Now that I'm home, I do look

forward to spending time with Mom and Dad. I hope to better support them, in person.

So, I've been thinking.… I find it very strange that most wars have been over whose god was the true God. That seems very elementary to me. The fact that we still have wars blows my mind. What happened to sharing and working together? Being the historian that you were Ethan, I'm sure you would have much to say on this matter! I wish you were here, so I could talk to you.

It is easy to understand that when a solider is hurt that he feels pain, but does the solider, too, feel pain when he hurts another? Not if he is taught to disconnect emotionally.

I haven't made a decision yet whether I am going to go into the military or not. Soldiers are taught to accept and obey orders without question, which doesn't sit right with me. I understand the importance of obeying orders in emergency situations, and possibly in times of war. In obeying orders, you can surrender to your job at hand, fully accepting the order, and responding with action. But, what if I was asked to complete a task that I did not agree with?

I looked out the window. There was never any snow before Christmas. I was feeling very uneasy. It's okay to ask questions, I reminded myself. I'm only eighteen and have a whole life ahead of me to figure these things out.

Where do I go from here? I'm good at the whole military thing. I'm naturally an organized freak. I can keep up physically, and I look great in uniform.… But it does seem like I have serious doubts about going into the service. Dad has encouraged me to follow his footsteps, expressing how the military isn't just about war, that I could have a nice job, see the world, and have college paid for.

But, I ask myself, do I truly believe in the military? What if I was sent overseas to a war I didn't support? I don't know.

I want to stay true to myself. If I was asked to complete a mission that I did not agree with, and I completed that mission, I would be betraying myself. If I chose not to fulfill an order that I was given in the military, I could get in serious trouble.

I sighed.

I was, in connection with CAF, already representing the United States military. I was representing a belief system and a way of life. Even with my contradictory thoughts, I fit in well as a cadet. As much as I get stressed at CAF, I do like the school. Now I'm just plan confused. What would Ethan say to me now? -Alicia

Chapter 26: Christmas with the girls

"You're telling me that you saw Seth and that was that?" Christine asked.

"Yep," I said and took a big gulp of the chocolate liqueur and cream Julie had brought over from her parents' house.

The four of us; Christine, Julie, Theresa, and I; were sitting outside on my parents' back porch. It was Thursday night and Christmas Eve. The weather was lovely. My parents had a beautiful backyard since Mom had hired a gardener. Flower beds outlined the back of the house, accentuating the edges and making the house feel colorful and warm.

My three friends looked at me with inquisitive eyes.

"You're way too calm about this, Alicia," Julie said. "Something is up."

"Smell a rat, do you?" I teased.

"Yeah, why are you so calm about all this? If I were you, I'd be a wreck," Theresa said.

"I know. I'm actually surprised about how I'm acting too. But to be honest, so much has happened and so much has changed. I wouldn't have survived CAF if I hadn't adjusted. It was only five months to y'all, but it was like *years* to me."

"But I remember how in love you were with Seth," Julie said.

"Honestly, I'm still in love with him."

"Then what gives?" Christine asked, not satisfied with my vagueness.

I broke my gaze and turned to them. "I basically can't do anything about it, can I?" I looked at each of them. "Seth broke up with me, remember? I've been doing my best to come to terms with that." I looked at my glass. "I thought a lot about him when I was away. The Tick Line sucks, which means I haven't had the luxury to mourn Seth *or Ethan*. Both situations could've easily destroyed me," I explained. "But I had to move on quicker than I would have, if I wasn't at CAF."

"But why didn't you—" Julie began, but I cut her off.

"Why didn't I ask him to take me back? Why didn't I just kiss him in the car or at the airport? I thought about it. Honestly, seeing him took me by surprise." I met Julie's eyes. "It was weird, you know? When I was away, I thought about him all the time. It was like he was my lifeline and thoughts of him helped me get through tough times. When he ended our relationship, all I had to hold onto from then on—was myself."

"Well, you sound a lot stronger than I would've been in your situation!" Theresa said.

"Yeah, you sound very logical and level-headed about this," Christine added.

"It doesn't mean that I don't love him or I don't want to be with him. I just don't want to put myself through all that again. *He* ended it, remember?"

"So no fun and innocent roll in the hay?" Julie asked.

"No! I have a little more respect for myself than that." I straightened my back. "Besides, it wouldn't work this time. Maybe one day ..." I smiled.

"So, that's it?" Julie asked.

"Yep."

"Well, I'm disappointed! I thought for sure you and Seth would get back together!" Christine said, lower lip pouting.

"Well, he's available, if you want some fun," I teased.

"No! Ewww. I'd never date anyone you've slept with. That just wouldn't be right!"

"Yeah, whatever." I dismissed her response. "So," I said, turning to Theresa. "Tell me about Jamie.... I'm dying to know."

"Okay, okay," Theresa responded, collecting her thoughts. "Jamie ... handsome Jamie ... tall Jamie ... strong and gorgeous Jamie ..."

"Yeah, yeah! Get on with it. Has he called you since the Hop?" I asked.

"Yes." Theresa smiled. "He's cool, but it's not like we can have a relationship or anything."

"See! I told you. At least Theresa knows firsthand that relationships at CAF are *impossible*."

"But I'm open to keeping in touch, chatting online, and he can call me anytime he wants to."

"No juicy details?" I asked.

"Not really. He was a perfect gentleman at the Hop and at dinner beforehand. We didn't even make-out afterwards, to my disappointment. All he did was kiss me good-night when he dropped me off at the hotel." She shrugged her shoulders.

"Really?" I said. "That's interesting. Did you feel a spark with him?"

"Oh, yeah. How could I not feel a spark with Jamie? He looks like a Scottish statue in uniform. I got flustered just looking at him!" She giggled.

"What about you guys?" I turned my attention to Julie and Christine. "Did you like Kenny, Julie?"

"Yeah, he was fun, a little nerdy, which I like, but smokes too much. Definitely cute, but I haven't heard from him since the Hop. No big deal. I was just happy to go, meet your Guides, and see your school."

"It meant a lot to me too that y'all saw my new life."

"And as for Toby ..." Christine paused, hesitant. "I don't think he's into women, Alicia." Christine's shook her head with a smirk on her face.

"*Really?* No way!"

"Yeah, I totally think Toby is batting for the other team," Julie said.

"For real?" I asked, my voice going up in pitch.

"Yeah," the three of them answered simultaneously, nodding.

"I had no idea!"

~

Christmas break flew by. I picked up the book *The Fifth Sacred Thing*, again. It was my ambitious goal to finish the five hundred page book before Christmas break was over. I continued journaling, enjoying the time to self-reflect.

Dear Diary,   *January 2, 1999*

I'm not looking forward to returning to school, and my time away doesn't seem long enough. I'm just finally starting to relax, to actually feel a separation from school. I love being with my friends. It is so nice to be around people who know me. Especially since they're not screaming at me, making me push, or telling me how worthless I am!

I feel like I'm another person here than I am at school. In the comfort of my friends, I can relax a little, probably because I feel safe and loved. At school, I'm a stranger, a Tick, and my self-esteem is low. Being at home with the girls, I've noticed how much I've changed. I'm much more sensitive, cautious, and tightly wound. I don't smile as easily as I did before. I'm no longer carefree.

I haven't really talked to any of them about the stress of school and how it is getting to me. They can't possibly understand it, anyway. I can't escape it and talking about it doesn't make it go away. I just have to suck it up and deal.

You know what I'm most surprised about? My personal response to the system. I didn't expect to be stressed all the time. I've completely shifted to survival mode. I knew the first year was going to be tough, but I find myself feeling scared, restless, and exhausted all the time.

I find myself angry a lot too. I'm angry at those Upperclassmen in the woods, especially the one that tormented me later—fuck him. And that asshole that came to our room.... What the hell did I do? It makes me feel so vulnerable and powerless. I'm angry at being abused by the Upperclassmen, which doesn't totally make sense. It's just part of the system that I willingly signed up for.

I guess I'm just angry at being pushed constantly beyond my limits. I'm not just physically exhausted. I'm emotionally exhausted. I feel like damaged goods, and there doesn't seem like enough time over break to piece myself back together.

I know Cadre reminds us every day that CAF is not for everyone, and that might include me. So, if it's not for me, someone that gives it her all, than who is it for?

CAF is the curse we fell in love with. Its hypnotic energy makes us compliant for the dream, for an existence so different and separate from the status quo. Image is important. It keeps alive the illusion, the illusion of perfection.

Cadets are forced to control their emotions while the human act of living consists of expressing how we feel. This is a tribe, like a cult, where all are expected to obey the higher power. The higher power isn't even the Upperclassmen. It is more than that. It is the belief system, the culture, the way of life dedicated to honor and the portrayal of the citizen-solider. CAF is a world of its own. In order to function accordingly, in order to survive, certain rules must be maintained. The Ticks obey all Upperclassmen, the power resides with the First Class, and the hierarchy follows from there. The cloud of energy that surrounds Barracks is intertwined with the past, a resistance to change, including the incorporation of women.

Personally, I feel proud to be part of the second class of women ever to attend CAF. My roommates are wonderful. There is a satisfaction in just getting through one more day. Each time I get through a personal workout from Upperclassmen, I feel like I've earned a gold star. I'm glad that I've survived so far, but how much of myself am I willing to give?

The mentality at CAF is to 'break you.' That means they, the Upperclassmen and Cadre, wish to take you to the point of no return, complete unconditional surrender, and obedience. It's the point where you feel like you're about to lose your mind. When you cross over that point, you no longer care about anything—but surviving. It takes away any desire to fight the system. You accept the madness as it is. You know the system's crazy, and you realize that you can't change a damn thing, so you stop trying. You surrender, thus 'you're broken.'

I'm past the point of being broken. Cadre didn't have to break me. It was the time around Ethan's death and Seth's letter that I felt the shift inside of me, and I started functioning by pure instinct.

I did my duties. I showed up where I was supposed to be, did what I was told, and I became very robotic. I was choosing to feel as little as possible; that way I kept depression at bay.

Being at home and by myself, those cumbersome feelings of sadness and depression are becoming more real every day. Mom is acting like nothing has changed. Dad, also, is keeping himself so busy that he doesn't have to stop and face the tragedy either: we practice avoidance as a coping mechanism.

I know I could call any of my roommates for moral support, but I don't feel like reaching out. I don't want to bring them down or to have them worry. Hopefully, they were coping well.

It is true that we could rely on and support each other. I'd been strong up to the point of leaving for Christmas break. Christmas break is something of a landmark, a point we all reached for, knowing that once we made it, we were halfway there.

And here it was Christmas break, and I'm thousands of miles away, but I feel like I've barely left. The thought of returning to the Tick Line makes me nauseous and my heart beat faster. I felt stressed, for real. I feel like my nervous system has been depleted. I'm on edge, extremely sensitive, and I possess a weird desire to run or hide.

I'm scared of returning to CAF and giving all of myself to a school that is so crazy; I'm scared of losing who I am.

I missed Ethan. He'd be the perfect one to talk to. He'd slap me back into focus. I so wished he was here.

I wished I could, for a minute, feel peace. Maybe it is easier to be a Tick in the Tick Line, getting through one more day, one day closer to the end, rather than waiting for the Tick Line to resume. -Alicia

～

"Oh my god, Alicia! *That's disgusting!*" Julie shrieked from the drivers' seat.

"Well, at least she doesn't have any hair for anyone to hold," Theresa laughed, slapping her right leg.

Julie pulled over to the side of the highway. I'd barely had time to unhook my seatbelt and get out of the car before my lunch came up.

"Are you okay?" Christine asked. "Did you eat something that made you sick?"

"No," I said, still hunched over.

"I'm glad you didn't do that in my mom's car!" Julie yelled.

"You're so considerate to think of me," I said.

When the waves of nausea finally passed, I stood up, took a deep breath, and climbed back into the car. As the car resumed its course, I leaned my head back and kept my eyes closed. Julie had rolled the window down next to me, and I could feel cool air across my face. "It's just my nerves."

"Well, if I was returning to CAF, I'd be throwing up, too. The Tick Line is the last place I'd want to be," Theresa said.

"You don't have to go back if you don't want to," Christine said.

"Don't tell her that! You're only going to make it worse for her," Julie barked.

I looked at Christine, feeling immediately envious of my friends who did not have to return to the Tick Line.

"Nah, I'll be okay. A girl's got to do what a girl's got to do."

"Will you be home for spring break?" Theresa asked.

"No, it's too short a break and too far to travel. I won't be home until summer."

~

At the airport and after all the good-byes, I sat down to wait for my flight. I pulled out the book *The Fifth Sacred Thing* and resumed reading. I'd hardly put it down all week and was almost done.

The story presented two different worlds. The cover simplified it: "Imagine a world without poverty, hunger, or hatred, where a rich culture honors its diverse mix of races, religions, and heritages, and the Four Sacred Things that sustain life—earth, air, fire and water—are valued unconditionally. Now imagine the opposite: a nightmare world in which an authoritarian regime polices an apartheid state, access to food and water is restricted to those who obey the corrupt official religion, women are the property of their husbands or the state, and children are bred for prostitution and war. The best and worst of our possible futures are poised to clash, and the outcome rests on the wisdom and courage of one clan caught in the conflict." (Starhawk, back cover)

I thought it was a fascinating contrast. I opened my journal.

Dear Diary,   *Sunday, January 4, 1999*
   Just reading about the lifestyle in The Fifth Sacred Thing *gives me hope. They honor themselves, each other, and nature. They grow food*

without pesticides, have clear streams that make water assessable to all, and work through conflict by talking and coming to compromises for the higher good. The utopian, pacifist, and peaceful society "chose food over weapons." (Starhawk, 3) They don't have a military. Instead, they have a society of elders, healers, teachers, business men and women that regulate and make sure everyone is taken care of, that all voices are heard. Their society honors all people, including children, as well as their ancestors.

Everyone was required to work, to work hard, and equally everyone is provided for, including a home, land, and job. People were required to work extra, if needed, meaning extra hours for a healer if there were sick people that need tending to. With everyone working and everyone sheltered, there were no homeless, poor, or illiterate people.

It makes sense to connect people to specific professions based on their talents, dreams, and desires. As such, a musician was put with the Musicians' Guild. Dreams were fulfilled because dreams were respected and nurtured.

Madrone, the main character was an awesome, strong, and independent woman and healer. She sometimes worked too hard, but her co-workers, as well as her many lovers, helped keep her balanced.

Just like I have always felt other people's feelings, most of the people in this society were in tune with each other. By being tuned into each other's feelings, the need for violence diminished and the collectivity of taking care of each other prevailed.

It is much easier to use violence against people you don't know, especially when they are labeled and viewed as "the enemy." It is harder to use violence when you see your connection with everyone, and in hurting another, you essentially hurt yourself.

"Who sees all beings in their own self, and their own self in all beings, loses all fear." (Starhawk, 34)

I love this book! Starhawk did an excellent job in painting a picture of a utopian society. She contrasted the utopian society with a nightmare society dictated by a controlling government; one that regulated what naturally should be available to everyone, what Starhawk labeled as the four sacred things: earth, air, fire, and water.

"When something is sacred, it can't be bought or sold. It is beyond price, and nothing that might harm it is worth doing. What is sacred becomes

the measure by which everything is judged … we will not be wasters but healers." (Starhawk, 18)

It is so fascinating to read about the nightmare society because our current world has some similarities: a large military, lots of pollution, and a lack of respect for Mother Nature. People value logic over emotion, while not being in tune with each other's feelings or sometimes even their own feelings.

A person who is strong in mind and passionate in feelings seems to be the most powerful combination, unified in logic and emotions.

I chose the College of Armed Forces because I thought it was the way toward greater success and fulfillment. The question, though, is will I become more of myself there or do I have the potential to lose who I am by disconnecting molding myself to their image? -Alicia

Chapter 27: Return to CAF

"Hey!" I yelled, when I saw Cathleen waiting for me at the airport.

"Hey you!" she said, giving me a big hug. "It's so good to see you!"

"Ditto!" I followed her out to her car. The air was damp, having just rained, and it much colder than Texas. "Has there been snow yet?"

"Nope, not yet, but soon I'm sure. My car is over there." She pointed at a small two-door, green Saturn. I chuckled when I read the stickers on the bumper of her car which said, "Serve Your Local Goddess," and "My other car is a broomstick." On the passenger door there was a sticker that read, "Stone Soup Bookstore & Café" with the phone number, which I assumed was on the driver's door as well.

"Do you want a *College of Armed Forces* bumper sticker too?" I asked.

Cathleen looked at me and laughed. "*Sure* ... why not? Do they have a bumper sticker that says, "My insane friend attends CAF?""

"Probably."

Cathleen unlocked my door for me, and moved the seat forward, so I could throw my rucksack in the back.

"I brought some civilian clothes with me. Could I keep them at your place?"

"Of course," Cathleen said, putting the car in reverse. We had a three hour drive back to Farmington. Cathleen turned to me, "So, how was your Christmas break?"

"It was good to get away. I'm sorry I didn't call. I spent a lot of time by myself. I did see my girlfriends, but I craved the alone time. I wrote in my journal constantly and finished *The Fifth Sacred Thing* on the plane ride."

"That's fantastic!" Cathleen rolled down her window to pay for parking.

I grabbed my wallet and handed her some money.

"Oh, no. Don't worry about it." She waved her hand at me.

"But it's for gas too. I really appreciate you spending your afternoon picking me up."

"No problem. I'm happy to do it."

"Well, thank you. How was your Christmas break?"

"Typical." She rolled her eyes. "Dad is remarried with two kids, a boy and girl. They're cute, *young*, eight and five, and I love them, but I feel like an outsider now. Dad's wife, Janine, hasn't really taken to me. I think she's been jealous of the relationship Dad and I have." Cathleen shrugged. "I'm happy for him, and he seems happy. After Mom died, it was just the two of us for years. When Janine moved in, it just didn't feel like home anymore, which is why I left at sixteen."

"That explains why you're so independent."

"Well, it's in my nature. I've always walked an independent path." She smiled at me, her chin up with a bit of pride.

"For your information, I think that IET you gave me really changed me. I'm questioning everything now!"

"IET is powerful stuff," Cathleen said, nodding, looking straight ahead and concentrating on driving. We turned onto the highway and headed south. "During my year of transition, I had seven IET sessions, and when that first year was over, I honestly felt like a different person. I healed and released so much. I almost changed my name, shaved my head, and ran off with The Twelve Tribes," she laughed.

"Really? Who are they? "

"Well, it's a ... cult, really. I only thought about joining them briefly, and I certainly didn't shave my head. I just got my nose pierced instead, to gently symbolize my transition."

"That's cool."

"So, tell me what you've been questioning."

"Okay. Um, I've been doing a lot of self-reflection. I've been questioning my choice of college, but it's more than that. Going home was very strange. It was the first Christmas since Ethan passed, and it was awkward. My parents didn't really talk about Ethan...."

"Really? Well, that's interesting. Dad and I talked about Mom all the time."

"You did?"

"Yeah, sure did. I couldn't imagine not talking about her. It would've felt like we were pretending she hadn't existed, which would've been devastating to me. Dad was smarter about it. He told me how Mom was in Heaven and wouldn't be coming home anymore. That was really hard to accept, but he said that she was happy, healthy, and could hear anything I directed at her. Even better than that, he told me that if I paid attention, I would feel her presence."

"You understood that, as a six year old?"

"Not right away. When I got older, I started writing letters to her just to connect. I wrote to her about school, and what Dad and I were doing, and how much we missed her. At first, I kept checking the mailbox because I thought she was going to write me back, but Dad told me that Mom was now an angel, and that angels communicate differently than people do."

"That was clever of him."

"Yeah, he told me that angels send happy feelings, like energy of love, encouragement, and comfort. He told me that I would feel her presence whenever I asked for it, and I could talk to her whenever I wanted."

"I see." I smiled at the sad, but sweet tale.

We rode for some time in silence, letting each other stew in remembrance of the ones we've loved and lost. Then, Cathleen spoke up.

"So, I didn't mean to start talking about me. I do actually want to know what you've been thinking about."

"Well, I've been questioning lots of things, like the choices that we make in our lives, like how I ended up here. I know that my thoughts create my reality; the book *The Four Agreements* reinforced that truth to me. What we think, essentially what we believe, creates our reality, so I've been analyzing the military."

"Whoa. I bet you could theorize about that for a good long while."

"Yeah, I can, for real."

"And what did you figure out?"

"Well, I'm a natural pacifist. I've always been, and I knew that going into the military environment, but I still felt very drawn to CAF."

"Uh, huh …"

"But I wonder … I wonder if by simply creating an army, we create a *need* for it."

"What do you mean?"

"Well, if our thoughts, feelings, beliefs and actions create our reality … I wonder if by creating a military we simultaneously create an enemy."

"Well, that's an interesting concept."

"It doesn't fully make sense to not have a military; that would leave us exposed. But do you think, we, as a culture, *create* conflict by supporting and funding a military?" I asked.

"I'm sure there is some truth in it. Well, which came first, the chicken or the egg?"

"My dad would argue that by having a strong military, we are actually preventing the cause of war because it prevents countries with smaller militaries from wanting to fight us."

"Have you read *The Secret*, yet?" Cathleen asked.

"Not yet, but I'm planning to."

"Well, it might help you answer these questions. *The Secret* describes the Law of Attraction, meaning we attract what we focus on. It's the same concept as with IET; your life reflects the energy you are sending out into the world. So, you're probably right. If we focus our intentions on creating a strong military, we then draw to us reasons to utilize it."

"Exactly! Wouldn't it be better to create a Peace Corp, rather than a Marine Corp, some organization that teaches how to resolve conflict, so the military is used as a last option? An organization whose goal was to resolve conflict and live together peacefully. Wouldn't it be better if all our money for weapons and tanks went toward teaching others how to work together peacefully?"

"Yes, of course. I completely agree."

"So why is our culture stuck in this old fashion view of living where we just kill one another when someone else doesn't agree with us?"

"Well, that sounds a little extreme...."

"Does it? If we are willing to go to war over issues, then we're willing to kill and put our families and friends in harm's way. Why can't we resolve issues peacefully?"

"Because we're not that evolved yet. Walking softly and carrying a big stick is as good as it gets now, with the U.S. as the strongest military force in the world."

"Well, then the U.S. has the greatest potential for change. It's our duty to set the example for the rest of the world. With great power, comes great responsibility."

"Well, maybe you should run for office after your affair with the College of Armed Forces, Ms. Randall!"

"Yeah, sure," I said snidely. "But doesn't it seem barbaric to still have wars in our time? We are intelligent beings. We need to start working together and honoring each other in order to create peace in our lives. Don't you agree?"

"Of course I do. Keep thinking what you are thinking. We're women. We have more of a natural ability to want to resolve conflict through talking rather than beating each other up. Guys are different. Maybe the solution is to inoculate all the men with testosterone blockers, and inject them with some progesterone?" Cathleen laughed.

"That doesn't sound half bad!"

"So, these new ideas of yours, has it impacted your relationship with your school?"

"Yes, I am conflicted. CAF is so crazy! We're taught to follow so many rules. It's purely a dictatorship, one that punishes you when you don't act and behave exactly how they want you to!"

"Yep."

"I'm sorry. I have to return there in a couple of hours. Let me bitch and get it all out of me before I have to go back to the precious Tick Line and behave like a good, little Tick. Yuck!" I made a face at her.

"You're going to be fine."

"I know I will be." I sighed.

"There are things I can teach you that might help you cope with the stress...."

"Yeah, like what? No more IETs until the Tick Line is over!"

"That's probably a good idea."

"So, what are you thinking?"

"Well, we're just a half an hour away. Do you have time to come over before I drop you off at school?"

"Sure, I just have to be there by sun down."

"Okay, great."

⌐

"Alright, take off your shoes. Stand up and plant your feet securely on the ground. Close your eyes. This is a visualization exercise for *grounding your energies*. It will make you feel more secure and less anxious. Imagine that your feet have roots, roots that go through the soil of the Earth, and grow deeper and deeper until they reach the core of the Earth.

"Feel the sense of grounding this Tree Meditation provides. Feel secure in knowing that you are connected with the Earth; you are *One* with the Earth and with Mother Nature. Feel your energies securely rooted in this moment in time.

"Take all the negativity in your life, your fears and worries, and push it down through the ground. Release all your concerns and give them back to the Earth.

"Take a deep breath. Know too that the Earth has the power to nurture you. Visualize the core of the Earth as a large crystal. Take in its healing power through your roots and receive the nutrients from the soil. Feel yourself energized by its vibration. As the healing energy passes through your roots, it recharges you with clarity, strength, peace, and balance. You are once again whole and complete within yourself. You are healed. You can open your eyes now."

I opened my eyes to find Cathleen looking at me with a pleasant grin.

"What?" I asked.

"Your aura has become brighter."

"Really? You can see auras?"

"Not all the time. I'm more intuitive than anything, but when I do see color around people, it's usually very faint. Your aura, though, is glowing."

"Really? And what color is my aura?"

"It's a deep blue, like mine," Cathleen answered. "You're an Indigo Child, like I am."

"A what?"

"Alicia, you're an Indigo Child. You haven't heard that before?"

"Nope ..."

"Well, I guess there's a lot for me to teach you! Sit down," she said, pointing to the sofa, "and I'll tell you."

I sat down and waited as Cathleen went to the kitchen and grabbed us a few drinks. When she came back into the room, she handed me a sparkling water and sat next to me, propping her feet onto the coffee table in front of us.

"A lot of the New Age thinkers write about Indigos. My favorite is Doreen Virtue's book, *The Indigo Children*. To summarize, Indigos were born as early as the 1950's, but most are coming into this world with our generation, children of the seventies and eighties. Indigos are continuing to be born now along with Crystal Children."

"Indigo Children? Crystal Children? What makes you so sure I'm an Indigo?" I asked.

"Your aura is a deep blue, the color Indigo. Indigo Children have an Indigo aura. Most Indigos are adults now, so the term "children" is just a phrase. Indigo Children, simply put, are warriors. We come in with a higher consciousness and vibrate at a higher frequency than the previous generations. Most of us are very sensitive to energies, so we feel when things are not truthful. A lot of us are intuitive and can feel when things are imbalanced, like when people have been mistreated. As a result, Indigos don't readily believe things. We have a healthy distrust of authority. Indigos are choosing to do things differently, more respectfully, like protecting the environment and working from a space of love."

"That's interesting."

"Yeah, Indigos are neat. We're often questioning things, seeking answers that our elders can't usually provide us, hence probably why you are questioning so much yourself. The reason I call Indigo Children *warriors* is because it is our mission to break down outdated systems, which takes a powerful and determined mindset. There are organizations in our world in academia, businesses, and governments that function with a specific sense of morals or belief systems that no longer work. If we are to grow as a species, to raise our consciousness, we have to evolve, which requires changing. The Indigos are the ones that walk between the two worlds, this physical world, and the spiritual world of greater visions and idealism. They are drawn into businesses and schools, and through choices of their own, start to break down old systems. It is with warrior-like strength that they cause great change, breaking down old systems that no longer work, so the Crystals can come in and rebuild better systems."

"What about the Crystal Children?" I asked.

"Crystal Children are sensitive like the Indigo Children, or even more so. Their auras are characterized as pink or crystal-like. I believe most of the Crystal Children are being diagnosed with ADD, Attention Deficient Disorder, because they vibrate at such a high frequency, that they have trouble functioning in our third dimensional world. They're having trouble putting their attention on things that we designate as important, like our academic structures, and are accused of being dysfunctional, when it simply could be that they learn or understand things differently. Things are starting to change, though, but not quickly enough. Americans like easy solutions, so diagnosing children and putting them on drugs has been the easy quick-fix solution, which is unfortunate because it is lowering the children's vibrations and preventing us from learning from them."

"That's interesting. I haven't heard that before," I said.

"You see, we're all different, and as much as Americans honor individual success, we are slow to understand that people learn differently, too. We need better approaches to education. Some people are oral or audio learners. Some are better at doing hands-on, rather than reading from a textbook."

"How did you come to these conclusions?"

"Well, when I was a kid, I was put in the slow learners' class, even though I was very bright. I read books all the time, but I didn't perform well on tests, so the teachers assumed I was dumb. Dad thought I was struggling in school because Mom had died. It wasn't until my sixth grade teacher had me stay after class one afternoon and verbally ask me the questions on an exam, that I received my first A."

"Wow."

"Well, now that I've talked your ear off, can I offer you something to eat?"

"No, thank you, that won't be necessary. I see its starting to get dark out. I should get back to Barracks."

"Oh, one more thing. I wanted to explain to you why I taught you the Tree Meditation."

"Okay ..."

"I assume at school, with other people having power over you, that you often feel stressed and imbalanced. I thought learning about the Tree Meditation would help you recharge. When you stay rooted in yourself, it can prevent you from being drained. Also, by feeling connected to the Earth, you can draw upon the energies of the Earth to fill you up when you do feel depleted. Does that make sense?"

"I see. Sounds great. Thank you for sharing, and thanks for picking me up from the airport and being such a great friend. I always feel good whenever I'm around you."

"You're always welcome." Cathleen smiled.

"I do hope I can continue to visit on Sundays. I'll try my best to e-mail you if I can't stop by. I'm hoping Sundays are still free of academic and Tick responsibilities."

"I understand. Just let me know if I should make two brie, pear, and honey sandwiches or just one."

"Definitely! Well, I need to get back in uniform, and if you wouldn't mind driving me to campus, I'd really appreciate it."

"Of course."

~

"Are you okay?" Cathleen looked at me from the driver's seat. We were parked on the side of Barracks, a few feet away from Marshall Arch.

"Yeah, I'm just ... what do you call it? Trying to ground my energies ... My stomach is doing flips, and I'm not ready to jump back into all that chaos," I said weakly, slouching down in my seat.

"Well, the best thing to do is keep breathing and feel your body. Feel your solidness. Understand that no one can hurt you. You will learn how to be calm in the chaos. You do not have to *be* the chaos. I promise you. I can read your energies, and I know the strength and potential you have. Ground your energies and walk in there feeling at peace, knowing your own determination to succeed."

"Thanks. You're right; I can do this," I said, straightening my back.

I climbed out of the car, pushed the seat forward, and grabbed my rucksack from the back seat. It felt slightly strange being in uniform again. I was wearing an identity. I put my cover on, waved good-bye to Cathleen, and headed straight for Jackson Arch, the only arch Ticks were allowed to enter. I saluted General Jackson, resumed straining, and went inside.

Barracks was so noisy; the shouts and chatter were defending. I quickened my pace, made an immediate left, squaring my corners, and ran up the stairs. I kept visualizing my room, my goal that I was trying to get to, without anyone noticing me. On the third stoop, I heard voices everywhere. Ticks were getting worked out, and cadets were shouting to each other across the courtyard. No one stopped me, so I kept moving.

I bolted into my room, panting, and startling my roommates.

"Well look who just strolled in," Brenda said, sitting by the window on her rack, her red hair standing on end.

"Hi!" I plopped my rucksack on the floor, pulled my chair out, and sat down.

Caroline was in the middle of putting her things away. "Hey, how was your vacation?"

"Weird. Yours?"

"How was it weird?" Dawn asked joining the conversation.

I looked at her. "I don't know. Christmas was weird. I hung out with my girlfriends which was awesome. They don't have a clue about my life here, but that's okay. Mom and Dad are acting strange, and I didn't spend much time with either of them. That's the short of the long. How about you?"

"I got to see my men." Dawn briefly looked up from her laptop and gave me one of her devilish grins.

"Are you talking to one of them right now on your computer?" I asked.

"Just one of them?" Dawn answered, one eyebrow raised.

"You just got back! Didn't they see enough of you over break?"

"Well, you know I couldn't give them *all* my time...."

I laughed. "What about you, Brenda? How was it going home?"

"Well, I was just telling Caroline that I'm jealous that Dawn had so much sex over Christmas break since I had none, and I don't know when Troy and I will be in the same place, at the same time, ever again!"

"Awe, I'm sorry. Did you and Troy at least talk on the phone?"

"Yes, we did. Once." She pouted.

I gave Brenda a pout of my own, in sympathy. "And who did you sleep with over Christmas break?" I turned my attention back to Dawn.

"No one!" Dawn said.

"Liar!" Brenda said, throwing her pillow at Dawn.

"Hey! Don't hit my computer, you bitch!"

That made me laugh.

"What about you, Caroline? How was your Christmas?"

"It was fine," she answered, occupied with what she was doing.

"Really?" I asked again. "Fine, huh?"

"Yeah, fine," Caroline answered, ending the conversation.

"Uh, huh." I shook my head.

"Ticks! Get on the stoop now!"

The four of us simultaneously looked up at each other.

"Shit!" Brenda said.

"Good-bye, my lovers ..." Dawn said out loud, signing off immediately, and slamming her computer top down.

"I guess I'd better change." I looked down at my class uniform.

Brenda and Dawn were already in their sweats. Caroline and I were not.

"Quick, pull down the shade!" I ordered.

"Ticks, on the stoop now!"

I looked up when I'd finished changing. Caroline was ready and waiting.

"You okay?" I asked.

"Yeah, let's get this shit over and done with," she stated calmly.

"Well, okay then."

"Ready?" Dawn asked us all. Caroline and I nodded.

Dawn pulled the shade, and it rolled up instantly. We stepped out of our peaceful room to enter the hellish doom once again, Brenda following in the rear.

"No one better piss me off tonight!" Brenda said, before the door slammed behind her.

Caroline and I glanced at each other, both of us straining and grinning.

"*What the hell are you laughing at, Randall?*" a voice approached me from the left.

Oh man, here we go….

Chapter 28: Rebuffing the Rat Race

"So how is CAF?" Cathleen asked, yawning. "I'm sorry. You're the one who is worked to death, and I'm the one yawning," she said over a cup of coffee.

We were sitting at the kitchen counter. Cathleen was dressed in a simple white, long-sleeve top with black cotton pants, something she probably slept in. She didn't have any makeup on since I showed up so early. I barely had enough time today to do all that was required of me.

"I'm back in the rat race of the typical Tick Line. I'm running on adrenaline right now, and I'm afraid if I stop, I won't be able to keep up with everything," I said, trying not to yawn myself. "And so, I've started drinking coffee again, *instant coffee*, unfortunately, but it's the only coffee I can keep in my food box. Cadre won't let us have the real stuff."

"Yes, the coffee god is a generous god." Cathleen looked at me with tired eyes.

"And this brewed stuff is *so* much better. If only I could sneak a coffee maker into Barracks." I smiled. "I'm sorry I woke you up so early. I have a lot to do, and I could've gotten up this morning and worked, but I wanted to see you instead. I needed a break, and I've been looking forward to Sunday all week."

"It's quite all right. You're welcome here at anytime. How's CAF?"

"Last week was hell, another hell week in itself. The Upperclassmen

207

feel it is important to remind us every day of our place in the food chain," I whined, rolling my eyes.

"Ha! And how does it feel to be on the bottom?"

"Annoying."

"So what did you want to do today?" Cathleen asked.

"Just hangout. I don't mind doing nothing, honestly. After doing everything and anything all week, I am perfectly content with doing nothing."

"Oh, I know what we can do!" Cathleen suddenly beamed with excitement. "Let's watch my most favorite movie in the whole world!"

"*G.I. Jane*?" I asked. "No, wait … that's *my* most favorite movie in the whole wide world."

Cathleen stopped and looked at me. "*G.I. Jane* is your favorite movie?"

I nodded.

"I can see that. Demi Moore was hardcore in that movie."

"Yep. That's why I love it! Whenever I needed motivation during high school, I'd watch a couple of scenes, listen to the music, and get high off of it. It's a kickass movie!"

"Yeah, Demi's character adapts to the environment by becoming very masculine herself, a powerful woman in a man's world, like something you're trying to do right now. She did a great job … almost made me want to enlist myself…." Cathleen paused and reflected.

"Really?"

"Yeah, for a split second," she laughed, "but then I got over it."

"Ha! So what movie are we going to watch?"

"*The Mists of Avalon*!" Cathleen sang. "I'm sure you haven't seen it," she said, dismissing me with her hand. "It's not necessarily your type of movie, but I know you're ready to see it, and you're going to love it!"

"Okay, whatever you say."

~

The movie was fantastic, but shortly after The Lady of the Lake took Morgaine to Avalon, I fell asleep, a type of deep sleep that took me away to another world.

I dreamt of walking the shores of Avalon, of exploring the rich growth of plants and trees. I walked quietly, fully observing the scenes around me. Birds sang and people in brown robes walked gracefully, as if in tune with the earth. They walked silently in their oneness with Mother Nature, communicating with a deep level of respect and reverence. I felt peaceful in my solitude and found joy in the colorful arrangement of plants and flowers, which adorned the landscape, like a touch of earth that'd never been damaged by human touch.

I felt so free, like nothing mattered. All life was important and to be honored. I felt the Earth call to me, not with a voice, but with a pulse that reverberated inside my heart and extended through my limbs, telling me that I was loved. I felt like I could do or be whoever I wanted.

I walked through the flowers, feeling delighted as the damp grass and soft flowers caressed my bare feet. I walked to a circle of stones where I felt the power of the circle vibrating all around me, as if I could be swept up at any moment into oblivion.

The circle lifted my energies so high, I felt I could fly. I climbed one of the rocks and stood up. I lifted my arms high to the sky, as if praying to the Almighty. With my eyes closed and my head turned upward, the sun warmed my face, and I stood on the strong steady stone. I felt blessed and so loved.

In my dream, I opened my eyes and looked across the valley to the homes below. I felt connected and detached from human existence. Rich green mountains accented the background. The world felt and looked so large.

If I jumped, I knew I would soar. In flying there is such freedom, to not be weighed down by an earthly body, but to feel light, almost transparent while floating through the sky. Light wind whirled around me. If I caught the wind right, I'd be taken higher. With my arms out and ready to take flight, I jumped.

~

I awoke with a jolt. I groaned out loud, displeased to be back in this world, my world.

I closed my eyes again, hoping I could return to the dream state. I couldn't, so I lay in between the two states of consciousness and allowed myself to gently wake up. My face was matted to the couch and my mouth had been open while I slept; there was a wet spot under my chin.

I rubbed my hands over my eyes and tried to wash the weariness from my face and sighed. I then realized that I didn't know how long I'd been asleep and jumped up in a panic.

"Cathleen?" I called out. I quickly looked down and grabbed my socks and shoes.

Cathleen came in from the other room. "Oh, you're awake," she said happily.

"I need to go. I have so much to do!"

"Okay, but how about you sit for a moment and ground your energies before your run off," she ordered me with her hands. "It's the best thing you can do for yourself."

"Okay, okay, but can you tell me what time it is?" I asked eagerly.

"A little after eleven. Please calm down. Your energies are all over the place. Ground them, so you can focus on what you want to accomplish," she spoke gently, but sternly.

"Okay." I sat down and took a few deep breathes. "How could you let me sleep so long?"

"Breathe, Alicia, breathe," Cathleen said, focusing her attention on me, and breathing deeply herself, setting an example. She sat down next to me on the sofa, providing a solid and calming presence. "I let you sleep because I thought it was the best thing for you."

"Yeah, I am tired."

"Tired? Ya think?"

"Yes, that's how I felt all last semester too. I just need to get this Tick Line over and done with, and then I can sleep."

"Or you can just sleep when you're dead," she said, making fun of my mentality.

"Yeah, there's that!"

"Well, look, this is just my opinion, so take it for what it's worth...."

"What's that?"

"Well, look how worn-out you are already, and it's only been the first week back at CAF. How about you slow down and pace yourself a little better, so you don't burnout so quickly?"

"I know. I'd love to not have to work so hard. I'd love not to give CAF all my time and energy, but I don't know how not to. The school is very demanding. It's a college, so there is homework, in addition to all the Tick responsibilities. I'm doing the best I know how, just trying to keep my head above water."

"I know, and I won't pretend to understand any of it. I think you're nuts for volunteering to be a Tick, but there are better ways to approach this."

"Like what?"

"Put your attention on what you want. The power to manifest is infinite. Your energy, like money in a bank account, is not infinite, but the power to manifest is."

"Manifest ... what do you mean by manifest?"   "Manifesting is like praying. Remember when we talked about how our lives are a reflection of the energy we are sending out into the world?"

I nodded.

"Well, as we continue to grow spiritually, we become more conscious of our thoughts and feelings. As we become more conscious, we become more aware of where we are directing our energies. This gives us choices."

I nodded for her to continue.

"Manifesting is essentially focusing your attention on what you want. So, if you're overweight and want to lose weight, you focus on thinking thin and feeling thin. You do not focus on how much you hate to be fat—that just keeps creating what you don't want. Listen closely, because what I am telling you is very powerful. This wisdom is becoming better known in our culture through books, including the book *The Secret* that speaks about the Law of Attraction."

"Well, it's not that simple," I said, sighing.

"Actually it is, but what is important to understand is *feeling* the reality you want to create, not just thinking it. When you feel and think it, even by pretending, you will manifest it into your life."

"Okay, so what should I do?"

"Focus on what you want, Alicia. If you want to slow down, focus on that. If you want to focus on being invisible in relation to the Upperclassmen, focus on that. I honestly didn't believe in the whole manifesting thing when I first heard about it. I didn't understand how

I could ask for what I wanted, and it could show up. So, if I were you, I'd just experiment and see what happens."

"And what have you manifested?"

"Lots of stuff, but the first thing I manifested was lavender soap," Cathleen grinned.

"Soap?"

"Yeah, I thought manifesting a physical item was easier for the Universe, so I kept it simple. I did it specific enough, too, so when it showed up, I'd recognize it," Cathleen explained.

"And how did it show up?"

"My grandmother mailed me a package for my birthday, and it included lavender soap."

"And didn't you just think it was a coincidence?"

"Sure, I could've looked at it that way, but how random was it really, out of all the things my grandmother could've bought me for my birthday?"

"Did you manifest other things?"

"Of course. I continue to manifest on a regular basis. I manifested this business, which has been my main focus for the past three years. I manifested everything that it took to get it up and running." Cathleen walked over to the kitchen.

"But, wouldn't you just call that hard work?"

"Sure, there has been a lot of hard work put into it, but when you're only nineteen and have no established credit, establishing a business is no small task. Getting loans, purchasing the books with little money, finding the right location, et cetera, takes a lot of manifesting."

Cathleen brought out some cheese, grapes, and crackers. I was thankful for the nourishment because I was very hungry. As a matter of fact, I was generally hungry all the time and was now used to eating every couple of hours.

"I spoke about manifesting during a sermon I gave when I was attending The New Seminary. There are five rules that I've come to understand that need to be present in order to manifest what I desire in my life. To me, manifesting is aligning myself with the Divine, in a clear act of intention. It is bringing something or some circumstance into my life, in an act of receptivity. It is participating in creating my own reality."

"Alright, what are the five rules?"

"First, allow yourself to receive what you have asked for. Second, use the word "desire" when you request it, because the word desire means "to know God." Third, be specific. Fourth, do not share your request with anyone because that diverts the energy. Fifth, after stating the request once, let go of it completely, and trust that it will come to you in due time."

"Wow. I feel like I should've written that down," I said in between bites.

"It's not necessary. I'll give you a copy of my sermon."

"Great! Thank you for the food. This cheese is delicious. What is it?" I asked with my mouth full.

"It's goat cheese. Haven't you had goat cheese before? This is a mild one, my favorite." She smiled.

"No, but it's really good," I said, wiping my hands on the napkin and getting up. "I really need to get my act together."

"Just wait a second. I'll get that sermon for you. It will help."

"Well, it certainly can't hurt," I mumbled to myself.

~

Once back at Barracks, I went straight up to my room. I had three papers due and one exam this week. I prayed that no one was in my room or if they were, they were studying. I could always go to the library, but all of my books were there, and I really wanted to stay put and not brave the chaos of Barracks again.

I walked in and was relieved when I found no one there. I changed out of white pants and class top and put on my sweats. I walked over to the window and opened it slightly.

I sat down at my desk and opened my laptop. Which paper did I want to write first? My least favorite task was studying for my Science exam, and the exam wasn't until Wednesday, so I opted for the history paper I needed to write. I was taking History 201 which consisted of the Reconstruction just after the Civil War period to present. I turned on my laptop and began to write.

Deep in thought, the door to my room opened without me noticing. I looked up, and in realizing it wasn't one of my roommates or one of my Fellow Ticks, I bolted upright and hit my right knee on the top of the desk.

"Damn Jamie, you scared the living daylight out of me!"

"I was looking for you today, Randall," he said. "All the other Ticks in the room have already been informed, that the First Class is going to do a Step-off this week. That's when the First Class takes over, and we take the power away from the Administration and gain some control within Barracks. I wanted to tell you myself because I require your assistance."

I sat back down. "What do you require of me?"

"I want you and Buxbaum to report to our room tonight, after lights out. We have a mission for you. It will test your character and your loyalty to CAF."

"And when has my loyalty to CAF been challenged?" I asked, holding back my annoyance.

"You've done a good job, but we have more task for you to do. I expect your full cooperation, do ya hear?" he asked, looking at me straight on.

"Yes, sir."

"Okay, see you tonight," he said and left.

"*Damn*," I exhaled.

～

I forced myself to put my full concentration back on my studies, but I couldn't because I was annoyed. Jamie didn't divulge any information concerning tonight's mission which had me a little concerned.

I grabbed a cigarette from my desk and walked over to the window. I thought of the tree meditation and went through the steps to ground my energies, to calm myself. It made me feel a little better. I can't give my energies away to the Upperclassmen anymore; I'd burnout unless I slowed down and paced myself.

It was essential for me to stay focused on what was important. Ticks have been kicked out, even at the end of the Tick Line, because they failed academically. I wasn't going to let that happen, *and* I wasn't going to let myself to be drained by those in power.

This whole Tick Line was a joke, a joke to stress me out and make me go crazy. Was there any way I could choose what I do rather than have the Upperclassmen tell me what to do? Not really, unless I wanted to suffer the consequences. If I chose not to show up at Jamie's room tonight, I'd get in a lot of trouble. At the very least, Dawn and I would be there together.

Chapter 29: When Everything Changed

"Okay Ticks, we have called you into this room tonight for a mission," Jamie said.

Quentin, Trevor, David, Dawn, and I were dressed in our sweats and sat around the room on various hays, giving Jamie our full attention. None of us knew anything, but showed up with blind obedience. Barracks was quiet, and it was past our bedtime, which meant we weren't even supposed to be out of our rooms.

I could hear myself breathing; I was nervous. Kenny, Toby, and Brandon, our Uncle Guides, were not there, and we didn't know why.

"Tonight's mission is very important. It will test your loyalty to us."

At least *my* loyalty wasn't the only one being tested tonight.

"Quentin, Dawn," Jamie said, drawing their immediate attention. "It is your mission tonight to sneak into the Commandant's office."

Quentin and Dawn looked at each other and back at Jamie.

"There's a list of names I need. It's the list of demerits and tours for the First Classmen. The list is crucial for when we take over the school. Quentin, you will stand guard while Dawn breaks into the office."

Dawn's eyes widened at the request. She didn't say anything, but it was evident that she was troubled.

"David and Trevor, I want you to destroy Bromley's room."

"The First Battalion Commander?" Trevor asked, his voice cracking.

"Yes. That's exactly whose room I'm talking about. Mr. Bromley has used his authority for breaking rules repeatedly, and I'm sick of having a scumbag as a so-called superior. His father is on the Board of Directors and pulls strings for his lousy son—who doesn't even want to be here. Cadet Bromley is making us all look bad. Tonight he is on leave—yet again—and his roommate is gone as well, so tonight is perfect for this mission."

Instantly, as if planned, our Uncle Guides, Kenny and Toby, entered the room carrying baseball bats, ski masks, and toilet paper.

"Give one bat to Quentin," Jamie said. "Dawn will sneak in while Quentin stands guard, and Trevor and David are attacking Bromely's room."

Kenny and Toby nodded.

"Here you go." Kenny threw two rolls of toilet paper at Trevor and handed a bat to David.

"What do you want me to do with the bat?" David asked.

"Whatever you need to," Toby said.

"Use it to smash Bromely's computer, his windows, his mirror … whatever…." Kenny chuckled.

"And Alicia, I have a very special mission for you," Jamie said, suddenly making my mouth go dry. I licked my lips and kept my attention on him. It was scary seeing Jamie in this state of vengeance as he plotted out these schemes.

"With your careful and sensitive touch, you are to decorate Stonewall Jackson's statue. Toby?" he asked, turning to find Toby pulling out a colorful array of lingerie.

"Eww. Whose underwear is that?" I asked.

"That's none of your concern. Here you go." Toby happily handed them to me, along with two rolls of toilet paper.

I moaned.

"Alright gang, any questions?" Jamie asked.

We were ordered to put on the ski masks and sent out the window before we could contemplate any repercussions. We were following orders.

Tonight Delta Company was on guard duty. One guard patrolled inside Old Barracks, one inside New Barracks, one outside Marshall Arch, and one more in front of Barracks, near Jackson Arch. In addition, the guard room was at the front of Barracks, where a handful of Delta Upperclassmen hung out during the duration of guard duty. The five of us; Quentin, Trevor, David, Dawn, and I; crouched down under the window with our ski masks on. Jamie had closed the window after we exited.

"I wished they'd been more specific about how exactly to accomplish these tasks," Dawn said, turning to me.

"Alright, Buxbaum, let's get this task over and done with," Quentin said.

"First, we have to get by the guard room and the front guard," Dawn whispered.

"We'll have to pass one at a time." Quentin wasted no time and started crawling along the side of the building.

I sat there with my back against the wall of Barracks. I was going to have to become invisible, not only to the front guard, but I would have to be quiet enough not to draw attention from the guard room as well.

It was freezing out and my hands were going numb. I held the lingerie, thinking how stupid I looked. I wished Jamie had at least given me gloves. The ski mask provided a little warmth and discretion. I watched Dawn follow Quentin's lead to the right. David and Trevor headed in the opposite direction, toward Mr. Bromely's room.

I took a deep breath and tried to focus. This was not a good time to be scared. I stuffed the clothes into my sweatpants and the toilet paper into my sweatshirt. I crawled to the right, toward the front of Barracks, and kept one hand on the wall to keep myself steady. It was very dark out, and though I could see lights in the distance, there were no streets lights on campus. That was probably a good thing; the darker it was, the easier it was for me to stay hidden.

I reached the front, peered around the corner, and spotted the guard. I quickly ducked my head and banged it on the corner wall. "Damn!" I winced in pain and could feel myself becoming angry.

Calm down, Alicia, I told myself, and took some deep breaths. As the throbbing diminished, I refocused my attention on the guard. He wore the long, black uniform jacket, black gloves, and a hat I didn't recognize. The hat covered his ears, like a Russian would wear, and I hoped it would help block out the noise of my footsteps.

I waited for him to walk toward me and turn around, just a few feet away from where I was. I stood up and at the right moment, took off running toward the parade ground. I didn't look back and slid into the wet grass behind the cannons.

The guard had to have seen me. I crawled up behind the last cannon and peered over. The guard was still walking the line, as if nothing happened. I low-crawled to the center of the parade ground, directly behind Stonewall's statue but still yards away. When the guard turned again, I took off running toward the statue.

This time I knew the guard saw me.

My heart was beating so fast. I forced myself to breathe. I listened and waited to hear if anyone was walking toward me. I actually thought I heard the guard laugh, so I proceeded forward.

I climbed up the back part of the statue. As I held on with my left arm, I pulled out the lingerie with my right. I flung up the bright, pink bra, hoping it would land on Jackson's head. It landed on Jackson's right arm. I threw the next two bras, one after another, and one landed on Jackson's shoulder, and the other fell to the ground. I climbed down to retrieve it.

I didn't like feeling so exposed and visible while doing something illegal. The guard made no attempt to stop me, so I continued. I threw the third bra again and got a lucky shot. It caught his ear and hung straight down. If I could reach up far enough to dangle the underwear from his hand, I'd be in good shape.

My hands were shaking from the cold, and I threw up the toilet paper as best as I could. It landed on the opposite side of the statue. I ran, grabbed it, and threw it up again. I continued to run around the statue, throwing up toilet paper, until Jackson was covered in white. I was out of breath by the time I was done and stood for a second, admiring my work.

"Randall!"

I turned around without thinking, ruining my hidden identity. I saw Mr. Rouge standing ten feet away, with his fists clenched, walking toward me.

In a panic, I took off running. I ran through Jackson arch, up the staircases, ignoring orders for me to stop, until I reached the fourth stoop. I crouched by the stairs and looked down, to see if anyone was following me. I was breathing hard. Upperclassmen were not allowed on the fourth stoop after hours, but Cadre were the exception. Luckily, Mr. Rouge didn't follow me. I took a deep breath and ran to my room.

~

To the opening of the door, Brenda and Caroline stirred in their hays. At the sight of me in the ski mask, Caroline let out an abrupt squeal.

I quickly pulled off the ski mask and looked around the room. Dawn had not returned yet.

"Oh my god, are you okay? What have you been doing?" Caroline asked quietly.

"You'll find out tomorrow. It's not a good sign that Dawn's not back yet."

"What were you doing?" Brenda asked.

"You don't want to know." I sat down and took off my sneakers. The less they knew the better. I was exhausted and more than anything wanted to sleep, but I was worried about Dawn.

"No word from Dawn, eh?" I asked.

"No. The last we saw of her was when she left with you," Brenda said.

"Okay. Thanks for putting down my rack," I said and laid my head on my pillow, appreciative to be in bed. It was important to put all the racks down and appear like everyone was asleep, and thus all were present and accounted for. It was against the rules to leave our rooms, except to use the bathrooms, between the hours of eleven and six.

I tried to fall asleep, which was never an issue, but I stayed fully awake, concerned about Dawn. We had obeyed our Guides, without question, and without mulling over the consequences.

CAF is different than West Point, I heard Ms. Doyle' voice in my head. *The Tick Line is run by the cadets, not the Administration.* That point seemed irrelevant over the summer, but now I thought about it. Who was in charge here? The Upperclassmen were, specifically the First Classmen.

In the morning, I awoke to the normal sounds of Barracks stirring. There was no point in setting the alarms anymore. Our bodies were programmed to wake up in the early morning hours, regardless of how tired we felt. Out of fear, though, we continued to habitually set the alarms—because we knew how tired we really were.

I immediately looked at Dawn's hay. She was here, thank god. I rose and asked her if she was okay.

"I'm fine," she said.

"When did you get in?"

"Around three," she said, rubbing her eyes.

"Damn. I was back in the room by one. Mr. Rouge caught me right after I'd finished TPing Jackson." I yawned and stretched.

"You what? TPing? You mean you put toilet paper all over Stonewall Jackson's statue?" Caroline asked, shocked.

"Yep, and bras and underwear, too!" I exaggerated, just to freak Caroline out. "Have any luck breaking into General Alexander's office?"

"*You broke into the Commandant's office?*" Caroline stood white-faced, staring at Dawn.

"Yep," Dawn answered.

"Did you get the papers?" I asked.

"Yes, but we got caught. How did they expect us to do something like that without getting caught?" Dawn asked.

I shrugged. "Who caught you?"

"The guard. I don't know who he was, but he asked both our names, and we told him, naturally. What else were we supposed to do?" Dawn said, throwing her hands up. "We were directed to return to our rooms at once, but I suspect it isn't over."

"Fuck. There has to be consequences for both of us," I said.

"I guess we'll just have to wait and see," Dawn said.

"Damn, who ordered you to do all that?" Brenda shook her head in disbelief.

"Our Guides," Dawn and I said in unison.

~

When we returned to our rooms that evening, there was a small white note on my desk stating I'd been written up to the Tick Disciplinary Committee; I knew Mr. Rouge had written me up. I felt disheartened, but also relieved that my punishment was simply reporting to the TDC. All Ticks were sent to the TDC, one way or another, so this didn't seem like a big deal.

There was no note on Dawn's desk.

~

The school was starting to change. As the Company Commander of Band Company, Jamie used his rank to rally immediate support from other First Classmen to take over the school. He used our vandalism as an example for the school needing tighter regulation over the lower classes. Even though the Tick Line was run by the Upperclassmen, the Administration still regulated the enforcement of strict standards every CAF had to abide by. Jamie argued that too many demerits and penalty tours had been given to the First Classmen, and he naturally received a lot of support from his classmates.

All cadets had to follow a clear set of rules, as basic as dressing properly and keeping our rooms immaculate, to as crucial as following the Honor Code and completing penalty tours. It was well-known that the Administration could kick a First Classman out—even on the day of graduation—if a First broke the Honor Code or had too many penalty tours left.

All cadets were obligated to report their own mistakes, like being late to formation, missing class, or not shaving that morning. It was considered lying if one did not report disobedience.

Jamie felt that the enforcement of these rules was being exploited by the Administration. With the intention of taking over the school, the First Classmen led a full Step-off, talking complete control over the daily administrative duties.

It was mesmerizing to watch the change of leadership. Now, Mr. Carr, the President of the First Class, had all the power. With the successful trashing of Mr. Bromley's room, Mr. Bromley was exposed to having been gone, when he had not reported his own absence. As a result, he was forced to resign his position as the First Battalion Commander—and most likely he was going to be kicked out for breaking the Honor Code.

Jamie, with his natural leadership and popularity, was promoted to take Bromley's place as First Battalion Commander. Kenny Dunn, my Uncle Guide, replaced Jamie as the Company Commander of Band Company.

My Guide's room was now the center of political turmoil. First Classmen, from all companies, came to the room to seek guidance from Jamie. Because our Guide's room was so hectic, Dawn and I decided to stay away for a while, at least until things died down. Besides, we'd done what we had been told to do. The Guides never spoke of the events of Sunday night, never expressing any gratitude or disappointment toward us for having completed the missions.

I couldn't help feeling that Dawn and I had been completely used for our Guides' political agenda. It was portrayed that it was *our* idea to cause trouble—not that we were following orders.

~

The banging open of our door startled the four of us. A tall Upperclassman, dressed in gray blouse, stood in the doorframe and addressed the whole room in a deep baritone. It wasn't anyone I recognized.

"Tick Buxbaum, you are to report to Room 135 to be questioned by the Honor Court. You have five minutes!"

We stared at each other. Dawn jumped out of bed, put her white dress pants and gray blouse on, and ran out of the room.

We were shaken silent with fear and apprehension. None of us had ever been questioned by the Honor Court before. It was so intimidating that we stayed awake until Dawn returned.

She was in tears.

"What happened?" I asked.

Dawn rolled down the shade to our door and began undressing. "I was questioned about Sunday night," she said, clearly embarrassed by her own tears.

"What did they specifically ask you?"

"They asked why I broke into the Commandant's office." She looked and sounded tired.

We were all exhausted.

"And what did you say?" Brenda asked gently.

"The truth. I told them whatever they wanted to know." Dawn climbed in bed and rolled over, toward the window. The rest of us looked at each other, shrugged, and followed her lead.

~

The next day, Dawn and I left for our Guide's room like we had done a hundred of times before.

"Buxbaum, Randall, you're not allowed in," Quentin whispered, looking as if he felt sorry.

Dawn and I stood frozen in the doorway.

"What … why?" I asked.

"He said, get out!" I heard Brandon say.

Scared, I didn't know what to do. Then Dawn grabbed my shoulders and turned me away from the door. I followed her out of Barracks.

Once outside, we relaxed our shoulders and walked casually. Dawn didn't walk toward Band Company formation, but turned right, so I followed. She walked straight into the library, and as soon as we went through the doors, she turned to me. Ticks were allowed to talk to each other in academic buildings, but not outside Barracks without permission. Rules were rules.

"What the heck do you think is going on?" she asked.

"I have no idea."

"That was so strange."

"I agree. Did you happen to see Jamie in there?" I asked.

"No, I don't think so."

"That's odd too."

We looked at each other, not sure if the lack of Jamie's presence meant anything, but something was of course wrong, and we didn't know what it was.

"We'd better get to formation. Want to meet at our room for lunch?" Dawn asked.

"That sounds like a good idea. I'll see you then."

~

After attending my ROTC class, I ran back to my room to meet Dawn. I was stressed to the max between juggling academics and the drama of the Tick Line. When I let my mind wander, I thought of Cathleen. She repeatedly reminded me *to focus my attention on what I desired.* While racing back to Barracks, I visualized reaching my room easily.

I entered Barracks, immediately strained, and walked the Tick Line. I turned left, squaring my corners, and ran up the first flight of stairs without any interference. While on the second stoop, I walked the wide width of the Tick Line, squared my corners, and ran up the second flight of stairs. I kept the picture of my room clearly in my mind. I was trying to ward off any Upperclassmen workouts, which could put me behind schedule. I kept my mind focused on my intention, getting to my room as quickly as possible.

I heard voices on the third stoop and anticipated being stopped. I reminded myself to stay focused, to keep visualizing my room and the feeling of relief. I made it up the last set of stairs without any trouble. Once I reached the fourth stoop, I ran to my room.

Wow. I'd made it to my room without being stopped!

I was surprised to find the room empty. I'd come all the way from the ROTC building, the farthest building from Barracks, and I'd still beaten Dawn back to the room. I started to feel sick. She might be getting worked out this very moment. I went to the door, opened it slightly and listened. Oddly, I didn't hear anyone getting worked out. Dawn must not have entered Barracks yet.

I waited. Ten minutes went by and no Dawn. I began to worry and started pacing around the room. As each individual minute passed, I started to panic.

My door flew open, but it wasn't Dawn. Tick Khawaja stood there breathing heavily and taking out his inhaler.

I knew something was wrong by the look on his face.

"Randall, Buxbaum is down at Sick Bay. She wants to leave!"

"*What?* How do you know?"

"I was getting a refill when I saw her there," he said, holding up his inhaler.

"Okay, I'm on my way. Thanks," I said, patting Khawaja on the back and ran down the stairs.

Sick Bay was blocks away, past the mess hall, on the very edge of campus. I was tired of running and was very hungry.

When I entered, I bypassed signing in. I wasn't there to see a doctor, to rest, or use the phone. I was there to find Dawn—before it was too late.

The building was very small; there were only two rooms with beds. I entered the first room and found Dawn lying in one of the four beds, alone.

"How did you find me?" Dawn asked.

"Khawaja came and found me," I said and collapsed on the unused bed next to her. "You're not allowed to leave."

Dawn looked at me, shaking her head. "I don't know how I can do this anymore. I'm sick of the bullshit."

I kicked off my shoes and put my head on the pillow. I felt like the wind had been knocked out of me.

"Talk to me, Dawn. Tell me what's going on."

"I went to class today, and I didn't care what the professor said. I didn't care about anything around me. I just wanted to scream or hit something," she said between clenched teeth. "I hate this school! I hate everything it stands for! I'm *so* tired. I'm sick of working so hard and always getting screwed."

"I know, honey." I looked up at the ceiling. "I feel the same way. The Tick Line is stupid—such a bunch of bullshit."

"Then why the hell are we doing this, Alicia?"

"I have no idea," I said honestly and shrugged.

"I'm just so tired."

"I know, me too. Over Christmas break I daydreamed about not returning."

"Then why did you come back?"

"Because I want to finish something I started. Besides, I promised

Ethan that I'd finish. And I came back for you and Brenda and Caroline. All for one, one for all, right?"

"Yeah," Dawn whispered.

"Please don't leave, Dawn. I need you here." I felt tears start to well up inside of me.

Just then, Brenda walked in. I was so relieved to see her.

"Hey, chicks. Now which one of you had the hair-brained idea of leaving?" she demanded.

Dawn turned away.

"Don't worry, Brenda. She's not going anywhere," I said.

"Well, that's good because you'd have to get through me first!" Brenda said, pointing to herself.

We started laughing. As tough as Brenda was, she was still only five feet tall. It was her spunky, stubborn, and tough attitude that balanced her unintimidating short stature. I could easily picture her harassing some innocent Ticks next year, making them pay for not taking her seriously.

~

I went to my next class on an empty stomach. I convinced myself I could make it through the next couple of hours until dinner formation. I hated being hungry, though. The three of us met up an hour later in the band room for rehearsal. I was relieved to see Dawn pick up her trombone. I couldn't imagine being there without her.

Band rehearsal was easy, like it always was. It was a lot different than high school band, though, where band had been more of a social event. Here Ticks were expected to be quiet and subservient, so it wasn't much fun.

I looked forward to getting back to my room, so I could eat and be with my roommates. I wanted all four of us to sit and talk together, to make sure everyone was okay. We were each other's cheerleaders and support systems.

I had swimming next, aka "Tick drowning," a freshmen requirement along with Boxing, which I took first semester. Swimming didn't require too much effort on my part, and it was the one time I could bless myself for being a woman and having natural body fat. The body fat allowed me to easily pass endurance floating tests, whereas the muscular males often sank to the bottom, causing them to fail.

I was grateful once SRC came because I was famished. After dinner, Cadre ran us up to the fourth stoop to be worked out. It felt like it never ended! Being worked out after dinner was a regular event so far this semester. Cadre wanted to remind us, over and over, that we were still Ticks and deserved to be treated as such. I think they were concerned that their initial intimidating stature had diminished. We were beyond the culture shock we'd felt last semester, and the Cadre were looking less scary.

I was surprised when I'd found out Tick Delphine, the other Band Company Representative, had not returned after Christmas break. He'd seemed dedicated and driven to be at CAF. Tick Anders and Tick Johnson had not returned either. I didn't allow myself to wonder why they'd chosen not to return because, for me, leaving was not an option.

It was incomprehensible and unfathomable to quit. Whenever one of the Ticks left, it was a blow and disappointment to us all. We relied on each other so much. It was "us" the Ticks, against "them" the Upperclassmen—at all times.

Cadre used those who had left against us. *"Do you want to be as pathetic as Tick Anders? Do you want to worm through the Tick Line like Tick Johnson did? Why don't you run home to your mommy like Tick Delphine?"*

We felt the shame of those who'd left. Fellow Ticks that we had supported now became worthless creatures who'd had no drive to succeed and no willpower to stay.

During our after dinner workout, I ended up pushing next to Tick Williams and Tick Khawaja, my neighbors. I felt very appreciative of Tick Khawaja, who'd performed the Tick Rescue for me last semester, and then had informed me this afternoon about Dawn being down at Sick Bay. It gave me great comfort that my Fellow Ticks and I were looking out for each other.

After the workout, I ran to my room, feeling free at last.

I switched on the light and stood still—*in complete and utter alarm.* Brenda and Dawn entered the door after me, accidentally bolting into me.

"Oh my God!" Dawn said.

"Did you know anything about this?" Brenda asked, turning to me.

My wide eyes stared at her in panic, pleading that it wasn't true.

"*Nooooooo!*" I screamed at full volume, letting it all out.

Caroline's wall locker was *entirely empty*.

She had left.

Chapter 30: Meeting with the TDC

The sound of the heavy metal music pulsated through my body.

"*Push, Tick, Push!*" Mr. McCavery shouted loud enough to be barely audible.

I'd been taken down below Barracks to a dark room that felt like a dungeon, along with a few other helpless Ticks, for our punishment by the Tick Disciplinary Committee. The floor underneath my hands was cold and smelled of body odor and urine. My arms were shaking. I could barely see, the room dimmed only by a small light in the corner. My head was starting to throb from the loud music and shouting.

I continued to push, trying hard not to fall on my face. I was so hot in the BDU uniform we were required to wear for our meeting with the TDC. My combat boots kept slipping on the dirty concrete floor.

"*You think you're something, huh, getting through six months of the Tick Line? Seriously, Tick! Is that all you're made of?*"

I felt queasy during these early morning hours. How could anyone get such pleasure out of tormenting another person? These men were sick. I felt sick. Oh how I wished I was anywhere but here.

"*You're worthless. Scum. Pathetic. The Tick Line is just getting started! The pain hasn't even begun!*" Mr. McCavery focused his full attention on me.

The workout lasted for what felt like an eternity. There were no breaks. There was no comfort from sharing this experience with my roommates or Fellow Ticks in Band Company. I knew there were other Ticks getting worked out too, but I felt completely isolated.

Mr. McCavery focused on tearing me down. He wouldn't stop.

"You need to leave, Randall. You don't belong here. You should be kicked out for vandalizing Jackson's statue. You represent the opposite of what this school stands for. You need to go home! You don't belong here. High Knees, Randall! High Knees, now!"

I got up from the cold floor and attempted to perform as ordered. My boots felt so heavy. As I pulled my legs up by the knees, my arms flopped around. I knew I looked insanely goofy, but I tried to give it my all, but I didn't feel good.

And what was the point of trying so hard? I got yelled at when I did poorly, and I got yelled at when I tried my best. The Tick Line was a joke. This mother-fucker thought he owned me, that he could mess with my head and break me down. It wasn't going to work! I thought to myself.

I tried to ignore him. This jerk wasn't going to get under my skin, I promised myself.

"Don't think I won't run you out of here. Now that you've messed up for good, you're mine. I have my eyes on you from now on. I'm going to run you out of here! You don't belong at the College of Armed Forces. We don't want any dyke here!"

It was a mind game, I reminded myself. He was full of bullshit. I didn't have to listen to a thing he said. *What? What did he just call me?*

"Don't think I don't know who you've been screwing. I've been watching you! That girlfriend of yours is bad news."

What the hell was he talking about?

"You and that little slut who owns the bookstore are going to burn in hell for your actions. Burn in hell, Randall, burn in hell. I'm not going to stand here and watch a bitch like you graduate from my school!"

I couldn't believe what I was hearing. How did he know about Cathleen? My heart began to pound rapidly. She was my friend, and I cared about her. This was really scaring me.

"On your face, Randall. Whores like you don't belong here!"

I got down and started pushing again. He then grabbed my arm and pulled me up.

"On your feet. It's time to teach you a lesson, Randall."

He dragged me up the stairs and out the door while I tripped over my own feet. I could see from the courtyard that the sun was rising. How long had I been worked out? Ten minutes? Half an hour? I felt like I should run, get as far away as I could from Mr. McCavery, but his grip on my upper arm was like a vice. He squeezed harder, and I winced in pain.

"You listen to me, Randall," he spoke between clenched teeth, his spittle landing on my face. "You don't belong here. I gave you a warning once...."

He dragged me across the courtyard and into Old Barracks. He kicked in a door on the first floor and shoved me in. He tossed me in so hard that I banged into a desk and recoiled in pain.

What the hell was going on? This wasn't right!

Mr. McCavery dragged a chair across the floor, scraping the concrete.

He was blocking the door, I realized, alarmed.

I backed away and immediately bumped into a rack. I continued to move, feeling my way, hoping to grab something I could use to protect myself.

"Randall, what are you doing?" He spoke so softly that I hardly recognized his voice.

He walked toward me.   I was thinking clearly—aware of his every move—and I knew I had to come up with something quick to get out of there. I inched backwards, near the window. I was fully visible by the small amount of light that shined in.

"Come to me, Randall ..."

He was instantly in front of me, putting his arm behind my back and pulling me closer. I momentarily panicked when he touched me. I couldn't believe this was happening. He kissed my neck—and I was horrified.

"That's a good girl," he breathed on my ear. "You need to be reminded how a man feels."

What? No, what I needed was *to get out of there.* He held me tight with one arm while his other hand wandered, reaching up under my shirt in seconds. His hand was warm on my stomach, griping my side and directing me backward until I hit the rack.

Where the hell were his roommates? Why were we alone? This can't be happening! Thoughts ran rapidly through my head, as I observed every sound, every feel, even the smell of his sweet cologne. He pushed me down on the bed with such sheer force that it momentarily stunted me. I was on my back: I knew I had to do something quick.

He unbuttoned his pants with one arm, but had trouble with the buttons. He let go of me for a moment and I seized the opportunity. I reached for his desk and swiftly grabbed one of his textbooks. I tried to swing, but he grabbed my wrist, stopping me from hitting him.

His expression shifted to anger. He pushed his lower body down suddenly to hold me. I tried to scream, but was choked into silence when his other hand wrapped around my throat.

"You will not make a sound!"

I couldn't breathe. I couldn't think. I panicked and started thrusting my legs with all the strength I had.

He let go of my throat, annoyed by my kicking. He grabbed and held both of my wrists down. I had my clothes on, protecting me—my one silver lining.

Determined to fulfill his mission, he pulled my wrists above my head, twisting my arms, and transferred both wrists to one grip. He used his free hand to unbutton my pants, and then his pants. He became fully exposed, showing his intense hardness.

I was horrified and felt completely helpless. I screamed as loud as I could. Within seconds, his hand was on my mouth, and I bit down hard. He flinched back in pain. I pulled my right knee toward me and kicked as hard as I could, hitting him squarely on target. It knocked the wind out of him.

I jumped off the bed and hurried a few feet toward the closest exit, the window. I yanked the window open, climbed up, and leaped out of it. I landed with a thud, hurting my wrist which broke my fall. Squatting in the grass, I instantly realized that I was on the backside of Barracks.

I crawled until I was under another room's window. I buttoned my pants. I didn't want anyone to see me. I continued to crawl until I reached the end of the wall. I stood up and ran through the nearest arch and up the staircase.

"Tick! Stop, Tick!" an Upperclassman yelled, noticing I had entered an arch only Upperclassmen were permitted to use.

I ignored him, kept running, and flew up each flight of stairs. I was so disoriented. Once I reached the fourth stoop, I looked around, careless of the Tick Line I was required to walk. I realized I was right near the bathrooms and darted inside.

The door flung closed behind me, and I fell to the ground. A toilet flushed, and one of the stall doors creaked open. I heard the water run and then turn off. I was trembling from shock. As the Tick walked towards the door, she noticed me.

"Hey! What's wrong?" she asked.

I didn't look up, my mouth hung open as I tried to speak. My eyelids drooped and tears streamed down my face. I could feel the throbbing of my heartbeat and the heaviness of my head.

She crouched down next to me. "What the heck happened to you? Are you okay?" she continued to ask, obviously alarmed by my appearance.

"What company are you in? Where's your room?"

I looked at her and swallowed. I tried to speak, but nothing came out. I rocked back and forth, my nose running. I wiped it with my sleeve and buried my head in my hands.

"I don't know what to do," I finally said, licking my lips.

"Where do you live? What's your room number?" she asked again.

"Band. Room 482," I finally got out.

She ran out of the bathroom.

Within minutes, Brenda and Dawn were by my side.

"What the hell happened, Alicia?" Brenda asked.

"It's okay, Alicia. We're going to get you cleaned up," Dawn said. "It's going to be okay now. We're here. We're going to take care of you."

～

Brenda and Dawn directed me back to our room where they helped me change into my class uniform. They forced me to Sick Bay where the three of us could sign in for accountability. This way we could talk and be together without being required to attend class. It gave us a few short hours to figure things out. Luckily, we found an unoccupied room.

I laid down in one of the beds while Dawn and Brenda spoke softly around me, deciding what I should do, as if I wasn't there.

My mind drifted to thoughts of Cathleen. How had Mr. McCavery known my connection to her? He must've seen me enter the store more than once. I didn't know anyone knew about our friendship, our relationship. Did we have a relationship? We had kissed once. I honestly hadn't thought much about it. I was so distracted by all that happened in my life: the Tick Line, Ethan, Seth, and pure survival. It didn't even cross my mind how significant a kiss might be.

Where did Mr. McCavery play in all this? He was a very sick man, *and* I was very lucky to have gotten out of there. I suddenly felt worried about Cathleen. I hoped he wasn't going to hurt her in any way.

"Alicia should report him to the General Committee," Brenda said.

"I don't disagree, but wouldn't that make it worse for her here? Mr. McCavery is on the TDC. He pretty much has free range at whatever punishment he wants to give out," Dawn said.

"Yes, but attempted rape is not one of the allowable punishments!"

"And how's she going to prove that? It'll end up being his word against hers! Of course I want the bastard to pay, but I'm not going to allow Alicia to sacrifice everything she has worked so hard for. Besides, who'd believe her?"

"But ... *damn it!*" Brenda threw her hands up in the air.

"Maybe waiting until the Tick Line is over would be better...."

"And let that bastard get away with it?" Brenda's face was the color fuchsia.

"I'd heard his voice before," I spoke up.

"You had?" Brenda asked, startled, and they both turned to look at me.

"You remember last semester when we had that mysterious visitor?" I asked.

"Do you think that was Mr. McCavery?" Dawn said, lowering her voice.

"That's my best guess. I don't have any proof, but I think it was him."

"How did you figure that out?" Brenda asked.

"Just by the sound of his voice," I said. "He knows about me going to Stone Soup, and my relationship with Cathleen."

"How could he possibly know that?" Dawn asked.

"I don't know, but he must've seen me. That's my only explanation."

"Shit! Well, this is complicated," Brenda said.

"It's not going to stop me from going to see her on Sunday. Actually, I should probably try to skip out and warn her tomorrow," I suggested. "Do you think I could do that?"

"What about parade?" Dawn asked.

"After parade then. I have to warn her."

"Okay, do what you have to do," Brenda said.

~

After parade, I put my saxophone in its case and left the band room determined to get into town without being seen.

Ticks were not allowed off campus on Saturdays, but I went anyway. There was no way I was going to put my friend in jeopardy. I would never allow her to experience what I had—or almost had.

I walked quickly through the streets. I kept my head held high, confident, impersonating an Upperclassman. I was wearing the black uniform jacket that zipped up in the middle. I was thankful for its warmth and discretion, though it didn't hide the fact I was only a Tick, making me vulnerable if anyone from CAF spotted me.

Rushing through the door of Stone Soup, I surprised Cathleen, and she immediately processed my look of worry and fear.

"Whoa, are you okay?" she asked.

"No, I'm not. Can we go upstairs and talk? Do you have someone to take over for you?"

"Sure, I'll be right back."

I anxiously paced back and forth in front of the counter, as I waited for Cathleen to come back. Yesterday's scenario continued to play over in my head. It still seemed unreal. How can one person be so cruel to another? Is this the type of person CAF breeds? Can I really stay here and allow this type of abuse—

Before I continued with that train of thought, Cathleen was back leading me upstairs to her apartment.

"Okay, what happened? Are you okay? I'm going to make you some tea, and you're going to tell me everything."

As I relayed the details of what happened, Cathleen sat next to me on her couch and held me. I told her my concern for her safety, how crazy Mr. McCavery had been, how much he knew, and the fear I had for what could happen next.

"Oh, is his first name Jerry?"

"I don't know. Why?"

"Well, there was this cadet, and I assume he's a Senior from all the stripes he has on his jacket. Anyhow, he asked me out a few times. I tried to be nice about it, but I said no. It's probably the same guy."

"Well, I'm worried about you, Cathleen."

"Alicia, don't worry about me. There's nothing he can do to me. I don't go to CAF, and he wouldn't dare try anything out here. Please, don't stress about my well-being. You have enough to worry about. I'm fine." While she talked, she softly petted my head to soothe me. Even though I felt like a child, it was comforting.

Her natural presence had a way of calming me down. The whole environment was peaceful. I was relieved to be in her apartment and know she was safe. I started to relax and move closer to her as she adjusted me under her arms. I placed my head in her lap and she continued to rub my head. It felt good.

I leaned up to hug her and found my lips touching hers. It was so natural. She didn't resist either. She took me in her embrace, and we kissed for what seemed a decade. Why had I waited so long for this to happen?

Cathleen pulled away. "Are you sure about this? You are already in trouble with the TDC and have so much other stuff on your plate. I don't want to—"

"I don't know. It feels right," I said. "What do you think?"

With that, Cathleen took my hand and led me to her room. I never noticed before how sultry and inviting her eyes were. Cathleen lit some incense and candles, then turned off the lights. We stood at the end of the bed staring at each other. She slowly ran her fingers up and down my arm and began to unzip my jacket. After slipping my jacket off, she kissed my neck slowly up to my ear, and our lips met again. I pulled her closer to me. I could feel her hard nipples against mine. Exhilaration filled me. This was amazing. The buttons of my white shirt seemed to want to come undone as quickly as I wanted them to. Cathleen pulled my white undershirt off, and I returned the favor by taking off her sweater.

I couldn't believe I was looking at her sexy, beautiful, and naked body. That thought made me even more excited. I remember having these feelings when Seth and I—but this was obviously different.

Cathleen and I gazed into each other's eyes. She helped me completely undress and then laid me down on the bed. She began to kiss my neck again. Her sweet kisses continued down to suck on my nipple. I heard myself moan slightly. As she continued further down and parted my legs, I almost climaxed right there.

I closed my eyes and enjoyed the sensations going through my body. Cathleen was taking care of every one of my needs. I tried to sit up and stop her, but she wouldn't let me. I started to feel her tongue inside me. *Oh my!* I didn't know how much longer I could wait.

"Oh …" I heard myself moan, the sound vibrating throughout the room. My heart was beating out of my chest now, and I grabbed a pillow to quiet my screams.

I howled as I felt my whole body peak.

Cathleen slowly worked her way back up, kissing me every step of the way. She made it back eye to eye with me. I leaned up to kiss her, but she turned away, embarrassed. I grabbed her and kissed her deeply and passionately. I flipped her on her back and began the same path she just took with me.

"I need some direction. I've never done this before. Can you guide me?"

"You don't have to do that. It's an acquired taste. Just lay with me."

"No, I want to. I want to make you feel everything I just did. That was *amazing*!"

As I caressed her breast, she grabbed my hand and pulled me back up to her. "You do make me feel that, being here, allowing me to feel your soft skin next to mine."

Cathleen pulled me on top of her, and we began to rock

simultaneously. The motions were the same as being with a male—which reassured me. I joined her in the movement, our lips kissing while our hands wandered.

I surrendered to everything that was happening, and the rest of the night was a blur. We stayed together for hours, connecting on so many levels. I felt so loved, recharged, and fulfilled. I never wanted to go back to Barracks.

Chapter 31: Facing the General Committee

"I'm scared to go back," I whispered, staring at the light peeking in from the windows. I was curled into a ball with my arms wrapped around a pillow. Cathleen's arms were around me, cradling me.

"I'd be scared too, if I were you," Cathleen mumbled, sounding like her eyes were still closed.

"I don't even know who I am anymore...."

"But I know who you are."

I rolled over to meet her eyes. "You do?" I asked.

"Yeah." Cathleen nodded. "You have a good heart, Alicia. You always try your best."

"What am I supposed to do now? Am I supposed to report *him*?" I didn't want to say his name out loud. "Or am I supposed to ignore what happened?"

"How much do you want to fight the system?"

"I don't want to fight anything. I'm broken. I don't have any strength left for CAF."

"It's a hardcore school. It doesn't seem like you can ever win. It's been an uphill battle, huh?"

"Yeah." The words I spoke sounded flat, empty. "I don't want to leave this room," I said.

"You can stay as long as you want."

"You're amazing. I can't believe I feel this way toward another woman." I looked into her eyes and reached down to gently kiss her.

Cathleen kissed me back and put her arms around me. She held me tight for what seemed like hours. I felt so loved, so understood. The thought of returning to the abusive environment of CAF seemed insane.

Eventually Cathleen shifted, released her arms, and stood up.

"I'm going to go make some coffee. Do you want anything?"

"Coffee would be fine," I said, watching her leave the room.

I sat there in a daze. I felt so raw and exposed, so vulnerable yet safe here. I wouldn't mind hiding out in Cathleen's apartment forever—which was impossible. Tears came to my eyes, tears of mixed feelings, from not knowing what to do.

I couldn't believe what had transpired between us. Her touch was so sensual. I could feel the warmth of her heart. Love vibrated off of her skin. How could I be so lucky? *And so fucked up?* I have to go back to school, I reminded myself. I'm not a quitter. I'm not a quitter. I am not a quitter!

I climbed out of bed and went to the bathroom. The bathroom was cozy with a soft purple rug that warmed my feet and an elegant white-purple flowered shower curtain. Cathleen had lit a candle in the bathroom and the flame danced joyfully. Here, everything was cheerful and warm. Even Cathleen's things were happy.

I looked at myself in the mirror. My breath caught short as I observed my appearance. I was wearing my white undershirt. The dark circles under my eyes revealed the hidden emotion inside me, the feelings I tried to keep stuffed down. I sighed.

I turned on the water and cupped my hands underneath. I splashed water on my face and ran my fingers through my short hair. Water droplets ran down my cheeks. The cool water had its natural affect of waking me up. I grabbed some toothpaste, put some on my forefinger, and brushed my teeth.

I looked at myself again. I didn't know whether to feel happy or sad and I realized—I'd been in this predicament before.

"I brought you coffee." Cathleen's voice perked up my spirits. I turned around and was greeted with a large cup of creamy coffee. "And let's talk for a minute before you have to leave."

"Of course. Can you give me a moment? I'll be right out," I said, smiling a half smile. I sipped the cup, thankful for its sweet and hypnotic haven.

"Sure," Cathleen said and left the room.

I collected the rest of my uniform and dressed. I stood in the room, looking at the messy bed, trying to process all that had happened. I quickly performed the tree meditation and grounded my energies. I took a few deep breaths and let it all go.

I met Cathleen out in the living room. She was sitting peacefully on the couch with her feet propped up.

I sat down on the couch, facing her.

"I have to return to my old life, even though I don't want to." I smiled, hesitantly.

"You can do it, Alicia. It's only a matter of time, and it will all be over."

"Yeah, but time's a funny thing. Once at CAF, time slows down considerably. Three months to you may sound like nothing, but three months to me sounds like *forever*."

"Better you than me!" Cathleen reached over and pulled me to her. "You don't regret anything that happened last night, do you?"

"No, absolutely not. I'm just having trouble figuring out what I'm going to do, once I'm back at CAF."

Cathleen nodded, and we both sat there for a few minutes in silence, holding each other, treasuring the last moments before I left.

"Does this mean I'm a lesbian?" I asked, turning to Cathleen. She laughed. "I don't know, are you?"

"You're the first woman I've been with."

"I know. I'm always converting straights to go gay." Cathleen shrugged her shoulders innocently.

"Ah!" I exclaimed and let go of her arms.

Cathleen pushed me onto the couch and got on top of me. She kissed me hard, controlling. I stayed stiff under her grip.

When she released me, she mumbled, "Since you're used to taking orders—"

"Ah!" I pushed her off me.

"I'm just teasing, Alicia."

"Yeah, yeah," I said, getting up.

"You're an amazing person. Don't let CAF change you too much." Cathleen waved her finger at me.

"Okay," I said. I was so awed by Cathleen's beauty. "Thank you for everything."

"Of course. I'll see you soon. Be careful and take good care of yourself."

"I'll do my best," I said and gently kissed her good-bye.

~

It was Sunday which gave me time to think and get my affairs in order, before the week started again. I walked back to campus slowly, not eager to face my fear again.

I rounded the corner, a few blocks from campus, and was surprised to hear my named called.

I looked up to see Brenda rushing toward me.

"*Where have you been?*"

"What do you mean? I told you where I was ..." my voice trailed off as Brenda grabbed me and pulled me into a small alleyway.

"Alicia. Listen to me. Jamie's been kicked out."

"*What?*"

"Yeah, and the whole school has been on Dawn's back. Your Guides have apparently kicked you both out of their room?"

I nodded and felt like the wind had been knocked out of me.

"Cadre has been looking for you. I didn't tell them anything, but I also didn't want to be forced to lie."

"Was there ... did we have guard duty last night? I thought ..."

"You should've gotten away with it, but *now* you're a target. I wanted to warn you and get you back as quickly as possible."

"But why did Jamie get kicked out?" I asked, my words sticking in my throat.

"All I know is that the missions your Guides had you do eventually went back to him. We're guessing that when he was questioned by the Honor Court, he lied."

"Why would he lie?"

"I don't know. Maybe he thought he could get away with it?"

"The whole plan was his idea!"

243

"I know, but he was pinning it on the Ticks."

I was feeling light-headed now. "We were just following orders!"

"Yes, I know, but there's little we can do about that now. Have you decided what you're going to do about … McCavery?" she asked cautiously.

"I don't have a clue." I felt completely overwhelmed.

"Well, this is just too much shit happening all at once. You might want to lay low for a while."

"And how do I do that?"

"Don't report anything, for now."

"*Really?* But I thought you—"

"I did," Brenda said. "But not now. Dawn was worked out continuously last night. I'm afraid she's going to break. It'd probably be in your best interest to pretend nothing happened, as awful as that sounds."

"Okay," I said, nodding. I took a deep breath and exhaled. "Alright, let's get back to school."

~

Returning to Barracks, Brenda and I ran up to our room. Dawn sat by the window with a cigarette in her right hand.

I laughed at the scene. "When did you take up smoking?"

"Since now," she answered, without turning around.

Brenda and I grabbed our chairs and sat by her. I grabbed the pack of cigarettes off of Brenda's desk, lit one, and handed them to Brenda.

I looked at Dawn. She was tired, the strain of the Tick Line clearly visible in her face and eyes.

"I'm glad you're back," Dawn said, turning to me.

"I was tempted not to come back. Are you doing okay?" It was easy to be there for my roommates. We relied on each other.

"Did Brenda tell you about Jamie?"

I nodded. "It's hard to believe. Can you imagine spending three and a half years here and then being kicked out?"

"I don't know why he lied." Dawn sounded weary.

"How did you hear what happened?" I asked.

"Trevor came to me. It was nice of him too because neither David nor Quentin are talking to me. I guess they were told not to speak to us."

"Damn. Well, that explains why Jamie wasn't there Wednesday morning. Ahh!" I said, my head falling into my hands. "What the hell do we do now?"

"Survive," Brenda said and started to sing. *"I'm leavin' on a jet plane … don't know when I'll be back again…."*

~

Days passed and nothing happened to me. Cadre acknowledged my presence, but I wasn't singled out or even yelled at. I continued to wait for the other shoe to drop. I knew something must happen from my Saturday AWOL, absent without leave.

Thursday night, coming back to my room from dinner, I noticed that a small white piece of paper had appeared on my desk. I approached the note as if it would suddenly explode and saw—as I dreaded—that I'd been written up to The General Committee. The paper stated that I was to report to Room 410 at 11:00 PM that night.

~

I shined my shoes. I polished the brass on my cover, shoulder bars, and breast plate. I dressed like we did for parades, decked out in my best with white straps crossing at the chest, the brass chest plate securely in the front, and holding the black bullet packet on the back. My hands shook as I held the Brasso in my left hand and the stained rag in my right. My absence Saturday night obviously had consequences. My mind went blank, so I focused on the task in front of me. I shined the brass like it was the most important task in the world.

"What are you going to say when they question you?" Brenda asked.

"I don't know. Will you help me with my uniform?"

"Of course," she said, getting up.

"Caroline's online!" Dawn beamed.

"Are you shittin' me? Instant Message her," I insisted.

"I did," Dawn said

"I wrote her once," I said, "but she hasn't written back."

"She says hi." Dawn said.

"Is she okay?" I asked.

"She says that she's sorry she left without saying good-bye. She was afraid that we wouldn't have let her leave," Dawn explained.

"Damn right!" Brenda said.

"She says she's really sorry."

"Tell her we miss her," I said, suddenly teary-eyed. "Damn!" I kicked my desk. The last thing I needed to do was cry right now. I missed her. We all did. The room had changed since she'd left. Her empty wall locker was a constant reminder of her absence. It felt, almost, as if she had died.

I turned away from Dawn and stood before the mirror.

"I hate this white tag at my throat. It always makes me feel like I'm choking, especially when I'm straining," I said.

"You look good, Alicia. You're ready," Brenda said.

"Alright, now all I need is some balloons and champagne and *let the party begin!*"

Dawn looked at me, shook her head, and laughed.

"Brenda, any idea what happens when you get sent up to the GC?" I asked.

"I don't have a clue."

"Well, it's probably not any scarier than an Honor Court proceeding," Dawn said. "And I survived that, so you'll be fine."

"But you weren't the one on trial!" I argued.

Dawn looked me up and down and shrugged. "That's true. Well in that case, *you're screwed.*"

～

I strained on the fourth stoop, while in line with Upperclassmen, waiting to be called in by the General Committee.

"What the hell did you do, Tick?" the Upperclassman in front of me asked.

I ignored him, not feeling pressured to answer him.

"She must have fucked up real bad to be sent up to the GC."

"I didn't know they sent Ticks up to the General Committee.

I thought the TDC handled all their behavior problems," another Upperclassman said.

My neck hurt from straining. My eyes were tired, so I allowed them to blur. I told myself to relax. Waiting for this punishment was like waiting for doom's day. How could the Tick Line honestly get worse for me? Maybe that was the point. Bad days can get worse, and the worst was always to be expected.

I wished I was in my hay, relaxing, and drifting off to a brief oblivion. Sleep wasn't just for resting the body, but for escaping CAF temporarily. More than that, I wished I was with Cathleen, snuggled on her couch watching a movie, or reading one of her books.

One by one, I moved forward in the line, until I was finally called in.

The room was bright compared to the darkness on the stoop. I walked in, straining, to the center of the room and kept my eyes forward. I stood there, taking in the surrounding with my peripheral vision. As a Tick, I was not allowed to divert my eyes. I looked straight ahead, with my chin in, my forehead back, and my arms pinned to my side. From what I could see, there was a line of cadets seated both to my left and a few feet in front of me.

"Tick Randall, you are charged with two counts. First, you are being charged with vandalizing school property. Second, you are being charged with being AWOL," a male voice boomed throughout the room.

I listened, embarrassed to be the center of attention, and prayed for this to be over as quickly as possible.

"Please tell us, Tick Randall, why you vandalized the sacred Stonewall Jackson statue?"

"This Tick was ordered to, sir!" I spoke loudly and in third person, as required.

"Who ordered you?"

"This Tick's Guide, Jamie Fraser," I answered. Jamie had already been kicked out, so there was no point in hiding him now.

Murmurs erupted around me. Clearly other cadets were surprised by Jamie's scandalous behavior.

"Very well. Now, Tick Randall, can you tell us where you were the night of Saturday, February 28th?"

The room went quiet. I didn't know what to say without jeopardizing Cathleen and her store.

"*This Tick will not say, sir!*" I couldn't lie, so I refused to admit anything. I heard a few murmurs to my left, but I continued to face forward.

"*Tick, you do realize that not putting forth the information we request automatically increases your punishment?*"

I sighed. "Yes, sir!"

"*Tick Randall, please tell us who you were with the night of February 28th?*"

"This Tick will not say, sir!" I answered, again.

"*I see. There is one more thing that needs to be addressed here, tonight. Tick Randall was seen off campus, entering Stone Soup, the local bookstore on Main Street, numerous times,*" he said.

I felt sick. I had no idea I was being watched. Apparently, they knew everything already....

"*You see, Tick Randall is under great suspicion. Not only has this Tick vandalized school property, having defaced Stonewall Jackson's statue, but this Tick has also been seen entering Stone Soup Bookstore during school hours.*" He paused and then spoke slowly and clearly, as if to make a serious point. "*This Tick is under great suspicion for participating in behavior unbecoming of a cadet.*"

What? I wondered.

"*Tick Randall, as a cadet at the College of Armed Forces, it is important that I ask you one question.*"

I held my breath, completely unaware where he was going.

He cleared his throat. "*Tick Randall, are you a homosexual?*"

I froze, my eyes widened. A homosexual? I'd barely had time to process what had happened between Cathleen and I—*oh god!* My head started to hurt. I didn't know what to do or say.

I tried to speak, but I couldn't. Apparently I didn't know who I was. Was I gay or straight? Did it matter? The room began to spin, and I felt dizzy. I tried to speak again.

Finally I got the words out. "This Tick will not say, sir." I tried to yell, but the words came out weak and powerless.

Suddenly, there was uproar! Everyone in the room started talking. I stood there, closed my eyes, and tried desperately to ground my energies.

I felt powerless and sick. Don't faint, Alicia, I told myself. I stood there, waiting for my punishment, waiting for them to decide my fate.

I wanted to feel free, to no longer feel trapped and controlled. God, angels; I prayed; I desire to manifest *freedom*. I imagined myself flying, flying high over the mountains and far above Barracks, far enough away that the school would never hurt me again. I felt carefree, light, and liberated.

"*Tick Randall,*" he said, drawing me unwillingly back into the room. "*You're found guilty today, March 5th 1999 at 11: 43 PM, for vandalizing Stonewall Jackson's statue and for being AWOL on February 28th 1999. Your penalty for this behavior includes two Number Ones. Each Number One consists of three months of confinement and sixty penalty tours. With two Number Ones, you have a total of six months of confinement and one hundred and twenty penalty tours. Do you understand your punishment?*" he asked, hurrying to finalize the meeting.

"Yes, sir!" I answered.

"*Very well, you are dismissed!*" He drew the meeting to a close, and I was directed out of the room.

Once outside on the fourth stoop, I took off running to my room.

～

"Is everything okay?" Dawn asked.

I shook my head, closed the shade, and undressed.

The door flew open, surprising us all, since the curtain was down. It was Ms. Doyle. "Holy shit Alicia. What the hell?" she asked.

"How do you know already?" I asked.

"I was there in the room. I'm on the General Committee!"

"Oh," I answered. "I didn't know that."

"Do you know you were this close to being kicked out?" she said, holding up her thumb and index finger in measurement.

"I'm doing the fuckin' best I know how. If that gets me kicked out, so be it!"

"Alicia! Don't make me knock some sense into you!"

I glared at her.

"So, when were you going to tell me you were a lesbian?" Ms. Doyle asked.

"*What?*" Brenda sprang up like a jack-in-the-box.

I sighed. I was not in the mood to defend myself anymore.

"And she's in a lot of trouble now, too," Ms. Doyle said.

"Ah! Enough!" I ordered.

Now Dawn and Brenda were both up in their hays, staring at me.

I sat down on my rack, feeling like I'd been run over.

"Alicia, please tell us what the hell is going on," Brenda insisted.

"And start with the lesbian part first," Dawn encouraged.

"Fine. I'm a lesbian, a horrible cadet, and a disgrace to the College of Armed Forces." I gave up and collapsed onto my bed.

"Come on, Alicia. What is this all about?" Dawn asked.

"Alicia is in a lot of trouble. She is being punished for Jackson's statue and more importantly, for participating in behavior *unbecoming of a cadet*." Ms. Doyle explained.

"But I thought you liked guys!" Brenda said wide-eyed.

"I do, but now I like Cathleen. Someone saw me entering Stone Soup on Saturday and reported me. I'm in a lot of trouble here, and I don't know what to do," I said.

"Yeah, *a lot of trouble*, Alicia. Your punishment is as large as the punishment one of my Fellow Ticks got last year—for pulling a gun on his roommate!" Ms. Doyle gave in and sat down in Caroline's old seat.

"Isn't that a little harsh?" Brenda asked.

"Yes, two Number Ones is extreme, but she had multiple offenses. I know you were just following your Guide's orders, but that's no excuse; you broke the rules. And where you are really getting screwed, no pun intended, is your sexuality. I know you're a good cadet, but this is a guy's school."

I rolled my eyes.

"Your punishment should have only been based on the fact you were AWOL Saturday night, nothing else. But they're trying to make an example out of you."

"Or trying to get you to leave," Dawn said.

"Are you trying to get yourself kicked out?" Brenda asked.

"No!" I said, insulted. "I've done my best here, trying to be the best cadet and Tick I can be. Why do I have to convince you, after all the shit I've been through?"

"You don't, Alicia. We know," Brenda said.

"But leaving campus was stupid," Ms. Doyle said.

"Ah! Get out! I've had enough. Leave me alone!" I yelled.

Ms. Doyle turned, clearly offended, and left.

We sat in silence for some time.

"I know I could have told Lalita about Mr. McCavery. I know she would have kept it confidential, but I just didn't have the desire to go there, yet," I said.

"You've gotten a ridiculous punishment, Alicia. If you do decide it's too much, I completely understand," Dawn said. "There is only so much any of us can handle."

"Bullshit! You're not allowed to leave!" Brenda said.

"Brenda! Stop thinking about yourself. Look at Alicia. She's lost her brother, her boyfriend, was almost raped, and now is being punished for liking a woman!"

I remained silent and retreated into my own world. This was too much pressure. How much more could I take—and was it worth it?

Chapter 32: Them Against Us

My punishment consisted of two parts, penalty tours and confinement. Confinement meant I wasn't allowed to leave Barracks for six months, except for authorized academic, military, or sports activities. Being a Tick, we were already confined to Barracks. This meant, though, that I could no longer see Cathleen. We had less than three months of the semester left, so I would have to make up the rest of my penalty tours and months of confinement during my sophomore year.

I felt myself dying a little every day, missing Cathleen with each passing moment. In addition, there were confinement checks that needed to be signed every morning and every evening in the guard room, recording my accountability. The thought of running down to the guard room every morning and night was daunting. Whenever I left my room, I was prey to any Upperclassmen that wanted to work me out, and right now I was a target. If I missed a day, however, I'd be written up again, and who knows what repercussions that could lead to, possibly even dismissal.

Dawn and I were singled out daily. Dawn was still unfairly blamed for Jamie's dismissal, and rumors about my sexuality spread throughout Barracks, sparking hatred and curiosity among the Upperclassmen.

Upperclassmen continuously asked me if "they could watch," or if they could participate in a "threesome with us." It was annoying. One Upperclassman even had the gall to say that I'd never been with a real man before, but once the Tick Line was over … he could show me what it was like….

Brenda and my co-Ticks got singled out too because of their association to Dawn and me. I felt really bad for what they were being put through. I came to learn that there was even one female Tick that got stopped continuously, because she resembled me. I honestly felt the school was trying to get me to quit. Dawn felt the same way.

Each day I got ready to face the cruelty and harshness. I was fatigued and past being burnout. I felt my body breaking down. The back of my neck and head hurt all the time. I continued to drink instant coffee every morning and carried packets in my bag. I was caffeine-crazed and attended class with dry, red eyes. My heart began to beat funny, whether from anxiety or sleep-deprivation, and I was caught off guard by things that weren't there. I was going crazy. I was truly losing my mind.

Apathy became my best friend. I didn't care about anything but getting through the day. I'd made a promise to my brother and damn if I was going to quit after getting this far.

During class, I dreamt about running away. The thought of grabbing my rucksack, filling it will all the food I had, and walking away from this school felt so liberating. No one would have to know where I went. I could change my name and become a whole new person. The thought of even being homeless felt freeing. I knew I was losing myself, and I questioned every day whether I was going to make it.

It felt shameful to have these thoughts. Going home to Texas wasn't an option. People were counting on me to finish, not just my roommates, but my family and friends. They were so proud of me! I had to stay until the end.

I started to hate everyone that loved me and wanted me here. What the hell did they know about going to CAF? I was sick of all the pressure, even when it was disguised in encouraging cards and letters. As a result, I stopped checking my e-mail and calling home.

I kept my negative thoughts to myself. I feared telling my roommates because I didn't want to bring them down. I knew they too, were burning out, like a cigarette that had been lit too long. We looked ragged and worn, and were aging rapidly.

⁓

One evening I gave in, ran down to Sick Bay, and called Cathleen. I couldn't suppress my dark emotions any longer. I sobbed the instant she answered. It had been a hellish three weeks since we'd been together.

"Alicia! I'm so happy to hear your voice."

I told her everything. I knew I sounded crazy, chaotic, and dysfunctional, but I couldn't help it.

"Oh my, Alicia, you sound horrible. I'm so worried about you."

"I'm worried about me too. I'm so sorry I haven't been able to visit. I wish I could, but I can't leave."

"I understand. Is there anything I can do to help?" she asked eagerly.

"Maybe. Tell me how to do this, how to get through this. I feel like I'm losing my mind. I'm delusional in class. I see and hear things that aren't there...."

"Oh honey, it's just because you're so sleep-deprived." Cathleen sighed.

"I don't have any energy left. I feel like I have given everything to CAF, and I have nothing left. What should I do?" I sounded hopeless.

"Well, be like Madrone in *The Fifth Sacred Thing*," she said. "Madrone used *love* to conquer her opponent, don't you remember?"

"Sort of, but tell me again ..."

"Okay. At the end, when the army comes in to take over the city, Madrone welcomes each person into the city, offering them food, shelter, and water. The people in the north used kindness and love to conquer their enemy. In truth, they never envisioned their opponents *as enemies*, but as fellow human beings, and welcomed them into the city like they would their own brothers and sisters. Eventually, the soldiers gave in—they surrendered—because Madrone was providing a life so peaceful and abundant compared to the world of regulated water, military dictatorship, and war. You see, you have to use *different tools* than the Upperclassmen use to defeat you," she explained. "If you pull from within, you'll find a kind of strength that is not from willpower, which you've already used up, but is from the Divine. Pull from within for support, peace, and security. You cannot find that without, in our world of things and people, especially at CAF. We can only find that within ourselves."

"Okay. I'll try."

"Hold for a second. I'm going to focus my attention on you, and channel as much positive light and love in your direction as I can. Allow yourself to receive and try to reconnect with your Divine source, okay?"

"Okay," I said.

"While I send you energy, think of something that brings you joy. It will uplift your energies."

"Alright."

I put the phone down and let it hang while Cathleen was still on the line.

I closed my eyes and tried to visualize something that would make me happy. I was brought back to a time when Ethan and I were kids. We were playing in the backyard in these large cardboard boxes. Dad had brought them home from work one day and gave them to us to create our own houses. We carved out windows and doors, so it felt like a real home. I had blankets and pillows, and I spent time painting and holding picnics. Ethan turned his cardboard box into a fort where he ran around shooting lifeless objects. We played endlessly in our worlds of imagination.

"Alicia … Alicia?"

My attention was brought back to the present. I felt a little better, uplifted. I picked up the phone.

"Hey, I'm here."

"Oh, you sound better," Cathleen said, amazed. "I sent you a lot of higher energy vibration. You sounded so depleted a minute ago, but now you sound a little better."

"I do feel stronger, thank you! When you were sending me energy, I was thinking about a childhood experience I had with Ethan."

"That's good. Draw energy from those happy moments. You can shift your energies from empty to full by drawing upon the right sources, like joy and peace. The universe will reflect whatever you ask for, whatever you envision. When you feel shame, draw upon a memory when you felt proud and strong. Switch your attention, so you can become what you are seeking."

"Okay, I'll try."

"Focus on what you desire to manifest and draw it to you. Whatever you desire to create, create it."

"Thank you for reminding me of my power. I will do my best," I said, feeling better than I had felt in weeks.

"Oh, and let me teach you one more thing," Cathleen said.

"What's that?"

"Another powerful tool is the ability to *cut chords* with people. You see, when we have a relationship with someone, we energetically connect with them too. Remember when I spoke to you about the chakras on the body when I described Integrated Energy Therapy?"

"Yes ..."

"Well, we connect with other people energetically through our chakras, the energy systems of our body. Imagine a rope coming from each of your chakras and connecting with another's energy field. If you want to end a relationship or get them out of your energy field, you can *cut chords* with them," she explained.

"When have you used this technique?"

"I've cut chords with ex-girlfriends, to disconnect and help us move on with our lives. I've also done it with my dad's wife. When they first married, Janine felt insecure about Dad and my relationship, so whenever I was around I felt like Janine was trying to compete with me. It was annoying, so I cut chords with her—to prevent being dragged into her little competitions."

"Do you only cut chords when you want to end a relationship?" I asked.

"No, cutting chords doesn't necessarily mean ending a relationship. All you are doing is ending what is occurring at that moment, shifting the energy to allow a transformation to occur, so if the energies were to reconnect, they'd have the potential to reconnect at a better place."

"I see. Well, I should probably cut chords with all my Cadre!"

"That'd be a good start. It will help shift the energies, maybe so you'll not be in such a victimized position."

"Is it possible to cut chords with the whole school?"

"I have no idea. I've only cut chords with individual people."

"So how do I do it?"

"Okay, well, just like manifesting, I ask for the presence of my guides and angels. I envision the person standing before me, and I visualize an energy exchange ... all my energy returning and giving back all their energy. Then I ask for the presence of Archangel Michael to cut the chords, and I picture a sword from the top of my head slashing down in front of me, cutting each chord one by one. I visualize this three times. To conclude, I envision crystals sealing the end of each of my chords, where my chakras are, preventing the energies from reattaching."

"Wow. Do you usually feel anything when you do that?"

"Generally, I feel relieved. Sometimes I feel dizzy until the energy is settled."

"That's fascinating. I'll definitely try that. Thanks."

"Anytime, Alicia. I'm glad I could do something to help. Manifesting and cutting chords are very powerful tools."

"Definitely! So, have you been doing okay?"

"Business is good this time of year. Everything is fine. When do I get to see you next?" Cathleen asked, hopeful.

"You don't, not until after Breakout." I sighed.

"Where's Breakout?"

"Ah, New Lexington Battlefield, forty-six miles from here. We're marching there. It will take three days. I'll be happy when all this is over!"

"Why New Lexington?"

"Because it's the only battle CAF cadets fought in during the Civil War."

"Oh, wow. Will you be sleeping in the woods too?"

"Yep."

"Better *you* than *me*."

"I'm sorry I haven't been able to see you. I do miss you," I said.

"I miss you too, solider."

That made me smile. "I'll try to call you again. If you don't hear from me, don't worry. It's just because I haven't been able to get to a phone."

"Sounds to me like we're going to have to learn how to communicate telepathically."

"Sure! Well, I should go."

"Be careful and take care, Alicia."

"I will. Bye."

I waited until I heard her hang up the phone. I sighed. I always felt better after talking to Cathleen. I reluctantly got off the stool, signed out of Sick Bay, and returned to school.

Chapter 33: Taking our Power Back

"Okay, I call a room meeting."

"Why, what's up?" Brenda looked up from a very large textbook that lay wide open on her desk. She was studying, like always.

"I want to share something I learned from Cathleen that I think will help us."

"So, you're finally going to tell us what it's like being with a woman?" Brenda said.

"What? I didn't know you wanted to know!"

Dawn and Brenda looked at each other.

"Well, it was really only one night.... The rest of the time we just talked," I said.

"Don't be so modest, Alicia. We want details!" Dawn said.

Just then a small, banging sound caught our attention. All three of us looked over toward the sink and noticed the door had flown open.

"Apparently they want the details too." Brenda laughed.

I got up and went to the sink and looked underneath.

"Hey Randall, do you guys have any lotion?"

I recognized his voice. "We always have lotion, Williams. It's a girl's room."

"Can I borrow some?"

"Of course."

"Okay, I'll be right over. Thanks."

I closed the door to the sink and grabbed my miscellaneous box.

"Hey guys," Tick Williams said, awkwardly smiling as he entered the room.

"Don't tell us what you're going to use the lotion for," Dawn said, dismissing him with her hand.

Grinning, he grabbed the container and quickly left the room.

"So," I said, drawing the attention of the room again. I explained the multiple things I'd learned from Cathleen, including how to manifest and cut chords.

"It's important that we all learn to redirect our energies toward what we want," I reiterated.

"Well, I'm willing to try anything at this point. I've surrendered to the fact I'm going to be miserable until summer," Dawn said.

"I know, I'm exhausted too. Every cell of my body hurts, including my brain," Brenda said, shutting her book.

"So, do you want to do all this together?" I asked.

"Sure," Dawn said.

"I'm game," Brenda said.

"Okay, I'm going put the shade down, so we're not interrupted."

"We should probably cast a circle," Dawn suggested, "a circle of protection around the three of us."

"That's a great idea. Do you know how to do that?" I asked.

"I saw the movie Practical Magic. I'll just imagine and request a circle of protection. I'm sure in witchcraft there are more details." Dawn shrugged her shoulders.

"Well, go ahead."

I watched Dawn walk around the room, holding out her hands with the intention of circling us with protection.

"I call in the protection of the spirits from the north, the south, the east and the west."

"Okay, good enough. Let's first start with cutting chords with the entire school. Imagine taking your energy back, all the parts of yourself you've given to the school."

We sat in silence for a few minutes with our eyes closed. It didn't take long to picture Barracks in my head and take back my energies. I envisioned a swoop of energy, like a blur of light, as if a ghostly aspect of myself returned. The energy kept coming, symbolizing how much of myself I'd given to the school. I continued to allow myself to receive and waited until the blur of light faded, and it felt complete.

I opened my eyes and looked at Brenda. Her eyes were still closed. I glanced at Dawn, and she nodded at me that she had finished. "What do you think about cutting chords with Cadre?" I asked.

"I don't know. Do you think it's necessary after already taking our power back from the school?" Dawn asked.

"Maybe we need to individually decide who we want to cut chords with. I know I need to cut chords with Mr. McCavery and our Uncle Guides," I said.

"Alright, I know who I need to cut chords with." Dawn nodded.

"Me too," Brenda said.

"Okay, let's do it. Let's call in Archangel Michael for assistance. State in your mind, who you want to cut chords with, and make sure to protect yourself by visualizing crystals at the ends of each chord when you're done."

"Okay," Brenda said, her eyes already closed.

We spent the next five minutes cutting chords. One by one, I took my power back and cut chords with Mr. McCavery, the Upperclassmen I met in the woods last semester, Jamie, Brandon, Toby, and Kenny. After the exercise, I started to feel a greater sense of peace.

When Brenda and Dawn's eyes were both opened, I began again. "I think the most important thing we can do is get back in touch with ourselves. This will help keep us balanced. Also, when we are in tune with our feelings, we can more readily interpret other people's feelings."

They nodded.

"I know I've been giving away my energies too easily, leaving me depleted and empty. So, my goal, now, is to be focused inward. I'm going to hold onto my energy, the essence of who I am, with ultimate protection now," I told them.

"How do you do that?" Brenda asked. "I'm sick of feeling insanely stressed and scattered."

"Well, to start with, we should probably discontinue pushing ourselves past our limits," I said. "Instead, we need to pace ourselves. We can't burnout. We need to be more like the turtle, slowly and continuously moving forward, no more sprinting. Haven't you noticed that even when we're giving our all, we still get yelled at?"

"Yes, it's so *frustrating*. I'm sick of kicking ass, and Cadre still wanting more," Brenda said.

"Their appetites are insatiable. By now, we can fully acknowledge that no matter how hard we try, we're never going to win," Dawn said.

"Exactly, they will never be happy with our performance. They will continue to criticize and demand more, regardless how much we give of ourselves. As a result, in order to protect ourselves, we need to stay balanced. I suggest—that we start channeling energy from within, from the Divine, and to each other, to keep us full and sustained."

"And how do we do that?" Brenda asked.

"Cathleen showed me that she puts her thumb and middle fingers together." I lifted my hands in demonstration. "She says that that movement creates a heart link between her and her angels, allowing her to channel in energy, and I'm thinking … if we want to channel energy to each other, we should visualize energy from the Ultimate Being, coming in through the top of our heads to our heart, and then out to the person's heart we are trying to help. What do you think?"

I went on to explain what I'd felt during the Integrated Energy Therapy session, and what I'd felt earlier that day when Cathleen sent me energy.

"That's really cool, Alicia. I hadn't thought about my personal energy before, but I'm very aware that I keep giving my power to the Upperclassmen, and it's pissing me off," Dawn said. "Ever since Jamie got kicked out, it's been a circus, and I feel like the opening act!"

"Yeah, I haven't gotten a break either. It's like the Upperclassmen have become more vicious. I personally don't think either one of you did anything wrong—I could've easily been in your shoes," Brenda said. "We can't let them win. We need to take our power back now."

"I'm very happy all three of us are in agreement. The last thing I want to practice is sending energy to each other. This will be really important if any one of us starts to feel weak during Breakout. Besides, it's a way for us to help each other, without anyone noticing."

"I'm starting to feel like a witch," Brenda said.

"We're using the healing powers each one of us already has," I said.

"I agree. I'm feeling witchlike too." Dawn smiled.

"Shall we heal in a circle? I'll send energy to Brenda, Brenda go ahead and send energy to Dawn, and Dawn will you send energy to me?" I asked.

"Sure," Brenda said.

"Yep, sounds good," Dawn said.

The next couple of minutes we sat in concentration. I visualized white light coming in through the top of my head and then directed it out of my heart, toward Brenda's heart.

"I don't know if I'm doing this right," Brenda said.

"I wouldn't worry about it. Cathleen says *energy follows thought*, so as long as your intention is clear, everything should be good."

Minutes later, I spoke up. "How do you feel?"

"Okay," Dawn said.

"I'm fine too … maybe more at peace," Brenda said.

"Really? That's fantastic. That's our goal! Now we have a technique that we can use and help each other whenever we need to." I felt hopeful.

"Well, when I'm with my horses, I can sense how they're feeling. I'm sure if I pay attention, I can do that with people too," Brenda said.

"I think *that* is really important to understand. When we are constantly running around, we can lose touch with who we are. We become so mind-oriented, we forget to check in with ourselves, on how we are *feeling*. When we slow down and pay attention, our intuition can give us a whole new perceptive," I said.

"I can be pretty intuitive too," Dawn said.

"I'm so glad you both are aware of that. I think everyone has the ability to perceive energy, to feel each other's feelings." I paused. I felt like I was really starting to understand something important. "And you know what? If we are taught to disconnect from our feelings and are taught to just obey who is in command, it is no wonder that wars occur. You know what I mean? If each of us stayed in tune with ourselves, then we could perceive how people around us were feeling, right? It just reconfirms that *we are all connected* and if we're all connected, there is no such thing as *an enemy*."

"That's an interesting concept, Alicia," Brenda said. "I wonder then, if we can channel energy to each other, if we can shift the energy of a room."

"What do you mean?" Dawn asked.

"Well, you know, if someone is angry, and I channeled energy to their heart, would they feel better?" Brenda asked.

"Probably. I mean, this is all new to me, but now you're giving us ideas," I said beaming. I was so excited about the possibilities.

"This is very cool, Alicia," Dawn said.

"Yeah, it is." Brenda nodded.

Chapter 34: Breakout

The change was instantaneous, like a light going from off to on. I was no longer the center of attention, no longer the wrath of the Upperclassmen. I became almost invisible, like a Ghost Tick. It was incredibly thrilling. I was learning how much I could change my life by shifting my energies—through the power of changing my thoughts and feelings. I finally understood how to play by the rules, without losing myself in the process.

What we focus on expands. You cannot fight an institution with the same mindset that created it. I could hear Cathleen's voice teaching me along the way. Even though we hadn't seen each other in over a month, I still felt connected to her.

I was fighting with new tools. I stopped giving all of myself and surrendering to the wills of those in power. Now I was in control of *my* destiny. I used heart-centered energy against those who challenged me, and I set clear intentions to create the outcome I desired. I played a key part in my reality. Now I could honestly say I was getting out of here alive and intact.

Each morning and evening, I put a wall of protection around myself and my roommates, with my mind full of my whole-hearted intention. I visualized a crystallized energy field surrounding us and keeping us safe. I was especially clear about my intentions of protection when I ran downstairs to sign my confinement checks.

The more in tune I was with myself, the more I felt connected with everyone around me. While walking the Tick Line, I wasn't allowed to divert my eyes; however, I could sense the feelings of the people around me. I felt like I was utilizing a sixth sense. The instant I felt someone's anger or fear, I channeled love, and everything shifted.

I was still worked out, but for the most part, Upperclassmen left me alone. I was still a Tick, but I was no longer painfully singled out. Occasionally, an Upperclassman stopped me to see what I was made of, but when he realized, whether consciously or not, that I was no longer surrendering to his power, I was no longer fun. I was playing the same game, but now I set the tone. Big Brother was still watching, but he could no longer control me.

Because I was liberated from the constant harassment, my attention returned to academics. Brenda was sweating bullets, more concerned about her academic standing than I was, because she feared losing her scholarship. My grades were below par, but I refused to stress over it. I was just happy that I was passing because if I didn't, all this wouldn't be worth much.

It was such a relief to no longer feel victimized. I felt a greater sense of peace and, interestingly, a greater sense of love toward myself. The more love I channeled, the more alive my heart felt, and I knew I was beginning to heal.

My roommates and I knew Breakout was coming soon because Cadre started waking us up in the morning, before breakfast formation, to work us out, which sucked, but I was also matter-of-fact about it, knowing we were just one day closer to the end.

The date of Breakout was unknown, so there was no countdown. Each year, the First Class decided when Breakout would be, depending on when they considered the Tick class to be unified. Some Tick classes broke out in February. Other classes didn't break out until the end of the semester.

It was now April.

After Breakout, we'd finally be recognized as Fourth Classmen and would no longer be Ticks. During class, my Fellow Ticks and I constantly talked about Breakout. We anticipated the finale, to finally start the collective march to New Lexington.

~

Wednesday night, in the middle of April, we woke up to the sound of exploding bombs and machine gun fire. This time, though, it was partially expected, so we didn't jump out of our hays in fear, but with anticipation.

I looked at my clock. It was four o'clock in the morning.

"I know I should be excited," Dawn moaned. "But I would honestly rather stay in my hay until morning," she said, rolling over.

"I don't think any one of us has a choice here." I yawned and stretched, encouraging myself to wake up.

"Oh, shit, I have a fuckin' exam tomorrow. Do you think ..." Brenda asked, confused.

"Brenda, I'm sure our professors were informed of Breakout, so I wouldn't worry if I were you."

"Oh ... yeah," Brenda said, sounding like she was still asleep.

Our door flew open, and Mr. Gray told us exactly what we needed for our trip. He spoke calmly, but firmly. "Change into your BDU's. Fill your rucksack with two sets of underwear, extra socks, a sweat uniform, poncho, blanket, and roll-out bed. Don't forget your rifle and report onto the stoop ASAP!" Then he left abruptly.

"Alright girls, this is it! The end of our hell," Dawn said, suddenly excited.

I was ready to get this over with. We were marching to New Lexington which would take three days. As a remedy to wake up, I pulled out packets of instant coffee and ate it dry. I wanted to get as much caffeine as I could.

Whether because of dehydration or lack of sleep, I started to feel dizzy. I tried getting up from my hay and a wave of nausea passed over me.

"Brenda," I whispered.

"Yeah," she said.

"I don't feel so well...."

"What's wrong, Alicia?"

"The room is spinning."

"Here, drink this." Dawn handed me a glass of water.

I drank it, but I didn't feel better.

"Alicia, you need to snap out of this!" Brenda ordered.

"Did you just eat those coffee grains straight, Randall?" Dawn asked.

I nodded.

"No wonder you feel sick. Keep drinking water, and eat this." Dawn handed me a granola bar.

I continued to drink and chewed the granola bar slowly. I got back into bed. After a few minutes, when the spinning subsided, I was able to get up, get dressed, and check my rucksack to make sure I had everything I needed.

Lining up on the fourth stoop during these wicked early morning hours, I was instantly taken back to Hell Week, just nine months earlier. I felt so different than I had then, and I was thankful I was at the end of this crucible, not the beginning. Life had certainly changed.

We ran down the stoops, formed up by company, and began the march. There were almost three hundred people: Ticks, Cadre, and Guides that had volunteered to join the march. Brenda, Dawn, and I stayed together, not allowing anyone to come between us. We were each other's lifeline.

~

Once the sun came up, I felt suddenly uplifted. I glanced over at Brenda. She too looked pleased and excited about the march. I smiled at Dawn.

I was thankful my rucksack wasn't too heavy, but just like a marathon, I knew I had to pace myself. I turned inward and checked on my physical body. I felt tired, no doubt, but I was happy to keep the slow and steady pace of the march.

Band Company was in the rear. We were holding our rifles, so I had to envision placing my thumbs and middle fingers together, as a sort of pray and intention to recharge myself with energy from the Divine. As an exercise, I channeled energy to Brenda for a few moments and then to Dawn. I felt more awake and more peaceful.

After marching a few hours, the line of Ticks took a detour into the woods where we settled and ate breakfast. Breakfast came in the form of MREs, meals ready to eat, filled with sustaining calories and salt. We had an opportunity to refill our canteens. Cadre ordered us repeatedly to drink water and check our feet for blisters. The three of us went deeper into the woods for privacy, to relieve ourselves, and took turns standing guard while we went individually.

Once we were back marching, my mind wandered. I could see it so clearly, as if a premonition, the three of us dirty and exhausted, running across the battlefield while holding each other's hands in victory. It was exhilarating to know the end was near.

I thought about Cathleen, and I ached for her. I thought about all the fear many held about whether or not I was a lesbian. I felt most of the Upperclassmen were just curious or liked drama. Were they threatened? I wondered. I had been punished because of the idea of being a lesbian. Why? *Was I a lesbian?*

Growing up, the idea never crossed my mind. I'd only dated guys; only ever thought to date guys. It wasn't that I didn't find other women attractive. I just never pictured myself dating them. But, obviously, this was before I met Cathleen.

When I'd been with Seth, I felt loved. I felt like he knew me, knew my goals and dreams, my friends and family. More than anything, we were linked through my brother, a connection we'd always have.

With Cathleen, something more momentous happened. In the mist of all the pain, all the struggle and hard work, I could go to her and feel nurtured both in body and in spirit. She didn't run away like Seth did. She was my rock, within the storm, and she helped me not lose myself in the Tick Line. I never felt more loved and honored than when I was with her.

With a few miles left, I was ready to collapse. The speed of the march had increased. During the fast moments, my roommates and I buckled down and increased the length of our stride. The line wavered like an accordion, sometimes slowing and bunching; other times, the pace hastened and the lines thinned, leaving us jogging to keep up.

Messages passed down the line, at first barely audible, then clearly heard.

"Tighten up the line!"

"Tighten up the line!"

"Tighten up the line," until the message reached Band Company.

Messages announced when there was a bridge crossing or a pot hole, to prepare us to pay attention. In following the person in front of me, I often dazed off and followed blindly.

Luckily, Cadre did not force us to march silently, so we sang songs or told jokes to keep each other motivated. Those that were hardcore naturally loved the challenge of the march. It was long and even Cadre looked haggard at the end of the day.

By the end of the first day, we had marched thirteen miles. That night, tents were set up all along the woods, one for each room. Brenda, Dawn, and I enjoyed the seclusion of the tent. Every muscle in our bodies ached with fatigue.

We took off our boots and massaged our feet. We took turns and massaged each other's shoulders. My hips ached because we often marched at a wider stride, to keep up with the guys, so I massaged my hips and legs too. We knew how important it was to take care of ourselves and each other.

"How are you feeling?" I asked

Dawn grunted, and Brenda half-chuckled. We were too exhausted to talk.

"I feel the same way." I yawned.

I laid down in fetal position and slept as if I was cuddled in a bed with silk sheets and feathered pillows.

~

"Oh, shit!" Dawn said.

"*What?*" I demanded, angry that she had made me jump.

"I have my fuckin' period!"

"That sucks." I couldn't help but laugh.

"Well, I didn't know when I was going to get it. My period has been messed up all year. Come to think of it, I don't remember when I had my last period—shit!"

"I'll go find an Upperclassman female or a nurse." Brenda sighed and left the tent.

Brenda returned five minutes later, pulling out very thick pads.

"What the hell are those?" Dawn asked, wide-eyed. "They look like diapers. No tampons?"

"Nope," Brenda said, handing them to Dawn. "Beggars can't be choosers...."

After breakfast, we quickly resumed the march. Hours later, we pulled out our ponchos because it had started to rain. Surprisingly, it didn't let up quickly, like many spring showers, but lasted for hours. By the time we took a break for dinner, many of us were soaked to the bone, having been that way most of the day. I was afraid I was going to break out in another rash.

Medical problems were a normal occurrence during the march. Ticks continuously twisted their ankles, so I forced myself to pay close attention to where I stepped. Fellow Ticks fell out of line all over the place, either from injuries, dehydration, illness, or exhaustion.

On the second day, Brenda started limping because her shin splints hurt. The three of us continually glanced at each other, one another's protectors. We had plenty of time during the march to send healing and supportive energy to each other. I enjoyed going inward, dreaming, and thinking about Cathleen. I wondered if she'd been thinking about me this entire time too.

That night, back in our tent, I took my wet BDU's off and happily changed into sweats. I was thankful Cadre had instructed us to bring extra socks. My socks were always moist, either from rain or sweat. Changing into dry clothes, especially dry socks, was heavenly.

The weather cleared up on the last day, as if to honor our upcoming victory. We were too worn out to emanate any sense of joy, but there was a slight feeling of anticipation building among us.

As we marched along the highway, I was tempted to put my thumb out and catch a ride. My feet ached. My arms hurt from the rifle. My back was sore from the rucksack, which now felt like dead weight. As I wallowed in self-pity of having to march, my spirit and motivation started to weaken.

For dinner, we entered the woods once again. Our formation dispersed, as some Ticks took the lead, plowing through the broken branches and mud. I had a tendency, especially when I was tired, to drag my feet, so I had to concentrate especially hard where I stepped.

I continued to look down, determined not to trip, and when I glanced up, I realized I was no longer behind Brenda. I looked around and didn't see Dawn either. Suddenly, panic ran through me. I wanted so desperately to stay in my little group. I tried to pick up my pace and tripped. My left hand went out to catch my fall, and I lost hold of my M-14 which hit me in the shin. I winced in pain, my eyes watering.

"You okay, Randall?" Tick Williams offered his arm to help me up.

"Thanks," I said. I limped, but the pain quickly dissipated.

I looked up and saw Dawn and Brenda walking toward me. I felt relieved. They had noticed my absence and had turned around to look for me. Once we met up, the three of us found a soft spot and sat down. I laid back on my rucksack to rest.

The chatter of voices and the rustle of MRE packets made my mind hypnotically drift. I couldn't wait to sleep. I couldn't wait to see Cathleen again. Just then, as I pictured her clearly, I felt my energy lift. Maybe, at this exact moment, she was thinking of me too, sending me energy, her way of communicating with me.

Okay, I can do this. I focused on the trees all around me, admiring their beauty and thanking them for providing me with air. I was determined to get out of my self-pity and to feel appreciative again.

I smiled.

"What are you thinking about?" Brenda asked.

"Nothing," I answered, still smiling.

"Yeah right," Dawn said. "She's probably thinking about her next booty-call with Cathleen."

"Ah, what?" I tried to slap Dawn, but I forgot to tell my arm to move.

"Yeah, you heard me," Dawn teased. "So, Alicia, you ever going to tell us what's going on with the two of you?"

"Well, haven't you heard?"

"Yes, but are the rumors true?" Dawn asked.

"I guess."

"So, you're a lesbian now?" Brenda asked.

I shrugged my shoulders.

"You know, you're not responding to all this *normally*," Brenda said.

"Really? Well, how should I be acting?" I turned to her.

"I just don't get it. How do you wake up one morning and all of a sudden you're gay?"

"Brenda, she's just experimenting...." Dawn pointed it out, like it was *so* obvious.

"And how would you know?" Brenda asked.

"Because I did that in high school too."

Brenda and I snapped our heads and looked at Dawn.

"What? Now you tell me!" I said.

"It's not a big deal. I mainly like guys, but I've had my moments, when I messed around with a woman or two," Dawn said, nonchalantly.

"*What?* Is everyone *gay* now?" Brenda asked. The shock on her face made her look so funny that I burst out laughing.

～

"*Is that it?*"

I looked up to see what Dawn was talking about. After passing the sign, announcing that New Lexington was three miles up the road, excitement reverberated through the line of Ticks.

"Thank god!" Brenda said.

"Are we there, *already?*" I asked.

Brenda tapped me with her rifle.

"Well, personally, I could do another ten," I kidded.

Brenda and Dawn exchanged glances.

"*What?*" I asked. "You know, I really think I've finally got the hang of this whole Tick Line. It really wasn't that bad...." I fluttered my lips at them.

"Oh *please*, Alicia!" Brenda rolled her eyes.

"She's getting cocky now," said Dawn.

"I know." Brenda shook her head.

"You keep this up, I'll have to kill you with my bare hands!" Dawn said.

"Dawn, stop being so serious. You need to loosen up. You should really take up drinking," I said.

"What the hell is wrong with her?" Dawn asked Brenda.

"I don't know, but I'm going to ignore her," Brenda said.

"I can't believe we are so fuckin' close!" Dawn said.

"I know. I'm ready to collapse," Brenda said.

I tried to get excited, but I felt more relieved than anything. I was so fatigued. I kept my attention on the ground, watching my step. It had become automatic to put one foot in front of the other, but I was being cautious.

Luckily, the temperature was mild. The grass and trees were so green, but I couldn't fully appreciate the beauty around me. To look around took too much energy.

"So what do you think you'll do this summer?" Brenda asked Dawn.

"Nothing. I want to lie around and do *nothing.*"

"And when you're done doing nothing, what do you think you'll do?"

"Take up drinking, like Alicia said…."

⁓

"We're here!" Dawn screamed.

"Sweet!" Brenda yelled.

New Lexington Battle was the only battle CAF cadets fought in during the Civil War, so the battlefield was symbolic twofold, as it was also the end of our journey.

Companies of Ticks ran across the field in front of us. When we reached the field, Brenda, Dawn, and I ran, more like hobbled, together across the field.

"Yeah!"

"Woo-hoo!"

Screaming erupted everywhere; our Tick Line was finally over!

When we reached the end of the field, I dropped all my gear and collapsed onto the grass.

I hope you're proud, Ethan was the only thought running through my head, along with feelings of utter relief.

"Alicia?"

"She's right there," I heard Brenda say.

I knew I looked silly lying on the grass, face down and all, but I didn't feel like moving.

"Alicia?"

I turned my head sideways, and I forced myself to look up. It was Cathleen.

"Hey. The Tick Line is done!" I yelled.

"Yeah, I can see that...."

"Come down here." I waved my hand. "The grass is *so* comfortable."

References

Byrne, Rhonda. *The Secret*. Hillsboro, Oregon: Beyond Words Publishing, 2006.

MacLaine, Shirley. *The Camino*: *a journey of the spirit*. New York, New York: Pocket Books, a division of Simon & Schuster Inc, 2000.

Ruiz, Don Miguel. *The Four Agreements: a Toltec Wisdom Book*. San Rafael, California: Amber-Allen Publishing Inc, 1997.

From the book The Four Agreements © 1997, Miguel Angel Ruiz, M.D. Reprinted by permission of Amber-Allen Publishing, Inc. P.O. Box 6657, San Rafael, CA 94903. All rights reserved.

Starhawk. *The Fifth Sacred Thing*. New York, New York: Bantam, 1993.

About the Author

Destiny Jennifer Ringgold, an ordained Interfaith Minister, from The New Seminary, started her college career as part of the second class of women at Virginia Military Institute. She received her BA from Northern Arizona University in Women Studies. Destiny has a passion for writing, music, spiritual counseling, and energy work. She currently lives in Lansdale, Pennsylvania with her partner Keith Moore and two precious sons, Thorbjoern and Thadeaus.